First Time Friends

By Jenna Avery

First Time Friends

Website: Jenna-Avery.com

For licensing, copyright, and other questions, email jenna.averys.email@gmail.com

Cover art by Ann Bugarin

First Edition

Contents

Dylan Thomas Quote 1
Dedication 2
Books By Jenna 3
Content Warning 5
1. Chapter One 7
2. Chapter Two 15
3. Chapter Three 26
4. Chapter Four 32
5. Chapter Five 38
6. Chapter Six 45
7. Chapter Seven 50
8. Chapter Eight 55
9. Chapter Nine 62
10. Chapter Ten 67
11. Chapter Eleven 72
12. Chapter Twelve 78
13. Chapter Thirteen 85
14. Chapter Fourteen 90
15. Chapter Fifteen 97
16. Chapter Sixteen 102

17. Chapter Seventeen 111
18. Chapter Eighteen 117
19. Chapter Nineteen 125
20. Chapter Twenty 133
21. Chapter Twenty-One 140
22. Chapter Twenty-Two 150
23. Chapter Twenty-Three 158
24. Chapter Twenty-Four 165
25. Chapter Twenty-Five 172
26. Chapter Twenty-Six 180
27. Chapter Twenty-Seven 186
28. Chapter Twenty-Eight 193
29. Chapter Twenty-Nine 200
30. Chapter Thirty 209
31. Chapter Thirty-One 220
32. Chapter Thirty-Two 227
33. Chapter Thirty-Three 234
34. Chapter Thirty-Four 242
35. Chapter Thirty-Five 251
36. Chapter Thirty-Six 254
37. Chapter Thirty-Seven 260
38. Chapter Thirty-Eight 264
39. Chapter Thirty-Nine 269
40. Chapter Forty 280
41. Chapter Forty-One 284
42. Chapter Forty-Two 291

43. Chapter Forty-Three 297
44. Chapter Forty-Four 301
45. Chapter Forty-Five 307
46. Chapter Forty-Six 310
47. Chapter Forty-Seven 314
48. Chapter Forty-Eight 319
49. Chapter Forty-Nine 323
50. Chapter Fifty 327
51. Chapter Fifty-One 331
52. Chapter Fifty-Two 335
53. Chapter Fifty-Three 340
54. Chapter Fifty-Four 343
55. Chapter Fifty-Five 349
56. Chapter Fifty-Six 361
57. Chapter Fifty-Seven 368
58. Chapter Fifty-Eight 373
59. Chapter Fifty-Nine 381
60. Chapter Sixty 390
61. Chapter Sixty-One 396
62. Chapter Sixty-Two 402
63. Chapter Sixty-Three 408
64. Chapter Sixty-Four 413
65. Chapter Sixty-Five 418
66. Chapter Sixty-Six 423

Acknowledgements 427

About The Author 429

Though lovers be lost, love shall not;
And death shall have no dominion.
~ Dylan Thomas

For those forced to gather themselves after the devastation of all Heavens and Hells, I write this for you.

Also Written By Jenna

My Ashes: Memoirs of a Misbehaving Woman
Come Back To Me: A Dark Romance Thriller
The Singularity
Through The Folded Stars
Skies of Avalon
Glittering Skies
First Time Friends

Content Warning

Welcome to Book Two in the Skies of Avalon series. If you've already read Glittering Skies, thank you so much for returning to this world. If you haven't read Glittering Skies yet, you are *not* required to do so in order to enjoy First Time Friends. However, the experience is certainly enhanced by going in order!

The initial three books in the Skies of Avalon series were written within sixty-three days. Yes, 63. It was unexpected, and as a result, I had no idea what I was doing, narrative wise. When Heimlock finished (the sequel to this story), I realized it was a downward spiral into myself. These books embody the trauma that's seeped into my molecular structure.

I've experienced an enormous amount of trauma in my too-long life. For the first time, it all makes sense. If I had to go through all of that to create this series ... I'd do it again. That's how much this series means to me.

That's also how deep this series is. First Time Friends really submerges into grief and trauma. There are moments of first person POV triggers and panic attacks, based on my own direct experiences. Some of Fynn's reactions, I pulled from my own husband's thoughts and behavior. All of that to say that this book, despite being in a fantasy world, is ***very*** realistic.

<u>This book is not like Glittering Skies.</u> That book, as beautiful as it is, should be considered an emotional primer. I've had people tell me *this* book made them feel something for the first time in months. I've received texts and emails from sobbing readers.

I don't put this out there to scare you; truly. It's more that I'm genuinely concerned about harming my readers.

Take care of yourself. Take breaks if you need to. It's an HEA, but a hard-won HEA.

And for the love of all twelve goddesses, send a DM if this changes your life. When I say I peeled apart my own soul into consumable slivers for these words ... Well, you'll be able to tell. I want to know who this book was meant for.

<u>CONTENT WARNING:</u> So, without further ado, **please be aware that you'll encounter** pregnant spousal death (off-page), domestic violence (on-page), deep exploration of grief, the memory of sexual assault triggering a panic attack (on-page in first person POV), and murder (on-page).

1

Fynn

Four Years Ago

The day my wife died, I was searching for ice cream. Not just any ice cream; the chocolate mint and pistachio kind. Not my favorite flavor — in fact, I hate it — but it was a random pregnancy craving for my wife, Rhuth.

Unfortunately, that was at 3:00 a.m. this morning. Naturally, no stores were open at that hour, so the moment she left for work, I struck out on an ice cream hunting adventure.

So while she finishes up one of her last days as a librarian, before her maternity leave, I've visited *three* markets to find this damn flavor.

It's not a popular one — for obvious reasons — so by the time I step through the automatic sliding doors of the fourth market, I'm frustrated as all Hells.

"Hello!" The female Orc clerk calls out, smiling as she scans a can of minced meat.

Lips thin, I give a little wave and look for the freezer aisle. It's a simple spot, with clean floors, bright lights, and organized shelves. The short line of patrons watch me with expressions of curiosity.

Walking up to the female Orc clerk, I send a prayer up to Fortuna for a frozen creamy dessert blessing. "You wouldn't happen to have any chocolate mint and pistachio ice cream, would you?"

The clerk, whose nametag reads *Virinia,* gives me a look of pity, her blue eyes softening. "How far along is your wife?"

Doing a double take, I chuckle. Shoving my hands in my pockets, I ask, "Do all pregnant women have this absurd craving?"

Virinia grins. "With my first two, it's all I had for weeks. My friend too. There's simply something magical about the flavors."

"If you say so," I chuckle. "So you have it?"

Virinia jerks her head of curls toward the back of the brightly lit shop. "Aisle thirteen, near the end."

Relief is a palm to my anxiety. "Thanks."

I turn to walk away; Virinia adds, "Buy three. Trust me."

Humming in agreement, I make the trek down the aisles, filling my arms with five pints. I'm not about to find myself at three in the morning coming here and banging on the locked doors, begging for a miracle.

Virinia's eyes crinkle at edges as she sucks air through her fangs, grabbing the first pint to scan. "A good man, you are. How far along?"

Pride wells up in my chest. "Eleven months."

She gives a low whistle. "The gestation period of Dragons always shocks me. She has two months left?"

I nod, thinking of my wife's round belly. "She's already tired of it." Motioning to the pints of ice cream as she shoves them into a bag, I continue, "I never expected being so impatient. Sometimes, I think I'm more impatient than she is."

Virinia laughs as she rings up the amount. I pull out corals, placing them on the scanner. Rhuth is going to be thrilled, especially if I pair it with a back rub. She loves those.

Handing me the bag of goodies, Virinia winks at me. "I assure you, no one is more impatient than a very pregnant woman. What's her name? Is it her first?"

Nodding again, I grab the bag, relief washing away my fear of failure. "Rhuth, and yes, it's our first, but we're hoping for more. I want four. She wants six."

"So you'll probably have five?" she asks with a knowing look.

"If the goddesses are generous!" I retort with a chuckle. Dragons aren't the most fertile of species, but with enough time, I'm sure we can pull off our dream of a big family. Imagining Rhuth with babies on her hips and toddlers at her thighs warms my already-burning heart.

"Well, good luck. Knowing the power of cravings, I'm sure I'll see you again."

I make a show of lifting the bulging bag. "This will probably last me *at least* three days."

We share a laugh; I wave goodbye, stepping out of the market with a whistle on my lips. Kneeling, I place the pints of ice cream into my insulated backpack.

Walking to the nearby launch pad, I shift into my sleek red dragon form. The world around me grows sharper; more colorful in vision and sound. Grabbing the pack with my claws, careful to not slice the strap, I pump my wings until I'm up in the air, joining the air traffic.

The floating city of Gondora reaches out before me, held in the palm of my goddess Fortuna, the Dragon Goddess whose breath elevated the earth to float in the skies. The domed roofs, sparkling metal buildings, and the rolling mists that never fully disappear, even on scorching days. Uniformed lines of traffic criss-cross at various speeds, making the city teem with life. It never fails to excite me, taking flight.

This is my home, and I love it here.

Falling into the line of traffic headed toward home, I keep an eye on the yellow orbs guiding the pathway. Deviations kill. As the man who owns the top Dragxi company in the city, Flaming Fares, I'd never live it down if I strayed from a path.

On the way, I see some friends flying customers around the city. I blow smoke out of my nostrils in hello, which they return. We aren't close enough to speak mind-to-mind, but the sentiment is the same. I'll see most of them tonight at Rhuth's surprise baby shower.

I've been planning it for months; everyone from my company, plus all of Rhuth's friends, is attending. Our home will be filled with love and laughter. Excitement courses through my veins in anticipation. Her smile will be worth the headache of RSVPs and making sure all diets are accounted for.

Finally, I turn off the major flight path to a side trail lit by blue orbs, deftly sweeping between homes decorated with flowers, ivy, and lush green grass. Our home is modest, set at the end of the trail. A large, clear dome arches toward the blistering sun, lighting up the main living spaces. Last year, we painted the outer walls sky blue, so in the right light, the home almost disappears.

Landing on our large lawn, I shift back to my bi-pedal form and pick up my backpack. Our front door, a beautiful dark blue, squeaks as I push it open. Scenting the air, I can tell Rhuth still isn't home. Smiling, I lock the door behind me. Everyone should be here in an hour. I've spent the morning setting up everything.

Resting on our oversized royal purple couches are new white velvet pillows I bought last week. Flowers decorate every surface; her favorites: peonies of every shade. Soft green and white chiffon streamers drape along the ceiling, and on the wooden kitchen table is a four tiered cake made of chocolate with a cherry ganache.

She's going to love it.

Whistling a tune, I walk into the kitchen. With deep satisfaction, I carefully place each pint of ice cream to the far reaches of the freezer so they stay extra cold.

Turning back to the decorated scene, I place my hands on my hips, taking in our home. Aside from the decorations placed by yours truly, Rhuth has painstakingly made it homey. She loves anything wooden — growing up in the forests of Talume, Rhuth's always favored wood — which means most surfaces are covered in plants.

Pictures of us line the walls. My favorite resides over the gray stone fireplace; it's a picture from our wedding day five years ago. My red scales stand out against the white suit Rhuth picked out for me. My muscular arm is wrapped around her slender shoulders, her light blue scales shining in the sun. Our wedding photographer, Luca, captured the moment where I was whispering into her ear that I couldn't wait to ravish her.

We both gazed at one another with adoration. Now that moment is prominently displayed in our home.

My eyes trailed to the clock on the wall. "Twelve Hells," I growl, rushing to our bedroom. People will start arriving any minute now; I still need to rinse off the day.

I make the shower quick, focusing more on my unkempt black hair. There are some dark circles under my gold eyes, mainly because Rhuth's tossing and turning keeps me up. She's incredibly uncomfortable at this point in the pregnancy, so staying up to do whatever eases her discomfort is the least I can do.

Tonight, I'll sleep like a baby knowing five pints sit in the freezer.

Smiling to myself, I dress in a simple buttoned henley shirt and some jeans that hug my ass, just like Rhuth prefers. She loves the way they ride low, revealing the base of my long ruby tail. If I'm lucky, she'll feel amorous after the party. No matter what she looks like, pregnant for almost a year or not, I'll always crave her body.

As I'm buckling my belt, there's a knock at the door.

Finally.

Jogging down the hallway, I pause to adjust a frame that is somehow slightly crooked. I release a deep exhale and open the door. On the doorstep is my brother, Trinte. A couple of inches shorter than me, the stocky Dragon has his signature toothy grin. His left eye is an iridescent gold glass orb. Long black hair cascades past his large shoulders, shaved above his ears.

His one blue eye widens as he takes in my appearance. "How do you look both exhausted and excited at the same time?"

I resist the urge to give him a brotherly punch on the arm. Instead, I step back so he can bring his blue-scaled ass inside.

"Get a pregnant wife and find out for yourself." He is a perpetual bachelor, so there is a fat chance of that happening.

Trinte scoffs, heading straight to the kitchen. "And have a dung-filled, diaper-wearing youngling screaming in my ear? No thanks."

I close the door behind him after making sure no one else is arriving. I'm desperate to keep this as a surprise for my wife. "Don't say that in front of Rhuth, brother, or I'll descale you."

He whips his blue tail, but grins, making the threat playful. "Maybe you'd finally qualify for most handsome dragon in Gondora."

As he sits on the barstool at the kitchen island, I head to where we store the alcohol. Grabbing the Minga, a spicy wine, I saunter over with two glasses in my other hand. "Beauty is in the eye of the beholder."

"No one understands that more than your wife," he retorts, still grinning.

I inspect his empty hands as I place a glass in front of him. As I pour wine, I ask, "Did you show up without a gift?"

"Check your email," he says smoothly.

Irritated at the non-answer, I pour my wine, then pull out my phone. There's a new email from a travel company. Excitement flutters in my chest as I open it.

My eyes slowly drag to his in disbelief. "You bought us a trip to Slous?"

Joy lights up his cerulean face. "Sure did. It's an open ticket, so you can either go before the birth or after when you need a break. I'll even babysit if you need."

Emotions war in my body, tightening my throat and burning my eyes with tears. We've never been overly affectionate, but I wrap my arms around his broad chest. He returns the hug fiercely, the fire in his chest meeting mine.

"I love you, Fynn," he says, voice raspy. "I'm proud of you."

A rebel tear breaks away from the corner of my eye. "I love you, Trinte."

As I let go, there's another knock at the door. Trinte lets go of me, clearing his throat and gazing at the wall. That's our yearly allotment of affection. Another knock comes; I give him one more grateful smile before heading to the door.

For the next thirty minutes, the knocks keep coming. Soon, my home's filled with laughter and tinkling glasses. I've turned on soft, relaxing music; it's Rhuth's favorite.

While we wait for my lovely wife to arrive, I go around greeting our friends. Gifts pile up in one corner of the living room. The nursery in our spare bedroom will explode with infant supplies after it's all over.

My phone rings. I excuse myself from a conversation with one of my employees and step outside. Scanning the skies, I answer the phone with a smile.

"Hello, beautiful. Are you almost home?" I'm expecting to hear her soft voice, telling me she's only a minute away.

Instead, there's silence.

Frowning, I check to make sure the call's still connected before saying, "Hello?"

"Hello?" The word is hesitant, delivered by a gruff male voice.

There are some moments in life where you know nothing will ever be the same ever again. My gut screams this is one of those moments.

I examine our little garden. Rhuth spends everyday tending to these flowers. This tiny, wonderful slice of life we've been building together.

"Mr. Gleanscale?"

The voice is now concerned.

My shaking voice reflects the earthquake shaking up my reality. "Y-yes? This is he."

Another pause, then the disembodied voice says, "Sir, I'm sorry to be calling from your wife's phone, but it was the only way we could reach you."

This isn't real.

"Where is my wife?" The Fyre inside me sputters out, leaving me as cold as stone.

"Sir, I think it's best if—"

"Where the fuck is my wife?" I roar into the phone, panic now coursing through my blood. The insistent desire to protect.

This isn't real.

Fury, unlike anything I've ever felt, clouds my thoughts and sizzles against my senses. This isn't real. It's a prank. My heart slams into my sternum, as if already in protest of the future. The Fyre in my chest roars, filling up every inch in my body, ready to explode and destroy.

This isn't real.

Behind me, the front door opens. Someone steps up to me: Trinte. He tilts his head, a groove of concern deepening between his brows. My mouth opens, then closes. What can be said?

On the phone, the man says, "Sir, there was an accident ..."

And just like that, my world crumbles, and I collapse to my knees.

2

Orliana

Three Years Ago

The bruises on my face are harder to cover up today than usual. Frowning, I pat the blending sponge against the concealer, willing away the purples and greens. My morbid sense of humor wants to point out that the colors really bring out my dark brown eyes, but I don't feel like smiling.

Wincing when I press too hard, I sigh with frustration. Maybe I should cancel with my best friend, Kyrielle; if she notices the bruises, she'll kill Mikan. She teaches self-defense classes for women in circumstances similar to mine. Which makes this deplorable situation horrifically ironic.

I've spent the last decade hiding this from her — I'm not about to reveal my predicament over a cup of coffee.

Yet, it's the first time I've been allowed to go do something for myself in weeks. The idea of dressing up and seeing my best friend sounds wonderful. A privilege earned. I deserve this.

Which is most likely the exact reason Mikan did what he did last night.

And the make-up isn't doing its job. Leaving the house won't be happening. From behind me, Moxie huffs quietly, resting on the toilet lid. I glance at my familiar, a dark purple ugopeg. One of her gold, cloven hooves paws at the porcelain as she lowers her glittering gold horn jutting from her forehead.

"I know, I know," I whisper, hating that she's here to see it all. A witness to the destruction of her best friend. She can't speak, but Moxie never fails to share her opinions in other ways.

With one more examination of the bruises, I know it's a lost cause. I pick up my phone and dial Kyri's number. She picks up on the third ring. Her sweet voice increases the guilt slithering along my ribs.

"Hello, my beautiful, fabulous best friend. Are you on your way?"

"Hey." My voice cracks, forcing me to clear my throat. When I'm positive I won't start crying, I say, "I can't go. I'm not feeling too good. I think Joulian brought home a bug from school."

Joulian, my ten-year-old son, has never made me sick. Which is probably why she's silent for a beat too long. We've been friends for fifteen years; she knows me better than anyone else.

Except for one very large, very painful detail.

"Joulian's sick?" she asks, her words slow.

My reflection nods, my springy black curls framing my face. Playing with the pendant around my neck, I say, "Yeah, some stomach virus. I'm really nauseous."

There's another moment of silence before she says, "Do you want me to bring some soup?"

I examine at the bruises mottling my burnished skin. Some are older than others. All are noticeable.

Swallowing hard, I say quickly, "No, it's okay. I don't want you to catch anything."

"I don't mind," she says carefully. I love my best friend; she's kind, fiercely loyal, and has a low tolerance for anything she deems as ridiculous or wrong. Which is why I could never tell her about Mikan. I don't need her to end up in a prison somewhere.

"It's okay," I insist, trying not to sound panicked or angry. "Mikan is bringing me soup. I'm sure he'll give me a foot massage, too."

Fat chance of *that* happening.

"Sure." She doesn't sound confident at all. "Well, give me a call if you need anything, okay?"

Forcing a chipper tone, I say, "Of course. I'll talk to you later?"

"Yeah. Love you."

"Love you, too." I hang up with a sigh of relief, stamping down the incessant guilt. I'm not confident she won't show up randomly with soup, but for everyone's sake, I hope she doesn't.

From the kitchen, a cabinet slams. I flinch, my heart responding to the sound with a painful skip. Mikan never went to work today. He's out there, most likely waiting for a second round of arguments and punishments.

And if I stay in here too long, he'll begin pounding on the door, demanding that I "stop acting like a coward and get the fuck out."

My body sags in defeat. This song and dance are predictable. Lifting the pendant, I turn the piece of green crystal in my palm, siphoning my anxiety into it. Instantly, my emotions ebb. Not that it'll last long, but it provides a sliver of bravery to go out there.

Putting away the makeup, careful to make sure not a speck is left on the gleaming surfaces, I practice my smile in the mirror. My teeth are sharp, but worthless against his fists.

Looking at Moxie, I whisper, "Stay hidden."

My sweet familiar flies up on furious small wings, landing on my shoulder. She nuzzles my cheek with her soft goat muzzle and bleats quietly in my ear as if to say, *be careful.* Then she goes invisible. As my familiar, she's there to support, guide, and obey. Mikan hates her, so she's invisible more often than not; a helpless observer.

Bracing for the worst, I quietly turn the doorknob, holding my breath. Blood pounds in my ears, muffling his frustrated mutterings. Another cabinet slams; surely he's not trying to cook.

Creeping down the hallway, I carefully peer around the doorway to our kitchen. It's brightly lit, all white. So much white. Better to show the fuck-ups in. I swear he chose this much white so he could seek out things to blame me for. A splatter of sauce. A stain not wiped up yet. A crumb.

Mikan paces near the farthest counter, twisting a towel in his hands. His blond hair's mussed, like he's run hands through it repeatedly. His pale skin flushes with anger, and I know if he were looking at me, his blue eyes would be full of scorn. Elves are notorious for their dispositions — it's rarely pleasant. I'd thought Mikan was different. We'd met twelve years ago, during the last year of university in the library. Back then, his aura sang of kindness: purples, pinks, and blues.

Now, it's blood red. It's almost always the color of what he tries to carve out of me, one punch at a time.

With jellied knees, I step into the room with a tentative smile. "Are you hungry? I can cook you something."

Like a predator locking onto its prey, his head whips in my direction. The look in his eyes quails my bravery. The tips of his pointed ears turn the color of tomatoes as he stalks over. "Where the fuck have you been?"

It's been fifteen minutes since he last saw me. Confused, I glance over my shoulder. "I-I was in t-the bathroom."

Stopping in front of me, he looms like a weapon ready to be wielded. Heat radiates from his body, but if I step back, it'll make things worse. It activates the actual predatory drive, so it's better to be as still as possible.

Sneering, Mikan squints, inspecting my makeup. "Did you even put any effort into being attractive today?"

Yeah, I wonder why. Instead of opening my mouth, I stare at the ground. Instantly, his hand is under my chin, gently lifting my gaze back to his. Kindness softens his features. I'm no fool — the demons in him are playing tug-o-war. Right now, the nicer one is in charge, but the other one is stronger.

His voice is gentle as he brushes a knuckle against my cheek. Lingers at the blooming bruise. Conflicting emotions skate across his eyes, almost like he regrets what he's done again. "You know I prefer you more natural, Orlee."

Orlee — what was once a beloved nickname has become a curse upon his tongue. Swallowing my fear, I say, "I was going to go out with Kyri, but I stayed home to spend time with you."

He cocks his head, running the knuckle from my cheek to my throat. "I love you so much." Her mouth twists with regret. "I hate fighting with you."

Lies.

"I need a release, baby." A pained expression tightens his features. In a plaintive tone, he begs, "Can you give that to me?"

Adrenaline spikes at his words; a conditioned response. It's a miracle I don't want up every morning in cold sweats. It wouldn't make a difference — he always gets what he wants.

Obediently, I nod. Staying as still as my shaking limbs will allow, I surrender to whatever comes next. Joulian won't be home for another few hours. I've kept him as protected as possible, even if it's becoming harder and harder. For years, Mikan promised to take him away from me. As a prominent lawyer in the city, I've had no choice but to believe him. So, I stay; for Joulian.

In our bond, I feel Moxie's spike of anxiety. *Stay away,* I silently command. She has no option but to listen.

Long, icy fingers wrap around my neck. A familiar collar of bone. Instantly, rage fills me from head to toe. It's consuming, lighting up my existence with a lust for violence. A desperate need to crush.

We hold eye contact as he squeezes my throat. Sweat slips down my spine as I'm devoured by his incessant fury. His hate activates my inherent nature — my power — as a Siphon.

It's called the somapath connection. An energetic flyway of sorts, linking my power to someone's emotions. As a Siphon, his emotions become my own. My flesh siphons it from his; in turn I channel it into my pendant. Some of it lingers, though, rooting into my brain like rot.

Mikan pants as he earnestly pours into me, greedy for relief. Unlike me, he finds peace in the end. He used to say it was better than a cup of coffee or any medication a doctor could prescribe.

I'm a resource. A punching bag. A vessel.

My knees weaken, but his grip only tightens, holding me up by the jaw. I'm overwhelmed by the emotional rampage swirling in his soul. It's what drew me to him originally; all of that pain ached to be healed.

Now I'm the one in desperate need of healing.

When he's done, a sheen of sweat coats his smooth forehead. He gasps as he lets go of my neck. It's consistently tender from his grip. I could use my hands to accept the emotions, but he prefers to shove it into me this way.

I swallow, wincing at the pinching sensation. The pad of Mikan's thumb brushes against my cheek; a gentle caress.

"You did such a good job," he croons. My body betrays me by leaning into the touch. It's disgusting how badly I ache for a kind touch. I whimper, scanning the gentle eyes of my husband. The same eyes that enraptured me all those years ago. A well crafted lie.

"Now," he says, sounding businesslike. Straightening, brushing away invisible crumbs on his shirt, he asks, "Who said you could go out?"

It's a trap. Alarm bells ring in my mind. He steps forward, pushing me back until I hit the wall. There used to be a painting hanging, a bucolic scene of Cyclops guarding sheep.

The frame broke the last time he slammed me here.

His aura flares to a bright red; the color instantly rattles my bones, shaking my body. "Y-you did."

Pressing his muscular frame against my soft curves, Mikan grinds his hips against my belly. "But did you earn it?"

Of course I did, but it's never enough for him. "No."

His breath is hot on my neck as he inhales my scent. "Then why do you think you get to leave?"

"I-I'm staying," I remind him. "To be with you."

One of his hands trails to my skirt, bunching it upward with his fingers. My thighs squeeze together instinctively, a pitiful attempt at protection.

"That's right," he croons, grinding against me again. "To be with me. Like a good girl."

He tries to kiss me, but I turn my head away, squeezing my eyes shut. His body freezes and another one of my pathetic whimpers escapes. When will I learn?

"Look at me." When I don't immediately obey, he roars, *"Look at me!"*

My eyes pop open, and I take in his calm expression. He enjoys this. Cold air touches my thighs as my skirt lifts to my waist. When his fingers find the skin of my thighs, I feel the disgusting lust boiling inside his body. His intentions.

"Mikan, please," I plead against my better judgment. "I'm still sore from last night. Can you please wait?"

"Wait?" His face twists with incredulity. "It's my *right.* I don't need to *wait.*" He spits out the word as if it tastes bitter.

Still, I squirm, trying to pull my dress down. "Let me cook you something. I'll make one of your favorites."

Fury darkens his eyes, like icebergs caught in a storm. Without warning, his hand whips out, slamming into my throat so hard that I can't breathe.

"I'm tired of your disobedience, Orlee." His free hand drops the hem of my skirt. My relief is short-lived as he unbuckles his belt.

My fingers try to pry his hand from his throat, but it's no use. My tongue swells as I try to speak. It's barely audible as I wheeze out, "I-I'm sorry ..."

"I'm sorry," he mocks, theatrically rolling his eyes. Leaning his face close to mine, he inhales from behind my ear and murmurs, "You may be sorry, but I'm tired, baby. So many excuses." The hair raises on my arms as his breath skates across the shell of my ear. "I've tried so hard to train you, but you just—" his hand squeezes tighter; something grinds in my throat. "—don't listen."

His murderous intentions transfer into me like a dark promise.

Mikan pulls back, his violent eyes assessing my face. "It's become a waste of time, baby." As my fingers dig frantically into his fingers, from far away, I hear him say, "I think Joulian will be happier without you."

Without you.

Knowing exactly what that means, a new level of fear roars into my chest, pummeling my heart. Now I claw at his hand in earnest.

He's going to kill me.

I kick out with my feet and reach for his face, hoping to gouge out an eye. I haven't fought back in years, but I can't leave Joulian behind. My son needs me.

A disturbing farce of a smile slowly spreads across his face, peeling away from his white teeth. A garish example of happiness. He won't be happy until he's crushed every part of me.

My mouth gapes open and closes as the world fades.

No!

With the last vestiges of strength, I buck my hips and kick out with my feet. He roars as my foot collides with his groin. His knees buckle, and he lets go. Oxygen fills my lungs.

There's no time to wait.

I scramble away on all fours. Gaining enough momentum, I stand. Stumbling to the drawer with knives, I open it. The world tilts. I shake my head, praying to every goddess available to keep me awake.

For Joulian.

With a grip weaker than string, I spin. Holding out the blade in front of me, I watch him stand. It's like watching a starving beast awaken from hibernation. Lumbering and disoriented, his gaze slowly drags to me. Then onto the knife.

I haven't cried in years, but my eyes burn with tears. This is it. I know it in my bones just as much as I know I love my son. It's me or him today. Resolve encases my bones, fortifying my muscles.

It will be me.

He lunges, closing the distance in three steps. His fingers squeeze my wrist. It snaps. I scream as the knife tumbles onto the tiled floor. I briefly notice a speck of blood on the white. *He'll be so mad.*

A fist pumps into my stomach, forcing air from my lungs. I fall to my knees.

Don't stop.

As he grabs my hair, I reach for the knife. My fingers barely miss it. Tears fall in earnest, spattering the floor, mixing with the spray of blood.

A foot collides with my ribs. There's a cracking sound, followed by blinding pain.

Don't stop.

I try again for the knife. He grabs the back of my neck, yanking me upright to situate me on my heels.

"Look at me," he says with deadly calm. My burning eyes rise to his. For the first time in a decade, I let him see my festering insides, where the unadulterated hate resides. Everything throbs, but I won't die without him knowing that there was a part of me he couldn't break. A part he never got to touch.

"Ah," he says, almost chiding. "I see I haven't done my duty as a husband. Well, let me correct this error."

Stars explode in my vision as he backhands me. My skull slams against the floor. For a terrifying moment, everything disappears.

When my eyelids flutter open again, I see the knife.

It's miles away.

Too far.

A black boot steps into my line of sight. I know this boot too well. It's closer, so I reach for it. Claw my way up the leg, dragging myself forward.

"Are you going to beg for your life?" he sneers. He thinks he's won. In some ways, he has. A part of my soul shriveled up permanently.

But today is the last battle.

I fall limp again, letting go of the leg. The boot steps closer. My breathing is shallow. The heart beating in my ears slows. Death is here. It's in the room with us. Watching. Will its grasp be cold? Or warm and welcoming?

"I'll take real good care of Joulian. My son will grow up knowing his mother was a weak cunt. I'll teach him how to make sure he never finds a woman like you."

My fingers twitch as I reach. They shake as I grasp.

Don't stop.

The boots shift away. My fingers tighten. The boots return, closer to my face. The rubber sole pushes against my face. He intends to crush me under his heel. Despair weakens my resolve for a split second, then Joulian's sweet face is there, renewing my fight.

Don't stop.

"Say goodbye, Orlee."

My cheeks are squished, my jaw shoved to the side, but I'm able to gasp out, "Fuck you."

I strike. Aiming for his Achilles' tendon, I slice the blade through flesh until I hear a pop, then a shrill scream of agony. Mikan's body collapses in front of me.

Don't stop.

Finding every last scrap of energy left in my body, I lunge for him, clawing up his feet; his legs; his chest. He's wailing like a baby, trying to reach for his ruined ankle. I can't even enjoy the sound. Only seconds stand between me and death.

The knife is strong in my grip. We lock eyes, and he knows. He fucking *knows.* But it's not fucking nearly enough.

Grabbing my pendent with one hand, I wrap the other around his throat. Just as he did to me every morning. Except this time, instead of receiving, I give. Pulling every saved emotion from the pendant, I slam them into him. Every hateful inch he's ever given me. I've saved it all, hoping for the perfect moment to return these emotions back to their master.

"All of that's for you," I croon with a sickening grin, returning the words he gave me every night in bed.

Mikan convulses, overcome by it all. It flows from the pendant, through me, into him. I feel his emotions, and while it morphs into devastation for him, I'm unstoppable. Like a goddess Hellsbent on revenge. For once, my power is a beautiful curse; his deliverance.

I snatch up the knife. He's too lost in the consuming emotions to notice, weeping like a baby.

Giving my abuser one last look, I snarl, "Say goodbye, Mikan."

With a heart made of ice and a deadened soul, I slice his throat.

For once, he's the one bleeding. It's beautiful.

Come.

Moxie responds to my silent command, appearing at my side, watching impassively. This moment is for the both of us.

As the knife clatters to the tile, Moxie sniffs the blood while I attempt to inhale oxygen. Everything in my body aches, and the headache is otherworldly.

Moxie paws the blood with a golden cloven hoof and, to my amusement, she hops into the hot liquid. Dancing, Moxie bleats with joy. The smile peeling apart my lips is genuine.

She hates him just as much as I do.

3

Fynn

Present Day

When my wife died, her belly full of our unborn son, she took a part of my soul with her. That's okay — it was never mine to begin with. From the moment I met Rhuth, I happily set aside a piece of myself, reserved for her smiles and laughter. A safe haven for her love.

So it was only natural for it to disappear the day she died.

Every day, I wake up, noting its absence, along with hers, and I think, *Yes, this feels right.* To be whole would be a betrayal.

And I'll never betray my wife.

It's been almost five years since she was stolen from me; a Dragxi accident, of all things. One of my now-former employees veered off the path and collided with a Pegasus carriage. There wasn't a body to recover, not from that height.

I've spent this entire time simply existing, waiting for my time to die. Today is no exception.

My eyes open to our darkened bedroom, the perpetually closed curtains blocking out the sunrise. Rolling onto my back, I stare at the ceiling. As usual, my fingers find their way to my wedding ring. Spinning it, I consider what needs to be done today.

There are new Dragxis to be trained. Paperwork to be pushed. Taxes are due in a month, and I've barely thought about it.

Every single day from the last time I hugged Rhuth steals a little more breath from my lungs. I practically beg time to move slower, to retain the receding sound of her laugh.

Flinging my long legs over the edge of the bed, I rub my face aggressively. Sleep has been an adversary since the night she asked for a pint of ice cream. I'd do anything to have one more night of being woken up by her and those ridiculous cravings.

With a heavy sigh, I start my morning routine, albeit it's less of a routine and more of a performative existence.

Ignoring one side of my closet, I pull out a shirt with the company logo, Flaming Fares, on it and a pair of too-big slacks. Dressing as I walk to the sink, I stare at my reflection. I've grown out my hair, but not by choice. With some care, the dark ringlets framing my face could really enhance my features.

Too bad I don't give a shit.

After quickly running a comb through the strands, I brush my teeth before making my way to the kitchen. Avoiding every picture hanging on the walls, I grab some yogurt and granola. It's all perfunctory, to avoid increasing the gnawing emptiness in my belly.

I sit at the table, chewing mechanically, staring into nothing. When the hunger subsides, I place the dishes in the sink. Halfway disassociated, I walk outside. The sun's warmth doesn't touch the chill inside me. The skies might welcome me as I shift before leaping from the cliff edge, but the golden light can't thaw what's wrong with me.

***

When the paperwork becomes too much, I decide to patrol for fares. It keeps my mind distracted. After shifting into Dragon form, I have the flight technician place the comms collar around my neck and cinch up a seating saddle. With everything in place, I sweep into the sky.

Taxiing fares was something I used to enjoy very much. Listening to the often-dramatic stories of others, then going home to relax, used to feel strangely fulfilling. Like I could experience the complexities of life before returning to my reliable sanctuary, no worse for the wear.

Since home is no longer a sanctuary, the skies comfort me the best way possible — space from the farce of existence.

Eager to waste away the day with mindless trips around the city, I track around the main shopping plaza in the center of the city. When my collar pings and Corsair reports my next booking on the collar, I skim the mist until I land on the platform. My fare, a green Forest Sprite, taps her foot with impatience when she realizes I'm her ride. A phone's glued to her ear and whoever she's speaking with is receiving quite the tongue lashing.

I wait patiently as she settles into her seat.

Looking at her, I mindspeak. ***Where to?***

The woman pauses in her frustrated conversation, barely looking at me. "Loreyll Rotunda."

Activating my magic to create a dome of protection around her, I jump off the cliff and glide into the traffic pathways.

With a whiny voice, she berates whoever is on the other line. "*No,* you *cannot* let him do that." There's a pause before she says, "I'm really goddess damned tired of this, Frederico. When he slept with my sister, I said, 'Whatever.' When he stole a thousand coral from me, I said, 'Whatever.' Now he wants to take Lucy? I bought that miniature manticore with my own money after selling my mother's trinkets after she died. *He can't have her.*"

Sometimes, I hear the craziest things as a Dragxi. Today is no exception, apparently. I can't wait to tell Rhuth—

No.

Shutting off the impulsive, stupid thought, I pretend to mind my own business, when really, I want to know who gains custody of Lucy. Trinte will probably appreciate the story.

The weight on my back shifts as the woman scoots to the other side of the saddle. "Is he there? I'm on a Dragxi; I can have it turn around. I will not let my *ex-boyfriend,* who slept with my *sister,* take my pet manticore too. What's next? *My mother?*"

I snort out smoke, hoping she doesn't notice. People often treat Dragxis as things, not as sentient creatures. Even though we can speak to them, sometimes it doesn't process that there's an audience.

The woman listens to whoever is speaking, then taps my neck. "Can you turn around? I need to go to Guiliden apartments." She pauses, then adds, "Please."

Sure.

I take the nearest turnaround spot to fly in the opposite direction.

The call ends soon after, and I can hear her nails clacking on the phone screen. As much as I want to pry about her boyfriend sleeping with her sister, it's not my place. Usually, the moment they remember a Dragxi is a person listening, they often turn angry.

So, I collect stories to share them with the right people. Rhuth used to find stories like this hysterical. She'd lament about me not asking exploratory questions. Her frustration at the lack of gossip on some days was so charming.

When I land at the apartment building, the woman hops off with a muttered thank you and no tip. *Oh well.* I take off without a backward glance, waiting for the next fare.

The next few are boring enough that I return to headquarters. After my gear's removed, I meander back to my office.

As I make my way through the hallways, I smile politely at my employees. Most are familiar faces, although some are new trainees. After ... the accident ... the training is rigorous. None of them become active fliers until I inspect their skill sets.

When I reach my office, I close the glass door behind me and exhale. Here, no one needs words or eye contact. My office is undecorated, with a desk cluttered with disorganized paperwork, a computer, and a single photo next to it. Sitting in my worn leather chair, I glance at the photo. Rhuth grins at me, encouraging me to chase my dreams.

Fynn, you should start your own business. You hate your boss, so why not become your own?

The words echo in the chasm of my broken mind. Without her, I might very well still be working at the dingy offices at Rutkers, instead of owning the most successful Dragxi company in the city.

"It's all for you," I whisper to her photo softly. Looking away, I wake up my computer and dig into the remaining paperwork.

Before I know it, it's time to go home, but not before I stop at my favorite market.

Virinia smiles as I enter. She's one of the few women I speak to willingly outside of work. When she found out what happened right after the first time we met, she took me under her proverbial wing and always ensured I've eaten. In exchange, she receives free Dragxi rides all over the city whenever she wants.

After checking out the patron unloading items, Virinia reaches under her counter and pulls out a glass container. "I made you your favorite: slivers of roasted piglet, some mashed corons, and leafy vegetables because I know you're not eating well."

She gives a pointed glance at my baggy clothes. They used to fit snugly. I ignore the comment, but offer a small, grateful smile as I take the container from her hands.

"Thank you. I've been craving piglet."

Her jutting fangs flash as she grins. "Eat all of it. Don't make me ask for photographic proof."

I grunt, rolling my eyes as I place it in my backpack. "Maybe I've just been busy."

Her eyes narrow on me before trailing to the patron walking up with a basket full of items. "Flying all day and playing video games at night isn't 'busy,' Fynn."

"Are you insulting Dragon culture now?" I tease half-heartedly. She always tries to draw out some playful banter, but it's usually a failure. She'd have better luck trying to converse with a pile of laundry.

A gleam enters her eye as she scans the items. "Tomorrow, I'll make worm soup to force you to eat something else."

"I like worms," I lie. "Don't threaten me with a good time."

She harrumphs, dismissing me. With another small smile, I thank her again before heading back outside. Virinia isn't wrong — my life is a disgusting display of bachelorhood, except worse. The depression sank its claws into everything years ago, refusing to let any form of happiness into my life.

And that's fine. If Rhuth isn't here to be happy with me, I don't want it.

4

Orliana

Present Day

After Mikan died, I got rid of everything white in the house. I took a hammer to the tiles. Painted the walls various colors when sleep was elusive. The white sheets were shredded with a knife in a fit of rage.

I removed every kitchen cabinet, preferring a more open design. All pieces of wood were painted whatever color I felt like at the moment.

As a result, our house has become a home, especially as I replaced every bit of art with pieces from local artists. Each is an explosion of color, nonsensical in its delivery, all except for one.

Situated on the wall across from my bed is an oil painting of a Dragon flying across endless skies with pillars of clouds. It caught my eye one day when Joulian and I went to a local farmer's market. Every day, I study it before leaving the bedroom, promising to never let my inner fire die ever again. There's something so powerful, yet solitary, about the image.

The way I've felt every day since I killed my husband.

Today's a little different. Instead of opening my eyes to the painting, I'm greeted with a purple ugopeg threatening to poke my eye out with her golden horn. Moxie flaps her wings in demand.

"What time is it?" Groaning, I run fingers over the coarse goat fur. "Can't you wait a little longer for a slice of bacon?"

She bleats her disagreement while hopping, that little tail flicking side to side. While she can't speak to me, Moxie can pass her emotions along our bond, and right now, it's hunger. She doesn't even need to eat — she just really likes bacon.

When she widens her stance and lowers her horn again, I'm tempted to bop her with a pillow. "Patience is a virtue, you know."

She snorts as she flits off the bed, giving me space to get out of bed. I don't even get the luxury of laziness; familiars can be quite demanding. At least mine is.

After going through my morning routine of styling my hair, washing my face, and putting on my favorite perfume — Mikan hated it, so I wear it daily — I choose from the endless options of clothing hanging in my closet. Skipping the makeup, I follow Moxie to the kitchen. She zooms around my mass of curls as if she can herd me toward the bacon faster.

When she misjudges the distance and grazes the side of my head, I glare at her. "You know damn well it's going to take a few minutes to cook up breakfast, your highness. Go wake up Joulian."

Moxie's golden eyes narrow; with a huff, she heads down the hallway to my son's bedroom. He likes to sleep in until the very last possible second, which allows me to have a quiet morning. I brew myself some tea and begin making pancakes, his favorite.

The large window, facing the center of Gondora, reveals traffic already intensifying. Dragxis and fliers sweep across the air in orderly rows. For the umpteenth time, I admire their grace and power. The goddesses did not see it fit to give me wings, but it doesn't stop me from dreaming. The freedom of endless horizons when you have wings ... the potential of power sounds intoxicating.

"Pancakes?" Joulian says, moseying into the kitchen with pattering feet. His blue eyes, stark against his dark golden skin, peer around my hips where the bowl of batter rests.

I stir enthusiastically, grinning. "It's your favorite, right?"

Joulian nods, pulling juice out of the fridge to pour both of us a glass. A brush has clearly been ignored, if his mass of messy, dark curls is any indication. I'm grateful every day that his features take after me, and not his father. Minus his eyes; they're as piercing blue as Mikan's.

Moxie flies into the room, coming right up to the stove, examining the slices of bacon sizzling in a pan. Satisfied, she lands on the counter and sits on her haunches, waiting. Right behind her is Greg, Joulian's blue crow familiar. He lands on the table, letting loose a loud caw.

Giving me a deep look of distrust, Joulian says, "It's my favorite, but why today? It's not even a special day."

"Every day you're alive is special," I sing, tousling his tight curls. He jerks away like a typical teenage boy, expression twisted in disgust.

"Come on, Mom. I'm not a kid anymore. I'm thirteen, you know."

"Forgive me," I tease, turning the stove on. "I forgot you're a grown man now. Will you pay bills, too?"

"I'm not that old," he says, serious as can be as he sits at the table. Moxie snorts.

"Good," I say, pouring batter onto the hot pan. "Because I don't cook for grown men anymore."

Joulian is quiet, but it takes me a second to notice. When he doesn't respond, I glance up to see him staring at his juice.

"You okay?"

I'm startled to find his eyes full of sadness. Pancakes forgotten, I rush over to him and kneel beside his chair, smoothing away a rogue curl. "What's wrong?"

"You used to cook for Dad," he rasps, lower lip quivering.

Blood freezes in my veins. We never talk about Mikan, not for years. In fact, Joulian has no idea what happened. He was young enough that it was easy to brush off Mikan's death as an unfortunate circumstance. Since it was self-defense, I didn't spend a moment detained. The blood was cleaned up while my parents watched him. The funeral was small and quick. Joulian never asked about him; a part of me has always been relieved.

But he's getting older, so it makes sense for this to start encroaching on our peace.

Moxie betrays our shared fear by laying flat on the counter, her long floppy ears like purple pancakes on the tile. Exhaling a loaded breath, I nod. "I did."

I smell burning, forcing me to hurry and flip the half-cooked pancakes. They're dark brown. He'll still eat them. When they're all flipped, I peek at my son.

He's cataloguing me, as if appraising exactly what question to ask next. Dread coils like an angry serpent in my gut. One day, he'll need to know what happened. *Just don't let it be today.*

It's cowardly, but I don't coax out anymore conversation. Instead, I flip the pancakes with shaking hands, carefully towering them in the center of his plate. While they cool, I make him scrambled eggs, every one of my nerve endings on alert. It's almost a complete fear response; talking about Mikan does that to me.

Pulling out Moxie's doll-sized plate, I break up a slice of bacon into small chunks. She springs from the counter, dour mood forgotten. The sound of tiny clopping hooves makes me smile as I place the feast in front of her.

When Joulian's plate is full, I look up, stalling as I see his determined expression. He's going to make it a thing today; I can tell.

Bracing, I bring over the food with a smile. Slowly, he grabs the fork, but the tension is thick in the air.

Taking a sip of my tea, I wait as it builds inside him. I want this to unfold naturally, without having to prod it out. He needs to explore this in a way that makes sense to him — not in a way that will relieve me of my emotional burden immediately.

Joulian cuts into his pancakes, chewing mechanically as he continues to stare down at his plate. He's a thoughtful boy, always examining emotions before giving them life.

Finally, his eyes meet mine. "What really happened to Dad?"

My knee jiggles with anxiety as I fight to keep the hysteria at bay. He needs his mother, not her trauma. Cautious, I say, "Why do you ask?"

"Gimer, my friend at school, said Dad was a piece of Minotaur dung."

I spin the tea mug, needing to busy my hands. That's certainly one applicable title for my dead husband. "Why would he say such a thing?"

Joulian shrugs, taking another bite of pancake. "Gimer is a dunghole, Mom. But..." He stares at the table, frowning.

"But what?"

His eyes meet mine again, appearing troubled. "I've been having bad dreams, Mom. About Dad. Where he's being really mean to you. I don't know if those memories are real."

As much as I tried to keep Joulian away from the worst of it, when he was younger he witnessed some attacks. I'd always hoped he was too young, but apparently not.

"That sounds really scary." I'm being a coward, but I don't care because what I need is time; time to regroup and rethink.

My answer is clearly unsatisfactory because he scrunches his nose and furrows his brow. "That's all you're going to say? It's scary?" Dropping his fork on the plate with a level of surprising force, he demands, "Did Dad used to hurt you"

I glance at the clock on the wall, shaped like an owl; a gift from my mother. "You need to head out for school, bubs."

Joulian explodes, shoving away from the table as he stands. When he slams his hands on the table, I flinch; I can't help it. He doesn't even notice, too wrapped up in his anger. "*Fuck* school, Mom. Did Dad used to hurt you or *not?*"

Where in the Hells is this coming from? Why now? Why today?

Moxie flies to my shoulder, lowering her horn to him in a threat.

"Easy." I bring my hand to her small back, settling her need to protect. She knows Joulian won't hurt me; I know he won't. But my body hasn't caught the memo yet, and that's what's triggering her. It was why she was required to hide more often than not around Mikan — she might've genuinely taken his eyeballs out, but he would've crushed her in his fist.

Struggling to keep the fear out of my voice, I say evenly, "First off, Joulian, fix your language. This kind of conversation isn't meant for a school morning. If you'd like to discuss this calmly later—" I raise an eyebrow at him, pretending that his outburst doesn't bother me. "—we can. But if you're going to raise your voice, please understand I will not tolerate this level of disrespect. So finish your breakfast and grab your things. This conversation is over."

"But—"

"Now."

Shoving away the remaining bites of pancakes, Joulian stalks out of the room. When I hear his bedroom door slam, I exhale a shaking breath. Interlocking my fingers, I press my hands into my thighs, willing them to steady. Fear claws up my throat, battering against my self-control. *Do not cry.*

Joulian's young. It's natural for him to want more information. Now that I know he wants said information, I can spend the day formulating a way to explain things in an age-appropriate way. He idolized his father, like most boys, so it needs to be done carefully.

When he emerges from his bedroom, Joulian gives me the silent treatment. Greg ignores me in solidarity, balancing on his shoulder. I try to muffle the sting as he refuses to look at me, even when the Dragxi shows up to whisk him away to school. No backward glance or small wave. Only rejection.

When I'm back in the house, I mechanically walk back to my bedroom. Tossing away the pillows, I crawl back under my comforter. Moxie joins me, nestling between my arms. Curling into myself, hugging my knees close, I focus on taking deep breaths. When the tears arrive, I wipe them away faster than they can fall, so it's like I'm not crying at all.

5

Fynn

The one thing I enjoy is playing video games. It's such a stereotype; a Dragxi who loves having a controller in his claws and kicking ass in virtual worlds with strangers.

On a microphone, my reality fades away, and I'm just Fynn — a typical Dragon consumed by bright screens, chattering voices in my ear, and a comfortable chair cradling my body.

Tonight is the Battlepalooza, a mega event involving thousands of Gondorans, and citizens from other provinces. The game of choice is Rukbegger, an open world game where players team up to fight opposing factions, using a plethora of magical weapons.

My team, the Threshers, is undefeated. Trinte is my co-leader with the job of recruiting the best of the best. Our core group comprises four other players: Curly, Synava, Euclid, and Burno. I have no idea where they live or who they are, despite playing together for years at this point. That's the beauty of gaming, I suppose.

After a long day at the office, it's a relief to arrive home with the generous meal from Virinia, by-passing the living spaces to head straight to my game room. Over the years, I've decked it out with up-lighting, an excellent chair, a top-of-the-line gaming system, and two screens mounted on the wall. The curtains, as usual, are pulled tight.

Flipping on the mood lights, I drop the food on the black desk. Next to my desk is a small fridge with drinks. Turning on my console, I sit in the chair and pry open the container.

It smells incredible. Guilt nibbles at my sense of self; I'm not nice enough to Virinia. I need to do something in return because honestly, starvation would've been an option without her. Half the time, I can barely make myself eat, but her kindness keeps this hollow body alive.

Taking my first bite, I settle into the chair and start up the game. Securing my headphones, I scan the screen to see who's on. Trinte — username: StupendousSkies, Curly: Churloulou, and Euclid: LazyWave. Grabbing my controller, I turn on the microphone. Selecting our group chat, I pause to listen. They're chattering excitedly about the tournament.

"Hey."

Together they say, "Hey TopDrag!"

Chuckling, I start Rukbegger. "Where's Synava? Shouldn't she be on right now?"

"Ugh." Curly makes a sound of disgust. "Her boyfriend invited her on a date." Curly sounds mildly jealous. "I can't believe she'd abandon us for dinner."

I eye my piglet. "Yeah, how crazy."

Trinte speaks next, a teasing tone in his voice. "Have *you* at least eaten today, Fynn?"

"I am," I say defensively. "Virinia had dinner ready and everything."

"Is she single?" He jokes, but I know what he's really asking: *would you date her?*

Biting back a growl, I say evenly, "She's engaged, dunghole. She's just nice to me."

"Yeah, can't women just be nice?" Euclid fires back. A smile quirks my lips. Euclid has a small, tiny voice that always belies a fiery attitude.

"Whatever," Trinte mutters. "Either way, we're down a person."

"I have a solution," Curly declares in a pleased tone. "I met a player last week, MeanCat. She's willing to join us."

It's my turn to make a sound of disgust. "*Ugh,* Curls, we do *not* need a new person today of all days. I *actually* want to win again."

"Is it because she's a girl?" Euclid accuses.

Even though she can't see it, I roll my eyes. "I play with you just fine, don't I?"

"Well, that's true ..." she says slowly. "But we do need another person. It's better than having an empty spot and being disqualified."

"True," I admit. With a sigh, I say, "Fine. Send her an invite."

"On it," Curly declares.

While we wait for the newcomer, I continue eating in silence, listening to them discuss their lives. Trinte is talking to a new woman, some Water Sprite from Slous. Euclid teaches grade school and regales us with a story about a young Gargoyle getting in trouble for giving piggyback rides, almost killing a fellow student. Curly ... Well, Curly does cam work. They've never told us where; I'm not even sure what species they are, but the stories are always amusing.

"And then his six tentacled dicks got wrapped together," Curly nearly screams with delight. "I could barely keep it together as the poor Kraken kept apologizing, trying to untie them. But you know how those suckers stick to everything."

Trinte makes a sound of disbelief. "Sometimes I think having one dick is a lot of work; I can't imagine *six!*"

Scraping up the last bite, I hear Euclid say, "I can't imagine dating someone with more than one dick. I mean, what do you *do* with the extras?"

"Get creative?" Trinte offers. "Dragons can thicken their dicks. It's not the same, but still a fun party trick. Just ask Fynn."

Just as I'm about to give him a solid tongue lashing, a soft, yet alarmed voice says, "Hello?"

Squeezing the bridge of my nose with two claws, I close my eyes. My brother is such a mess sometimes. As the main leader, it's my job to greet newcomers and smooth over any insanity that might occur. Like the discussion of genitals.

"Hello MeanCat," I say smoothly. "Welcome to the Threshers. You came at the right time; my brother Trinte was about to apologize for inappropriate commentary."

I hear Trinte swear under his breath. "Sorry for talking about our inflatable dicks, Fynn."

"Trin," I warn. "I'll block you for the day."

He knows I mean it, too. I take mic etiquette seriously. MeanCat could report us for inappropriate behavior as well. I'm not about to lose my entire team's standing because my brother wants to poke at the metaphorical sleeping Dragon. It's not like I'd even have an interesting answer, audience or not; I haven't touched my dick in years.

MeanCat chuckles. "Oh, I love a good sex conversation. But yeah, maybe we should spend this time catching me up on protocols, plays, and the game plan?"

I'm relieved to hear her blow past the inappropriateness. "Sounds good. Euclid?"

Turning my mic off, I listen to the team give MeanCat the rundown on everything we have planned. Trinte does most of the talking since it irritates me to no end, speaking more than necessary.

The countdown begins at the top right corner. Grabbing my drink, I resettle in my chair. The player count in the bottom left corner shows twenty-thousand. That means there are over thirty-three hundred teams competing.

By round two, that number's halved. We're steadily creeping up to the top one hundred. Our avatars hunt down the others in a joyous virtual murder spree, and even I can't resist a gleeful crow of victory as I wipe out three teams at once with a well-placed spell.

"That was great, TopDrag!" MeanCat chirps.

I smile at the compliment. "Took five years to master that one."

"I can tell," she says, a smile in her soft voice. "Watch this!"

To my surprise, her avatar leaps into the air, slams her broadsword into the grass, and wipes out twenty players at once. Their decimated remains flung to the furthest reaches of the map. I can imagine the screaming occurring on other mics. The thought makes a tiny smile pull at my lips.

"That was impressive," I say begrudgingly. "How'd you do that?"

I click on the message that pops up. Inside are command instructions from her.

"Just sent the code to you!"

"I want it, too!" Euclid pleas. "To show these men what's what!"

MeanCat laughs. "Okay, I sent it to the whole team."

I download the code to use later. In a voice rough with determination, I say, "Okay, let's get this final push going. If we all activate that same move, we can ravage these dungholes into all twelve Hells!"

So we do. Within thirty minutes, we're in the top five. Then top three. Finally, it's between us and the MercurialMercs, a team we've beaten repeatedly. Now that there's only twelve of us, they're on mic, too.

"Who's the bitch using that fucking WideBerth casting?" a nasally voice demands.

"Hello there, Xeno," I say smoothly, eager to put the pup in his place. He's always gotten on my nerves, and using foul language over mic really pisses me off. "We all have. Are you going to cry your way through this massacre?"

Xeno snorts. "Well, actually, I am glad to know it's all of you. I can't wait to tell my wife how I beat your asses tonight."

"By wife, do you mean your mom?" Trinte taunts.

MeanCat cackles. "Ooohhh, burn!"

"Shut up, bitch," Xeno snarls. "I'm married, okay?"

"Is she a hydra?" Euclid says sweetly. I notice her avatar sneaking up behind him, wielding her glowing staff.

Distracting him, I guide my avatar in front of him and draw my sword. Fire spreads across the blade. Even though it isn't real, I love knowing how deadly the weapon is.

"Come on, Xeno. Why don't you tell me how you love being married to your mother?"

His avatar lunges while my team engages the others. Vibrant balls of spells fly across the scream. Curly screams dramatically when one of the opposing team stabs deeply into their avatar.

"Sonofabitch," Curly swears. There's a loud clanging sound as their controller undoubtedly flies out of their hands.

I bite back a chuckle, focused on distracting Xeno. "What are you waiting for?" I taunt. "Your mommy's permission?"

I wince as Euclid screeches with fury, her avatar crumpling onto the digital grass. She was my game plan. Xeno's avatar and mine slam blades together, and I try to see where MeanCat and Trinte are. They aren't in my field of vision, so I'm forced to focus on Xeno.

"Got 'em!" MeanCat hoots with glee.

"How many?" I grin, my fingers cramping from the furious movement required to engage in the battle.

"Two left, including him," Trinte reports.

"Easy," I say dryly. Xeno's at a higher level than me, so when he overpowers my avatar, I break my own rules and swear over mic.

"That's right," the skeezy player purrs. "Come to Papa."

"Xeno?" MeanCat says.

My avatar loses an arm; it takes every ounce of self-control to not roar with frustration.

"What?" Xeno says, hacking off my avatar's leg.

"That's what your daddy said to me last night," MeanCat says gleefully, stabbing his avatar right through the chest.

It's a glorious vision and, forgetting myself, I holler with excitement, thrusting a fist in the air, happy for a split second. It's why I love playing video games — sometimes, the achievements feel like actual accomplishments. Like my life isn't a total loss.

Reality snaps back into place and I swallow the joy escaping from my mouth. Resettling my attitude, I say, "Great job, MeanCat."

"I live for the thrill of the kill," she crows, then breaks into a fit of cackles. I gnaw on my lips, refusing to smile.

"That was cheating!" Xeno declares.

"That was skill," I correct. "Now quit being a baby and apologize for your rudeness."

He leaves the game, as expected. Sore loser.

"What a pussy!" Trinte hollers, and I jerk back at the loudness in my ears.

"Language," I growl.

"Sorry, but he is," Trinte jokes. "MeanCat, you're welcome back at any time!"

"Thanks everyone! I had fun!" Her soft voice is filled with laughter.

I glance at the clock and groan. It's later than normal. "I have to go. Good game, everyone."

Everyone says their goodbyes, and I log off. The silence of the house layers over my senses like a wet blanket. My focus returns to the controller still in my hand.

Turning the console back on, I resettle in the chair. It's better than allowing the silence to choke me.

6

Orliana

Joulian doesn't bring up his father when he comes home and I'm relieved. After spending the whole day considering how to broach the topic, I was coming up blank. It's tense throughout dinner, and by the time he goes to bed, my heart aches.

When I'm sure he's asleep, I lock myself in my bedroom to call my mom. She's always able to find a way to offer comfort. As the phone rings, I curl up on my bed, pulling a thick pink blanket over up to my hips. Moxie appears at my side, immediately resting her head on my hip. I run my nails through her soft fur, enjoying the soothing motion.

Mom answers on the fifth ring. "Hello my sweet, wonderful, beautiful daughter, how are you?"

I let out a heavy, exasperated sigh, earning a chuckle.

"Oh no, what happened?"

Diving right into it, I say, "Joulian asked about Mikan."

She inhales sharply. "About what?"

Closing my eyes, I grasp at the dregs of my strength to say, "Whether or not he used to hurt me. He's ..." I trail off, struggling to say the words. "He's having nightmares that sound like memories."

"Oh, muffin, I'm sorry to hear that. What did you tell him?"

Shame slithers under my skin. "I ... I avoided discussing it." I bite the inside of my cheek, pushing down the deep grief still simmering in my soul.

Mom sighs. In a gentle but firm tone, she admonishes me with, "Orliana, you need to talk to him about it."

I curl into my mound of pillows, half-hoping one will suffocate me into a nap. "What do I say? 'Sorry, but your father tried to kill me and before that, he beat me when you weren't around'?" I make a sound of disgust as I flop onto my back. "No little boy wants to hear that, Mom."

"I agree, but if he's old enough to ask, he's old enough to know."

I'm not sure if I agree with that sentiment. "He's only thirteen."

"I know how old my grandchild is," she chides. "And I stand by what I said. Joulian is intelligent. He might surprise you."

It's not that I want to hide this from him forever; I know that isn't possible. But a part of me worries that I've already fucked up enough of his childhood — I want him to retain what innocence he has for as long as possible.

Staring at the small crack in the ceiling, I nibble on my lip. "Maybe I can tell him a little bit. Not all of it." I pause, then, "I'm not ready for him to view me differently, you know?"

Mom's voice is mournful when she says, "How would he view you differently?"

I squeeze my eyes shut, the muscles in my already-tired body clenching. Moxie nuzzles my hand. Her soft muzzle plays with one of my fingers, a habit she's had since we were young. "That I'm weak, Mom. That I let Mikan rule us with an iron fist and I never left."

"Orliana Veritas," she says sharply. "Do you honestly believe that about yourself?"

"Yes." The answer is swift and honest. "I do. Maybe if I'd told you or Kyri or *somebody,* maybe things would've changed. If I'd left after the first punch ..." The words freeze in my throat.

When she realizes I'm unable to continue, Mom says softly, "Mikan was one of the best manipulators I've ever met. He could manipulate his aura, for goddesses' sake. We're Siphons and neither of us caught on. As for not leaving, how could you? He would've chased you to the ends of Avalon for his son. You stayed for your son; it's a choice most mothers would make."

She's definitely not wrong about Mikan being a talented manipulator. Our ability to read auras and know if someone is being dishonest works with almost everyone. The issue with Mikan, to the best we can surmise, is that he truly didn't think he was doing anything wrong; therefore, he technically couldn't reveal dishonesty because he believed all of his own lies. The most dangerous kind of psychopath.

My eyes trail to the painting across from my bed. "He never touched Joulian, but what if he had? I should've *left*. It's made me doubt my ability since, Mom. I can barely tolerate being around people, let alone men. How do I explain these things to Joulian?"

"Well, you don't," she says simply. "He's most likely already noticed that you rarely leave the house. Correct me if I'm wrong, but your only friend is Kyri."

I wince, hating the truth. Nowadays, I avoid the truth more than is healthy. I've had enough pain to last me seven lifetimes; I'm okay with not facing certain things now.

"I keep my circle small," I say defensively. "As the guardian assigned to Joulian's trust, I'm able to stay home to take care of him as much as possible. I can't exactly be there for my son if I'm off gallivanting, can I?"

Mom scoffs, cutting to the core of my truth. "You're so afraid of being hurt, Orliana, but you're also slowly rotting away in that home."

Anger flares, and I sit upright, gripping the phone tightly. "I called you for comfort, Mom. Not a psychological dissection."

"Is that so?"

Unlike me, Mom always digs for the foundational truths of everything. "Just as I know you, sweet daughter, you know me. You didn't call me to coddle you and say it's okay to hide things from Joulian."

Ugh. She's right. I'm too stubborn to admit it though. It's childish, but I say it anyway. "Maybe I want to rot in this house. Have you ever considered that?"

"Orliana, don't be ridiculous. You're thirty-five; there's still so much more life to live. There's time to find a new partner; a better one."

A bitter laugh escapes before I can stop it. "I do not want a new partner, Mom. I'm happy being alone."

"Are you?"

Instantly, my eyes flick to my nightstand where my battery-operated boyfriends reside. "Yes. I'm fine. I promise. I don't need to go find someone."

"And if I want more grandbabies?" she says, sounding a little frustrated. She means well, but she's on husband number three — she's not a shining example of sensible romance. Although she'd argue otherwise.

"Mother," I say, exasperated. "Please let me live my life as I see fit. Right now, I'm okay being alone. I prefer it."

Emet is going to strike me down from her heaven for being dishonest. She's a benevolent goddess, but as a Siphon, one of her Chosen, it's taboo to lie. Guilt pools in my gut, stirring itself into a stomachache.

"I don't believe you," Mom says primly. "I think you need to find things to do. Go out and see the world."

Bone-deep exhaustion weighs down, sinking me into the mattress. "I'm going to sleep. Tomorrow, Joulian has a career fair."

"A career fair?" she says, incredulous. "He's thirteen."

"What happened to his being mature?" I say snidely, then wince. "Sorry. That was petty. It's an introduction to some careers; some kids may find their passion early."

"Sounds boring," she says, her voice finally back to its normal cheer. "Do you want company?"

I want to say no, but she'll probably call me during the event, asking all sorts of questions. Better to appear more amenable immediately. "Sure. It begins at ten."

"I'll see you both there. So much time has passed since I've seen Joulian; is he taller?"

"Mom, you saw him three days ago," I say dryly.

She chuckles. "At that age, three days can equal three inches. Let me fuss over my only grandson."

"Goodnight, Mom." It's a feat hiding the irritation from my clipped tone.

"Goodnight, Muffin."

But ending the call, I don't go to sleep. No, instead I stare at the painting, watching the dragon's wings halfway disappear into a dark gray cloud. When I close my eyes, I can almost feel the air on my face, the sound of leather wings against gusts of wind.

For the millionth time in my life, I wonder what it'd be like, being that free. To have nothing above or below, with only silence and space to keep you company.

I bet it's wonderful.

7

Fynn

I hate flying.

It's not the only thing I hate; the list has grown over the years. But the skies hold memories. Some clouds are similar shapes to the ones we used to fly past, ripping off the barely scabbed wound that is my heart. Scents cemented in my mind become almost-daily assaults. Even certain colors of the blue sky reminds me of her soft skin.

A Dragon who hates the sky might as well be dead.

Sometimes, I wish I were.

Then I'd be where my home is.

Melancholic thoughts plague me as I wake up, groggy from a late night of gaming. A quiet part of me knows this is no way to exist; Rhuth would be absolutely furious with me. She would've flung a plant at me, demanding I get my head out of my ass. I'm even growing sick of myself, sick of this pathetic attempt at living.

A change is needed.

Some day.

Not today.

After getting dressed, I collect the watering can from a cabinet in the kitchen and begin the process of tending to all of Rhuth's plants. It's time consuming. Some days require more work than others, but I've only lost one plant since she ... died. That loss was almost as profound as actually losing her, so I'm determined to keep every single leaf green and healthy.

It takes the better part of an hour. By the end, my back aches from bending over. Being forty is no joke. My father always warned me that age creeps up faster than shooting stars. Now, as I rub my lower back with a wince, I begrudgingly realize how right he'd been.

With the plants watered and fed, I make time for a quiet breakfast, staring into nothing. Right at eight in the morning, I'm on my way to the comms building.

Trinte meets me at the landing pad before I've even shifted, which doesn't bode well. Scowling, I stride toward him. He's wringing his hands, a pained expression full of dread prickling my unease.

"What?" I bark out the word, knowing I won't like whatever he says.

He rubs a hand against the back of his neck, looking away. "Yeah, so I forgot I have a doctor's appointment today; I've waited six months for it."

"So?" I put my hands on my hips in disbelief. "Go to the appointment."

"Yeah ..." Trinte grimaces, peeking at me from the corner of his eye. My stomach rolls with apprehension. "So I promised Gretchin that I'd attend the career fair today at the local school."

"No." I take a step back, my pulse quickening. "Absolutely not."

Now he turns to face me, going in for the kill. "You know we've owed Gretchin since she got us that emergency permit. We can't back out now."

"No."

"Please?"

"No."

Trinte whips out his phone and thrusts it toward me. "You can tell her a booth will be left empty because you don't want to stand there for a couple of hours and hand out brochures."

I growl as anxiety buzzes under my skin. I don't want reminders of my loss. "You know I'm no good with kids."

"You're fine with kids. Just, I don't know, *smile?*" The last word's said weakly, as if he's suddenly remembered who in the Hells he's talking to.

I cock my head. He makes it sound so ... simple. *"Smile?"*

He lowers the phone, tucking it back into a pocket. Sensing an opening, he says in a rush, "Yeah. Just ... smile. Most of the kids won't even qualify through their species limitations, obviously. It's more performative than anything. Just stand there."

"And smile." I say flatly.

This elicits a rough sigh of exasperation. "You used to do that. A lot."

"Do what a lot?"

"Smile," he says angrily. When my head rears back at the insult, he inhales sharply and hangs his head. "Sorry. I shouldn't have said that." His eyes meet mine again, and there's earnestness in his expression. "I can't cancel this appointment. I'd fully planned to go on my own; there was no intention of trapping you into this. Please. It's only for a couple of hours."

With another deep-throated growl, I shove past him. "Fine. Send me details."

"Great!" He jogs to catch up to me, pulling out his phone again to send the details. "I've already had Nicko setting things up."

Irritation grinds my jaw. "Why couldn't Nicko do it, then?"

Trinte scoffs as he sends me an email. "Nicko has the personality of a Slogoth."

"And someone who has forgotten how to smile is any better?" I say, unable to resist the barb.

He winces. "I'm sorry I said that. It was unfair. But..."

Opening the door to the comms center, I let him step into the building. "But what? Just say it, brother."

All around us are employees hustling to wherever they're supposed to be, but some pause. When I send them a glare, they scurry away.

Trinte lowers his voice, cognizant of listening ears. "But it's true. I haven't seen you really smile in years."

"My wife is dead," I say dryly, refusing to let the truth sting.

Apparently that excuse is dried up, because he doesn't even try to look abashed. "Yes, but that doesn't mean you need to join her before your time."

The fire in my chest roars for the first time in a very long time. He's right — I know he is. Mere minutes ago, I was thinking the same thing. But coming from his mouth pisses me off.

"I'm still alive. I didn't take matters into my own hands. Let me grieve on my own."

"In less than a month, it'll be five years, brother." He says the words softly; sadly. "Rhuth would hate how much you've allowed yourself to wallow in her death. She might even have walloped you upside the head for it."

Again, he's not wrong. The fire peters out, turning back into embers. My shoulders slump and I swallow hard, trying to shove down the different emotions suddenly appearing. Numbness has been a gift I've indulged in for far too long.

I clap a hand on his shoulder roughly. "I'm not ready yet. You need to respect that. There's no timer on healing; so telling me how many years have passed only helps mark the time, not make it disappear."

Trinte at least appears contrite. "Okay. I'm sorry for pushing." He looks thoughtful, eyebrows rising with each passing second. "What are you going to do at the Weyr reunion next month?"

I'm unable to hide my surprise. "Reunion?"

He gives me a sideways glance. "Yeah. Aunt Teale sent out the invites over email last week. Did you not receive it?"

I'm loath to admit that even though I'm playing video games every night, I almost never check my email. Grunting, I pull out my phone to find the email. Sifting through the other ignored emails, I find it.

"Sonofagorgon," I curse. "We haven't had one of these reunions in years. Why now?"

Trinte shrugs. "I think it's because of ..." His voice trails off, not willing to poke at that open wound again, but his look implies it's related to Rhuth's death. He recovers quickly. "I think they're hoping enough time has passed that everyone can get together without it feeling like a funeral."

He winces at the last word, and I hate myself for making my brother treat me like I need to be coddled. I'm the oldest — he shouldn't be the one comforting me, even if we're only a handful of years apart in age.

Going to the Weyr reunion sounds like a nightmare. It's most likely going to be exactly like this conversation, except repeatedly. Over and over again, people will falter on words like *dead* and *death.* They might not even mention Rhuth's name in fear of setting off some miserable chain of events.

There's no way I'm going. None. I'd rather slice through the membrane of a wing than endure my aunt asking if I've found anyone — *never* — and when I'll get married again — *never.* I'm willing to bet a thousand corals she'll ask about nephews or nieces. I'd rather cut off my wings than hear that goddess-forsaken question. There's no way in all twelve Hells I'm going.

Trinte must see this decision in my expression because he sighs heavily, but doesn't push the issue. Instead, he checks his watch. "You'll need to be there in twenty minutes."

Right. The career fair.

Giving him one last nasty glare, I stalk over to the landing pad. This was not how I expected to spend my day, but Trinte has been nothing but patient with me for almost five years; longer than that, if I'm being honest.

It's the least I can do.

8

Orliana

Mom meets us at the front of the school, beaming when she sees her grandson. The school grounds teem with families. A large banner above the main entrance says *Welcome To Your Future.* It's a beautiful day, with a balmy breeze brushing through my hair. A welcome relief from the heat caused by my sweater and gloves.

Opening her warm arms, Mom bundles Joulian up in a hug, lamenting on how tall he's already grown since last week. Greg flies lazy circles around them, landing next to Mom's fox familiar, Tess. Moxie sits on my shoulder, making tiny goat noises while nibbling on my earlobe.

I roll my eyes at the way Mom fusses, waiting for my turn. She might drive me crazy, but my mother's hugs are the best. She lingers and squeezes, always ending with a slight rub between the shoulder blades. It feels like home every single time.

Today is no different, and after the tense morning, it's a welcome respite. He's still giving me a semi-silent treatment. He'll answer questions, but won't engage in any attempt at conversation. It makes me want to lay everything bare to him, but this conversation needs to not be motivated by emotional desperation. The facts deserve more than that.

"How is he?" she whispers into my ear. He's watching us, so all I can do is give a quick shake of my head. She releases me far too soon. Putting her hands on her ample hips, she says, "Let's go find you a job, shall we?"

"Gammy," he whines with a toothy grin. "I don't need a job!"

Mom pretends to look startled and gives me a sly glance. "Are you sure? I was just telling your mom that you are really mature for your age. I apologize for assuming."

Joulian's eyes light up. "You did?"

She nods emphatically. "Sure did. So it's time to pay bills."

He rolls his eyes this time. "Come on, let's go inside."

Mom grabs my gloved hand, an anchor in the crowd. I loathe going into crowds or being around people. One brush of skin and I could be easily overwhelmed by a stranger's emotions. As Joulian opens the door, flourishing an arm dramatically to usher us inside, my heart races. A child screams and I flinch. Mom squeezes my hand in silent support. She knows this isn't easy for me, which is most likely why she offered to be here in the first place. I squeeze her hand back and take in a shuddering breath. *I can do this.*

The flow of foot traffic heads into the school's gymnasium. As soon as we enter the space, Joulian bolts to the first booth where air traffic controllers explain their job to a mob of children. He's always been fascinated with everything Dragon related. We're similar in that regard.

"Does he have any booths he specifically wanted to visit?" Mom asks, scanning the options. Her eyes light up at a local restaurant's booth where food samples are being handed out. She tugs me in that direction.

I laugh. "Are you sure you came here to support him?"

Stopping at a short line offering food samples, she gives me a mischievous smirk. We look fairly similar, except her eyes are a darker brown and she has short hair. "Of course, but that doesn't mean I can't have any benefits."

Handing me a sample, Mom nibbles on her confectionary dessert. I do the same, enjoying the explosion of sugar on my tongue. I'm not normally fond of sugary treats, but in a crowd this size with all these sounds, I need every emotion boost possible.

As another stranger bumps into me, and renewed gratitude flares for the multiple layers. I have no desire to accidentally siphon or bestow emotions right now.

Joulian runs up, face full of excitement. A few tendrils of curls dangle in front of his eyes. I absentmindedly go to brush them away, but he jerks his head out of reach. It takes everything to hide the sting of his rejection.

Without missing a beat, he rushes out, “Come on, they have a Dragxi booth!” He runs off down the aisle, waving to friends.

“He’s a teenager,” Mom says quietly, noticing the entire exchange. She misses nothing.

I shrug it off, swallowing the tears threatening embarrassment. “He probably doesn’t want to be embarrassed.”

“Exactly.” She pauses. “He knows he can’t be an *actual* Dragxi, right?”

I force a smile. “Joulian has never been the type to take ‘no’ as an answer.”

Mom chuckles, tugging me along to where Joulian stands. He’s the only child at this booth, already chattering the ear off of the Dragon patiently listening to him. The man is the color of rubies in sunlight. His golden eyes flick up to us as we approach, but he doesn’t smile.

Joulian’s talking a mile a minute, with each passing second appearing to widen the Dragon’s eyes. “And I’ve always wanted to fly, and I know I can’t, but I heard Dragxis still need teams to prep for rides, organize fares and—”

I squeeze his shoulder. “Kid, slow down. Take a breath.”

For an instant, he must forget he’s an angsty teenager because he doesn’t even jerk away from my fingers. Instead, he peers up, face full of eagerness. “Mom! Look! They have an OJT position!”

He grabs a brochure off the table, handing it over.

I frown, opening the slip of paper. “OJT?”

“On-the-job training,” the man says. His voice resonates with patience. I scan the information. It appears they have a training program for kids, specifically for this kind of event.

“Can I *please?*” Joulian begs.

Swallowing hard, I look at the man. He's watching me with those sunset eyes. His aura is mostly neutral blue, but a deep grayish blue hugs his frame tightly. Grief. It's always sad to see grief clinging to people. Who has he lost?

Mom squeezes my hand, prompting me to say something. I didn't realize I'm staring.

"Um," I nibble on my lower lip. My heart flutters with anxiety. Can I really let Joulian go spend time with a stranger? "I think it could be okay ... if I can come along?"

The man's expression doesn't change, but he nods. "Of course. Parents are more than welcome to escort."

"I won't be in the way?" I ask, glancing at Joulian, not wanting my fears to dampen his experience.

The man shakes his head. "Not at all." He smiles. At least, it's probably supposed to be a smile. It appears to pain him enough that it resembles more of a grimace.

My eyes track his hand as he offers it for a handshake. "My name is Fynn. I run Flaming Fares; I assure you that my brother built the program so the kids are safe."

I stare at the hand, unwilling to touch him. Even wearing gloves, I do not want to chance touching another man's skin. Trying to make the rejection as gentle as possible, I offer a soft smile.

"I'm Orliana."

Something undefinable flickers across Fynn's expression, and he drops his hand slowly. Yet, he doesn't appear to be annoyed at my rejection; most people usually do, so this difference furrows my brow at the way I'm both confused and intrigued.

Mom clears her throat, expression positively devilish. My heart skips for a different reason now — when she has this look on her face, it never bodes well.

She cocks her head at Fynn. "How long have you owned this company, Mr... ?"

"Gleanscale," Fynn says roughly. "For ten years."

He still won't look at us, instead watching Joulian paw through a flyer for upcoming Dragxi training classes.

"Are you married, Mr. Gleanscale?"

This steals Fynn's attention. We briefly exchange bewildered looks before we share expressions of horror.

Why does *he* seem horrified?

My cheeks growing hot, I hiss, "Mom. That's not relevant or appropriate."

Fynn holds up his trembling right hand. Nestled on the middle finger is a simple silver band.

His throat works, as if trying to digest a lodged emotion. Finally, he says, "Yes, ma'am, I am."

His aura doesn't change at all, offering no clues to his slow response. Why would a married man seem reluctant to admit he's married? Is he ashamed of his wife? Does he hate being married? Sometimes Mikan liked to pretend he wasn't married right in front of me to start a fight later.

My stomach rolls, and suddenly, I don't want Joulian to spend time with him.

Gently steering Joulian away from the table, I say tightly, "Thank you for your time, Mr. Gleanscale. I apologize for my mother's inappropriate question. I'm sure you're busy."

Fynn's brow furrows. "Did Joulian want to sign up for the program? We have an opening this weekend."

"No," I say sharply; *too* sharply. All three of them stare in surprise. I clear my throat, evening out my tone. "We'll talk about it."

"Moooom," Joulian whines. His aura swirls, mostly in shades of red. My anxiety spikes as he says, "Come *on.* It's only for a few hours this weekend."

"We'll talk about it later," I repeat more firmly.

Joulian is undeterred. The red around his body darkens. Anger twists his features. For a split second, he resembles Mikan as he spits out, "You always do this. You never let me go anywhere or do anything fun."

The bitterness in his tone is like a blow to my sternum. It steals my breath; I flinch, seeing my ex in his face. Will it be like this from now on?

"You shouldn't speak to your mother with that tone," Fynn interrupts, giving my son a severe look. His voice is quiet, but brooks no argument. "She deserves more respect than that. Disrespect is not tolerated at my company."

Joulian's eyes widen as he deflates. Not shrink, but more like he realizes how cruel he was being. "Yes, sir." He turns his beautiful eyes to me and whispers, "I'm sorry, Mom. I just really want to do this."

Emotions war in my mind. Fynn overstepped, but it was also a teaching moment for Joulian; I can't begrudge that. Even when admonishing Joulian, Fynn's aura doesn't change. As if offering stern guidance, neither takes nor gives him anything.

Fynn turns his gaze to mine. "We focus on helping kids learn responsibility. In our industry, mistakes—" He seems to catch himself, his expression twisting with fleeting bitterness. Then he says, more quietly, "—mistakes kill people. So we are very stringent in our training, even if it's for a single afternoon."

The way he says mistakes kill people makes me wonder if he's accidentally killed someone as a Dragxi or knows someone who has. It creates another concern. "Is it safe? Will he be flying?"

Fynn raises a black eyebrow in amusement. "Is he of Dragon descent?"

"I wish," Joulian grumbles, crossing his scrawny arms. "Mom's a Siphon and Dad was an Elf."

"Joulian," I admonish. I see Fynn's eyes scan my fully covered body, pausing on the gloves. He gives me an understand, empathetic look.

To Joulian, he says, "Well, we need technicians. No flying involved, but you'll help us keep people safe. How does that sound?"

"Yes!" Joulian rounds his eyes, and I swear his pupils dilate as he intertwines his fingers in prayer. "*Please,* Mom? I'll do extra chores! I'll be good! Please let me do this!"

Mom brushes fingers against my elbow; a quiet censure against refusing. Relenting, I exhale hard. "Fine." While Joulian whoops with joy, I ask Fynn, "What time?"

Fynn frowns, pulling out his phone. "Let me check."

While he sends off a text, I turn to Mom and whisper, "Do you think it's actually safe?"

"I think so." Mom observes Fynn thoughtfully. "He seems to take his job seriously."

I don't know how she gathered that opinion based on less than five minutes of conversation, but it still makes me feel a little better. She's usually an excellent judge of character. As a therapist who siphons emotions for clients, she's become excellent at reading people.

"Nine," Fynn says, tucking his phone away. "It'll be for about two to three hours, if that's alright."

"That's fine," I say, folding the brochure still in my hands. "We'll be there."

"Will it be you?" Joulian says, sounding hopeful.

Fynn visibly cringes. "Um, I—"

"Come on, bubs," I say to Joulian, attempting to steer him away from the table by his shoulder. "Mr. Gleanscale is probably really busy."

"But will you?" Joulian refuses to move. This newfound teenage obstinance is going to take a bit getting used to. Fynn rubs the back of his neck, watching my son with indecision twisting his expression.

"Joulian," I admonish again, becoming exasperated. "Let's go to the other tables."

Joulian continues to refuse, giving Fynn a pleading look. My mother's incredibly amused, because of course she is.

"Yes," Fynn finally says. "I'll be there."

"Yes!" Joulian pumps a fist, finally relenting to my grip. As he turns away, he looks up at me. "Thank you so much, Mom."

A lump in my throat thickens; all I can do is nod. With one last glance over my shoulder at Fynn, I catch him watching me. There's nothing showing in his expression, but his fists are tight, ridged at his sides. Like the entire interaction was so painful, his body can't let it go.

9

Fynn

I watch the three of them walk away, feeling emotionally exposed. The kid, Joulian, wanted me to be there during his on-the-job training. Me. Why? Even after I overstepped with the admonishment, he wanted me there.

And the way Orliana scrutinized me throughout the entire process, as if I were about to attack, leaves me unsettled. I've never met a Siphon before, but surely our inter-cultural classes in school would've mentioned if they struggled to trust or touch. She was covered head to toe; it was all colorful attire, but still.

The rest of the career fair is blessedly uneventful. Joulian was the most excited kid to appear, but it's still a relief when it's over. Nicko appears with a wide smile, shooing me away as he packs up.

It's an unfamiliar comfort to take to the skies; I haven't felt solace in the clouds in years, but at least up here, a mother isn't watching me with fear.

Maybe I should go home, but instead, I head back to headquarters. It might be nice to put on a saddle for some fares. Empty my mind, perhaps gather some stories.

No one meets me at the landing pad, so I'm able to slip into the building without interference. Some employees wave at me; I dip my chin in acknowledgement, but I'm too overstimulated for pleasantries.

My life seems full of unwanted surprises because when I open my door, it's Aunt Teale sitting across from my desk. Her purple eyes find mine the moment I stall at the doorway. Dread dips heavy in my stomach. I recover quickly, closing the door and striding to my desk. She tracks my every movement with predatory intent. Even though she's smiling, I know exactly how this conversation will go. I glance at the photo of Rhuth, silently begging for strength.

"Aunt Teale," I say evenly, sitting in my chair.

She's wearing her typical gaudy attire with jewels on each finger and dripping from the cartilage of her ears. Her pink scales are complemented by the bright purple jacket with gold trim. "Fynn."

My name already sounds like an admonishment. I lean back, bracing my hands on the armrests. "What is the reason for this invasion?"

Her eyes flash in warning. "An invasion? Is that what you consider family now?" It's difficult to not squirm as lilac irises scan me from head to toe. "You seem ... different."

The power dynamics between older and younger Dragons are dictated not just by a subtle hierarchy, but magyck as well. It's taboo to wield this power over one another in general circumstances, but Aunt Teale is a commanding matriarch. Her love's given in equal measure to her expectations.

So, as much as I want to be snarky, it would be an egregious insult. Instead, I bite back my irritation. "Different how?"

"Diminished."

My head snaps back in shock. That one word cuts like a blade between my ribs. While I'm not permitted to insult her, she has no such compunctions, apparently. To call a male Dragon diminished is no better than a physical blow.

"Aunt Teale," I say calmly, with enormous effort. "Please speak plainly as to why you're here. I've had a very long day, and I did not expect to return to my office to receive insults."

"You are the first to insult me," she says primly, cocking her head with narrowed eyes.

"How?" I answer hotly. "I haven't seen you in ..." Realization dawns, stealing the wind from under my wings.

She smiles like a victor being handed an award. Tucking a strand of magenta hair behind an ear, she says, "Years, I do believe. Not only that, but you ignored my reunion invitation. So, really, there are multiple insults. I've decided that it's become intolerable."

My claws dig into the wood of my chair. It creaks in protest. "Perhaps you missed the death of my wife, but I've been focused on grief—" I motion to the walls with a hand. "—and making sure this business doesn't fail. People rely on me. Entire families depend on this business thriving."

She sniffs dismissively. "It's been almost five years, Fynn."

"As people keep reminding me," I grit out. "What is an acceptable time for grief, Aunt Teale? One year? Two? Three? Why is four too many?"

"Because Rhuth would be ashamed of you."

Dragons are known for speaking plainly, but she's going too far. I lean forward, bracing my arms against the pile of papers on my desk. A growl loosens in my throat, the instinct to fight back trying to free itself. My aunt is unbothered, knowing full well I won't do a thing to her.

Yet, I snarl, "How dare you come in here to tell me what *my* wife would think or feel about the way I grieve."

The worst part is that she isn't wrong. Rhuth would knock me upside the skull and tell me to stop slowly killing myself with loneliness.

"Dragons are not meant to be alone, Fynn. We exist in Weyrs for a reason. To stay connected to our roots." Despite riling me up, she still continues to be unruffled. Perhaps because we both know she's going to win in the end. "But you have disconnected not just from your Weyr, but from yourself as well."

Shame pulls at my heart just as roughly as the lingering grief. "And what would you have me do? Go find a new mate tomorrow? Have more babies? Forget about Rhuth entirely?"

"Mind your tone," she snaps. "Or I'll mind it for you."

I sit back again in an attempt to add the illusion of distance between us. Despite my angry outburst, I refuse to apologize. Crossing my arms, I repeat quietly, "What would you have me do?"

Her chin lifts as her mouth thins. "Come to the Weyr reunion."

I desperately want to scream my refusal. It was foolish to think it would be easy to avoid this situation. But she flew all the way here to force an agreement, which means a refusal now would be unforgivable.

Grinding my teeth, I try to come up with an excuse. *Any* excuse. "I don't want people asking me when I'll find a new mate. That's too painful for me."

"Then bring someone," she says simply, as if that wouldn't be equally painful.

"No."

She raises an eyebrow. "Why not?"

"Because I'm not *with* anyone, Aunt Teale."

The matriarch huffs out a laugh. Motioning to my appearance, she says, "Of course not. Look at you. You've lost weight. Your clothes are mis-matched. Your hair is too long. *Clearly,* there is no feminine touch involved."

"I don't want a woman responsible for keeping me together," I retort. "I'm not a child."

"Then stop acting like one."

I close my eyes, asking Fortuna for patience. When I open them, it's to gaze at the photo of Rhuth. While I refuse to agree that it's time to stop grieving, perhaps it *has* been too long since I've connected with the Weyr. The pit of loneliness that aches every second won't be solved by being around family, but Dragons need connection. It's how we remain strong.

Looking back at my aunt, I say, "Fine. I'll go."

"Will you bring someone? I would like a correct headcount."

"I have no idea who I'd bring."

She stands, signaling her mission's complete. She waits as I rush over to open the door. "I'll optimistically assume you'll find someone." Her expression softens. "We all miss her, Fynn. She was a light beyond measure. But you need to live your life, nephew. Bring a friend for moral support."

Her eyes narrow. Tone dry, she adds, "And that does not mean your brother."

At this, I crack a small smile. I've missed her abrasive personality, even though it's currently aimed at me. "I'll be there regardless."

She offers a curt nod. "See that you are. I'd hate to have to pull rank."

Brushing a respectful kiss against her wrinkled cheek, I murmur, "Don't act like you wouldn't love it."

Her chuckle is raspy. "This is true." Bringing a weathered hand to my cheek, she says, "Find someone. You have a month."

With that, she's striding down the hallway, the whimsical fabrics of her skirt fluttering behind her. When she turns the corner, I close the door, locking it firmly.

The leather chair groans as I collapse into it. I'm more exhausted than before. Today has been the most challenging day in a long time. Who in the hells will I bring to this reunion?

Who would agree to spend time with a grieving widower who simply wants to be left alone?

10

Orliana

The next few days, Joulian is in a great mood. He doesn't bring up his father at all, and true to his word, he does extra chores despite not actually being assigned any. During our meals together, he chatters about the research he's done on Dragxis. According to him, Fynn Gleanscale owns the top Dragxi company in Gondora. Explains why Flaming Fares Dragxis seem to be everywhere.

He's utterly thrilled to be learning from the best of the best. Honestly, I'm a little impressed as well. I've never accomplished anything like that in my life. At this point, I'm not sure I ever will.

When the day finally arrives, Joulian is already up by the time I pad into the kitchen. The sun's shining into the cozy space and to my surprise, Joulian has a cup of tea ready to go. Moxie makes an immediate beeline for the bits of bacon already prepared.

"Thank you, sweetie," I take the hot mug from him. "You're up early."

He nods, settling at the table where two plates of scrambled eggs and half-burnt toast await. I frown at the blackened bread, but say nothing as I sit across from him.

"I'm really excited. Do you think Fynn will take me flying?"

I prod the burnt toast with my fork. "You've ridden on plenty of Dragxis, Jouls."

"Yeah, but what if I ask to go do tricks? Like somersaults?"

"Absolutely not," I say firmly. I scoop a modest amount of eggs onto the less-burnt side. He watches me for my reaction. I nod with a tight smile.It's dry, but he never takes initiative with cooking, so I sip my tea, swallowing the dry lump with effort.

He's shoveling eggs into his mouth as I say, "That's delicious. Thank you."

Joulian beams, then pleads, "What if he says it's safe?" A chunk of yolk flies out, landing on the table as he says, "I'll be really good, I swear."

"Eat with your mouth closed." It's clear already he's going to test my patience today. While I want him to be happy, and I know Dragons use magyck to keep people safe on their backs, I'm definitely uncomfortable letting him on a Dragon's back doing acrobatics.

This is probably the hardest part of parenting: making the smart decision while feeling like a dunghole.

"Come on, Mom."

I close my eyes and inhale slowly, counting down from ten. I've always loved being a mother, but this new begging version of my son has me on edge. I can't teach him that it's okay to keep badgering someone until they say yes.

Opening my eyes, I say, "If you ask one more time, we won't be going at all."

His face falls as his mouth purses. There's no more backtalk as he digs into his breakfast. Guilt flickers through my chest, but I ignore it. It's moments like this where I wish there were someone else here to back me up. It's exhausting to always be the bad guy.

It's better than Mikan, though. He would've encouraged Joulian to challenge me.

The rest of breakfast is in silence. When our plates are emptied, I bring them to the sink while he goes to find some shoes.

Gathering my purse, phone, and keys, I wait by the front door. As he comes down the hallway, he still refuses to look at me. Anger flares, but

I bite the inside of my cheek, refusing to take it out on him. He's only a kid.

Maybe if I keep reminding myself of this enough, I won't want to scream at him, at the skies, at the heavens.

The pre-arranged Dragxi waits patiently, its blue scales beautiful in the golden morning light. Definitely not Fynn. We climb onto the seating saddle, and a pocket of still air envelops us, absorbing any jerky movements or wind. Moxie curls up in my lap while Greg sits on Joulian's shoulder.

As we fly through Gondora, I'm struck by how beautiful the city is. When my parents moved us here twenty years ago, they'd practically dragged me kicking and screaming. We lived in Britner, the land of unforgiving mountains. It was frigid all year round, with mountains casting long shadows, making it hard for anything to grow.

Which is probably why the lush, verdant, floating upside down mountains of Gondora are so appealing. Anything and everything can grow with this much sunshine. I've always wanted a garden, but Mikan purposefully killed everything I've tried to grow, and I haven't had the energy to try again.

The Dragxi landing is smooth, and we're greeted by Fynn waiting patiently right outside the loading zone. He's wearing a white henley shirt, the sleeves pushed up to his elbows, and a pair of loose fitting jeans. The tip of his tail flickers in agitation, the lone insight into his feelings.

Joulian unloads first, sprinting for Fynn with a frantic wave. Fynn's mouth flickers with the ghost of a smile, but that's the extent of his greeting. As soon as my feet are on the ground, a group of technicians runs over to the blue Dragxi, releasing the saddle.

The blue Dragon doesn't wait a second longer before shifting, turning into a handsome man who resembles Fynn, with long black hair shaved at the sides and a similar nose, but where Fynn is more scowls, this one is all smiles. I'm fascinated by the sunburst orb in his left eye socket. It catches the light, with a soft glow shining from within itself.

"Hey, I'm Trinte, Fynn's brother." He strides over with a grin. When he's close enough, he holds out a hand.

I glance at it, then back at his face, offering a smile that feels like a mask. "Hi, I'm Orliana."

Unlike Fynn the other day, Trinte doesn't miss a beat. His hand drops, and he motions for me to follow to where Joulian is asking Fynn a million questions. Greg hops around, eyeballing everything with too much interest, reflecting his bonded's energy.

The red Dragon stares down at my son, hands on his narrow hips, both wide eyed and perhaps a little lost. Fynn looks up and I smile, knowing at least a little bit of how he feels.

"Just to warn you," I say to Trinte. "Joulian loves to ask questions, sometimes before you can answer the previous one."

Trinte chuckles. "Oh, Fynn will love that."

A flicker of worry has me shooting a glance at the red Dragon. "Will Joulian bother him?"

He shakes his head. "Fynn is incredibly patient. If he doesn't know the answer, he'll just grunt."

I pause in my steps, frowning. Trinte keeps walking, stopping at Fynn's side. Standing next to one another, it's hard not to compare. Fynn has about three inches of height over his brother, with broad shoulders that narrow into a tapered waist. Trinte is stockier, with a thick waist that leads to even thicker thighs.

Fynn casts his brother an unreadable look as Joulian continues chattering. Trinte rolls his eyes. Anxiety threads through my nerves, and I speed walk to close the distance, putting a protective arm around my son's shoulders. Fynn watches the gesture and frowns. I don't care if he feels offended.

Joulian's alight with glee. "Fynn says I'm going to learn how to saddle *and* unsaddle Dragxis today, Mom!"

I squeeze him into my torso, smiling down at him. "That sounds so exciting." I glance at the brothers. "Where should I be while he does all of this?"

"At the Dragxi scale wash?" Trinte offers.

Fynn shoots him a dirty look. “Knock it off.” To me, he says, “We have a seating area you can wait in. Or if you’d like, I can find you a chair to sit in so you can watch.”

“I’d like the chair, please.” Tension I didn’t know existed melts from my shoulders, making it easier to breathe. Having Joulian out of my sight created deeper dread than I’d realized.

Fynn nods, and Trinte jogs into the headquarters. Fynn motions for us to follow him into the large metal hangar where everything Dragxi related resides.

11

Fynn

I love children. It was one of the first things Rhuth and I agreed on; lots of children. Before her death, I imagined the pitter patter of young feet running through our hallways, or the giggles from tickle fights. I wanted endless breakfasts in bed with a cup of coffee and cuddle piles.

Joulian is the first kid I've interacted with in almost five years, and it feels like I've bitten off more than I can chew. *Why does he ask so many goddess-damned questions?*

"What's that?" he asks for the twelfth time in five minutes. He's pointing at a hose in the scale wash.

"That's to help clean off Dragons if they get dirty during a shift."

"How do they get dirty?"

I shrug. "If it rains, dirt can get caked on the scales."

"It doesn't go away when they shift?"

"Unfortunately not."

He runs over to the large hose. Without asking, picks up the large nozzle, his small fingers wrapping around the handle. I hold up a hand, lunging forward. "Don't—"

The pressure from the hose is so intense, he skids backwards. The water hits me straight in the face, covering my body. It stings against my bare skin, soaking me instantly. I hold up my hands, trying to protect my eyes. It hurts like all Hells.

From behind me, I hear his mother scream, "*Joulian!* Oh, my goddess!"

The onslaught stops. I gasp, spitting out water. Leaning against my knees, I cough. Frantic feet run over to Joulian. Squinting, I see Orliana skid to a stop in front of her son, yanking the nozzle out of his hand. His eyes are wide with fear, shock paling his face.

Next to him, the blue crow cleans itself in a puddle. The purple ugopeg splashes in the same puddle, but keeps an eye on me, as if she can't decide to have fun or poke out my eye with that horn.

"What were you thinking?" Orliana chastises, glancing over at me. Fear is written all over her face. The words quaver as she says to him, "Look at what you did! You can't *do* things like that, Joulian!"

"I-I'm sorry," he sputters, ready to break out into tears. I straighten and peel my soaked shirt off my chest. My magyck can dry it within seconds. But first, I turn my focus back to Joulian and his mother.

"Don't say sorry to me; say sorry to Mr. Gleanscale." Orliana gently places the hose on the ground. The ugopeg trots over to smell it.

"I'm sorry," the boy whispers, watching me fearfully. Both of them are. Maybe it's my imagination, but it appears Orliana's shaking. Her arm curls protectively around him for the second time, like she expects me to take my anger out on them.

I'm confused; why would they think I'd be angry over some water? Holding out my palms as a sign of safety, I say, "It's alright. I promise, it's fine. It's just water, buddy."

Joulian's lower lip quivers, but Orliana's shoulders relax a fraction. Not enough for my liking. So instead, I give them both a soft smile and begin walking toward them, but freeze when Joulian steps in front of his mother. He's shaking like a leaf, but lifts his chin, ready to defend her. Like she's needed defending before.

Putting my hands up, I slow my steps. His wide eyes watch me as I kneel in front of him, the cement digging into my knees. Orliana's arm tightens around his shoulder.

Grabbing the nozzle, I offer it. His brown eyes flick from the nozzle back to my face.

"I'm really sorry," he whispers. "It's my fault you're all wet."

Tears glisten in his eyes, one breaking free when a violent shudder works through his bones. What has happened that this kid thinks something like this is the end of the world? The strangest urge to give him a hug overwhelms me, but I resist.

In a stern but calm tone, I repeat, "It's just water, buddy. But you can't go around grabbing things that aren't yours." Lowering my voice, I ask, "Do you remember what I said about disrespect?"

Joulian nods slowly, glancing up at his mom. My heart clenches at the paleness of her face. There's a light sheen of sweat on her forehead.

"It's okay," I repeat to them both. To Joulian, I say, "This is your first warning, alright? Next time you touch things that aren't yours, your mom will have to bring you home. Sound fair?"

He nods a little more enthusiastically, clearly relieved that he can stay. Orliana exhales with matching relief, her clenched fingers on his shoulder relaxing. Who hurt these people?

I stand slowly, making sure my movements stay predictable. Glancing around the empty hanger, I point toward the saddle cleaning station. "I'll meet you both over there. Give me a few minutes to change."

Orliana begins walking to her chair, but I intercept her with a raised hand. "Don't worry; I'll grab it on my way back."

Chocolate brown eyes gaze up at me, her brow still furrowed with insecurity. "You sure? I can do it. I don't mind."

Offering another comforting smile — at least, I hope it's comforting — I say, "Of course. I'll be right back."

I turn to head back into the comms building, but her quiet voice stops me. "Thank you."

Looking over my shoulder, I frown. "For what?"

Her eyes darted over to her son, then back to me. The ugopeg appears at her shoulder, precariously balancing on all four hooves on the slender slope of muscle. "For not yelling at him."

This time, the smile is easy in a wholly unfamiliar way. It's jarring and makes my heart thump hard against my ribs. "It's only water, Orliana. Why would I yell at him?"

She stares down at her feet and, to my dismay, her shoulders bow forward an inch. The ugopeg nibbles on her earlobe, but she doesn't appear to notice.

If not for my excellent hearing, I might not have heard her murmur, "Because for some people, it would be worth yelling about."

"Not me," I say firmly. I wave my hand to catch her attention. "I can't remember the last time I yelled." That's a lie, but she doesn't need to know about the times I've screamed my grief into a pillow. "Joulian is safe with me, Orliana. I swear it."

Right in front of me, her face transforms from one of apprehension to calm. A tightness still clenches at the edges of her almond-shaped eyes, but the edges of her mouth relax a fraction. The ugopeg stares at me with one gold eye, flicking her blunt furry tail with agitation.

Something inside me stirs, shattering the moment.

It's too much. I stumble back. "I'll be right back."

Orliana's gaze is solemn as she gives a small nod. Striding into the comms building, I aim straight for my office, locking the door. Breathing rapidly, I lean against it, wrestling with my hammering heart.

I'm not ready to comfort people, especially not a mother and her son. Having them here was a mistake. My eyes trail toward Rhuth's photo on my desk. I spin my wedding ring frantically, trying to calm the thoughts racing through memories of Rhuth and my grief. Of my promise.

It takes more than a couple of minutes to relax my body enough to use my magyck and dry the outfit. I focus on steadying my breath. They're only here for a couple of hours. Then I can go home, go to my game room, turn on my console, and focus on a different reality.

***

The two hours passes faster than expected. Joulian's on his best behavior, and Orliana watches from her chair, her knee pumping rapidly. When Joulian's training experience finishes, she whisks him away after giving me a heartfelt thank you.

Watching them load onto one of my Dragxis, there's a mix of relief and something else I can't quite identify whirling around in my chest.

Refusing to examine it, I hunt down Trinte. He's in his office, tapping away at the keyboard. When I rap my knuckles against the doorway, he looks up. Sitting back in his brown leather chair, he appraises me.

"You don't seem too worse for▯ wear," he says with a smirk. "Did you remember to smile occasionally?"

I grunt, sitting across from him, slinging an ankle over a knee. "Yes. Three, to be exact."

Trinte steeples his fingers, raising an eyebrow. "That's impressive. Did it hurt?"

I bend my middle finger against my palm in a rude gesture. Even so, I grin. "Fuck off."

He lets out a loud laugh. "You appear to be in a good mood. Will you be taking point on training all the kids going forward?"

"Absolutely not," I say quickly. "The kid soaked me at the washing station. He asked an impressive amount of questions."

"Oh no," Trinte says with mock horror. *"Questions?"*

"Shut up," I growl. "It was practically one every ten seconds."

"The mom was a looker, though."

"I wouldn't know."

He scoffs. "I don't believe you. She was gorgeous, Fynn."

I shrug, sitting back in my chair. "I'm married."

At this, a flash of irritation crosses his face. His eyes flick to my fingers worrying the silver wedding band. I lift my chin in a silent dare to say something, anything, about my ring. I haven't taken it off in ten years.

Trinte is smart; he says nothing. Instead, a muscle feathers in his jaw. It's a stare-off I refuse to lose. I'm tired of people telling me to move on. To act as if Rhuth is someone I can just get over. As if the skies could move on if the sun disappeared forever.

He breaks first. "Okay, so you won't be spearheading a new training program? Am I understanding that correctly?"

Exhaling my anxiety, I smirk. "You understand correctly. I'm also never going to another career fair."

He shrugs. "We'll see."

"No 'we'll see.'" I snark, standing. "I'll be here for the kid's days, as promised, but that's it. No one else." I jerk my head toward the hallway. "I'm headed to lunch. Want to come?"

Trinte waves me off. "All the paperwork you refuse to do has to be done, regardless. I'll catch you later."

Pulling the door closed behind me, I give my last parting words. "I'm kicking your ass tonight."

My brother laughs. "I'll simply use one of MeanCat's spells on you."

"See you then," I promise and shut the door.

12

Orliana

Joulian is safe with me, Orilana. I swear it.

Fynn's promise echoes in my mind, over and over again. I don't know the man whatsoever. I'm not even sure why my mind fixates on it.

Joulian is quiet on the way home, pensive as he watches the city pass by. I watch him observe the world, still processing everything that happened at the washing station. I'm appalled Joulian grabbed the hose. It was an impulsive thing to do, completely out of character for my son.

Are teenage hormones to blame? Or is my lack of transparency around Mikan to blame?

My instincts tell me he's aching for someone who isn't his mother. How could he not be?

I've never bought into the idea of children needing a masculine guide in their life, but what I believe and what my son actually needs are at odds. It creates a sense of helplessness in some ways.

True to his word, Fynn moved on from the situation with mentorship. Joulian responded to it immediately, never touching anything without permission first. He didn't bicker, whine, or complain. He accepted Fynn's guidance with eagerness.

He deserves to know about his father.

Guilt churns in my stomach, and I look away from my son. It took great effort to calm my reaction when I saw Fynn covered in water. Fear, like I hadn't felt in years, surged, rattling my bones and pounding my heart. Fynn has been so stoic since we met him, but I've learned men are never quite what they seem. It's not like I can trust their auras anymore.

So when Fynn knelt in front of Joulian, I didn't know what to think. At first, I assumed he was going to eventually snap, but he didn't. Instead, it turned into a lesson about boundaries. When Fynn moved slowly, seeing our fear, something in my soul cracked. Even when I thanked him, he was more taken aback that his behavior resulted in gratitude at all.

My thoughts still swirl with the smile on his face by the time the Dragxi lands and we hop off. Joulian bolts inside without a backward glance. Greg and Moxie follow him, both finding their cushy, elevated beds for a rest.

I find Joulian in the kitchen, scarfing down some cookies.

As I take off my gloves and long-sleeved shirt, I frown. "I was about to make lunch."

He shrugs. "I'll eat that, too."

Chuckling, I ruffle his hair as I walk to the fridge. To my surprise, he doesn't jerk away. Maybe it's just in public? "Okay, one more. Then put the bag away."

"No."

Holding the fridge open, I close my eyes. Bitterness clenches my jaw; he gave Fynn more respect in thirty seconds than toward his own mother. It's difficult to not think this isn't a learned behavior from Mikan, who did everything he could to undermine me, especially in front of Joulian.

Closing the fridge, I face my son. He's assessing my reaction with a blank expression. Like my response will set the tone of his next outburst. His aura is a chaotic mess of blue, red, and orange.

Inhaling through my nose, I clench and unclench my hands before saying, "So this is the new version of you I have to look forward to everyday now?"

Joulian cocks his head; a curl falls across his forehead. "New version of me?"

Deciding this won't become some high noon stand-off, I turn back to the fridge and begin pulling out sandwich supplies. "Yes. The one who disrespects me at every opportunity, including in front of strangers."

As I pile items onto the counter, he says, "I'm not being disrespectful."

Placing slices of bread onto two plates, I say blandly, "So you're going to gaslight me, too?"

"I'm not gaslighting you!" Joulian exclaims, rounding the counter to stand across from me. I glance up and take in his confused expression.

Grabbing a knife from a drawer, I begin spreading mayonnaise onto a slice. "Do you know what gaslighting is?"

His nose scrunches as he crosses his arms. Looking too much like Mikan. "No."

"Then how do you know you aren't doing it?"

His expression flattens. "I don't. Are you going to tell me what it is or not?"

"Well," I say slowly, pulling out slices of meat. "It means trying to convince someone something isn't true, despite both of you knowing it is true."

Joulian scoffs. "I didn't do that."

"No?" I pause, lazily pointing the knife at him. "So when I tell you to put the bag away after one more cookie and you tell me 'no', that isn't disrespectful?"

"No."

Emet, give me strength. "So the other day, when you threw a fit at the career fair, telling me what a terrible mother I was in front of a stranger, that wasn't disrespectful?"

"No," He says the word too quickly; he knows it's a lie. His aura shows it through browned edges and flares of red.

"And when Fynn told you that you were being disrespectful, did you think he was overreacting?"

"No."

Chuckling, I place slices of cheese on top of the meat. "Is this the only word you know now?"

A pause, then, "No."

Raising teenagers isn't for the weak. Grabbing slices of lettuce, I say, "I think you know exactly the way you're behaving, Joulian." I purse my lips. "And I don't deserve it. I am your mother. I treat you with respect, and I expect it in return. Is that not a fair expectation?"

Right in front of me, my son transforms. His burnished gold skin darkens with anger, and his blue eyes turn flinty.

"How can I respect a liar?"

So this is how it's going to go. Hot anger, born of deep triggers, appears, scorching up my insides. For a split second, I'm consumed with rage. Not necessarily at Joulian, but at the unfairness of it all. You can try to protect your kids all you want, but if they don't understand it, they'll never appreciate it. Mikan is the cause of all this fuckery, and yet once again, I'm the one left to do the clean-up.

"Joulian Svaltar Veritas," I say sharply, slamming the knife down. He jumps, all bluster lost instantly. I rarely raise my voice at him, but I can't let this attitude or belief continue any longer. Forgetting the almost-done sandwiches, I round the counter to stand in front of him. Even at thirteen, he's almost as tall as me, but still, I duck my head to make direct eye contact.

His wide eyes track my movements. There's a split second of shame for scaring him like this, but I don't have the energy to let this behavior continue. It needs to be nipped in the bud immediately.

Keeping my tone even, I say, "You will *not* speak to me like this. If you have questions or a problem, we will talk it out. But don't you *ever—*" I point a finger in his face, lowering my voice to a deadly tone. "*—ever* call me a liar, *ever again.* There are a great many things in this world and about your father that you don't understand. Some of which you aren't old enough to know."

"But I want to know," he says, voice cracking. All of his earlier bravado is completely gone, replaced with tears and a wobbling lower lip. "Why won't you tell me?"

I straighten, letting my hands fall to my side. He's visibly shaken, shattering my frustration. I can't resist wrapping my arms around his scrawny frame, feeling his fear and confusion.

Against his ear, I murmur, "I'm sorry. It's no excuse, but I don't know how to do this, okay? I've never had to tell my son about his abusive father before."

Joulian's arms tighten against my rib cage. In a small, boyish voice, he asks, "So he *was* abusive?"

The onslaught of memories catches the air in my lungs. Punches. Kicks. Screams. Assaults. The daily rage siphons.

I hug him tighter. My voice cracks as I say, "Yes. He wasn't a nice person."

"I remember some things, Mom," he says, chest shaking with unshed sobs. "I remember seeing him grab you once. I didn't understand what was happening. I got so scared, I ran to my room."

His admission weakens my knees; he follows me to the ground, still crying in my arms. I rock us both in a soothing rhythm, running fingers through his curls. I had no idea he'd seen anything. *You failed to protect him.*

The realization is a wrecking ball to my confidence. Once again, the shame and guilt rear their ugly heads like a rabid hydra. Somehow, I resist the urge to abandon these feelings and siphon them into my pendant. Instead, I force myself to sit in the emotions, even though it feels like swallowing glass.

Even as I try to assimilate my beliefs, he continues. "I'd hear you crying, Mom. You cried a lot when you thought no one was listening."

"Oh, baby," I weep into his hair, inhaling the scent of his fruity shampoo and the smell that is distinctly my son. "I'm so sorry I put you through that."

He jerks away from my arms, giving me a furious look. "*You* didn't, Mom. *He* did. *Dad* did." Emotions war in his expression before he hisses, "I'm *glad* he's dead, Mom. I'm *glad* he slipped and fell. He *deserved* it."

Slipped and fell. We've never outright discussed how his father died — I have never felt driven to admit I killed Mikan. He's somehow assumed it was an accident, which makes sense because no child would immediately jump to murder as a reason. Right now isn't the right time to correct him, either.

Does it make me a coward? Perhaps.

I smooth hair away from his face, bracketing his cheeks with my palms. His tears fall hot onto the back of my hands. "I'm still sorry, regardless, Joulian. You didn't deserve a childhood where you grew up seeing and hearing those things."

His blue eyes search my face, wholly confused. "But if he was mean, why didn't you leave?"

Why didn't you leave? The question too many people have asked. Some never even gave the question a voice — I could see it in their eyes. Especially in that first year, where people acted like my not telling them was a personal affront. An insult because I didn't beg them to be my saviors.

The answer is both easy and complicated. I give Joulian the easiest answer. "Your dad was a really angry man. He told me if I tried to leave, he'd take you away from me."

"Because he was a lawyer?" Understanding seems to be slowly dawning.

I nod my head. "Because he was a lawyer. He also worked hard to make me appear crazy to everyone who knew us."

"Is that why I haven't seen Granny or Grampy?"

At the mention of Mikan's parents, something sharp lodges in my chest. A spike of anxiety forgotten, yet never removed. "Yes. They aren't nice, either."

Understatement; they'd fought for custody the first six months, believing all the lies Mikan had given them over the years. I can't necessarily blame them for being worried about their grandson living with a potentially unhinged, murderous woman, but they never even once asked me for my side.

Joulian sniffs, wiping his nose with the back of his hand, looking ten years younger suddenly. My heart aches for him; for both of us. A mere four feet behind him is where his father died. The entire floor has been replaced, but my imagination will never forget the pool of blood. Sometimes, in my weakest moments, I swear it reappears to taunt me.

I sit up on my knees and reach for a napkin on the counter. Handing it to him, I sit back on my heels, wiping away my own tears. "Do you feel better?"

His nod is forlorn, but I'm relieved he feels a little better. Standing, I hold a hand out. He gently grabs my fingers, accepting the assistance. Running my hands from the crown of his head to his shoulders, I'm relieved to have him safe in my hold. I lightly read his emotions, noting that the intensity has waned. To dig deeper would be a violation, but grazing the gist of his emotional state is more of a check-in than a deep dive.

Exhaling heavily, I force a happy expression. "What do you say we go have lunch on the terrace today?"

Joulian nods again, still wiping away tears and snot. "Okay." When I turn back to the sandwiches, he says, "Mom?"

Grabbing the knife to slice the sandwiches in half, I say, "Yes?"

"I'm sorry I was gaslighting you."

My heart expands with pride. He's a sweet boy trying to learn how to navigate the world. I love how much empathy he has. One of the few things he didn't inherit from his father.

Sliding over his plate, I give him a soft smile. "Thank you, bubs."

13

Fynn

"He's kicking!" Rhuth's excited voice calls from the opposite side of the house. I bolt upright and rush down the hallway, smacking some plants with my tail. I grin, excited to feel the kicks through the soft mound of her belly.

Ignoring the sound of one falling over, I call out, "I'm coming! Where are you?"

"In here, silly!" she calls again, but I can't tell where her voice is coming from. I keep running down the hallway, smacking more plants. A sweat breaks out, and I pant as I run and run and run.

"Where?" I plead, trying to open locked doors. Nothing budges. My fingers are coated with sweat, slipping against the metal in my palm.

From everywhere and nowhere, her teasing tone kick starts my heart. "In here! Hurry, he's kicking up a storm. I swear he'd fly out if it were possible!"

None of the doors open. The hallway never shortens. I'm frantic as I yell, "Rhuthy, where are you?"

"In here ... " Her voice fades, and I let out a sob, running faster and faster.

"Where?" I cry out. "Where are you?"

Then there's nothing but the sound of my claws on the tile and plants crashing from their stands.

I wake up with a scream between my lips, unable to breathe. The sheets are soaked with sweat, twisted between my legs and tail. Darkness fills the room; I lean over to turn on a lamp. Light hurts my eyes; it scares away the shadows, although never the ones in my mind.

Rubbing my face roughly, I focus on calming my breaths. It feels like my heart is about to burst from the thumping speed. Grabbing a dry corner of my sheets, I blot my forehead. It comes away stained with sweat.

The nightmares always increase near the anniversary of her death. It's usually the same one every single night. A sense of helplessness and loss trails me through the days, sealing my fate when I close my eyes.

Glancing at the time on the clock, I groan. It's six in the morning. Only four hours of sleep. I'd stayed up late playing games, thinking my alarm at eight would give me plenty of time.

There's no way sleep will come now.

Fuzzy brained, I swing out of bed and saunter to the bathroom. Turning on the light, I walk to the sink, bracing my hands on the porcelain edges. Glimpsing my reflection, I'm disgusted with the puffy dark circles rimming my eyes and the haggard appearance of my scales. My hair is in dire need of a cut.

Aunt Teale wasn't too far off in her brutal assessment. If I'm going to be at the Weyr reunion next month, I need to get my shit together. Less questions if I don't resemble a pile of dung.

Stepping back, I examine my appearance. The muscles that used to wrap my tall frame have shrunk to a less-than-impressive state. My scales are dry and ashy. All in all, grief has feasted and fattened itself on my misery. It's a miracle Trinte hasn't called me out more than he already has. But I know the Weyr will.

I need a physical overhaul before enduring the scathing commentary.

For the first time in years, I make my bed, giving Rhuth's old pillow an affectionate pat before getting dressed.

Now that I'm paying attention, it's obvious how much my clothing doesn't fit anymore. Ugh. I hate shopping. Rhuth used to buy all of my clothes, but now I'll need to go do it without her. Dread appears, simmering in my stomach. Maybe I can convince Trinte to go do it?

Who am I kidding? He'd froth at the mouth for the chance.

Tightening the belt on my narrow hips, I pad down the hallway to the kitchen. Absentmindedly, my fingers catch the leaves of plants, careful to not topple any of them over with my tail.

The sun has yet to rise, although my instincts tell me it's soon. The sky is a deep purple, signalling the same. Turning on the coffeemaker, I fill it with grounds. Grabbing one of Rhuth's mugs, one she made in a pottery class seven years ago, I place it on the counter as I wait.

Turning to lean against the counter, I eye the kitchen critically. In the last five years, not much has changed. I keep the wooden counters polished, but the hairbrush Rhuth forgot to put away still rests in the same spot she left it. Same as the pair of shoes by the front door. And the sweater draped over a chair at the kitchen table.

I haven't been able to bring myself to move any of it, as if a small, irrational part of my brain hopes she returns to put it away for me.

All of it, from my appearance to the sweater dangling on the chair, is a daily reminder of my loss. I'm finally recognizing how it's a prison of my making.

What kind of man does that make me?

My whole life, I've considered myself to be a logical man. While there will always be better decisions that could've been made, for the most part, I've always chosen to thrive.

These last five years do not reflect that drive. Five whole years of my life were spent enshrining myself with the essence of Rhuth, but all I've done is force myself to exist within an in-between of living and death. Everyone is pressuring me, but there's something inside me aching to be recognized. Maybe it's my old self begging for attention. Perhaps the new version of myself is eager to be born.

While I've never been one to cave into peer pressure, regardless of their status in my life, I can't help but admit that when *everyone* is telling you the same thing ... Maybe it's time to pay attention.

Filling the mug, I take it with me as I slowly walk around the house. Rhuth is everywhere in this tomb I call home. The pottery she made, filled with her plants. A painting she found at a flea market a few months before she died. It depicts a beach in Slous, with bright blue water and pink sand. On the wall by the fireplace is a broken wooden clock she squealed over, insisting she'd get it fixed one day.

I fucking *miss* her. When we first met, she was immediately all I could think about. My brain barely knows how to function without her inside it now.

Everything in this house is evidence of this. It's all evidence of a shrine to a goddess long gone. Am I really expected to get rid of it? What does it take to move on? How could I possibly move on?

There's no easy path leading beyond grief — I just need to figure out mine.

Shoulders sagging, I sit on our purple couch, leaning against one of the white pillows. Taking the first sip of my coffee, I stare up at the wedding photo above the fireplace. If I concentrate, I can almost recall her flirty laugh paired with a soft hand on my arm. Lace rustling against the grass. Lips against mine, eager for more.

Bitterness gnaws at the edges of happiness daring to appear. As if the grief can't stand to make space for anything else, like a jealous only child refusing to share.

With a growl of frustration, I get up to pace. Every few steps, I sip my coffee, but I'm focused on these unrecognizable emotions emerging.

There's a squeezing in my chest as I contemplate how I've spent the last few years. I can't continue to live like this. At this point, I have two options: dive headfirst off a cliff without shifting or learn to move on the best I can.

I pause, truly considering the first option. While the idea of being greeted by Fortuna and my mate sounds incredible, a part of me revolts at the notion. Somehow, that gives me relief. My soul isn't so lost that it wants to abandon this realm.

I resume pacing, drinking the last dregs of my coffee. There's probably a support group somewhere, but I can't picture myself sharing my feelings with strangers. It goes against my nature.

Maybe there's an activity group available? I could try a new hobby. But what kind? The only hobby I've ever had is video games. Whatever it turns out to be should be around other people. *New* people.

I miss the person I was before Rhuth died. No one will want to converse with the broody Dragon.

Making a sound of disgust, I stalk back to the kitchen, restless from all this indecision. By the time I'm done watering the plants, the sun's fully risen. When I go to make another cup of coffee, I'm dismayed to discover I'm out of coffee grounds.

Grabbing my phone, I head out the door, determined to grab a cup of coffee at a nearby shop, then visit Virinia when the market opens. She'll probably have some ideas on how to move on, and if I'm lucky, she'll have a meal available, too.

A muffin alongside coffee sounds like a great idea, if my grumbling stomach is any indication.

For the first time in years, I allow myself to enjoy the shift in the sunshine. Everything becomes sharper, including the sensation of wind under my wings. Earth bows under the pressure of my long, curled claws as I step to the edge of the landing pad. Faint sounds of the waking city comfort me in a way they haven't in a really long time.

A small kernel of fire sparks inside of me, warming my heart. Teetering over the edge, I allow gravity to embrace my form as I pitch forward.

Today, I remember what it's like to enjoy being a Dragon.

14

Orliana

The house is quiet; too quiet. Last night, Joulian spent the night with Mom upon her recommendation. Today, he's going back to the Dragxi headquarters for his second training session, so I'll head out to grab him soon.

But after a slow wake up with Moxie, who protested when I made the bed over her prone form, I'm energized enough to go to my neighborhood coffee shop. It's been too long since I people-watched.

It's still early by the time I walk into the cozy cafe. Moxie never behaves in public, so it's no surprise when she flits into the space and zips up to every patron for a hello. Luckily, most people find my ugopeg familiar charming enough to return the greeting with a chuckle.

A female Satyr in line even hops with excitement when Moxie reaches her, holding out a short, stubby palm for Moxie to land on. The purple ugopeg marches around, bobbing her head, eliciting a giggle from the Satyr.

Coming to stand behind the woman, I smile. "Sorry, she's a little too friendly sometimes."

The Satyr looks up with chestnut brown eyes, her curly dark hair a mess between her horns. "Oh, she's just the sweetest thing. Besides, aren't familiars just an extension of a bonded's soul?"

I chuckle. "This is true, although I can't say I'll sit in your hand to say hello."

This causes the Satyr to laugh. "Please don't. No offense, but you won't fit."

We both share another laugh, and Moxie flies off her palm onto my shoulder. I pet my familiar as I say, "No offense taken."

While the Satyr gives her order, I scan the shop. It's one of my favorites, the theme being rainbows. The owner is a Glyridite, so everything is colorful glitter to the extreme. The chairs sparkle, each in different iridescent colors. The ceiling itself is a simmering rainbow clouds, and the floor is black tiles marbled with glitter veins.

This cafe is unique because with each cup of coffee, they add glitter. It grosses out some people, but I think it's a unique aspect of the service here.

Plush seating fills the space, with one laptop bar at the main window. I spot a small table next to a smaller window and send a prayer to Emet that no one takes my preferred spot.

The Satyr waves goodbye, and I step up to the counter. The female Glyridite, with purple, white, and pink hair, beams. "Welcome to Bows and Brews. What can I get for you?"

Moxie lands on the counter and stabs a wrapped snickerdoodle cookie, piercing the wrapping. Sighing, I grab the cookie. "I'd like a Glitzy Latte with sparkling cold foam." I hold up the assaulted cookie. "I'll take this and ..." I point at the electronic menu. "I'd love the razzle dazzle raspberry muffin with white chocolate drizzle."

The barista hums in agreement, her pink eyes lighting up. "Those are *so* good. Ten corals, please."

I hand over the amount, looking at Moxie. "No more stabbing things. Up on my shoulder."

She snorts, then flies up to perch on my shoulder. The barista giggles. "She's *so* cute. What's her name?"

"Moxiellie, but I call her Moxie."

"What an interesting and adorable name," she gushes, the glitter veins on her body lighting up. "I wish I could have a familiar."

I hold up the cookie again. "It costs money sometimes."

"At least you're never alone, though," she says with a wide grin. I return it with one of my own and step away to wait for my order among the group of waiting patrons.

Keeping a nervous eye on the still-empty table, I unwrap the cookie. Taking a small bite, I offer it to Moxie. She bleats with gratitude and nibbles on the piece.

"We've talked about your stabbing habit," I murmur. She ignores me, closing her eyes, as if that will make me stop talking. She'll never stop, and we both know it. I could order her to stop, but unlike some Siphons, I don't aim to control my familiar. She's as much a part of me as I am of her. Punishing her would be like punishing myself — I do enough of that already.

However, I'm not opposed to making her rest in the Ether when I can't handle her destruction and curiosity.

At the counter, a Sprinkle appears, drying her freshly washed hands. She has pale pink hair with cream-colored streaks through it, springing from her head in tight coils. Two gold hoops adorn each side of her wide, flat nose. Her dark pink eyes crinkle at the edges as she examines the order ticket.

Looking up, she asks, "Razzle dazzle raspberry muffin with white chocolate drizzle?"

I raise my hand. "That's mine."

The Sprinkle, whose nametag reads *Sundai,* raises her dark brown hand. Hot pink nails stand out in contrast against her skin tone. Flattening her palm, the air shimmers into a tornado of glimmering sugar. It thickens as colors appear. Within seconds, my muffin rests in her palm.

Placing it on a blue, glittering plate, Sundai hands over my purchase.

As I reach over to grab it off the counter, I say, "I'll never get tired of seeing that."

She winks, pink eyelashes fluttering. "I never get tired of doing it."

Grinning, I toss a thanks over my shoulder and whisk our food away to the table, grinning with victory when I sit down. Moxie lands next to my coffee, sniffing it.

"Do *not* drink that," I command. "The last time you had coffee, you kept me awake until four in the morning. Almost twenty-four hours after one sip. *No.*"

Somehow, this tiny little goat pouts, but I don't care. Caffeine's not meant for familiars. Opening the rest of her cookie, I place it in front of her so she can feast while I consume my own muffin.

Leaning back, I watch the foot traffic pass. It's still early, but there are plenty of Gondorans heading places. I watch a Cyclops walk his pet chimeragon on a bedazzled leash. A pair of Orcs stroll, holding hands. A family of Seraphim walking by, the toddler with its tiny useless wings flapping in vain while the father tosses her into the air. Each instance of joy warms my heart.

As a Siphon, my purpose in life is to connect with others. Before Mikan, I dreamed of becoming a professional Siphon, like Mom. Helping people process their reactions to situations, connecting with them on a level no one else can.

Now that Mikan isn't here, maybe it's time to entertain this dream again.

I'm amused to find that Moxie has consumed half of the cookie, despite it being bigger than her.

"Moxie!" I admonish, keeping my voice down.

She burps, flopping onto her side, the fat lump of her belly grotesque. Shaking my head, I peel the wrapping off my muffin. She eyes my breakfast, and I point at her. "No. You've had enough."

With a heavy sigh, she closes her eyes, ready for an early morning nap. I watch her sleep, deep affection warming my chest. The Glyridite wasn't wrong — it's nice to never be truly alone. Sometimes, I wish she could talk, but she'd *never* shut up if that were possible.

Taking a bite of the muffin, I watch people coming into the coffee shop. That's when I spotted him — Fynn.

He hasn't seen me yet because he's stepping back to hold the door open for a pair of Elves walking out. It gives me a second to notice that something seems a little different. I've met him twice now, and neither time was a long conversation, but before, he seemed morose.

Focusing on his aura, I see it's still blue and the grief still exists, but today, there's a tinge of red mingling with the blue. Something is changing for him.

This is the first time in a very long time I can see a flicker of newfound happiness in someone, and I let myself revel in the empathy.

Fynn walks into the coffee shop and stands in line, still not noticing me. I'm not sure if I even want him to. *He's married.* The silver ring on his middle finger glints, a reminder of why it's stupid to want him to see me.

But it's difficult to not take in the fact that he's taller than almost everyone here — Dragon males usually are — and the richness of his red scales is impossible to ignore. He's wearing a black T-shirt and jeans, both of which appear to be too big. How odd.

Moxie opens an eye, feeling my curiosity.

"Mind your own business," I mutter, pulling off a piece of the muffin and stuffing it into my mouth.

After placing his order, Fynn stands at the delivery counter, hands shoved into his pockets. Even though his expression is blank, he rocks on the balls of his feet, as if the energy coursing through him is uncomfortable. The little bit of red in his aura begins to flicker out. I frown. Why is it disappearing?

He thanks the barista and walks toward the front door. Just as I think I'll get out of the situation unnoticed, our eyes connect. Damn. Fynn hesitates, looking between me and the door, but he makes a quick decision, heading in my direction.

My heart pounds, waking Moxie. She's up in a flash, ready to fight whatever has my nerves lighting up.

"Be good," I grit quietly through a forced smile. To Fynn, I say, "Hey. Fancy seeing you here."

Fancy seeing you here? Emet strike me down before I make a bigger fool of myself.

He stops next to the empty chair across from me. Moxie bleats loudly, and the corner of his mouth twitching. "Never been here before. My other shop had a line out the door, and I didn't feel like waiting."

"Ah. That makes sense." My knee bobs with anxiety. He's going to be teaching Joulian later today, so there's no need to draw out this conversation.

"What's her name, by the way?" His eyes cross as he tries to watch Moxie, who has taken flight, hovering in front of his nose.

"Moxie," I chide, silently telling her to back off through our bond. Since it's not an order, she lands on his shoulder. Thank the goddesses that her touching others doesn't transfer to me.

"I'm so sorry," I say in a rush. "She has serious boundary issues. Moxie, get off."

His chuckle is smooth. "It's alright. Curious little creature."

"That she is," I mutter, taking a sip of my coffee. Moxie tries to nibble on his hair, but Fynn jerks his head away.

"No, thank you," he says softly, smiling. "I need a haircut, but your teeth are probably not the best instrument."

I examined his black hair; it could use a trim. When he looks at me again, I see dark crescents cradling his gold eyes. "No," I agree. "That is definitely not her profession."

Moxie catapults off his shoulder with a snort, showing off with a flip before landing on the table. Taking advantage of the audience, she trots over to my muffin and takes a bite.

The awkward silence stretches between us, each second heightening my anxiety. I begin spinning the coffee cup, trying to busy my hands.

"Do you want to sit?" I offer.

At the same time, he says, "Well, I should get going."

I resist the urge to slap my burning cheeks. "Of course, sorry. I was being polite. I know you're married, and I wasn't trying to cross a boundary, I promise."

Fynn's expression is unreadable. The hand with the silver ring on it twitches. The bit of red in his aura is but a spec now.

Finally, he sits down. My brow furrows deeply; I'm stunned as he gets comfortable.

"Wait," I say, eyes darting around to see if anyone is watching. "You're married, and I'm not trying to get in between that. Please don't misunderstand me."

"Why did you offer, then?" he asks, clearly curious.

"Because I'm anxious and wasn't thinking when I opened my mouth." The truth spills out before I can catch it.

His eyebrows jerk upward at the confession. Those golden eyes flick over my layers of clothes, my gloves, the coffee, then Moxie.

After taking a slow sip of his coffee, Fynn asks, "Why are you anxious?"

The coffee cup keeps spinning between my fingers, and I look away, unwilling to see his expression or aura. "I don't want to mess anything up for Joulian. He's really excited about working with you. Please don't punish him because I spoke without thinking."

"You won't," he says softly. A red scaled finger appears next to my cup. He taps the short black claw on the table to catch my attention. I'm surprised to see empathy softening his eyes. "It's just coffee, Orliana."

If Mikan were still alive, 'just coffee' would have earned me a sound beating. His wife must be very trusting for him to feel comfortable saying that. For a split second, I'm jealous of the freedom they must have together.

"Is your wife going to be okay with it?"

Fynn pauses, appearing to consider his next words, spinning the silver ring. The red in his aura flickers out entirely as he says, "Rhuth was never jealous, and I never gave her anything to worry about." My stomach drops at the use of the past tense. It plummets when he continues. "At the risk of being overly morbid, I must admit my wife is dead. So technically, I'm not married."

Twelve Hells.

15

Fynn

The second the words are put into existence, I want to snatch them back. She just seemed so flustered about inviting me to sit; I want to give her peace of mind. This is the exact opposite of said goal.

Orliana's shocked expression is exactly why I never mention Rhuth being dead. People are normally immediately uncomfortable, expressing how awful it must be. Pity interlaced with the unspoken relief that it's not their loved one gone.

My fingers find the silver ring, spinning it over and over again. A habit I picked up after our wedding. I watch Orliana process my words; her expression shifts from one of shock to understanding.

To my absolute astonishment, she says, "My husband is dead."

I can't help it; I laugh. It's brief, but loud. She flinches, then smiles.

"I have to admit," I say, still grinning. "I did *not* expect that response."

"Let me guess," she says contemplatively. "People usually tell you how sorry they are, that they know how you feel, despite having never lost anyone?"

I nod emphatically with an odd sense of relief from this unexpected camaraderie. "Exactly. I once had someone tell me their pet sphinx died, and that they knew exactly how I felt."

Orliana scoffs. "Someone once said that they lost one of their favorite earrings, as if my husband was a piece of misplaced jewelry."

I point to the pendant around her neck. "You mean that doesn't hold his essence or something?"

It's meant to be a joke, but something dark passes over her expression before disappearing. She grabs the pendant, but almost like it's absent-minded as she says softly, "Some of him is."

Having an idea of how she feels, I hum in understanding. "I've kept all of my wife's plants alive. I don't even like plants."

This breaks her reverie, eliciting a look of surprise. "How many plants? For how long?"

Grimacing, I say, "Fifty-four. And in a few weeks, it'll be five years."

She gives a low whistle. "You hate plants, but you've taken care of them for almost five years? You must have loved her a lot." Her eyes widen. In a rush she says, "I mean, of *course* you loved her! I don't even know why I said that."

My heart squeezes. For a second, I contemplate mentioning our son, but I've already brought down the mood, so all I can say is, "I did. Very much."

"What's her name?"

Already, Orliana has thrown me for a loop. There's no pity in her voice or expression. Only simple curiosity. According to Joulian, she's a Siphon, which means heavy emotions are relatively easier for her to handle. Not that she doesn't feel them, but according to my old professor, Siphons seek out connections, even painful ones.

Is that why she wanted me to sit with her? She can sense my pain?

The thought is both troublesome and comforting. Everyone else wants me to move on, like my grief is a personal affront. Not for Orliana, if the open curiosity on her face is any indication.

"Rhuth," I say, enjoying the taste of her name on my lips. I never get to say her name out loud much anymore.

"Rhuth," she repeats. "That's a beautiful name. How long were you together?"

"Fifteen years." It's distracting when my heart picks up speed.

"So you've spent fifteen years dedicated to the same woman? That's incredible. Not many men can say that." She looks impressed.

After taking a sip of my coffee, I say, "I never thought about it that way, but yes. But if you had met her, you'd understand why it's so easy."

Orliana smiles, but sadness pulls at the edges of her brown eyes. "She's very lucky."

Why does it feel incredible for someone to speak about Rhuth in the present tense? I know it won't bring her back, but for a split second, I can pretend she's about to walk into the coffee shop and steal my coffee as her own.

Suddenly, I'm unable to continue talking about her. I glance away, swallowing down the incessant grief threatening to make me cry in a goddess-forsaken coffee shop. My face heats with embarrassment.

Clearing my throat, I rasp out, "Apologies. This is not the kind of conversation I intended when I sat down."

"It's okay." Orliana's soft voice guides my eyes back to hers. Her lips stretch into a smile, albeit a tight one. "I don't mind; truly. I'm not a small talk kind of girl. I'm more of a 'tell me all of your traumas' on the first date kind of girl." Shock pales her face. "Oh my goddess, no, sorry. I didn't mean that. This isn't, I mean, a date or anything. I can't believe I said that. You're sitting here, talking about your wife, and I say *date* like an idiot."

Her eyes dart around as if seeking an escape. Moxie squeaks and hops over to the muffin to take another bite. The coffee cup in Orliana's grasp spins so fast it might take flight.

Leaning forward, I bring a finger to the lid of her cup, careful to not touch her gloved hands. The spinning cup stops.

"It's okay," I say quietly. "I knew what you meant. No offense taken, I promise."

Tension leaks from her body. She sighs. "Still; sorry about that. Sometimes my mouth has a mind of its own, I swear."

"I can't say I have the same problem," I say wryly. "I'm not much of a talker, to be honest. This is probably the longest and most honest conversation I've had in a long time." The truth of it stings. I swallow hard before admitting, "Although, now that I think about it, most of my other conversations revolve around work or Rhuth. I can't remember the last time I discussed anything else."

Orliana tilts her head quizzically. "That sounds ... awful. You don't have any hobbies?"

I nearly smack my forehead. "Of course. Sorry, I also play video games. Like your stereotypical Dragxi, of course."

"Oh!" Her face lights up. "I do, too! What do you play?"

A level of excitement I haven't felt in years surges. "Really? I love playing Rukbegger."

Orliana nearly topples out of her chair; she's squirming like it's on fire. "*Really?* Me, too! Maybe we've played together? What's your username?"

"TopDrag?" I hold my breath. There's no way we —

"Oh, my goddess!" She nearly screeches. *"I'm MeanCat."*

My jaw drops. "No."

"Yes!"

Her enthusiasm is infectious. For a split second, I forget my desire to keep the world at arm's length as I playfully accuse, "I don't believe it. Prove it."

With a face shining with glorious happiness, Orliana beams as she says in a now-familiar voice, *"That's what your daddy said to me last night."*

I slap a hand on the table in jubilation. She flinches, then returns my grin. "I can't believe the sheer luck required for this serendipitous moment," I declare. "You're an incredible player, MeanCat."

She dips her reddening cheek toward her shoulder as she says shyly, "You're pretty great, too. You have a great team of players. Do you know them all in person?"

I shake my head. "Only Trinte."

Somehow, her eyes get even wider. "Trinte plays, too?"

"StupendousSkies."

"Oh, sweet goddess, what are the odds?" she says, bewildered.

For once, I have good news to share with my brother. "Trinte is going to lose his mind."

"Are you going to play in the tournament tomorrow?" she asks.

"Absolutely. I think Curly can't come; would you like to fill in?"

She smirks. "Curly already sent me an invite, so it's a yes."

"Excellent."

We grin at one another, caught up in the thrill of finding an online friend in real life. I notice how long her black eyelashes are; the way they frame her caramel-brown eyes. Such an interesting contrast against her skin tone.

Moxie breaks the moment by flying into my field of vision, somehow appearing angry at me. She bleats and rushes forward, forcing me to jerk my head back.

"Moxie!" Orliana admonishes her familiar. "You're being rude. Knock it off."

The ugopeg narrows her gold eyes with an obstinate snort. Secretly, I'm relieved for the interference. Guilt is already tearing into my grief. For a moment, I forgot about my wife. The realization is like an anchor clamped around my ankles as someone throws me overboard.

I clear my throat. "It's okay. She's right — it's getting late." I make a show of checking the time. "Joulian will be at headquarters at nine?"

Her head nods robotically. "I'm going to go pick him up right now, and we'll head straight there."

Standing, I pick up our trash. "Okay. Well, it was a pleasant surprise to chat with you this morning, Orliana." To my dismay, I mean it, too. "I'll see you in an hour."

She also stands, looking unsure. "Yeah. See you soon."

I watch her leave, unsure how to process the warring emotions inside my chest. As I throw out the trash, I realize I never asked about her husband.

16

Orliana

When Fynn's smile lit up the room, it tilted my world on its axis. My heart sped up. For a split second, thoughts disappeared. I've never seen his full smile and had no idea there were dimples on both cheeks. His fangs only add to the masterpiece.

Men cannot be masterpieces. I need a man in my life like I need a hole in the head. Though Fynn seems nice enough, so did Mikan.

Mikan. As I left, I realized he never asked me about my dead husband, but I'm glad for it. He's essentially a stranger, and even though it was in the news reports, I don't want it to affect Joulian's experiences with the Dragxi headquarters. I've taken away enough from my son.

If Moxie hadn't rightfully interrupted, I don't know what I would've said or done.

I'm shaking as the orange Dragxi flies me through the city to Mom's house. I barely notice anything, too wrapped up in my worries. It was nothing. A cup of coffee. Sure, we have dead spouses and love playing video games, but that's not much to go on.

By the time I'm at Mom's, I've resigned myself to keeping a distance between Fynn and me. The way he seemed uncomfortable, he's probably thinking the same thing. He's clearly still very much in love with his deceased wife.

An ache in my heart festers as I remember the way he spoke about her. It was full of longing, the grief in his aura turned almost black. He's a man still in mourning; I refuse to judge him for it. We can't control things like that.

All thoughts of dimples are forgotten when Joulian rushes out of Mom's home, backpack smacking his shoulders. "Mom!"

After asking him to wait, I hop off the Dragxi. It's a delight when he allows me to bundle him into a hug.

"I missed you, buddy," I say into his hair. "I had the whole house to myself and barely knew what to do."

"Are we going to the Dragxi headquarters now?" he says excitedly, ignoring my words, ripping out of my hold. By the time I open my mouth to answer, he's already rushing to the Dragxi.

Well then.

I wave at Mom, who waves back. I'll give her a call later, but Joulian clearly won't wait a second longer than necessary. I join him on the seats, and direct the Dragxi to Flaming Fares headquarters.

Joulian can barely sit still. Greg matches his energy by hopping all over, being a nuisance. When the blue crow hits me with a wing, I admonish Joulian.

"Love of my life, you need to control your familiar."

My son cuts me down with a glare. "Like you do with Moxie?"

Moxie's sitting between us, surprisingly not joining Greg in the ruckus. She kicks Joulian in the thigh as if to prove a point. It has all the power of flicking someone; Joulian merely frowns, then gives me a pointed look.

"Point taken," I concede. "Just keep him under control at the headquarters. Don't forget what Fynn said, alright?"

"Got it." He turns super serious. "I'm going to be really good today. I promise."

I sling an arm around his shoulders. "I know you will, buddy."

To my delight, he snuggles into my chest. Everything freezes, including the air in my lungs. *Don't spook the teenager.* He hasn't willingly given this kind of affection in ages. The curse of adolescence.

The moment breaks as he shifts, pulling out an ache of homesickness with him. I miss the young boy who was always giggling and hugging me.

Fynn's already waiting by the time we land, watching us with crossed arms. The smile that woke up a piece of me is nowhere to be seen, but that's okay. Two times in one day might kill me. Instead, he watches Joulian rush up with a vaguely amused expression. Over the mass of Joulian's black curls, his eyes reach mine and pause a second longer than necessary.

I look away first.

Like last time, there's a chair for me to sit in. The Dragxi that brought us here volunteers to sit in the washing station so Joulian can learn how to properly use the hose. I watch for any signs of Fynn losing his patience, but it never happens. Even as Joulian asks question after question, the Dragon remains steady, explaining everything in a way a thirteen-year-old can understand.

As I listen to him speak, I can finally match him with the voice over the microphone last week. As team leader, TopDrag was patient and thorough as well.

That's when I suddenly remembered what the team was discussing right as I joined: Fynn having a big dick.

My eyes trail from his face down his flat stomach to between his legs. It doesn't *look* like a giant dick nestled there, but I'm wholly unfamiliar with Dragon anatomy and how that works with shifting. Frankly, I'm not *that* familiar with dicks. Mikan's the only partner I've ever had, so there's nothing to compare it to.

I know, with Mikan, sex was basically not enjoyable; that much is certain. The last couple of years before his death, I never wanted it, but as my husband, he took advantage of any chance possible. Honestly, I thought it was completely normal until Kyri told me it wasn't.

It's not something worth thinking about.

Pulling out my phone, I text my best friend. I haven't seen her in a couple of weeks; she keeps pretty busy with teaching self-defense at the local battle arena and also helps women escape dangerous situations.

Orliana: Hey. How's life?

Sometimes she shares crazy stories, which are always interesting. It takes a few minutes, but eventually she responds.

Kyri: I was just about to text you, actually. Not too bad. Just finished pommeling the punching bag. You?

Orliana: Watching Joulian do the Dragxi thing. Boring stuff.

Kyri: Fun. Give the kid a hug from his goddessmother. What are you doing this evening?

Orliana: You know me. Hitting up a couple dozen parties. Smoking a lot of gibbonroot. Joining an orgy.

Kyri: So, in bed by 8pm with a book?

Orliana: Yup.

Kyri: You lead such a daring and exciting life.

I scoff. Kyri's younger than me and lives her life to the fullest. She had a rough childhood. After Mom and I discovered her outside a convenience store in the rain, she struggled to find her equilibrium. One thing she's always made clear, though: she hates relationships with men, and she doesn't want to have kids.

There's always been a tiny bit of envy there, wishing sometimes I'd made different choices. I'd never give up the chance to have Joulian, but everything else? I wouldn't mind a do-over.

Orliana: I'm a thirty-five-year-old single mom. What in the Hells do you want from me?

Kyri: I want you to get laid. You've never even had good sex.

Orliana: Don't remind me.

Kyri: You've never even had good sex.

Orliana: You're the worst.

Kyri: I know. Hey, you should come to the club with me tonight. I'm going on a date with a Gargoyle. He'll have the hook-up at the door.

Orliana: First off, a *date*? Also, I'm not sure I really want to be a third-wheel, Kyri.

Kyri: Okay, 'date' is generous. The pomp and circumstance he prefers before fucking. He buys me drinks, then provides orgasms. Anyway, he's invited some friends. Come on, it'll be fun. Invite others, if you want.

Orliana: Yes, I'll just call up my roster of friends. It'll be a hoot.

I haven't gone out in years. What would Joulian think? Fynn is showing him scrubbing techniques, gently curling his fingers around the handle of the brush to show the proper hold. He looks up, those golden eyes catching my stare. I pretend to observe some brushes.

Kyri: I'm ignoring your sarcasm. So, are you in?

Orliana: I have nothing to wear. I can't leave Joulian alone.

There's a couple of minutes before she responds. I watch Trinte exit the headquarters, heading toward his brother. He sees me watching and grins, offering a wave. I return the greeting, relieved that there's someone here as a buffer for my imaginary tension with Fynn. My phone buzzes.

Kyri: Your mom agreed to watch him.

Orliana: That's low, even for you.

Kyri: Proud belly crawler over here. I'll courier over a few dresses. I can't meet you ahead of time, but I'll make sure your name is on the list.

Orliana: Kyrielle! You're ridiculous. I didn't even say I wanted to go.

Orliana: I'm going to "accidentally" spill a drink on your dress.

Kyri: He'll probably just suggest I take it off.

Orliana: Nevermind.

Kyri: 9pm at Hottie Patottie.

Orliana: Maybe.

The part of me I'm struggling to acknowledge is excited about the prospect. The other part is sick to my stomach. I'll have to shield against every single brush of skin and automatically siphon whatever I can't block. I'm so out of practice.

Yet, maybe it could be good for me. The only way to not be out of practice is to, well, *practice.* Plus, I've never been to a club. Mikan never allowed it. Realizing this, it solidifies my decision to go. Because *fuck* Mikan.

Fynn's eyes are on me again. This time, he's walking with his brother and Joulian over to where I'm sitting. I stand, flustered, as I put my phone into my purse.

Smiling at Joulian, I say, "How was it?"

Joulian's blue eyes shine like the afternoon sky. "Mom! Did you see? I washed the Dragon! I even accidentally tickled him."

Fynn grunts out a low chuckle. "Evan wasn't pleased, but it's okay."

I smile. "That's great, buddy." To Fynn, I ask, "Is he good for the day?"

Fynn nods, but it's Trinte who speaks. "He's doing a good job. Does he want to come next weekend, too?"

Joulian appears ready to fight me if it's a no, so to keep him on his toes, I say smoothly, "Of course. Same time?"

Fynn's mouth twitches in amusement. "Same time."

"Great!" Looking at Joulian, I say, "I'm afraid you're heading back to your grandmother's again. I'm apparently going out tonight."

"Okay!" Joulian grins with excitement, probably because my mother spoils him rotten.

"Going out?" Fynn asks.

For a second, I'm taken aback. Then I remember we're tentatively friends. Right. *Friends.* "Yeah, my best friend invited me out to a club tonight. It's not really my thing — I've never even been to one — but she's hard to say no to."

Fynn snorts, eyeing his brother. "I empathize."

Trinte gives a low whistle, clearly intrigued enough that it makes me wary. "A club, you say? I love clubs."

I give him a sidelong look. Is he aiming to be invited or something? "Yeah, well, she has VIP access thanks to some rich guy and asked me to go."

Trinte's eyebrows go up. He nudges his elbow into Fynn's side, but the red Dragon only glares at his brother.

"No."

Whether it's the idea of going to a club, or being VIP — because he apparently assumes he can tag along — Trinte juts a thumb at me. "You're really going to let her go to a club for the first time, all by herself?"

Wait, what? "Um, no, it's okay. My friend will be there."

Trinte gives me a disbelieving look. "You're going to third-wheel on a date?"

"Other people will be there," I say defensively.

"I'm sorry, he was dropped on his head as a baby," Fynn says, trying to step in front of his brother. Trinte ignores the jibe, elbowing his brother's ribs.

"So you're with a bunch of other strangers while your friend is on a date?" Trinte actually looks disgruntled at the idea.

Well, when he puts it that way. I nibble my lip, considering my options. Kyri *will* be distracted with a date. She's a great friend, but unless she ignores him entirely, I'll be alone more than will probably be comfortable.

Sighing, I cross my arms and raise an eyebrow. With an exaggerated drawl, I say, "Trinte. Fynn. Would you like to come to the club with me so you can laugh at me being extremely uncomfortable in a VIP lounge?"

Trinte doesn't even hesitate. With a mad grin, he says, "Absolutely!" He looks at his brother, who is decidedly less thrilled. "Come on. You should get out of your comfort zone, too."

Fynn shoots him daggers with those golden eyes. With a mix of reluctance and amusement, as he grits out, "Sure."

I can't help it; I smile. Pulling out my phone, I ask Fynn, "What's your number? I'll send over the details."

When he recites it, I shoot off a quick hello text and put my phone away again, releasing a sharp exhale. "Well. I guess I'll see you both this evening."

"Hells yeah!" Trinte hollers, acting like he's won some sort of award. It's actually a little alarming.

Fynn rolls his eyes as he turns his attention to Joulian. "Alright, I'll see you next weekend. Sound good?"

Joulian nods, totally oblivious. "Yes, sir. See you then."

Giving the Gleanscale brothers one last meaningful look, I walk Joulian to the launch pad, wondering what in Emet's Hell I've agreed to.

17

Fynn

As soon as Orliana is out of earshot, I whirl on my brother. *"What. The. Fuck."*

True to form, he looks unperturbed. "What? You deserve some fun."

"You put her on the spot, Trinte. What if she didn't want us to go?" The thought of imposing makes me sick to my stomach. Hells, the thought of going to a club might actually make me throw up. "I don't *want* to go to a club, Trinte."

"Have you ever *been* to a club?"

Gritting my teeth, I ground out, "No. You know I haven't." Rhuth and I were more homebodies, focused on our careers and building a family. The idea of sweaty dancing and hangovers was never appealing. It still isn't.

"Then it's time to start something new."

"I'm too old to do something new."

"You're forty."

"My left hip aches when it rains. My knees crack when I climb a flight of stairs."

My brother, with the thick skull he was apparently born with, is too stubborn to know when to quit. "Wear a knee brace. Take a tonic. I don't care. You're going." He pauses. "If you come tonight, I'll tell Aunt Teale you're doing better."

This stops me in my tracks. Not because he'll tell her I'm doing better, whatever that means. But because that means he spoke to her about me before.

"Did you tell her I wasn't going to go to the Weyr reunion?" The way his eyes flick away tells me enough. "I can't fucking believe you. You know how she is ..." I stop speaking as realization hits. With a glare, I snarl, "You let her into my *fucking office*, didn't you?"

Trinte waves away the accusation. "Like she wouldn't have gotten in on her own, anyway. *You* know how she is."

For the first time in a long time, I'm mad enough to fill his mouth with my Fyre, just to put him in his place. "Don't *ever* do that again."

Tired of the discussion, he walks away, forcing me to trail after him. Over his shoulder, he says, "What time are we meeting her?"

"9pm. But I'm not going, Trinte."

He whirls around. No longer playful, he stalks up to me with a snarl. Even though he's shorter, his fury makes him suddenly taller. "Yes. You are. Because I want my fucking brother back, Fynn. I want him *back*."

The last word cracks, and he growls away the emotion clogging up his throat. I stamp down the urge to hug him with an apology.

It's finally dawning on me how much my grief has stolen. Not just from me, but from him, as well. Our mother died giving birth to him and our father ...

Trinte deserves better than what I've been giving.

"I'm trying," I say quietly, hoping the earnestness shows in my expression.

Swallowing hard, he's finally able to say, "I will continue to fight for you, Fynn, even if you don't want me to. I want to experience your first club with you. I want to drink an overpriced beer with my brother, check out beautiful women, and maybe dance a little bit." When I open my mouth to say I will *not* be dancing, he cuts me off. "*I'll* dance. You can brood in a corner. As long as you're there with me, okay?"

I want him back.

It's those words that finalize my decision. "Fine. But I have nothing to wear. All of my clothes are too loose." It's painful to admit, but this morning showed how badly I need a new wardrobe.

Trinte's smile is devious. "I guess we'll have to go shopping."

***

I'm quickly reminded why I hate shopping. Trinte drags me out to a clothing market, tossing items at me. I barely pay attention, trying things on, dismayed to see the smaller numbers on each piece. How did I let myself waste away like this?

It's three hours of torture. By the time we're done, my arms have lost circulation from all the bags. Shirts, pants, shoes; you name it, he's forced me to buy it. I never spend money on myself anymore, so it's not like it puts a dent in my bank account.

It's late afternoon when we part ways, going to our respective homes. I'm forced to take a Dragxi — there's no way my Dragon form can carry all of this. When we land, the Dragxi, an employee whose name is Elchor, looses some smoke as he rumbles out a chuckle.

I didn't know you were a shopaholic, boss.

"I'm not," I grumble, almost dropping the bags more than once. "This is Trinte's fault."

Sounds about right. Have fun tonight.

I look up sharply as he takes off. How does he know about tonight? We can mindspeak, but we aren't mind readers.

Trinte and his big mouth.

Making a sound of disgust, I carry the shackles of consumerism back into my home.

Yet, as I walk through the door, it feels different. Like a single boulder, from the pile of many, was lifted off my shoulders. Was it just this morning I had a horrific nightmare and decided to do something different with my life?

So far, I've had coffee with a new friend and gone on a shopping spree.

Who am I?

Dragging the bags to the bedroom, I toss them onto the bed and glimpse the photo of Rhuth on the nightstand. Touching her face with a finger, I smile.

"I'm going to a club tonight. Can you believe it? That brother of mine is too convincing with guilt trips."

I can almost hear what she'd say: *Don't let him convince you to get drunk and jump off high rises again.*

I used to live life as full as possible. While I never went to clubs, I've been to plenty of parties and bars. I used to have fun; I used to *be* fun.

Padding into the bathroom, I reassess my reflection. A haircut is required. Pulling my phone from a back pocket, I text my brother.

Fynn: I need a haircut.

While I wait for the text, I jump in the shower. By the time I'm toweling off, he's responded.

Trinte: I'm sending my barber.

Fynn: What's the address?

Trinte: He's on his way right now.

Fynn: You're kidding.

Trinte: I think this could be a good haircut on you.

He sends a photo of a bald Vampyre.

Fynn: I hate you.

Trinte: No need to be rude. Just say you don't like it.

Fynn: I actually don't know what to do with my hair.

Trinte: It's long enough you could do anything.

He sends another photo. This time, it's an intriguing haircut, with the sides cut up short and the top left shaggy, but not too much in the face.

Fynn: That's not too bad.

Trinte: I don't want to spend time with an ugly person.

Fynn: Avoid reflective surfaces.

Trinte: har har

There's a knock at the door. Still wearing only a towel, I walk down the hall and peer through the peephole. A dark-skinned Elf waits patiently on the other side. How in the Hells is the barber already here?

Looking down at my towel, then at the door, I sigh. Trinte owes me a few drinks tonight. Opening the door, I look around the edge.

"Hey, uh, are you the barber?"

The Elf nods, white eyes already examining my soaking wet hair. He hasn't even noticed the towel. "Sure am. He said it was an emergency?"

I suck air through my teeth. "*Tch.* You could say that." I step back to let him come in. "Give me a second to get dressed. I honestly didn't expect you to be here at all, let alone so fast."

The Elf is already walking toward the kitchen like he owns the place, carrying a large bag, presumably full of haircutting tools. Without looking over his shoulder, he says, "The name's Zerif."

"Uh, I'm Fynn?" This is one of the oddest interactions of my life.

Zerif simply says, "I know," before setting up at my table.

Before he gets too cozy, I call out, "Don't touch that sweater."

"Got it."

I don't trust him, though, so I dress in a hurry, tearing off tags. I settle on a see-through black button up collared shirt, open at the first three buttons. When Trinte picked it out, I flat out refused to buy it. He threatened to tell Aunt Teale that I want to be matched with someone.

I bought the shirt.

I pair it with black slacks that actually fit. Inspecting my reflection, I'm surprised at how much well-fitting clothes already change my appearance.

There's a tentative pep in my step as I meet Zerif in the kitchen. He's covered the table's surface in an array of tools, and a chair's already pulled out. Rhuth's sweater is in the same spot as it always is.

Relieved, I sit in the chair. "Trinte sent a photo for a suggested haircut."

Zerif gets right down to business, running his fingers through my still-wet hair. "Got it and I agree; it'll look good on you. He said you like to brood and this front fringe will help with that."

"I do not brood," I mutter and grind my teeth when I realize I'm brooding about being accused of brooding.

"Whatever you say," Zerif says, sounding amused. "So you're okay with me taking all of this off on the sides."

I stare into the mirror he's set up, seeing him hold up over six inches of hair. I nod. "Get rid of it."

And take the grief with you. A haircut can't cut out the grief, but it can soften it.

Zerif grins, revealing gems in his fangs. "Let's take you from sad to smolder, shall we?"

18

Orliana

I'm going to kill her.

I stare at the three dresses Kyri sent. Each is a different style, but not a single one of them fully covers a body part. She also sent shoes. No, not shoes. Deadly weapons disguised in the shape of torturous heels. I've never worn a pair of heels in my life and these are at least four inches each. I'm going to resemble a newborn Centaur in these things.

Silently cursing her name, I settle on the champagne-colored dress, with a decadent slit down my sternum. It's the only one that reaches mid-thigh, forcing me to choose exactly which part of my body to reveal more. It's backless, hugging the generous curves of my ass.

Examining my reflection, I have to admit I'm beautiful. I've been going to the gym since Mikan died, so it shouldn't surprise me to see small muscles flexing everywhere. I still have a tummy from carrying Joulian, but all in all, I look fantastic for thirty-five. I'm not the type to stare at my reflection very often, so I'm genuinely pleased.

Maybe this won't be so bad.

For the heels, I chose the matching set in the color of burnished gold. Together, the ensemble looks incredible. I add some delicate hoop earrings and allow the mass of curls to be as uncontrolled as they like.

My phone buzzes — I'm surprised to see it's a text from Fynn.

Fynn: I'm wearing a see-through shirt. Trinte made me wear it. Please don't judge me.

I grin. I've been apprehensive about them coming along, but with that one little text, Fynn has settled some of my anxiety.

Orliana: No judgment. I'm wearing a dress that might actually be a fancy napkin.

Fynn: I don't know how to respond to that without sounding like a creep, so I'll just say that I hope you like wearing a fancy napkin?

Orliana: Now I'm just thinking of all the creepy things you could be saying.

Fynn: Please don't. Me and my lizard brain are not always on the same page.

Orliana: Fine. Are you wearing a fancy tablecloth or are you also going to be wearing a napkin?

Fynn: Definitely a fancy runner, at least.

Orliana: Scandalous.

Fynn: Do you want us to come and pick you up?

Orliana: You're going to Dragxi me to the club? Isn't that a little too on the nose?

Fynn: Of course not. I'd actually pay the fare. Which is almost like just paying myself, but I'm not going to look too deeply into it.

It'd be nice to have an escort, especially in this outfit. Grabbing my sheer black gloves, I put them on.

Orliana: Okay, that sounds good. No wiping your greasy hands on my napkin.

The second I press send, I regret the text. It's too flirty. The man is in mourning, and I'm joking about his hands on my dress. Fynn immediately texts back.

Fynn: Keeping hands in lap was the plan.

Fynn: MY lap. Not yours.

Fynn: Not that there's anything wrong with your lap.

Fynn: Please ignore the last three texts. We're on the way.

Orliana: See you soon.

Butterflies slam into my rib cage; the anxiety is almost too much to bear. I sit on the bed and focus on my breath while Moxie sits next to me for support.

That felt flirty.

It was definitely flirty.

Does that mean tonight will be flirty?

Am I ready for that?

My breath speeds up as sweat soaks my palms. Maybe this was a mistake. All of this is too much.

Stroking Moxie's back, I murmur, "I don't think I can do this. I mean, look at me, Mox. I don't even look like myself."

Moxie carefully nudges my hip with her horn as if to say, *it's still you.*

"I know, I know." I let out a heavy sigh. "But going out with two men I just met? That's *definitely* not me." I gnaw at my lip. "Maybe I should just cancel?"

The thought gives me both relief and dread.

Moxie snorts, jerking up from my side. I watch her fly over to the bottom of a dresser. Curious, I kneel next to the drawer where she's slamming her horn into.

"What on earth are you going on about?" I slide it open.

It's an old drawer full of various pieces of clothing. I shuffle through, then stop when Moxie cannonballs into the fabrics, then roots around like a mole, bleating furiously. When she stops, she continues calling until I push aside the clothes, revealing my old, worn diary.

My blood goes cold. "Why are you showing me this?" I sound accusatory because this is an awful time for her to remind me of this diary. Of what's inside. "This is cruel, Moxie. Get out of the drawer."

She obeys the command, but glares at me. Since we're rarely truly at odds, it's uncomfortable to feel what she's sending through the bond. It's a return accusation, one of cowardice. It pisses me off so much, I yank the diary out of the drawer before slamming it shut.

"Fine. You want me to fucking look at it?" I seethe, teeter-tottering on the heels until I can sit on the edge of the bed. I open up the diary, thumbing through the pages. "What is it you think I'm refusing to consider?"

Moxie lands on the diary. Shoving her horn into the direction of the comforter top, I place the diary on the bed. She uses her muzzle to turn pages. I'm fascinated to watch her read, searching for something. I didn't even know Moxie could read.

"This whole time, you could be distracting yourself with books instead of bothering me?" I ask, incredulous.

She ignores me, searching for the unknown. Finally, she hops frantically, stabbing a page with her horn. I pick up the book and she tumbles onto the bed with a sound of protest.

"Serves you right," I murmur, scanning the pages. It's from five years ago.

Today, Mikan told me it would be impossible to go to Siphon therapy school. He claims Joulian needs me at home. I promised it would be only a couple days a week and during the day, when Joulian's at school, but he still refused.

I'm so tired of feeling like there's nothing out there for me. As if all I'm good for is being a vessel for him. A vessel of sexuality. Of rage. Of pain.

I don't know how much longer I can take it. Emet strike me down, but sometimes, I imagine what it'd be like to leave him with Mikan. To escape. Then I want to cut my own heart out, because that would be easier than leaving my son.

But by the time Joulian is old enough to leave the house, I doubt there will be much of me left.

Tears plop onto the page. I wipe them away furious, ruining my makeup. I remember that day so clearly, which is probably why Moxie insisted that I read it. The way I begged Mikan for the opportunity to go learn. The desperation rationalized asking the question I already knew the answer to. The conversation ended with a kick to the stomach and a threat of worse if I asked again.

And what did I do after he died? I curled into myself. Retreated from the whole damn world. Even without Mikan, I didn't pursue my dreams.

I stayed home to take care of my son and maybe that actually meant something those first couple of years. But it's been over three years now, but I'm no closer to my dreams. There's no one else to blame but myself.

The realization is devastating.

"Oh, Moxie," I sob, reaching for her. She crawls into my lap, whimpering. She did it because something about tonight feels ... *big.* I don't know why, but it just does. I needed the reminder of where I come from.

And where I want to go.

Placing the diary onto the bed, I hug my familiar a little tighter. She happily snuggles deeper.

"I love you."

She gives a tiny honk, her way of saying it back. Then my phone buzzes, shattering the moment. I grab it, then swear.

"Ugh, they're almost here." Bolting upright, I rush over to the mirror. My mascara has smeared under my eyelashes.

"Emet, give me grace," I mutter, snatching up a towel to blot at the black smudges. It's mostly under my bottom eyelashes, refusing to move. Damnit. I don't want to scrub too hard or I'll ruin the other bits of make-up still clinging.

Stepping back, I examine the mess. In the dim light, it could pass as an intentional smokey eye of sorts.

I look at Moxie. "Be honest. What do you think?" She bobs her head and paws at the ground. A seal of approval. "Okay, I'm trusting you."

There's a knock at the door. Blood freezes in my veins and all thoughts cease. Then my heart catches up and I inhale sharply. Tonight feels monumental and for a split second, I recognize the shift. Like opening the front door means more than just stepping outside; it's like stepping into my destiny.

"Okay, it's just a night clubbing, you sappy idiot," I mutter, checking the dark red lipstick one more time. Peering over my shoulder, I admire my curves once again. This may be my first time at the club, but it definitely doesn't look like it.

Grabbing the small gold purse, I tuck my phone, lipstick, and pepper spray. Moxie trots after me, but I hold up a hand. "No, ma'am. Not tonight; not at the club. I'll have to focus on shielding, not keeping an eye on you."

Moxie squeals with fury. I know she wants to see the club, but I just can't risk it. If I lose focus on not touching people, I could absorb terrible emotions without warning.

"If I find a reasonable spot that makes sense, I'll call you."

There's another knock at the door. Moxie bolts toward the sound. I sigh, following her on wobbling heels. "Don't make me order you."

I'll have to, though. We both know it. She's the embodiment of my inner child. She knows my every thought, good or bad, *and* is just as smart as me. Yet, she will always be more childish in her decisions. Which is why tonight, I'll have to command her to hide.

Letting her have a couple more minutes of freedom, I allow her to ram into the front door until I swing it open.

Fynn stares down at me, expressionless. Not a word passes his lips, but that's okay, because I'm busy taking in the new haircut. It's shorter on the sides, with the remaining hair on top is shaggy with faint curls adding texture. The longer fringe brings attention to his golden eyes.

He looks ... good.

Really good.

"Hey," I say faintly, leaning against the door because I don't trust my knees right now. "Nice outfit." What I really want to say is, *did you really have to leave three buttons undone?*

Fynn peers down at his clothing, then back up. His mouth opens, then closes.

Confused, I furrow my brow. "Are you okay?"

He clears his throat. "Sorry, yes. That's just the fanciest napkin I've ever seen."

I toss my head back with a laugh. "Clearly meant for royalty."

Wincing, he leans down to grab his ankle. "Oww."

"Moxie!" I exclaim, watching her stab him. She ignores me, charging toward his other ankle, hitting true.

"What the Hells?" Fynn groans. "Why is she attacking? Is it because I complimented the napkin?"

I scoop up my rebellious familiar. Through our bond, she shares her murderous intent. I laugh. "I think she's trying to tell you that if you do anything to me, she'll hunt down and kill you. Or cut off your feet. It's not quite clear."

Fynn gives my familiar a solemn nod. "You have my word; the napkin wearer shall remain safe."

To my surprise, Moxie snarls, revealing her buck teeth. Laughing again, I kiss her little cheek. "Okay, friend. It's time. Go hide."

She gives a mournful sigh, but disappears.

Fynn looks around, confused, still massaging an ankle. "Where did she go?"

I wave into the air dismissively. "Wherever familiars go until they're called back."

He straightens. "Wait. You've had that option the whole time?"

"Yep."

The expression on his face darkens as he glares at his ankles.

"Problem?" I chirp, feeling silly and playful for no other reason than the fact he's not actually mad at my familiar, despite his fake scowl. The red around his heart began burning brighter the second he saw me. It's burning brighter still at my teasing.

His eyes meet mine, expression softening. "No. Not at all."

"Great. Let me just lock up." I pause, resisting the urge to chew my lip. Lipstick on teeth would be a tragedy right now. "Can you catch me if I fall?"

He stares at me. "What?"

I point down at my heels. "These things might actually kill me by the end of the night."

At this, his mouth twitches. "I've never saved a damsel in distress; it could be a night of many firsts."

My anxiety flares again as I slide the key into the lock. Barely audible, I murmur, "Maybe."

19

Fynn

I've spent almost fifteen years not looking at another woman. I'm a true monogamist — Rhuth was my everything. She still is.

Yet, when that front door opened, I looked at another woman. I took in those curves, the dark glimmering skin, the curls, the lips ... and I *looked.*

Words failed as she peers up at me, smokey eyes lit up with anxiety and excitement. That dress ... whoever gave her that dress should be given an award. It's a gift from Fortuna, no doubt about it.

And as she slips her arm through mine, I stand slightly taller. Because having a beautiful woman on your arm is one of the most incredible feelings possible, even if she's just a friend. I have no doubt she'll catch attention at the bar.

Which is fine. I know she's not interested in me, at least; I'm fairly certain she's still mourning her husband. She didn't want to speak about him and understood my deep pain. On top of that, *I'm* not ready.

Plus, every time we made eye contact today, she looked away. I'm surprised she invited us to the club at all. Although Trinte sort of coerced her into it.

Speaking of, said brother is watching her with an expression that makes me bristle. When I catch his eye, his eyes drop. Almost as if I won't like what he's thinking.

I don't know how that makes me feel.

Averting my eyes as Orliana climbs into the Dragxi, I wait until she's seated before climbing up after her.

When we're finally settled, the Dragxi takes off, heading toward Hottie Patottie. Trinte was thrilled when he discovered which club we were headed to, so it must be fancy. Orliana sits between us, quiet and pensive. Trinte tries to coax her into conversation, but she's reluctant with responses. The way her knee jiggles, I know she's nervous.

Honestly, so am I. A forty-year-old going to the club sounds ridiculous. Yet, despite the apprehension, a kernel of excitement ignites.

I'm the first to get off and avert my gaze as Orliana climbs down. When she has both feet on the ground, I offer my arm again. She smiles gratefully, sliding a slender arm through mine. This is the most skin she's ever shown; I'm curious to know how she's going to deal with inevitably touching strangers.

While we wait for Trinte to pay, I ask, "Do the gloves help? With accidental siphoning?"

Orliana appears startled by the question, then nods. "It's probably going to be exhausting, shielding most of the night, but the gloves will help. When people aren't trying to give me emotions, it's easier to block everywhere else but my hands."

"What do you mean, *give* you emotions?"

Something inscrutable darkens her expression before disappearing. "People can force me to feel things if I'm not shielding fully or at all."

My nose wrinkles. "Isn't that a violation?"

"Yes," she says softly, suddenly sad. "It is."

Immediately, I decide to keep her in front of me so she has one less direction to worry about.

Instead of admitting this, I say, "Well, if you get overwhelmed, let me know. We can leave."

This time, her expression is more uncertain than anything else. "I can take care of myself."

Her words sound rote instead of true. Yet, I nod. "Yes, of course you can. But sometimes, an almost seven-foot-tall Dragon can be an excellent buffer."

Finally, a small smile tugs at her red lips. "I'll keep that in mind."

Trinte trots up, slapping his hands together like a gambler eager for a new hand of cards. "We ready to go cause some trouble?"

Orliana gives him a dry look. "Am I going to regret inviting you?"

"Yes," I say.

"No," Trinte says at the same time.

She rolls her eyes. "Alright, let's go."

Per her instructions, we breeze past the long line and greet the male bouncer who holds a clipboard in his hand. Glowing green eyes assess us when we come to a stop. "Name?"

"Orliana Veritas."

He checks the list, then glances at me and my brother. "Names?"

"Oh, they're my plus ones."

The bouncer raises a thin eyebrow. "There is more than one."

"I'm with Kyrielle Veritas."

The bouncer checks the list; his eyes go wide. Rushing forward, he pulls back the rope. "Of course. Please forgive me. If you had said that from the start, I—"

Orliana smiles. "It's fine. Thank you."

Whoever Orliana's friend is, or whomever she's on a date with, must be very rich indeed. We pass by the long line, ignoring the protests. Trinte leads, with Orliana between the two of us. I bite back a smile as she almost trips; I pretend not to notice when she peers back at me. She's like a doe learning to walk for the first time in those heels.

The further down the dark hallway we go, the louder the music is. When we enter the main dancing room, I'm assaulted with scents, sounds, and sensations. Thumping music along with the smell of sweaty arousal. Everything is lit by red lights, glowing. Flashing white lights move to the beat of the music, lighting up the dance floor thick with gyrating bodies.

That's not the only thing thick in here.

Freezing in place, I realize too late what kind of club this is. By the time my brain processes what I'm seeing, Orliana gasps as she takes a step back.

Sex. There's so much sex. Groups and pairs fucking on different surfaces, with a large crowd undulating in skimpy clothing as they dance to the music. Species of all kinds enjoy each other's appendages and skill sets. They play on various bits of furniture; even a revolving bed laden with black silk sheets.

Is this a fucking *sex club?*

Reaching around Orliana, I yank at Trinte's elbow. "Brother, is this what I think it is?"

Trinte's eyes brighten. "Oh, yeah!"

A deep growl reverberates in my throat. "You couldn't have mentioned that little detail?" I glance at Orliana, who appears as shell-shocked as I feel. "I assume you also had no idea?" The way her head slowly turns from side to side is almost comical. "Do you want to go?"

She opens her mouth, but before she can answer, a lilting voice says, "Are you with the Regar party?"

A blue-skinned siren approaches, her blonde hair in lush curls around her dainty features. Orliana nods, apparently unable to speak. The siren waves us to follow, her hips swaying side to side in the revealing black dress. I focus on the path in front of us.

We're being led up a set of stairs and this time, I stay one step behind Orliana to block the view for anyone looking upward. When her elbow hits my chest, she glances over her shoulder, irritated.

"Sorry," I murmur. "Just giving you some privacy up the stairs."

Understanding dawns, and she flashes an appreciative smile. "Thanks."

"Of course."

When we reached the second floor, I put a few paces between us, not wanting to overwhelm her. The hostess walks us further down another dark hallway until we stop in front of a door. She turns with a smile. "Here is the Barbarian Suite. Enjoy."

Something about the term barbarian being related to this sex club suite has me hesitating. But we're here now, and I'm not leaving Orliana here alone, not with Trinte or anyone else. It's not that Trinte would harm her — I'm positive of this — but he would push her boundaries, encouraging her to do things she might not otherwise consider doing.

"I'm ready for shots!" he declares as the door opens.

Case in point.

The suite is dim, but sensually inviting with unobtrusive music. Its walls are black and decorated with red velvet furniture, a bed in the corner, and seating in front of a one-way window overlooking the entire club. Groups of people chat amongst themselves in the suite, glancing at us as we step in.

"Orliana!" a feminine voice squeals as we step into the dim room.

A Fire Sprite with orange gossamer wings and alabaster skin jumps from the lap of a Gargoyle lounging in a large chair designed to accommodate his nine-foot-tall wings, rushing over to Orliana, arms wide.

While they embrace, I give the Gargoyle a once-over. His black hair separates into braids tight against his scalp, with a green drink in one clawed hand. He observes me with curiosity. I can't tell if he thinks we're all going to strip and copulate; I'm hoping that conversation won't even be necessary. Coming to a club was already out of my comfort zone — fully participating in a sex club is a whole other comfort zone I'm not interested in entering.

When Orliana releases her friend, she looks at me. "This is my best friend, Kyri."

I shake the Sprite's hand, careful to not squeeze too hard. "Hello Kyri, I'm Fynn."

She inspects me with fire-colored eyes. "Well, hello Fynn. Orliana didn't tell me you'd be so ..."

"Tall?" I supply.

She giggles until Trinte comes into full view from behind me. She freezes. Trinte does the same. There's a tense moment of silence.

Swallowing hard, she says evenly, "Trinte."

His eyes trail from her face down to the snazzy heels wrapped around her muscular calves. A muscle feathers in his jaw. "Kyrielle."

Orliana and I exchange looks. What in all Hells?

Turning toward my brother, I ask, "Do you two know one another?"

With an edge to his tone, Trinte says, "You could say that."

Kyri scans the crowd of people, pretending to not listen. My brother watches her with an unfamiliar intensity. Since neither of them seem interested in sharing how they know one another, I step forward.

"Who is your friend?" I say loudly, interrupting their weird stare-off.

Kyri's fixation on the crowd breaks, and she gives me a faint smile. Swaying her hips, she walks over to the Gargoyle, motioning for us to follow. "This is North."

Coming up behind the chair and in front of a wing, she stretches an arm around his neck as she bends down to kiss him on the cheek. I swear Trinte growls deep in his chest.

Pointing at us, she says, "That's my best friend Orliana and her two friends, Trinte and Fynn."

I *definitely* hear a low growl from Trinte now. The Gargoyle eyes Orliana for an inappropriate time before nodding and raising his drink.

A ghoul attendant appears from the shadows, ready to take our orders. "What would you like to drink?"

Looking at me, and *not* Trinte, Kyri says, "I'm glad you came. I don't really know these other people." She grimaces. "North is a little ... more territorial than expected."

"We're happy to be here," I assure her. "My brother Trinte loves having a good time."

Her orange eyes flick to him with a frown. With a tight tone, "Well, there are plenty of things at the club to make that happen. I'm sure he'll enjoy himself."

"I will," Trinte says quietly, tone equally full of unspoken whatever the fuck is between them.

Kyri narrows her eyes and refocuses on North.

On *that* incredibly odd note, I order a whiskey, while my brother orders a bottle of Heimlock. Orliana gives the crowd of strangers a nervous glance and asks for water.

As the ghoul floats away, I sidle up to her. "If you want to let loose and drink, I'll only have this one whiskey and you can have some fun."

Her mouth twitches, like she wants to nibble on her lip, but resists the temptation. "You sure?"

"Of course." I'm not a fan of hangovers, and this will be my first drink in ... I don't know how long. When she continues to hesitate, I offer, "You can babysit me next time."

This seals the deal. She grins, and when the ghoul reappears with our drinks, she asks for a glass of champagne. While we wait, each of us finds a chair, forced to pick from the ones overlooking the orgy down below. I notice Orliana giving the scene furtive glances, as if a burning curiosity drives her to watch, while shame makes her look away.

Studying the scene below, I don't blame her. Rhuth isn't the only person I've slept with, but before her, there's only been a handful of partners. And never once have I watched others have sex. I catch her sneaking a peek again. When she realizes I'm watching, she looks away so fast, I'm surprised her head doesn't fall off her slender neck.

I grin, accepting the whiskey from the ghoul as she passes it over. Trinte leans over, holding his glass out. "Cheers, brother."

I clink our glasses together, but give him my best glare. He's casting furtive glances at Kyri. The way he watches her, with a mix of anger and yearning, has me concerned. As far as I can recall, he's never mentioned her. Why is he acting so ... territorial?

Trying to distract him, I say, "You guilted me into coming, knowing full well what this place was."

His attention drags back to my face. After taking a sip of his drink, he responds smoothly, "Not at all. If you recall, I had no idea what she'd texted you when I guilted you."

The truth's irritating, so I say, "Well, I'm not interested in watching you fuck anyone."

"Noted." His gaze flicks to Kyri. She's giggling with the Gargoyle. He frowns.

"Have you met her before?" I murmur, watching Kyri kiss North. Trinte surveys the orgy; his knuckles crack from clenching the armrest of his chair.

"Yes." He's still staring down at the orgy, but it's like he's staring through it.

"Do you want to talk about it?"

Kyri giggles again, and his blue scales flush darker. His tail thumps with frustration. "No, I really don't." He jerks his head at the orgy. "I might join down there, though."

"Let me know when so I can look away."

My brother's demeanor shifts and, the pest that he is, smirks. "So you'll be watching until then?"

"Shut up," I grumble, my eyes tracking the ghoul delivering Orliana's drink. After thanking him, she takes a sip from her champagne. The second it touches her lips, her eyebrows arch in surprise. She takes another sip, this one longer than the last. As if she's never had champagne. The way her face lights us makes my heart skip in a way that strikes painful guilt in my gut.

Kyri strides over, dripping with sensuality. Stopping in front of Orliana, she holds out a hand. "Come with me to the bathroom?"

Orliana passes me a glance before standing. "Sure."

I watch them walk out of the room, then glance at my brother, surprised to catch him watching them, too.

We lock eyes, and there's a spark of something inside my chest. It's uncomfortable, but not as uncomfortable as my refusal to name it.

20

Orliana

"So, you didn't tell me you were coming with Dragons," Kyri exclaims, guiding me to the bathroom. She's kind enough to let me lean on her arm because I'm still unsure how to walk in these heels.

"I didn't think it mattered." Instead of engaging that topic, I hiss, "You didn't mention this was a *sex* club, Kyri. You should've seen Fynn's face when he realized." I laugh at the memory. "You should've seen *my* face."

She laughed, her orange hair swaying. "I'm sad to have missed it. And it's not just a sex club. There's dancing and a small restaurant you can visit when you're hungry."

"What's going on with you and Trinte?"

Kyri stumbles. "Um, it's nothing. One-time thing ages ago. Just didn't expect you to walk through the door with him."

"You slept together?"

Stepping into the bathroom, she shakes her head. "It doesn't matter. A one-time thing might as well not be a thing."

But there's something in her tone. I don't know what, but it's something. "Is it weird that he's here and you're doing ..." I motion in the air. "... whatever with North?"

"No." Something undefinable flickers through her eyes of fire, but her tone brooks no argument. I know better than to push.

Wobbling, I step into the luxurious bathroom, admiring everything made of black marble with gold veins. "Sweet Emet, this is the nicest bathroom I've ever seen."

Kyri laughs, strutting to a stall. "This is my first time, and now I want to travel across town every day to use it."

"Let me know so I can join you," I joke, checking my reflection. To my delight, the smeared mascara does look pretty hot. The mirror's lined with bright lightbulbs, casting glamorous lighting. Straightening, I take another moment to admire myself. This is probably one of the first times I've ever actually felt sexy. It's oddly powerful.

Kyri reappears behind me. "Girl, you are smokin' in that outfit."

My first impulse is to denigrate myself, like Mikan preferred, but my newfound sense of power overrides the old training. "I do, don't I?"

"Fynn can't take his eyes off you," she says, reapplying lipstick. "Is he single?"

I give her a sharp look. "Do not meddle. He's a widower still very much in love with his wife."

She watches me in the mirror, brow scrunching. "His dead wife?"

"Yes," I say flatly. "And don't bring it up. It was just as hard for him to come here, and the last thing he probably needs is a reminder of why it was hard."

Kyri holds my glare unapologetically. "But you like him."

"No." The word comes out sharper than intended. Softening my tone, I add, "I barely know who he is, let alone who I am, Kyri." Sitting on the Chesterfield sofa, I let out a sigh. "Moxie made me read one of my old diaries right before I left."

She brushes a piece of dust from her wing. "That's odd. Why?"

Looking at my lap, I say, "I think she was trying to show me something."

My best friend raises her eyebrows in curiosity. "Show you what?"

Why is it so hard to say? Shame is front and center, but also something deeper. I take a second to examine the unfamiliar sensation. It's an ache so acute it takes my breath away.

"Orliana?" Kyri sits on the edge of the sofa to avoid crushing her wings. "What's wrong?"

The tears have returned. It's the second time today — a recent record. After years of refusing to shed a single tear, my mind and heart have teamed up against me. Kyri knows this, so when she catches a tear sliding down my cheek, her face slackens with alarm.

"My goddess, Orliana. What is it?"

"I've done nothing with my life, Kyri." The words are like razor blades on my tongue, cutting so deeply that I never want to say them again. "It was from the day I asked Mikan to go to school to become a Siphon therapist."

A darkness clouds her ethereal face. "What did he do?"

We've talked about what Mikan has done, but shame has held back a lot of the details. I shake my head. "It doesn't matter. But it made me realize how much I've still let him control my life. How I've allowed fear to hold me back. And any time I did something for myself, it was normally to spite the memory of him."

Those last words break me. I sob, placing my face in my palms, too ashamed to make eye contact. A soft hand gently touches my shoulder. Instantly, I sense her energy, but she's careful to neither give nor take anything. As my best friend for over fifteen years, Kyri learned a long time ago how to offer physical comfort without harming me.

"Orliana, you can't keep blaming yourself for what he did to you."

I stare up at her blurry face. "Of course I can. I'm a grown woman who made an impossible choice, but even after all of that, I still chained myself to the trauma."

"Then don't."

I give her a look of disbelief. "Just like that?"

Her full lips split into a beautiful smile. "Of course not, but every choice you make going forward should reflect who you want to be. You can't become your future self until you make decisions like that version of yourself."

"I guess that makes sense." I glance at my reflection with a groan. "I've ruined my makeup again."

"No, you haven't," Kyri assures me. "Come on, let me fix you up so we can get back to the party."

When she's done, Kyri escorts me back to the Barbarian Suite. All three men appear relieved when we return, and I note a strange tension in the air. North's jaw ticks until Kyri is back at his side, crawling into his lap with a grin. Trinte tracks her move across the room, knuckles whitening against his armrests.

When my gaze catches Fynn's, a small slither of pleasure snakes down my spine. He watches as I sit; I resist the urge to adjust my skimpy dress.

Pausing in his observations of my best friend, Trinte leans in close. "Everything good?"

I give a thumbs up. "Just girl talk."

My half-full glass of champagne enters my line of sight, held by Fynn. Grinning, I take it from him with a grateful smile. I've never had champagne before, and it's quickly becoming a favorite. It feels incredible as the bubbles go down my throat and light up a buzzing under my skin.

"First time?" Fynn asks, eyeing my lips as I take another sip.

Nodding, I say, "Like you said, it's the night for a lot of firsts."

His focus trails to the performance on the dance floor. "There are some firsts I'm not quite ready for," he admits, looking back at me. A vulnerability lingers in his golden eyes as he says the words.

"I understand," I say quietly.

The ghoul reappears with a polite smile. "Would you like another round?"

Trinte and I order another round, but Fynn declines. It's a surprising comfort to see a man follow through on what he says he'll do. Mikan was the type to promise sobriety and be the first one drunk.

Within five minutes of the drinks appearing, Kyri's straddling North, her white low-cut dress riding up her ass as she grinds into his lap. Trinte can barely peel his eyes from them, blue cheeks flushing dark as his lips purse.

Checking, I'm surprised to see a mix of grief, anger, and lust intermixed in his aura. What in the Hells happened between them.

Before I can ask, Trinte slaps the armrests, like a decision has been made. "I need air. Let's go dance."

Fynn grunts, shaking his head. "Not happening, little brother."

After chugging the rest of his Heimlock, Trinte stands. Grip tight on the empty bottle, he glares at his brother. "So, you want to sit up here and watch people fucking?"

Fynn frowns, his gold eyes flicking to me before glaring at his brother. "No, I told you I wouldn't dance."

Shoulders slumping with defeat, Trinte nods. "Okay." His face transforms with a brilliant smile. Holding out a hand, he says, "Orliana, will you join me on the dance floor?"

Fynn stands so quickly, his chest slams Trinte's arm out of the way. "Fine. One dance."

The Gleanscale brothers stare expectantly.

I swallow hard, thoughts racing. "I-I don't dance. I've never danced."

Over her shoulder, Kyri pauses in her ministrations to give me a pointed look, as if silently reminding me of our conversation from the bathroom. Is dancing really that big of a deal? Does Future Me dance?

Since I have no idea of exactly what Future Me is like, it's impossible to say. The only way to find out is to, well, go dancing.

I slide my gloved hand into Fynn's, allowing him to help me stand. "I have no idea how I'll dance in these things."

Fynn hesitates. "I'm a little more worried about people touching you."

Trinte glances between the two of us, confused. "Why are you afraid of people touching her?"

'Why do you care about her?' is probably what he really wants to ask. He's right; Fynn and I barely know one another.

Fynn looks at me. "Have you told him about your ability?"

Oh. That's what he means. The pleasure of being seen warms my skin. "I'm a Siphon."

His eyes drop to my gloved hands, and his face lights up with understanding. "Got it. So, touching strangers at a sex club could get tricky?"

"Just a little," I say with a small smile.

Trinte shrugs. "So just dance with us. We'll keep the grabbers away."

"I'll be fine," I assure him. "If it becomes too much, we can always come back up here."

Fynn peers over my head at Kyri and North. When I do the same, I'm shocked to discover that North's hands have disappeared between her legs.

When she moans, Trinte sucks air through his teeth, then growls, "Let's go."

Following Fynn down the stairs, I already sense eyes roving over my body. The air smells like so many things, from sweat to sex. Blood pounds in my ears in rhythm with the loud, sultry music. I'm suddenly aware of every inch of skin on display, from the way my breasts slightly swing with each step to the breeze of a fan on my bare back.

It's electrifying.

At the bottom of the stairs, Fynn patiently waits, already offering an arm for me to balance on. He's rolled up his sleeves half-way up his forearm, so I carefully touch his covered elbow.

My body goes rigid when his warm breath caresses my ear. "Ready for a first?"

It's all I can do to nod, too distracted by the way anticipation vibrates my bones. There's so much energy in this room, I don't even need to touch anyone to feel it. Lust infests everything.

With Trinte following right behind, Fynn guides me toward the middle of the vast, dark room. Pulsing lights match the beat of the bass; something in me awakens. The surrounding energy provokes an instinctual Siphon response. It blooms into a craving for *more.*

We pass groups of naked people entwined. Over the music, I can hear sounds of pleasure. It's unlike anything I've ever experienced; my head swims as I try to take it all in.

Just as we're about to step onto the busy dance floor, Fynn stops to face me, tilting my head up with a finger under my chin. The touch is a surprise, but is light enough that I can shield instantly. He frowns, those golden eyes scanning my face.

Over the throbbing sounds, he yells, "Are you okay?"

Energy shakes my body; sweat slicks the shallow groove of my spine. "I've never been around this many people before," I admit, hoping he hears me.

Dragons have excellent hearing, thankfully. Fynn signals something to Trinte. The blue Dragon walks into the mass of people, using his bulk to create a barrier. He stays right at the crowd's edge, bringing his large palms to the ass of a pale pink Elf.

Trinte jerks his head at Fynn, I'm led through a group of four people fucking, then Fynn gently spins me so Trinte is to my back as he dances, leaving Fynn in front of me. Understanding hits me like a lightning bolt — they're reducing the chances of me being touched by strangers.

The realization cracks the hard exterior of my heart, knowing they're simply being protective. They barely know me, yet they're offering protection without me having to ask.

Relief is a profound balm for the deep ache lodged in my soul. It's so easy to grin at Fynn. I mouth, *thank you,* and he returns the gratitude with a quirk of his lips.

And then we dance.

21

Fynn

Dancing is decidedly not my thing, but dancing with Orliana? She resembles the light of dawn, with the shimmering gold dress against her dark gold skin. As she begins to tentatively move her hips, I'm hypnotized by the motion. Wrapping my tail around one of my legs to prevent it from being stepped on, I keep a few inches between us as I join in the swaying.

When she closes her eyes, losing herself to the music and energy, I can't help but wonder what this feels like for her. Over her head, I catch Trinte glancing at Orliana, then back to me, wearing a stupid smirk. If he wasn't helping me keep Orliana comfortable, I'd tail whip him. But we have an unspoken agreement to let this woman experience the club as safely as possible.

Like her, I close my eyes and allow myself to be in the present; to just feel.

This moment feels like scratching an itching wound. I know it'll make things worse, but I also can't resist. This is simultaneously the most alive I've felt in years, and also the most guilty I've ever felt.

Is it betraying Rhuth by being here? Near Orliana? Watching people have sex openly?

The answer is impossible to find, and it's driving me crazy.

Stay present.

Redirecting my thoughts, I attempt mindfulness, relishing the energy around us. Happiness still feels too far away, but the ghost of it appears, tugging at the corners of my mouth. Lust also feels unattainable, but the sensuality blanketing the club shines a light on the desire hidden away for years.

What could it be like to want someone again?

Have a new future with someone else? With new shared dreams, experiences, and secrets?

To no longer have Rhuth be the last person who touched me intimately?

For a moment longer than I want to admit, I imagine it's Orliana touching me. Not here, not now, but in the future. Her soft hands roving across my body. Our mouths as tangled as our limbs.

My pulse quickens as an unwelcome bolt of need shoots down to my groin. It's followed by a cramp in my stomach, the manifestation of my guilt. It's a blight against the temporary peace that barely had a moment to breathe.

Her brow furrows. She opens her mouth, most likely to ask what's wrong, when a male Orc stumbles and falls into her, accidentally touching her bare shoulders.

Multiple things happen at once: The Orc rights himself, apologizing. Through the overwhelming sounds, I hear a sharp intake of breath; she moans with pleasure. My bare hands come to Orliana's arms, catching her before she falls. Her knees buckle, and I'm forced to touch more bare skin to prevent someone trampling her. She's so soft, but I can't pause to appreciate the sensation.

Orliana's tear-filled eyes fly around in a panic. Is it me? Is it my grief that's hurting her?

I roar Trinte's name. When he sees Orliana half-collapsed, he releases the Elf in his hands to crouch next to us.

"Is she okay?" He sounds so worried for her.

Orliana is sobbing now, reaching for her pendant. I push her toward him. He's gentle, bundling her in his arms. She moans again. Trinte looks distressed. She needs her skin covered. Without hesitating, I rip off my shirt, the buttons flying in different directions. I motion for him to pass her back, and when she's in my lap, I wrap her from neck to mid-thigh.

Lifting her in my arms, I stalk through the crowd. Anyone in my way quickly moves, clearing a path to the stairs. Maybe we should go outside, but then an entire line of people will see her being carried. I can't imagine she'd prefer that over finding a quiet suite to collect herself.

Trinte bolts ahead of us, taking the stairs three steps at a time. When I'm at the top, he's talking to an attendant. The attendant sees Orliana's body in my arms. In a rush, she grabs a set of keys from her waist and opens the door right across from the Barbarian Suite. Would Orliana want Kyri? What's the best thing to do right now?

Her knuckles are white from clutching the pendant so hard.

"Hang on," I murmur, striding through the door straight to a chaise. Kneeling, I lay her on the plush fabric, careful not to touch her again.

"Is she okay?" Trinte repeats from behind me.

There's the sound of the door closing, and I say, "The Orc fell into her. It was an accident, but I think she absorbed his lust. Then I touched her and—" The words catch in my throat. She's crying because of my grief. I just know it.

Trinte comes to kneel next to me. "What were you feeling?"

I look at Orliana's pained expression. "Nothing great."

The pity on his face makes me sick. My focus returns to Orliana. She's stopped crying, but now she's shaking violently.

"What can we do for her?" Trinte asks, sounding anxious.

I peer over my shoulder, annoyed to discover the attendant is gone. "Can we get Kyri?"

He shakes his head. "The Do Not Disturb is on, and it's protocol to never interrupt unless in the most dire of circumstances."

"Can you wait out there? The moment it turns off, alert Kyri?"

He nods and stands. With one last, long look at both of us, he leaves. Orliana doesn't even appear to be aware of our conversation. Her teeth chatter; her eyes can't squeeze together any tighter. It's breaking my heart. It was too much, bringing her down there. She wasn't sure, but we pushed her.

When her body shakes violently again, it's impossible to resist rubbing her covered arms. After a quick scan of the room, I'm frustrated to discover there are no blankets in here. Directing magyck to my palms, I allow them to heat and rub them over her limbs.

Slowly, the shaking dissipates. The tension clenching her body eases. Her breathing evens out. My heart skips when one bright brown eye opens. I can see her brain trying to process everything; when it finally clicks, she bolts upright.

"Oh, goddess," she groans, hugging my shirt around her tighter. "I'm so sorry. This is so humiliating."

The moment her eyes opened, my hands returned to my lap. As much as I want to touch her arm, to show how much it doesn't bother me, I can't.

Orliana grimaces as her hand releases the pendent, revealing an imprint through the glove into her palm. She flexes her hand with a wince. "*Emet*, that hurts."

I hold out my hand. "If it's okay, let me see."

Hesitation makes her pause, and then she places her hand in mine. Instantly, I'm massaging the still-white skin, encouraging blood flow. She draws her knees up to her chest with a groan. Placing an arm on her knees, she rests her chin. While the tears are drying up, she still looks haunted.

"What happened?" I ask quietly.

Her eyes dart to mine, then away. "I didn't shield enough."

I'm desperate to ask her if it was me, my grief, that caused her so much pain. How could it not be? I was the only one not reveling in lust, not like the Orc or my brother.

"I'm sorry," I whisper, not trusting my ability to speak louder.

Her nose scrunches as her brow furrows. "Why are you sorry? You helped me."

I switch to her other hand, careful to not pull her arm off its resting spot. It's painful to ask, but I do it anyway. "What made you cry?"

When realization widens her eyes, I'm forced to look away, full of shame.

I knew it.

"That ... that was you?"

I nod mutely, still massaging her hand, but not willing to say anything else. Instead, I remember the way she sobbed the second I touched her. At that moment, I'd been thinking about what a betrayal it'd be, wanting someone else. The disgust and grief were at their peak when we touched.

She was an unwilling vessel for my internal state at that moment, letting out a keening sound that embodied exactly how my soul feels every second of every day.

"Oh, Fynn," she murmurs. "You feel like that every day?"

Would it be inappropriate to bolt out of this room, fly into the skies, and keep going until I landed on one of the moons? I can't speak, too afraid of what will come out.

I'm jarred out of my thoughts when she pulls my hand away. The rejection stings until I realize she's turning to face me, sitting on her heels. Using every ounce of courage, I meet her gaze, terrified of what I'll find. Will it be disgust? Pity? Hate? Anger? I don't think I can bear any of it.

None of that exists at all. She's smiling, face full of wonder and compassion. I'm speechless as she removes her gloves, placing them neatly on top of one another.

"You love her so much, Fynn. I cried because I've never felt anything so achingly beautiful. I'm also extremely out of practice, so it was overwhelming."

"That was just their lust," I mutter, wanting to pull away, even though she hasn't touched me yet.

Her laugh is soft. “I’m positive what you felt was more than fleeting lust like that Orc.” Uncertainty twists her lips. “Can I feel it again? You can say no.”

My stomach rolls. “How does it work?”

She wiggles her fingers with a smile. “Well, you know Siphons can absorb and read powers, right?”

“Yeah ...”

The pendant swings gently as she leans forward, hovering her hands on each side of my head. “When I touch you, you’ll feel us make the somapathic connection. It might feel odd since it’s not a part of you. Just try not to fight it. If you fight too hard, I’ll break the connection. Is that okay?”

Inside my soul, I frantically hide it all as I nod. I don’t want to hurt her again. She’s just being nice, like everyone else. I don’t believe for one second she thought my pain was beautiful.

Her soft hands are warm on my cheeks. Thumbs brush gently along my cheekbones as she spreads her fingers. I close my eyes, lost in the sensation of being held. Then I feel it: a curious sensation plucking at the strings of my emotions. Her somapathic connection explores my mind like roots digging for a perch. I sense the second she finds what I’ve been trying to hide.

The roots sink deeper.

Yet she doesn’t avert her eyes. Those dark brown irises drink me in as small muscles twitch in her face, reading me.

I’m splayed open, as if my rust-covered heart is worth something.

“Think of her,” she says softly.

It’s the easiest thing in the world, thinking of my wife. I close my eyes and remember beautiful blue scales that reflect rainbows in the sun. A ridiculous food fight in the kitchen that took days to clean up. Silky strands of hair in my fingers as we made love. My heart existing out of my chest, walking freely in the world, sharing compliments and smiles with strangers.

My body jerks as my heart aches so deeply, it feels like it's being carved out. Thoughts of Rhuth have been off-limits. Too scalding; too raw. The somapathic connection pauses.

"Do you want me to stop?" Orliana's hands loosen.

Half of me screams for this to end; the other half desperately wants out of this self-imposed Hell. I need to deal with this. For the first time since Rhuth died, I'm being given a real opportunity to examine my grief.

My hands fly to hers, pressing them harder. All I have the capability of saying is a rasping, *"No."*

Exhaling a shuddering breath, I refocus on the memories. Sit inside the agony. Making a nest inside the most rotted, aching parts of myself.

A radiant Rhuth walking down the aisle.

The moment she told me about the pregnancy.

Building the cradle.

Picking out possible names.

Feeling Titus kick against her belly button.

Finding her those pints of ice cream, feeling a false sense of victory.

I'm overcome with the memories, allowing the gaping hole inside my soul to widen, its greediness eager for more. It's the most excruciating, yet beautiful thing I've ever experienced in my life.

Rhuth was my everything. My son was ... my reason. At least I thought he would be. But as awful as it is to admit, if he isn't here, and I am ... then there must be a different purpose for me here. Fortuna must have an alternate future in mind.

The realization is excruciating. It's the reality I've refused to accept, but I *need* to. There's no possible way to forget them, and I would *never* want to, but I need to do more than survive.

I need to live without them.

That chapter of my life is closed.

My former self peels apart like flecks of old paint, fluttering in the wind.

The overwhelming pain of it rips a groan out of me. Every muscle in my body contracts until I'm in a tight ball. Air can't reach my lungs; it burns, but not more than the loss.

From somewhere, I hear, "Would you like me to take some?"

I cradle the grief for Rhuth like a gift. Orliana's connection observes it alongside me. Can she see my memories? I find that I don't care either way.

Taking a mental step back from it, I whisper, "Yes."

The curious thing observing my internal destruction begins coaxing the terrible devastation away. No more than crooking a finger and suggesting that maybe, just maybe, if it wants to leave, it has a new place to go.

Little by little, Orliana leeches it out and, to my shock, the gaping maw of pain shrinks. Muscles relax for the first time in ages. I suck in a breath of air, and for the first time in almost five years, I'm grateful for the oxygen in my lungs.

"There you go." Her tender thumbs massage my temples, loosening the tension even further. Orliana gently severs our mental connection.

My eyes peel apart, staring at pink painted toes settled in gold-colored heels. I'm still in the fetal position, which should be embarrassing, but ... it isn't.

The hands leave my temples; I sit up with a groan. Everything aches; a wave of exhaustion weighs heavily on my bones. I open my mouth and my jaw pops from the released tension.

Orliana watches me, tears leaving streaks down her cheeks, but a joyful smile splits her face. Right now, I'm numb, but it's not the kind of numbness caused by grief — it's something far more neutral.

Rubbing a hand over my heart, I croak out, "What did you do?"

Wiping away tears with the back of a hand, she uses the other to point at her pendant. "I put it in here."

"Will it hurt you?"

She shakes her head. "My body is built for this."

"Why did you do that?"

Her smile is so gentle when she says, "It's what I am, Fynn. A Siphon's purpose is to help others heal. It brings me great joy; most of the time."

Dismayed, I say, "That gave you joy?"

She laughs; it's a sound made of sunrises and gentle breezes. "Deep grief can only be made with great love. My mother likes to say that grief is simply love with no place to go."

"Except you took some," I say, still bewildered at the way I feel.

Am I betraying Rhuth by losing some of that grief?

Orliana nods. "Yes, I did. At any point, if you want, I can give it back." She taps the pendant again. "It's here; never gone."

"So if I asked for it back right now, you could do that?"

She tilts her head, considering. "Yes, absolutely. Do you want it back?"

Do I? If I lose the grief ... will I lose Rhuth as well?

I take stock of my emotions and find that it gives me solace that she has a little of Rhuth in the pendant. Still existing somewhere else in the world.

I shake my head. "You can have it."

Compassion softens her face even further. If I hadn't seen her expression firsthand, I wouldn't believe that she is grateful when she says, "Thank you for the gift."

What's an appropriate answer to that? *You're welcome?* That feels wholly insufficient.

Thankfully, the decision's taken away from me as the door opens and Kyri tumbles in with Trinte.

"Orliana," Kyri gasps, rushing over. She frowns, jerking her head back in surprise — I'm sure she's never seen a crying male Dragon — then sits next to her best friend. "Are you okay? What happened?"

"I'm fine," Orliana says quickly. "Better than fine, actually."

Robotically, I stand, feeling ready to pass out. Orliana ignores Kyri, watching me struggle to stay upright. To Trinte, she says, "Keep an eye on him, please."

"Huh?" Trinte comes to my side, perplexed at the sudden switch in who needs care. What I've experienced took more than expected.

While Kyri checks Orliana over for injuries, we continue to stare at each other. There's no way to define exactly how I feel right now.

No, that's wrong. As Trinte steers me out of the room, my feet freeze of their own accord. "Thank you."

Kyri pauses in her ministrations of checking over Orliana, staring with furrowed brows. Her eyes flicker between my brother and me with a frown.

Orliana's mouth quirks. "You're welcome."

Our stare lingers long enough for Trinte to shift, pressing against my shoulder. "Come on, brother."

I allow him to lead me out of the room. When the door's secure, cutting us off from the women, he asks, "What in the Hells happened in there?"

It feels like my insides have been scooped out and replaced with a refreshing sense of levity. Surprising us both, I place a hand on his broad shoulder, giving it a squeeze.

"I'm glad we came tonight. Thanks for being obnoxious enough to make it happen."

Trinte's dark eyebrows pull together, his blue and gold eyes scanning my face. "I can't tell if this is a trap."

His eyebrows jump when I laugh. "No trap. But I *am* ready to go home."

Stepping out of the club feels as if I'm stepping into the unknown. The fresh air holds an unfamiliar promise.

Of what, I'm not quite sure yet.

22

Fynn

The next day, morning comes too quickly. Everything aches; even my nerves are tender. Yet, when my eyes open, an unfamiliar eagerness for the day exists. While the weight of grief hasn't disappeared it's certainly eased enough that walking past the plants lining the hallway doesn't hurt. Drinking from Rhuth's mug doesn't feel like a punishment.

It's a new reality I'm struggling to process.

I don't think it's an overstatement that the last twenty-four hours have been life altering. Going from a terrible nightmare about Rhuth to curling up on the floor of a sex club, faced with the pain I've avoided for so long ... It sounds almost unbelievable.

After my morning routine, I take to the skies, deciding to take the long route to headquarters. It's still relatively early, so most of Gondora continues to sleep. The sun's blotted out by fog, offering an eerie backdrop.

Just like yesterday, I'm relearning to enjoy the sensation of mist rolling off my scales. It's a renewed pleasure to whip my long tail back and forth as a lazy rudder. Winding through the pathways lit by orbs, I make my way to a relatively empty slice of sky.

When I'm sure no one else is around to get hurt, I skim the edges of the mist and close my eyes. It's been far too long since I reconnected with my Fyre, the source of ferocity and magyck for each Dragon. The day Rhuth died, it winked out of existence; it's been almost five years since my tongue tasted of sulfur and smoke.

It's a tiny ember, waiting in silence. Using my rediscovered sense of excitement, I breathe new life into it. It glows inside my chest, slowly but surely morphing into a roiling inferno. Filling my lungs to their maximum capacity, I lose a torrent of dripping magma and flames.

My sleek body plows through the fireball like a baptism, turning this past season of my life into ash. If I could grin with this mouth, it would be ear to ear. Instead, I let out a shattering roar. The greedy mist swallows the offering. I'm made in Fortuna's likeness, and the clouds are her flesh; the wind her breath.

By the time I land at headquarters, shifting into my bi-pedal form, my skin buzzes and my chest burns from the Fyre begging for more.

I'm a Dragon again.

Headquarters is still quiet, since there aren't a lot of requests for fares at this hour. To my surprise, Trinte is in his office. I lean against the doorframe with a short knock. He looks up, his expression shifting from confused to suspicious.

"There's something different about you," he says, looking me over. "Are you feeling okay?"

It's the same question he asked before depositing me at the front door of my home late last night.

I nod. "Better than okay. I think I'm going to take some Dragxi fares before the tournament this afternoon. Will you be playing?"

He stares at me, dumbfounded. "You ... just ..." He shakes his head before nodding. "No. I mean, yeah. I'll be playing."

"Good. Orliana will be there, too."

At this, he does a double take. "What? Why?"

My smile broadens. "I know who MeanCat is."

Trinte's jaw drops. "No."

"Yup. Found that out yesterday over coffee."

Closing his mouth, Trinte leans back in his chair, appraising me. "You had coffee with her?"

I wave away the words. "Just happenstance. She was already there, and we chatted for a few minutes."

"You chatted?" he says flatly. "You're a chatter now?"

I laugh; his eyes widen at the sound. "It was nothing. Stop making a big deal about it."

"No big deal," he says slowly. "Just ... surprised, is all."

A small part of me feels irritated at his confusion, then I remember what he said yesterday.

I want him back.

Lowering my voice, I say, "I'm trying, brother."

He swallows hard and nods slowly. "I'm glad for you."

Not wanting to make it an even bigger deal, I push off the door frame. "So, 4pm?"

"4pm," he confirms, still looking bewildered.

With one last smile, I make my way to the saddle station, eager to find a story I might be able to share with Orliana.

***

I don't have to wait long for an interesting story to appear. The first two fares were normal and non-talkative, but on the third fare, I hit the jackpot.

It's a pair of witches — I didn't catch what kind — but they're whispering to one another. They probably assume I can't hear them, but in this form, I can hear a piece of paper drop from a mile away.

One of them, with a high-pitched voice, says, "I can't believe you gave him the potion, Tilda."

Tilda sounds hysterical as she says, "I didn't know it was *permanent*, Sel!"

"Did you add the laurel leaf?" Sel hisses.

There's a sharp intake of breath before Tilda admits, "Yes. I did."

"That's Brewing 101, Tilda. You never use the laurel leaf unless you want them to be in love with you forever. How did you even get it? It's banned on the entire continent of Avalon for this very reason."

Tilda's deeper voice is now panicked. "Professor Belham gave it to me. I had no idea it was banned; he said it would make the spell stronger."

"The professor gave it to you?" Sel sounds dismayed.

I tilt my head, a subtle attempt to watch them. These are the kinds of stories I love collecting.

Tilda, who has black hair streaked with blue highlights, looks ashamed as she says, "It might've been a punishment."

"Why is he trying to punish you?" Sel says evenly, her pale cheeks red with anger.

"Because," Tilda squeaks. "We were sleeping together, and I broke it off."

"What?!" Sel shrieks, not even trying to hide her angry words now. "You slept with our professor, then told him you wanted help with a love potion? Are you mad?"

Orliana is going to love this story.

"He said he was fine with it," Tilda says defensively, but embarrassment makes her look away.

As I bank left, heading toward the market they requested, Sel says, "Well, clearly he lied. And now Maximus is in love with you until the day he dies. Do you even like him that much?"

Tilda sounds morose as she whispers, "Not really. I just thought it would be fun for him to be in love with me while we had a one-time hook-up."

"That's unconscionable," Sel hisses. "You have to admit what you've done."

Unfortunately, this is when I reach the landing pad.

Here's your stop, ladies.

Both of them look at me with surprise, clearly falling victim to forgetting that I'm not a beast of burden. I swivel my head to look at them, taking in Tilda's stricken expression.

"I-I ... y-you aren't going to say anything?" Tilda says, looking ready to fall on her knees and beg for my silence.

It's the Dragxi code of honor that what's said between the breeze and the clouds stays there.

Not entirely true — if someone had admitted to murder or assault, I'd turn them over without a lick of guilt. But it sounds like Tilda will pay her penance soon enough without my help.

Sel laughs, then slaps a hand over her mouth. Tilda cracks a small smile. "Thank you."

I'd get rid of that laurel leaf, but that's just me.

They exchange a look and quickly disembark. Tilda hands over extra corals, placing them in the payment satchel. "Thanks for being discreet."

Good luck.

Tilda grimaces, rushing off with her friend. Whoever Maximus is, I hope he sues her for every penny, but if she's even slightly good at potions, he'll love her too much to hurt her like that.

Satisfied to have a good story to share, I return to headquarters. When the saddle's removed, I shift back and pull the extra corals from Tilda out of the pouch. Walking over to one of my employees, Curtis, I hand him the corals.

"Heard you have a baby on the way," I say gruffly.

Curtis' eyes bulge at the amount in his hand. "This is too much, boss."

I shake my head. "Babies are expensive. Take it — I don't need it."

"Thank you," he says in a rush. "Serena will be so excited. She's been eyeing this crib, and it's insane how much they charge for those things."

I think of the crib sitting in my home, ignored for almost five years. "I remember."

At the mention of my unborn son, Curtis pales. "I'm sorry, I didn't mean to bring up—"

I slap a hand on his shoulder and give him a friendly shake. "It's fine. Go buy her the crib, Curtis. Make her day."

Curtis grins so wide, all of his sharp teeth gleam in the morning light. "Yes, sir. I'll make sure she knows it comes from you."

"You do that," I say with a smile of my own. "Tell her I said hi."

"I-I will, sir. Thank you again." Looking down at the corals again, he thumbs through them.

I leave him to it, growing uncomfortable with the way his eyes shine. Mainly because it makes *me* want to be emotional, and I've had enough of that in the last twenty-four hours.

This time, when I shift and start flying back home, it's with a lightness in my heart.

***

When I log onto Rukbegger, only MeanCat is logged in. Clicking on her name, I turn on my mic. "Hey, you."

There's a beat of silence before Orliana says, "Hey, yourself."

Ignoring the way her voice flutters inside my rib cage, I ask, "Are you ready for the tournament? I heard Xeno is ready for a second chance at kicking your ass."

She laughs. "He's welcome to try, the sniveling little nerd."

There's an awkward pause. Do I bring up what happened last night? Tell her how I feel today? How much she's helped me? That it finally feels like I can move forward with my life?

Maybe she might want to do the same. Perhaps we could do some things together, as friends. Someone else who understand this difficult journey.

It takes a couple of seconds for me to decide. "Hey, do you want to go get coffee or a drink on purpose this week?"

Orliana is silent for a few beats before saying, "Sure, that could be nice." I hear the hesitation in her voice when she asks, "How are you since last night?"

Well, so much for breezing by the uncomfortable conversation. "Honestly?"

"Always, please."

If she always wants honesty, it's the least I can do. Even though it makes my heart pick up speed with anxiety, I admit, "I haven't felt this good in years, Orliana. It feels like I can breathe again."

A loud exhale rumbles against her mic. "I'm so glad to hear it. It's something I've always wanted to do for others, on my terms, and I meant what I said."

I think of everything that was said between us. "That it was a gift?"

"Absolutely. Plus, if you ever want it back, it's yours."

Initially, when she took it, that gave me relief, but today, the idea of taking back that chunk of grief sounds nightmarish.

"It doesn't hurt you?"

"No," she says firmly.

My first impulse is to ask for it back, anyway. But ... I've felt incredible since she siphoned out some of the grief. Rediscovering forgotten parts of myself. Taking it back would not only be counterproductive, it would be self-harm.

"I don't ever want it back," I say softly. "Is that okay?"

"Of course." There's a smile in her tone. "Grief is better shared with others; it makes it less of a burden. I truly believe that's why Emet made Siphons."

Others have said this before, but coming from her, I finally believe it. "So, coffee or a drink?"

There's a moment of silence, as if she's considering the pros and cons. With a layer of hesitation in her tone, she says, "This is just as friends, right?"

"Absolutely."

There's a beat of silence, then, "A drink, then."

A grin splits my face. "I'll ask Trinte for a recommendation."

The sound of a beep stops me from saying more; Trinte has logged in.

"Hey you two," he says cheerfully. "What spot? Where are we going?"

"You're not invited," I growl. "You need to stop inviting yourself to places."

"I'd never go anywhere, then," he complains with a laugh.

"Maybe that's a clue," Orliana says dryly. Giddiness makes me squirm in my chair, listening to her fire back at my brother. Not enough people put him in his place.

"Now there's two of you?" he exclaims, sounding genuinely dismayed.

"Guess so," I say.

He sighs. "Great. Goody for me."

More beeps sound, and the team begins loading in. Grabbing a drink from my fridge, I open the can and take a sip. While MeanCat is given instructions on how to approach this particular event, I listen in silence.

Wondering what kind of path I'm walking down.

23

Orliana

It's been a few days since I siphoned away some of Fynn's grief, and I'm still on a high unlike any other. When I siphoned from Mikan, all of that rage was putrid and unclean, born from hate curated over his lifetime. He never shared its source; something tells me it was nature rather than nurture.

But Fynn's grief was born of deep love. As such, I've felt invigorated since. When he said he hadn't felt so good in years, I was relieved because I half expected him to accuse me of stealing. When he hadn't, it only added to the natural high this sense of accomplishment provided.

So much so that I began looking into Siphon therapy training schools, an idea supported by my mother's encouragement.

Today, I'm meeting with Fynn for a drink, and I'm eager to tell him about the possibility.

Unfortunately, I've spent the afternoon fretting over my outfit. He said it's not a date, and he's seen me in that fancy napkin called a dress ... but this is drinks. At a bar.

But it *isn't* a date.

It takes far too long to decide, but I settle on a form-fitting V-neck shirt and jeans. Before I walk out the door, my eyes pause at the collection of gloves I keep in a basket. My fingers twitch to grab a pair, but it's time to build my power again.

No gloves tonight.

Fynn's already waiting for me outside the bar, hands in his pockets while he watches people pass. It's a simple spot, with no theme and literally called No Name. I've never been, but he assured me Trinte said the drinks are worth it.

I take a peek at his aura. It's a shock to see how different it is. While the deep blues of grief still exist, the reds around his heart have expanded significantly, filling most of his chest. The exterior aura is still blue, but it's a lighter shade.

When he spots me, I'm gifted with a smile so wide, those deadly dimples appear. Everything inside my body lights up with anticipation. I have no idea why he wanted to meet for drinks, but he's clearly happy, so it must be for something good.

Fynn's wearing a simple form-hugging black T-shirt and dark blue jeans. Before the night of the club, he always wore clothes that were too big, but Trinte clearly did a good job during that shopping spree. It makes me wonder if the grief wilted away his form. Eyeing the visible muscles, I can't imagine him filling out the old clothes, but he must've.

Which has me more secretly impressed than I'll ever admit.

"Hey," he says.

Stopping in front of him, I peer into his golden eyes. "Hey."

There's a moment of awkwardness. Do we hug? Shake hands? I've helped him, assuming we hug now is a bit too presumptive. Frankly, I'm not sure I want to do either; he must understand my hesitation because he walks over to the door, opening it for me.

Relief loosens a breath from between my lips, and I offer a grateful smile as I step into the dark bar.

Just like the exterior, the inside is simple. Dark sconces dot the black walls. Booths line one side of the space, with a long bar top on the other.

In the middle are tables, mostly empty. We're one of a few patrons, lending a sense of intimacy.

Fynn points to a booth. "Want to go over there and I'll get us some drinks?"

"Sure. I'd like to try a martini."

He grins. "Another first time?"

I laugh. "They look so fancy, so why not?"

While he heads to the bar, I slide into one side of the booth. My knee jiggles with anxiety; it feels like a pool of tar lining my stomach. Why am I so nervous? It's Fynn. He's not going to hurt me — at least, I'm fairly certain.

The reminder doesn't help my apprehension, though.

Instead, the anxiety builds until he sits down, passing a martini with one olive over to me. "The bartender told me it's the best."

I eagerly grab the glass, drinking half of it before putting it back on the table. Then begin coughing viciously. It burns, and is a little disgusting.

Fynn raises an eyebrow. "You okay?"

Nodding, I place the glass on the table, enjoying the rush of alcohol in my bloodstream. Wiping my mouth with a napkin, I nod. "Honestly?"

"Always."

"I'm really nervous," I admit. "The other day was really intense for both of us, and I actually wasn't sure if you'd want to see me again. I know you're still grieving, and I respect that. I don't want you to think I'm trying to push anything romantic."

He sips his beer, expression steady. "I appreciate that. The invite here was for a platonic experience, first and foremost. So if you're afraid I'm considering this a date, please rest assured, I'm not."

Emotions duke it out in my mind. Part of me is relieved, and the other part wants to ask what's wrong with me. I ignore both.

"That's good to know. You didn't feel like you were remotely ready to date."

"Not yet," he confirms. He takes a sip of his beer after clearing his throat. I wait for him to continue.

Finally, he says, "The other day, before I saw you at the coffee shop, I promised myself to dig myself out of this hole I've existed in."

I nod, knowing exactly what he means. "Did you discover how to do that?"

Fynn's gaze dances around the room like he's contemplating what to say next, before resettling on my face. "I realized that doing the same thing, day in and day out, won't help me get out of this rut. I need to step out of my comfort zone to really make a change. I'm not quite ready to date, but I *am* ready for change."

I couldn't relate more if I tried. "Is that why you went the other night? To get out of your comfort zone?"

He snorts. "That and Trinte is very convincing when he wants to be."

"I've noticed," I say dryly.

Fynn grins. "His intentions are good. I mean, he's watched me waste away for years. Can't blame him for pushing his brother to live life again."

I think of how much my mother and Kyri have done the same. "I get that. I'm also tired of being afraid to live, you know?"

Recognition lights up his expression. "Exactly. Which is actually why I invited you here. Well, there are two reasons. The first being the realization that I never asked you about your husband. All we've done is talk about my grief, but what about yours?"

Every muscle freezes; I stare hard at my drink. Trying not to let my voice shake, I ask, "What about him?"

Oblivious to the conflict tearing apart my thoughts, Fynn continues. "Well, I'm curious about when he died. I should've asked already, and I'm sorry for not doing so."

My fingers spin the martini glass. Tongue like sandpaper, I say, "Three years."

Sympathy softens his face, and I hate every bit of it.

Still unaware, he asks, "How did it happen?"

Hoping to distract him from this line of questioning, I ask, "How did Rhuth pass?"

Fynn cocks his head. "Do you really not want to talk about your husband?"

Shame reddens my cheeks. I find it impossible to fully admit what I've allowed to happen to me. "Mikan ... was not a nice person."

His brow furrows. "What do you mean? Like he was impatient? Rude to people?"

I let out a bitter laugh and sip my champagne before responding. "Honestly, that would've been a relief, Fynn."

It's clear he's trying to decipher my short answers. Lowering his voice, he asks, "Was he abusive?"

Memories assault my mind; I close my eyes, trying to block them all. I grab my pendant to siphon away the deep rage simmering in my gut. Rage not just at Mikan, but at myself for staying.

When I open my eyes, Fynn is watching me with an intensity that makes me want to bolt out of this bar. "Orliana, what happened?"

Bitterness stalls the words. I can't tell him. People don't want to be friends with murderers. Kyri is an exception, but there's a reason why I haven't made many new friends these last few years. It's not only because I struggle to open up, but because when people find out, they slowly fade away.

"Yes," I finally say. "He was abusive."

Something sharp flashes in his reptilian eyes. "Did he hurt Joulian, too?"

"No," I say quickly. "I would have never stayed if he had." Confusion twists his face, and I can't stand this conversation anymore. "Do we have to keep talking about this?"

"Absolutely not," he says firmly. Just like that, he pivots the topic. "The second reason I invited you here is that I want to make a proposition."

Immediately, I'm wary. "A proposition?"

"Yes. Maybe I'm making an enormous assumption here — and please tell me if I am — but maybe you might want to try some new hobbies with me?"

"Hobbies?" I echo. It's a relief to stop discussing Mikan, but now I'm even more confused.

Fynn leans forward, resting on his forearms, amusement twinkling in his golden eyes. "Yes, hobbies. Some things are better done with others, and since you already understand me better than anyone, I thought maybe you might want to join me?"

He grimaces. "Sorry, that sounds selfish. We barely know one another, and it's a huge assumption."

"Yes," I say quickly. "I mean, no, it's not a huge assumption. I need to get out of the house more. Kyri is great and all, but ..."

Fynn gives me a small smile. "But they just don't get it, right? Trinte is the same way."

"*Exactly.* They try—"

"But it's not the same?"

"Right."

We stare at one another, letting the words simmer between us. Having a friend to do activities with, someone who won't constantly push me to move on at an uncomfortable pace, could be refreshing.

Eventually, he'll want to know more about Mikan. Maybe he'll see the news reports before I gain the courage. Today doesn't feel right to share, though.

Trying to buy time while I think, I finish my martini. Fynn sips his drink, allowing me to process. It's ... comforting.

Knowing he isn't trying to date me helps make my decision. "Okay, but we're just friends?"

"Only friends," he confirms. "And if at any point you want out, just say so."

I feel a mix of relief and disappointment. "Same goes for you."

He sits back, scanning the space around me. "Where's Moxie, by the way?"

Silently, I summon my familiar. She appears on top of his head, prancing in glee. Fynn jolts in surprise with a laugh.

"I wasn't sure, but if this ended up being a serious conversation, a ugopeg wasn't going to enhance the situation," I joke. Moxie snorts, then flies to the table's surface.

"I like her," he admits. "Even when she's leaving bruises on my ankles."

Moxie bleats, wagging her little stump of a tail. I pet her affectionately. "Be careful what you wish for. Moxie is sure to deliver."

This time, when Fynn locks eyes with mine, it feels significant in some way I can't quite describe. Something flutters in my belly when he says, "I look forward to it." His sunrise eyes glance at my empty martini glass. "Would you like another?"

I shake my head, sticking out my tongue in disgust. "No. I'd like another champagne."

Fynn laughs, motioning for a waitress to come over. While we wait, Fynn's face lights up. "Do you want to hear a story from a Dragxi fare I had the other day?"

I lean forward, bracing against the table, grinning. "I'd love to hear any juicy gossip you've picked up."

Something flickers across his expression as he leans closer, lowering his voice. "Let me tell you about a witch named Tilda ..."

24

Orliana

Fynn: I have some ideas for hobbies to try

Orliana: I don't want to crochet, by the way. I've tried and I'm terrible at it.

Fynn: Crossed it off the list.

Orliana: What are the others?

Fynn: Painting, People Watching Club, poetry, bowling, ceramics, walking chimeragons at a nearby shelter, and poker.

Orliana: I like people watching, but doing it in a group sounds creepy. Can you imagine twelve people watching you walk by?

Fynn: Okay, crossed off the list. Any others?

Orliana: I'm allergic to chimeragons. I'm interested in trying bowling. Maybe painting.

Fynn: Want to try bowling? I'll cover the beer and snacks.

Orliana: Five days from now?

Fynn: See you then.

The day we're set to meet at the bowling alley, I meet Kyri and Mom at a local boutique. It's been ages since the three of us shopped together, and it's refreshing. Joulian's still at school, so I'll have to go pick him up soon. For now, I'm a show pony for these two.

Mom loves taking advantage of an opportunity to dress me, then bicker with Kyri about whether something will flatter my figure. Moxie floats around the store, stabbing dresses she likes. All of them have paisley patterns, so they're immediately rejected.

"Your familiar has terrible taste," Mom complains. Her own fox familiar runs past with a yellow hat in its maw.

Kyri hums in agreement, pulling a dress from a display, holding it up to her chest. "I'm seeing North again tonight. The man is insatiable. Do you think this will look good?"

With a snort, I take in her petite but muscular figure. "Kyr, you'd look good in anything."

She beams. "Thank you!"

As if she isn't already aware. It's difficult to not roll my eyes. Instead, I use them to peruse the racks, thinking of how Trinte dressed Fynn. We're planning to go bowling tonight as our first get-out-of-our-comfort-zone experience. Which I have yet to tell Mom or Kyri about. I'm actually unsure how they'll respond.

Mom ushers me into the changing room, hanging a dozen items on the hooks. She'll want to see every single piece before deciding. In a way, it's a relief to not have to decide on my own. However, it's also annoying to spin on command to check every angle of fabric.

Undressing, I say through the curtain, "So, I'm hanging out with Fynn after this."

"Who?" Mom asks; at the same time Kyri exclaims, "You are *not!*"

Pulling on the first dress, wriggling so it slides over my hips, I say, "Yeah. We decided to do some activities together. Apparently he's trying to get over his wife by trying potential hobbies."

I push back the curtain and step into the light, allowing Mom to inspect me. Kyri is still getting dressed in the stall beside me. Through the blue curtain, she says, "Orliana, you didn't tell me you're into him!"

"I'm not," I say quickly. "We're friends."

Mom scrutinizes me, but I don't think she's focused on the dress. "Why does that name sound familiar?"

Kyri steps out, wearing a floor-length pastel orange dress. With her creamsicle hair, fire burst eyes, she resembles a creamy dessert. "She brought him and his brother to the club the other night. Both are handsome as all Hells."

"They're attractive," I hedge.

Kyri scoffs, glancing over her shoulder in a mirror. Her eyes briefly meet mine. "You're protesting too much, Orliana."

"Oh, yeah?" I fire back. "Want to share about what happened with Trinte?"

"Nope." She pops the P, giving me a smug smirk.

"How did you meet him?" The excitement in Mom's voice actually spikes my guilt. There's too much hope in that question.

"You already met him," I say, wincing. "The Dragon from the career fair?"

Mom twirls her finger; I spin. She shakes her head, forcing me to change.

"*That's* where you met him?" Kyri says in the stall. "What is his career? A stripper?"

I laugh, unable to imagine Fynn being an exotic dancer. "He runs a local Dragxi company."

"Oh," Kyri says. That single syllable leaves so much unspoken. I think she's going to leave it at that, but she says, "So, he's really good at giving rides?"

"Kyrielle!" Mom practically shrieks her name in admonishment. "Don't be inappropriate."

"Sorry," Kyri says, not sounding sorry at all. "But you've seen him; you weren't thinking the same?"

"Well, maybe a little," Mom admits.

Stepping out of the dress, I call out, "Knock it off, you two. We're just friends."

"She's definitely protesting too much," Mom declares.

I grit my teeth in frustration, trying to hide the irritation as I step out for another inspection.

"Oh, I love that," Mom says, beaming with approval. "You should wear it today to go bowling."

I peer down at the floral print sundress. It shows off my shapely thighs and complements the roundness of my belly with a smooth bodice. "This seems a little skimpy, Mom."

"Nonsense," she says dismissively. "Where did you say you're going again?"

"Bowling."

Doubt flickers in her expression, but she can't resist the potential of me being on a date, even though I've been clear it's not a date. "Well, I'm sure it'll be alright to wear."

This time, I do roll my eyes. Already sounding like a broken record, I repeat, "We're. Just. Friends."

Kyri breezes out of her stall wearing a periwinkle dress with the slit up to her hip.

I grin. "That's the one for North."

"You think so?" she says, nibbling on her lip. "He said we're going to an opera tonight before dinner."

"It looks excellent, dear," Mom says, eyeing the outfit appreciatively.

Thankfully, they drop the subject of Fynn. With all the dresses tested, I settle on three, still wearing the floral one Mom suggested.

As we walk out of the store, I ask Kyri, "You sure you don't want to share about Trinte?"

"There's nothing to tell," she says breezily.

But I know my best friend. There's something in the tone of her voice that betrays a hurt. She'll share when she's ready.

I give her a hug, then turn to Mom. "You'll be picking Joulian up at five?"

She gives me a hug. "Of course. Text me when you're done bowling with that handsome Dragon."

I open my mouth to say we're only friends, *again*, but the two of them beat me to the punch, saying at the same time, "We're *just* friends."

No matter how much I insist it's true, they refuse to believe me.

***

This dress is *not* appropriate for bowling. Every time I bend over to swing the bowling ball into the lane, air licks the back of my thighs. After years of never baring my skin, it's far more exposing than normal.

I'm going to kill Mom for recommending this dress.

So far, Fynn hasn't said a word. Nor have I caught him ogling. Instead, he ordered pitchers of beer, some fried foods, and I'm fairly certain he's going to win this game.

The bowling ball wobbles, landing in the gutter. I groan in defeat.

Fynn chuckles. "So are we scratching bowling off the list of possible hobbies?"

"I'm not *that* bad," I insist, sliding my glove back on. The look he gives me tells me exactly how much he believes that statement: not at all.

He picks up the pitcher of beer and tops off my drink. "It's okay to admit you're not good at something."

I lift my lip in mock offense. "I've never played before."

After sipping his beer, he says, "So you're loving this?"

"Well, no," I admit, grinning. "I actually hate this."

He tosses his head back and lets out a throaty laugh. “Okay, so bowling is out. Do you want to call it quits?”

My mouth twists with uncertainty. I’m enjoying spending this time with him; will he want to go home if I say yes?

He must see something in my expression because he adds, “We can go do something else if you want. There’s a nearby pottery shop I’ve always wanted to check out.”

I perk up. “As in, we can make the pottery?”

“I think so. Want to finish up these beers and check it out?”

The beer already in my system feels like helium under my skin. It feels incredible. I can finally understand why people enjoy drinking. “Sure.”

We abandon the game of bowling. It’s difficult to decide what to say next. I focus on a safe topic.

“How did you start Flaming Fares?”

He leans back in his chair, slinging an ankle over his knee. He rubs his hair, the muscles in his arm flexing. Today, he’s wearing another T-shirt, and I swear in the last two weeks he’s gained muscle.

“It was Rhuth’s idea,” he admits. “I was working for a competitor at the time, but I was miserable. She made it sound so simple.” In a high-pitched voice full of humor, he says, “‘You could do so much more on your own.’”

I laugh at the impression. “She sounded just like that, huh?”

He grins, showing off fangs. “She’d kill me if she heard that impression. Really, though, she’s the sole reason I have the company now.”

“It’s great,” I admit. “Joulian is loving his training.”

Fynn nods. “He’s a good kid.”

“He is,” I agree. “I got lucky with that one.”

He tilts his head, considering his next words. “Is it difficult being a single mom?”

“Sometimes,” I confess. “As good as he is, there are still times when he presses the boundaries and, no matter what, I’m the one having to always be the bad guy. Mom helps, but she’s definitely a push-over.”

He grins. “You’re doing a good job, though.”

“Thanks.” Heat blushes my cheeks. “I try.”

"No," he says, leaning forward, suddenly serious. "I mean it. Your hard work is noticeable."

Words are suddenly difficult, so I take a long sip of my drink, refusing to make eye contact. It's not that discussing being a single mom hurts, but it's another reminder of what I've taken away from my son.

We spend the rest of the conversation talking about our favorite books and music. It's a relief to not discuss our personal circumstances. Sometimes, I just want to be Orliana, the woman, and not Orliana, the mom. I love my son, but something tells me I need to focus on Orliana, the woman, in order to move on.

If it's even possible.

25

Fynn

Since bowling's a bust — seriously, who likes that game? — I lead Orliana to the pottery shop. It's pretty busy, but after I hunt down the hostess, I'm able to secure us two pottery wheels for a group lesson about to start.

As we move through the crowded room, I walk in front of her, clearing the space so it's less likely for people to touch her. The sundress she's wearing is sinful, featuring too many bare curves. Less than the dress at the club, but yet somehow more.

Because we're last minute additions, we're seated across from one another. She looks panicked, and I have to resist touching her arm as a comfort as I point at my seat. "I'm right there. Perfect distance to throw things if you want."

Her shoulders relax as she grins. "Thanks for the idea."

The teacher hands us both aprons before we sit down. As I'm settling on my stool, I glance at Orliana. All thoughts dry up as she spreads her legs. There's a flash of silky beige between her thighs; I stare at the floor. When I peek up a few seconds later, she's situated the dress to cover up the view. I don't think she realizes what I saw — I'm going to keep it that way.

It's like when she bent over to throw the bowling ball, showing more golden skin than she probably realized. Since she's normally dressed head-to-toe, I wasn't sure if it was actually on purpose. It never reached a fully inappropriate view, so I decided it was easier to stay silent.

The teacher showing us how to pedal the pottery wheel interrupts my thoughts. Each of us has a clump of clay. She shows us how to wet the clay before shaping it with our hands.

One thing I didn't quite expect was how sensual this would feel. With spread legs and wet fingers, it's more erotic than expected.

Orliana watches the teacher with rapt attention, strands of hair falling from the messy bun she's piled on top of her head. When she turns to look at another student asking a question, I notice the curve where her neck meets her shoulder. The way one of the straps of her dress threatens to tumble off said shoulder.

Looking away, I focus on the project. Yet, I can't help but peek up again a few minutes later. She catches me staring and grins. When she motions toward what should be a pot on my pottery wheel, she gives me a thumbs up.

I'm too busy not breathing to respond back. Ducking my head, I studiously work the clay, struggling to focus.

We're friends.

I don't want to date her.

That isn't the purpose of these times together.

She needs to heal as much as I do.

But these newfound emotions are difficult to wrangle.

When she told me her late husband was abusive, I almost asked the location of his grave so I could dig him up and turn him into ash. The idea of a single bruise on her body makes me want to roar with rage. Considering how she reacted when I asked if Joulian suffered, I now understand the reason both of them panicked when he soaked me with the hose.

It explained why they responded like I was a hairbreadth away from violence.

I'm sick to my stomach that I acted in any way that made them consider it an option. I know logically it was a trigger for them, but it still makes me ill.

She deserves to enjoy life. Both of them do.

And she doesn't need someone like me, a man still trying to figure out how to exist without his wife, fucking things up for her.

For her sake and my sanity, we have to remain friends.

When the pots are done, I finally look at her. She's frowning at me. Maybe she just realized how awful this goddess-forsaken pot in front of me is. I point at the warped clay and grimace dramatically.

The frown breaks, morphing into a grin. When she points at hers, I nod in approval. It decidedly looks better. After washing our hands and returning the aprons, we take tickets that tell us when to return to pick up the pots later, once they've spent time in a kiln.

Stepping outside into the night air, I inhale the scent of blossoms. Orliana stands beside me, doing the same.

A sudden sense of awkwardness has me rolling my lips, trying to figure out what to do or say. Even though we're friends, how do we end this? The old me would've offered a hug to a friend, but none of those friends were Siphons.

"So," she says, breaking the train of my thoughts. "How do friends say goodbye?"

"I was thinking the same thing." I motion at her dress. "You have a lot of skin uncovered, so I figure a hug is out of the question."

Her eyebrows draw together as her mouth twists with uncertainty. "You can hug me, if you want. I'm confident I can shield if you don't want me to feel anything."

Do I want to hug her? My gut response makes me uncomfortable. Wanting to hug another woman, even as friends, feels almost ... like a betrayal. Rhuth genuinely wouldn't have cared if I'd hugged a woman.

But knowing the deep-seated motivations on my end, even if I refuse to acknowledge them, makes it feel disloyal.

When a group of people step out behind us, I touch the small of her back to coax her out of the way. She jolts at the touch; I snap my hand back. It was an impulsive, yet natural thing for me to do, but I shouldn't have done it.

"Sorry," I murmur. "I didn't want them accidentally running into you."

"It's fine," she says, walking out of the way. "I appreciate your thoughtfulness, Fynn."

"I fear I'm being so thoughtful, this entire interaction has become awkward."

Orliana's mouth quirks to the side. "I think we're both trying to be considerate of the other. That's not a bad thing."

"True, but this is a lot of build-up to a hug," I muse. "Can you teach me how to shield?"

When she looks confused, I rush to say, "I mean, if we're going to hang out more, it's probably wise for me to learn. In case I accidentally touch you."

She cocks her head, considering. "Let me see your hand. I'll show you how to shield." When she sees me hesitate, she's quick to add, "I promise I won't take anything."

That wasn't my concern, but I'm not about to admit there are other emotions I'm too nervous to show her. Our palms press together like two magnets. Unlike the last time we did, there's no sensation of something peering inside me.

"Can you share an emotion with me?"

Her skin is warm against mine; I resist the urge to curl my fingers shut. "Like what?"

"Anything. Maybe, if you have it, some happiness?"

If you have it. Orliana has felt the depths of my grief and isn't sure there's room for anything else. Except these last few days have shown otherwise.

Closing my eyes, I think of how it felt to rediscover my Dragon Fyre in the mist. The moment it's at the forefront of my mind, the curious thing reaches inside me and caresses it. A shiver runs down my back, raising the hair on my arms.

"Ah, that's lovely," she murmurs. "What's that from?"

Still keeping my eyes closed, I whisper, "My Dragon Fyre."

"Wonderful."

Her words strengthen the heat of my Fyre. I feel it the second my palm warms in hers.

She inhales sharply, running her fingers along mine. "Okay, so imagine your skin itself is a shell that holds that fire in. Since it's actual fire, let me know if it's too difficult."

"It won't be," My voice is deeper than expected. Rough.

Taking her advice, I imagine my red scales hardening. My tail thumps in protest; the Fyre doesn't like being controlled. Yet, for her, I do it anyway. It takes focus, but I'm able to draw the Fyre in enough that my skin cools.

"Incredible," she whispers.

My eyes flutter open, finding hers peering at my chest. There's a faint orange glow on her face; my Fyre is visible through my T-shirt.

She stares so hard I think she's about to peel apart my ribs to examine the Fyre. I take her hand, carefully keeping the movement as neutral as possible, and place it on my sternum where the center of my Fyre exists.

Her fingers spread wide, slowly running up between my pecs. The wonderment on her face tells me she's not even thinking about how she's touching me. I'm frozen, unable to breathe. No one has touched me like this since Rhuth. Why in the Hells did I put her hand there?

Her power prods my Fyre, and when my Fyre bites back, she jerks her hand away with a laugh.

"Is it a living thing?"

She has no idea what she's doing to me. My mouth is dry; words are difficult. Since she isn't touching me now, I release the control of my Fyre, exhaling from the effort. I'll need to practice more to get better at it.

Because deep down, I know she's going to touch me again.

"Are you okay?" she asks, searching my face for clues as to why I haven't spoken yet.

Swallowing hard, I say, "Yeah. It has a mind of its own a lot of the time. It's the core of Dragons, where our magyck comes from."

"Dragon magyck varies, right?"

Finally, something I can actually talk about. "Yes, all Dragons have magyck, but the skill set varies."

She claps her hands together with the cutest hop on her toes. "Like what?"

Despite the emotions ripping me apart inside, I smile and lift a finger. A breeze immediately swirls around us, lifting her hair in the air like a tornado. She giggles, peering up at her silky strands dancing above her head. By Fortuna's grace, the dress doesn't follow.

I release the simple magyck. Everything goes still. She glances around like it'll reappear.

"We can bend air to our will, like Dragxis do for fares. Of course, there's fire. We're impervious to it. The more powerful Dragons can manipulate clouds, which essentially equates to being able to control the weather."

"Can you?" she squeals, scanning the sky as if I'll command lightning to strike.

I chuckle. With a stronger pull at my magyck, I raise the finger again, guiding mist to crawl toward us like an ominous blanket.

Orliana literally cackles. It should be disturbing, but it's utterly charming.

"You should know, I don't command the elements for your amusement."

She places her hands on her hips. "And why not? This is way better than being a Siphon."

"We can agree to disagree," I say, grinning. With a flick of my wrist, the mist shrinks. "Besides, I'm not supposed to do those sorts of things in the city. It's frowned upon."

"Can we go somewhere else another day so you can show me more?"

"I can show you all sorts of things." The words come out lower than expected. They hover between us, crackling like the unshed lightning waiting for my command. "That came out differently than intended."

"It's okay," she says softly. Pulling out her phone, she checks the time, then swears. "I have to go. Mom's watching Joulian." Looking to her side, she says, "Come out."

Moxie poofs into the air, clearly ready to bicker with her bonded. Then she notices me. Squealing, she flits up to my shoulder and lands. To my surprise, she rubs her face against my cheek. It's incredibly soft.

Orliana laughs. "There was no way she would've behaved at the bowling alley and *definitely* not at the pottery shop."

My hand reaches up to pet her, then freezes. "Am I allowed to touch her?"

Orliana hesitates. "Yes, if she lets you."

Moxie catapults into my hand, stabbing the fat of my middle finger. I hold my palm flat so she can stand on it. Bringing a finger to her back, I give it a little rub. She bobs her head up and down in approval.

Offering Moxie back, I say, "I need to get going, too." An idea appears. "Tomorrow is Spawn Point and I have some extra VIP tickets. Want to go?"

Orliana watches Moxie, twirling a curl. "That could be fun. Can I bring someone?"

"Of course. I'll leave the tickets at the box office."

The awkwardness grows as we stare at one another a beat too long.

Heart in my throat, I ask, "Did you still want to try a hug?"

Her voice is so quiet, anyone with lesser hearing would've missed it. "Maybe next time?"

"Next time," I agree.

As much as I want to watch her walking away, I focus on getting to the landing pad as fast as possible. My flight home has never been so quick.

The invading thoughts are overwhelming. Smiles meant for me. A delighted cackle as the mist rolled in. A nibbled lip. Twirled hair.

Over and over again, my mind taunts me, boiling me alive.

This time, stepping through the door doesn't quite feel like a tomb. In fact, it feels like a refuge because my body *burns.* My Fyre is lashing against my insides with fury, demanding release. When it's like this, it demands a different kind of release. One that doesn't involve letting it loose in the sky.

It hasn't been like this in years, but between reawakening it and Orliana poking at it, my Fyre *needs.*

Sweat slicks my skin as I undress, lust pulsing in my blood. This is exactly why I pounded down my Fyre into submission for years. Connecting with it has consequences, ones that are easy to deal with when you have a consenting partner.

But I don't have a partner.

Because until this very moment, I haven't wanted one.

By the time my slacks are around my ankles, my cock is harder than diamonds. It bobs proudly, throbbing with desire.

The Fyre commands me to thrust into *something,* so I grab it with a fist, reacquainting with this long-forgotten part of my body. Its heat meets the burning of my palms, jerking my hips forward. Gasping, I drop to my knees, lost in the pleasure. I've spent so long forcing myself to feel dead inside that it's like being punched in the face, remembering what I tried to hide away forever.

Unable to control the pace, I work myself the way I remember liking, and as my mind attempts to visualize something to increase the pleasure, it's Rhuth that appears. The salacious memories of my wife having me crying out with sadness, longing, and desire. I work myself harder and faster, wishing it were her here.

Yet, as I reach my climax, it's the thought of beige silk panties between two golden thighs that shoves me over the edge. When the orgasm rips through me, satisfying my Fyre, all that's left in its wake is shame, guilt, and the painful realization that maybe Orliana means more to me than she should.

26

Orliana

Orliana: Do you want to go to a video game convention with me? Fynn gave me VIP tickets. Him and his brother are in a competition.

Kyri: Ooo, I like VIP. Will we be around Trinte?

Orliana: Yes? Will that be an issue? You don't have to come if you don't want to.

Kyri: No, it's fine. We're adults. I'll meet you there?

Orliana: Sounds good.

***

"This is way busier than I thought it would be," I murmur to Kyrielle as we head to the VIP line. It's shorter than the general line, but not by much. Spawn Point is the largest video game convention in Gondora, so thousands of people are trying to get in.

One of the main reasons I've never been, even though I've always wanted to. It features competitions, sneak peeks into unreleased games, people in costumes as their favorite characters, and even vendors offering food from famous games. Thousands of others had the same idea as us. My skin already tingles with anticipation.

Kyri slaps her orange fingertips together. "If any men get too close, I'll light them on fire."

I roll my eyes, bumping my shoulder into hers. "Down, killer. No fire lighting today, please. Focus on finding a cute nerd or something."

Kyri huffs with displeasure and lowers her hands, muttering, "My offer still stands."

After tugging my sleeves over my gloves as we step into line, I check my texts, unsurprised to find no alerts. The Gleanscale brothers are in the middle of a competition right now. They'd offered to let me join, but it was easy to decline. Having a few hundred strangers watch me play? No, thank you.

"Are we just going to watch them?" Kyri says, scanning the crowd. Her fiery eyes are always searching for potential issues.

I shake my head. "We'll stop at some vendor tables, too. Joulian asked for some T-shirts. Fynn mentioned trying out the pop-up pub that is designed like the one in Verile: The Deeds of Houra."

Kyri's nose scrunches. "The deeds of what now?"

"Houra," I repeat. "It's a game about two Vampyres that hunt—" Her eyes immediately glaze over, so I stop explaining. Instead, I put it succinctly as, "Big men beating up enemies, and resting for drinks between battles."

Her eyebrows shoot up. "Ah! Okay, that makes sense." She pats her belly. "I wouldn't mind some food. I'm famished after last night's battle."

I smirk. "Kick another man's ass?"

She tosses creamsicle curls over her shoulder. "Rumor has it I fractured his femur."

I wish it were possible to say she doesn't intimidate me, but it would be a lie. My best friend is an absolute badass. "Sad to have missed it."

The line shuffles forward as she says airily, "Well, you were making pottery with Fynn." With a smug look, she adds, "How's that going, by the way?"

"Still friendly," I say flatly, knowing where she's going with this.

"Sure," she says, sounding wholly unconvinced. "Men and women are really good at being friends, especially when they're both single and attractive. Happens all the time."

I swat her arm. "We *are* friends. How about you tell me what's going on with Trinte, if we're up in each other's business."

"Oops, we're next in line," she says breezily, motioning for me to pull out the tickets in my pocket. "Let's not keep the people behind us waiting."

Rolling my eyes, I hand over the tickets to the bored attendant. He mutters a thanks, jabbing a finger into the convention center.

The entrance hall to the convention center is almost shoulder-to-shoulder. It instantly makes my skin crawl; I'm relieved to have had the foresight to cover myself head-to-toe. Even Kyri tucks her orange wings tight to her back, frowning.

"There are this many nerds in Gondora?" she says, eyes wide as she takes in all the advertisements, sights, and sounds.

I grab her hand, determined to plunge through the crowd toward the convention hall door. "Apparently. Come on, let's go find the brothers."

It's a struggle to find them, especially as Kyri continuously gets distracted by the different booths. There are vendors selling gamer chairs, console accessories, costumes, and merchandise for the largest fandoms. The aisles between booths are wide, but that doesn't matter when a family of Centaurs meander down the center, tails smacking bodies without a second thought. Groups of pixies flit around, and the musty stench in the air tells me a Tiddy Munn is somewhere nearby.

Kyri gasps as a Cyclops almost knocks her over, only to nearly fall backward into a family of Elves. I'm wing-checked by a teenage

Seraphim who clearly hasn't realized how much space his wings take up.

I spit out an orange feather, frowning at my best friend. "I don't know if I want to stay here."

"Let's find the brothers and demand they use their Big Bad Dragon privileges," she declares, hopping on her toes. "Can you see them?"

"Not yet, but I think there's only one competition area."

The sound of cheering from one corner of the convention hall has us hustling through the crowd. To our relief, Fynn and Trinte are sitting at a console set up, microphones slung over their heads, eyes focused on screens mounted in front of them. A hundred onlookers chatter excitedly, pointing and urging them to do certain moves. If I weren't already overwhelmed, I'd probably join in.

Not wanting to distract them, we wait outside the barrier preventing people from crowding them. The brothers are locked into the game they're playing. Trinte grins broadly, saying something to Fynn, who frowns. They're so diametrically different, but I'm learning to appreciate it.

I'm unsurprised to see Kyri watching Trinte. She's never *ever* focused on men like this. Half the time, I'm surprised she dates at all, considering most men would crumble under her strong personality.

When the crowd cheers, my attention snaps back to the brothers, pleased to see them resting their controllers on a table. I wave, immediately catching Fynn's attention. He grins, hopping out of the chair and striding over. Trinte spots us; his smile melts into a frown when he sees Kyri.

"You made it!" Fynn ushers us past the barrier, waving away security. To Kyri, he says, "Nice to see you again."

Trinte's approaching, albeit with slow steps. Kyri looks at him, then back at Fynn. "Um, yeah. I'm not into video games, but I'll never pass up a chance to hang out with Orliana."

Something I can't identify glints in Fynn's eyes as he says, "I understand."

He understands? As in, he also can't resist an opportunity to spend time with me? *It's fine; friends like to spend time with one another.*

Pushing away the thought, I motion to the gaming setup. "Did you win?"

"Technically, I got the killing blow," Trinte says, stopping next to his brother. Giving me a playful waggle of his eyebrows, he adds, "This fucker was lazy. We should've invited MeanCat."

I laugh, jerking my head toward the crowd. "I would've embarrassed myself."

Trinte opens his mouth, and Fynn elbows him hard enough for the blue Dragon to double over. "Keep your mouth shut."

Rubbing his ribs, Trinte grumbles, "I was just going to say that you—"

Fynn's tail smacks Trinte's. They square off, but just as I think they're about to have a brotherly brawl, Kyri clears her throat.

"If you two insist on being children, please excuse me while I go get an adult beverage."

The brothers pause, looking down at my best friend. Trinte's the first to speak. "I'm in the mood for a Heimlock."

Kyri freezes, and a small muscle in her jaw flexes. "How funny — I'm in the mood for a glass of femire."

"Heimlocks are cheaper."

"I think there's a solid 'your mom' joke in here, but I really am thirsty," she says, pushing past them. Trinte watches her walk off, a glint of hunger in his gaze.

Unable to resist, I ask him, "What *is it* with you two? How do you know one another?"

Trinte turns his mismatched eyes on me. "What did she say?"

"Nothing."

Shoving his hands into pockets, he shrugs. "Then it was nothing."

Fynn steps in front of his brother, appearing both irritated and pleased. "Time for drinks?"

"Yes, please," I say with a loud sigh. After that entire exchange, I need at least two.

The three of us follow Kyri, who is already at the concession stand, ordering the largest glass of femire available. She and Trinte lock eyes as he orders a Heimlock. Fynn and I exchange a glance as we take our glasses of femire from the bartender.

"What is going on with them?" I whisper, hoping neither hears me.

Unfortunately, both of them do. Still staring at one another, Kyri and Trinte simultaneously say, "Nothing."

"I've never seen 'nothing' be so ... 'something.'" Fynn murmurs back, earning a glare from his brother.

Jaw clenched, Trinte takes a sip of his Heimlock. The tension between my best friend and his brother is so thick, it makes me want to take a step back.

Fynn must sense the urge because his broad chest fills my line of sight. Pretending to not be a buffer from the weird stand-off behind him, he asks, "So, is there anything you want to do here today? There are some booths I want to visit; I need a new headset and they're giving out discounts for my favorite brand."

Shoulders loosening, I nod. "That sounds great. Joulian wants a T-shirt, so let's find a clothing vendor."

Fynn scans the bar. "Where's Moxie?"

I flick my hand, and she appears, prancing on my palm. "She might be helpful in getting through this crowd."

My ugopeg hops happily across my fingers, then zips up to Fynn's shoulder, rubbing into his cheek.

Fynn grins, watching her out of the corner of his eye. "Well, let's leave those two to be weird together and go find Joulian a shirt."

Smiling, I nod. "Can you use your Big Bad Dragon privileges?"

Fynn holds out his arm. "I'd be delighted to intimidate everyone who dares get in our way."

Sliding my arm into his, I ignore the way my heart flutters at the immediate safety he offers. Until Fynn, men have never been safe for me.

It's difficult to admit, but it's lovely to have one who I'm positive would burn down this convention center to keep me safe.

27

Orliana

When it's time to take Joulian for his fourth job training experience, butterflies cause such a racket in my belly, I can't eat breakfast.

It's been two days since the video game convention. In that time, I haven't heard from Fynn at all. I've been a coward, refusing to text first. We'd spent the afternoon at the convention, going on a small shopping spree while Kyri and Trinte stayed at the concession stand, presumably glaring at one another the whole time.

By the time we headed home, things between Fynn and me felt even easier than before. Like we're developing a genuine friendship.

I'm ashamed to admit that when I touched his Fyre the other night, I caught a deeper glimpse of his feelings. It's no longer grief encompassing everything, but there's more — an awakening. There was longing, and it wasn't just for his wife. Since I can only feel emotions, and not the reasons for them, I can only speculate what that longing is.

Joulian chatters non-stop during the Dragxi ride, but I barely hear him over the thoughts in my mind. Even Greg's squawking and hopping from seat to seat doesn't phase me.

Maybe Fynn and I are pushing things too hard. While it sounds great to heal together as friends, there's so much he still doesn't know about me. I'm positive once he knows I'm a murderer, he'll never look at me the same.

When we land at the headquarters, instead of Fynn greeting us, it's Trinte who waits. He smiles and waves, the blue scales of his body gleaming in the early morning light. Joulian hops off and lopes toward him, unfazed that Fynn isn't here.

When Trinte meets my eyes, there's something in there I don't like. Something that prickles along my spine.

As Joulian runs ahead, I walk next to Trinte and murmur, "Where is he?"

"Elsewhere." His tone is flat and unrevealing.

Dread sticks like tar in my gut. "Is he okay?"

His blue eye flickers with something I can't name. "He will be."

For the last month, Fynn has been here every Saturday. My anxiety spikes, unnerved by the change in pattern. "Should I call him?"

Trinte leads us to the comms center. Joulian pauses at the door, having already learned he can't just run into spaces anymore. Beside me, Trinte walks slowly, hands clasped behind his back.

A few paces away from my son, he gives me a long look. Staring up at him, I see so many similarities and differences. Where Fynn has more full lips, Trinte's have a wide-set cupid's bow and a full bottom lip. His nose is also straighter.

He sounds genuinely curious when he asks, "Do you *want* to call him?"

Making sure Joulian isn't listening, I say, "I don't know *what* I want."

"You both are so similar, you know." Amusement crinkles the edges of his eyes. "He doesn't know what he wants either."

I furrow my brow, trying to decipher what exactly he's trying to convey. "If there's something you're trying to say, can you please just say it?"

Trinte's eyes flick to Joulian, who is watching us and growing impatient. His mouth thins as he contemplates his next words. Then, "I love my brother. He's the only thing I have left in this world that means something to me. And I want him to be happy." He blows out a breath. "And today, he is not happy."

"What's today?"

Joulian runs up, brow furrowed with confusion. "Are we going to go into the comms room, Mr. Trinte?"

The Dragon transforms his expression to a happy, friendly one. "Of course, little man. Give me one more second, alright?"

Joulian looks at me, and I offer a reassuring smile. "We'll catch up in a second. Let us finish talking, okay?"

"Okay, but hurry up," he says, showing that newfound teenage attitude before marching off.

Trinte pulls out his phone. "What's your number?" When I hesitate, he huffs in frustration. "I'm not hitting on you. I'm going to text you his address." *Oh.* I give him the number, and my phone pings with a text. "Don't call him. He's just going to tell you not to come."

"But what's *wrong,* Trinte?" I plead, trying not to beg. Anxiety is a living thing inside me now, rushing toward the worst possible scenarios.

The infuriating Dragon shakes his head. "Either he'll let you in, or he won't. It's up to him to tell you."

I let out a growl of frustration. "Has anyone told you what an infuriating *dunghole* you are?"

He smirks and turns toward Joulian, who is now tapping his foot in frustration. "Since the day I was born." He pauses. "If you want, Joulian can stay here and you can go to Fynn."

Indecision rips at me, but a Siphon instinct says I need to go to Fynn. "You won't take him flying?"

Trinte laughs. "No. We'll go over the comms training and clean some saddles."

I responded to his text with Mom's number. "This is my mother's contact information. If you don't hear from me by the time you have to do something else, call her, okay? Promise?"

He nods, actually serious for once. "I swear it."

Joulian watches, those blue eyes seeing too much. He's apparently heard more than I realized because he says, "It's okay, Mom. If Fynn needs help, you should go."

I point a finger at him and Greg. "The two of you *behave.* Am I understood?"

Greg squawks, and my son gives me a salute. "Yes, ma'am."

Trinte chuckles and steers him into the comms room, closing the door behind them.

***

The Dragxi ride to Fynn's house feels like it takes years, even though it's only a few minutes. The second the Dragxi lands, I pay in a rush. Once the Dragon flies off, I survey the house where Fynn lives.

While most of the yard is dead, a few bushes of peonies bloom in various colors. The house itself is a beautiful blue, with a clear domed roof that probably lets in a fair amount of light inside. Yet, as I approach, I see peeling paint and cracks in the foundation.

The door, a dark midnight blue, features chips and scuffs. I raise my fist to knock, but hesitate. Is this inappropriate? What if Trinte is overstepping, like he normally does? It seemed serious for him, and I don't doubt he loves his brother, but what if I'm not what Fynn wants or needs right now? I could literally ruin our friendship by knocking on this door.

My hand is halfway to my side, my heel ready to spin me away, when I stop.

In the last month, Fynn has been nothing but kind and understanding. No matter what's happening on the other side of this door, he's not going to take it out on me. He's *not* Mikan.

Still, my hand shakes as I knock. It's met with silence. I wait a minute before doing it again. Nothing. I send a text to Trinte.

Orliana: He's not here.

Trinte: Yes, he is. Make him answer. I promise he's there.

That actually pisses me off. If Fynn's ignoring my knocks, then that's just rude.

This time when I knock, I pound against the wood with force. "Open up, Fynn! It's me, Orliana! I know you're in there!"

I hear a faint curse inside; something falls to the ground. Finally, the door unlocks and opens up a crack. One dull golden eye examines me.

"Fuck," he mutters. The door widens, showing him wearing wrinkled pajamas and with unwashed hair. It's the worst I've ever seen him. When I peek at his aura, I'm devastated to see only grief. There's nothing else filling him.

He sounds exhausted as he says, "Why are you here, Orliana? Better yet, how did you get this address?"

"I'll give you one guess."

He rubs a hand over his face with a sigh. "He's a meddling dunghole." Fynn's shoulders sag. "You wasted a trip. I'm fine. Tell Joulian I'm sorry for missing today, but I'll be there next week."

He goes to close the door, but after seeing his aura and appearance, he's going to have to throw me off the cliff to get rid of me. I put a foot against the door. He glares at my foot, then at my face.

There's no trace of amusement when he says, "You don't want to be here, Orliana."

"And if I do?"

"You don't," he says flatly.

When he tries to close the door again, I refuse to move my foot. Instead, I give him my best glare. "I'll just sit out here, waiting. So you might as well let me in."

To my dismay, he actually growls at me. My heart picks up speed, and the shaking in my hands quickens. His tail thumps with frustration. "I don't *let* people in."

"So I'm 'people' now?" I challenge. "I thought I was a friend."

Something flashes in his eyes before he narrows them. It's a side I've never seen of him; it's both interesting and nerve-wracking. "We *are* friends, Orliana. But today is *not* a good day."

"Friendships don't exist only on good days."

He opens his mouth, then closes it. I've made a good point, and he knows it. I lift my chin to show that I won't be leaving. We hold the stare for at least thirty seconds before he sighs and walks away, leaving the door open.

Taking it as an invitation, I step inside, closing the door quietly. Instantly, the energy overwhelms my senses. It's ... desolation. It smells clean enough, and there's no trash or clutter. He heads down the short hallway and turns right. I trail behind him, taking stock of the well-tended plants — all of Rhuth's plants. The hallway opens into a large living room with a purple couch, more plants, and photos on the wall.

I pause to study the one above the fireplace. It's a picture of Fynn, but featuring an unfamiliar version. As I suspected, he was more filled out, with longer hair. His expression as he peers down at Rhuth is downright devilish. She's as beautiful as I imagined, with stunning blue scales that remind me of a spring sky. Her light blue hair falls past her shoulders, resting against handmade lace.

Looking to my right, I see Fynn standing in the kitchen, staring at the fridge. Approaching with caution, I quickly take in the space. It's earth tones and homey. No dishes in the sink; not a crumb on the floor. Thinking of the peeling exterior, it's clear where his priorities lie.

"Fynn?" I say his name quietly, not wanting to spook him. Alarm bells ring in my mind when he doesn't move a muscle. My brain screams to *run!*, but I think this is a trigger born of conditioning rather than being an actual danger. He might be motionless, but it's not like Mikan right before he struck. Fynn stands as if moving would be too exhausting.

Coming to stand next to him, I check to see if there's something else he could be staring at. There's nothing. His eyes practically bore a hole into the freezer.

"Is there something in there?" I murmur.

Arms slack at his side, he whispers, "Yes."

“Do you want me to open the door?”

“No.”

"Will you open it?"

"Eventually."

We stand like, listening to the tick of a clock, that until my knees ache. Outside, a child laughs. A hound howls. The shadows grow long.

Surely, he’s in pain too, but he doesn’t move. What could be in there? A severed head? It’s literally the only thing I can think of. What in the Hells else stops a grown male Dragon like this?

When my lower back burns like it’s on fire, I decide to take hold of the situation. He’s clearly too frozen with some emotion I don’t understand. But Trinte thought I could help, and there’s one specific part of me capable of doing just that.

Holding up my hands so he can see, I drag off my gloves, letting them fall onto the floor. The sound of them landing is disproportionately loud against the painful silence.

When he says nothing, does nothing, I lower my hands, grabbing one of his fists. I spread my fingers in invitation. For a moment, I think he’s going to refuse, but then his fingers unfurl, allowing our fingers to intertwine. To my surprise, his fingers curl between mine.

I close my eyes and lower my shield.

It’s ... unspeakable.

28

Fynn

"Sir, there's been an accident. Your wife was killed. She's ... dead."

Trinte catches me as my knees buckle. He takes the phone from me.

"Hello?" He sounds so confused. As the man speaks, his arms tighten around me. He lets out a choked sob. "What do you mean she's dead? What happened? Where is she?"

Everything inside me is dying. I swear the blood in my veins turns to ash. From everywhere and nowhere, I can sense my reality shifting. Cracking. Shattering. Everything I was thirty seconds ago is gone.

This isn't real.

My fingers dig into the grass, claws coming out to dig into the soft earth. My lungs scream — I haven't taken a breath yet. I can't. I can't take another breath in this realm without my wife. I refuse. I bite my lips closed, digging my teeth into the flesh. My fangs pierce the skin; blood fills my mouth.

And yet, I refuse to breathe.

My son. Titus. My beautiful son is dead. So small and innocent, yet to take a breath. For him, I still won't breathe. For both of them, I refuse oxygen.

Someone's pounding on my chest. I squeeze my eyes shut. No. *I don't care. She's gone. He's gone. My whole fucking goddess-damned life is over.*

"Breathe!" Trinte screams, shaking me.

I shake my head as the world narrows to pinpoints. Roaring in my ears deafens my thoughts. Something is shredding my ribs, cracking them into shards that slice into my heart.

"Fucking breathe, Fynn," he pleads. "Don't leave me here alone."

My elbows buckle. I curl into a ball, clamping my lips down harder. My brother shakes me, then screams to all those people waiting inside. An impromptu funeral. What would've been a wonderful moment will become a collective moment of devastation.

And still, I refuse to use my lungs ever again.

My tail curls into my body as I hug my arms close to my chest. Turning into a ball. Making myself small.

She's gone.

When the world goes dark, I pray to Fortuna that I never wake up.

***

The next couple of weeks might as well have not existed. Trinte took care of everything, from the funeral arrangements to filing necessary paperwork. He let me lie in bed and stare at the ceiling. Each night, he slept next to me, saying nothing. In hindsight, he was probably worried I'd kill myself. Honestly, I probably would've. It was a repeating thought in my head every single second of every single day.

Because it's my fault.

The pregnancy had a few complications, so the midwife had recommended that she avoid shifting. This meant Rhuth needed to use

Dragxis. On that day, I was supposed to schedule one, but forgot, so lost in my determination to find that ice cream.

I normally assigned the most experienced fliers, but because I didn't call, the operator didn't know any better. They sent a rookie.

He deviated from the path, causing a mid-air collision.

Not having a body to mourn made it worse.

If I hadn't been so focused on fucking ice cream, she'd still be alive. My son would be here, almost five years old, running around with a tiny tail dragging behind him. Next year, we would've started flight lessons. Maybe Rhuth would have another baby rounding her belly, begging for nightly foot massages.

Instead, I live in this mausoleum. A desiccated soul walking around until it's time to die.

But first, it's time to eat the ice cream.

Inside this freezer is the last pint of ice cream; the fifth from the day she died. Every anniversary of her death, I make myself eat the entire disgusting pint. The first time, five years ago, was a horrific choice on my part. Since then, it feels required to do this to myself. It's both a ritual and a punishment. That first pint was self-flagellation, consuming each bite with unfettered sobs in the dark. Each year, there are fewer tears, but perhaps because I drown myself in other ways.

All of that doesn't change that this is the last one.

What will I do next year?

I don't know — which is why I can't bring myself to open this freezer. Once it's gone, a piece of her is gone. *Another* piece. One day, I'll have to put that sweater away; that hairbrush. Eventually, every single plant will die.

And in the end, it'll be like she never existed.

Starting with this pint of ice cream.

When Orliana shows up at the door, demanding to be let inside, it's definitely not something I want her to witness. Only Trinte knows how bad this day gets for me, so if he sent her here, it's either to make a point or because he thinks she can help.

Probably both.

But I can't even speak of what I let happen. The words are impossible. So when Orliana shows the gloves coming off, I know what's coming next. Sure, she'd stop if asked, but I don't want to ask. I just need someone else to understand, to feel what it means to have a vortex of yawning despair in my chest all the time.

I squeeze her fingers like they're a lifeline to the last dregs of my sanity. There's no way she expected me to shield, so instead, I give it all to her. Every kernel of annihilation.

She says, "Oh," as her fingers tighten until I lose feeling in my own fingers. I don't care, because even in my state, I can't help but pay attention. To make sure it's not too much; that I'm not too much. I can't hurt her too.

We stand there until my entire body aches. She simply continues to siphon, taking whatever I send, storing it into the pendant.

When the early evening light hits the mirror on the wall, I know we've been here for hours. I loosen my grip, but she clings harder. I take in her tear-filled brown eyes, rimmed with long lashes. A tiny freckle rests beneath her left eye. I'd never noticed that before. Her mouth parts, like she wants to say something, but doesn't know what.

When a tear falls, I reach up to catch it with my thumb, leaving my hand on her cheek. It's impossibly soft.

"Thank you for coming," I say, my voice hoarse.

Her other hand comes to hold my wrist. "Thank you for letting me in."

For the first time since we met her, I fully realize how beautiful she is. And it's not only her curved lips, or high cheekbones. It's the way her expression is serene, as if she's simply happy for me to share with her. The pain I thought for sure would rip her apart doesn't affect her the same. To her, it's a gift. To her, my pain is beautiful.

I don't know how to feel about that.

Her smooth voice asks, "Do you want to tell me what's in there?"

Losing myself in those dark caramel eyes was a beautiful respite, but I can't continue procrastinating. It'd almost be worse to not eat it at all.

"It's ice cream."

Her eyes flare in surprise. "Ice cream?"

"Chocolate mint and pistachio, in fact." Her nose scrunches. My mouth twitches at her attempt to hide her disgust. "Go on; you can say it."

The disgust disappears, replaced with a false innocence. "Say what?"

"It's a horrendous flavor," I said flatly.

She huffs out a laugh. "I mean, I wasn't going to say it, but ..."

"It was Rhuth's favorite." Her mouth snaps shut, and the grip of her hand around my wrist tightens. I lower the hand from her face and turn to face the freezer again. "The day she died, I bought her five pints. It was her favorite, and I wanted to make sure there was enough. So each anniversary of her death, I've eaten a pint."

"And this is the last one?"

"This is the last one," I confirm. "So, you can see my dilemma."

"Definitely. Although I'm glad it's ice cream."

"You're glad?"

She grins. "I thought maybe it was a head."

Despite everything, I laugh. Somehow, this woman has made me laugh on one of the darkest days of my life. "A *head?* Do you take me for a serial killer?"

"No, but what else could have a male Dragon refusing to open the door? It was a logical assumption."

"Instead of ice cream?"

I love the way she smiles as she says, "Well, if I had known it was chocolate mint and pistachio, I actually would've assumed that first."

"Over a severed head?"

She gives me a mock look of surprise. "Mr. Gleanscale, I can't appear to win with you."

"You always win, Orliana," I say softly.

Her smile fades; she squeezes my hand, where our fingers are still intertwined. "Do you want company for the ice cream?"

"You'd eat this abomination of a flavor?"

She gives a sharp nod. "It's what a friend would do. We'll go into battle together."

"I don't think the pistachios fight back."

"Better safe than sorry."

Breaking our stare, I study the freezer — an inanimate object guarding the most precious cargo in the world.

It's time.

Still holding onto Orliana's hand, I open the freezer.

The container sits in the far corner, crusted with ice. I pull it out, ignoring the biting cold on my fingers. Placing it on the counter, I close the freezer door; open the drawer, and pull out two spoons. Grabbing the three items with one hand, I lead Orliana to the living room. We sit when we reach the couch, still holding hands.

Without saying a word, I hold out the pint, and she uses her free hand to pull back the lid. If it weren't such a serious moment, I'd laugh. This morning, I assumed I'd be eating this pint alone, but she's here peeling back the seal. In more ways than one.

With the dark green frozen cream revealed, a sliver of pistachio sits on top. She eyes it, then plucks it off. When she locks eyes with me, her intent is immediately clear. Bewildered, I open my mouth, and she tosses it inside. My jaw snaps shut to chew. A smile tugs at the corner of her mouth when she sees my grimace.

Orliana looks down at our hands. "It might be difficult to properly dig into the ice cream with only one hand each." She takes in my expression as she says, "Do you want me to let go?"

My answer is immediate. "No."

"Okay," she says slowly. Pointing at the back of my neck, she says, "I could continue holding here? You can share whatever emotions you're having, but have both hands free."

I frown, not sure how I feel about her hand on my neck. It'll just be another body part that Rhuth won't be the last to touch. Hands are one thing — everything else is another.

Orliana must see the hesitation, because she says quickly, "It's okay if you don't. I'm just offering a solution that doesn't involve accidentally getting ice cream on this really nice couch."

She has an annoyingly excellent point. Rhuth adored this couch. Eventually, someone is going to touch my neck. It's better if it's Orliana.

"Okay."

When she lets go of my hand, I grab the ice cream. As I dig a spoon into the crusted top layer, her fingers rest on my neck, sliding across my skin to find a good spot. Everything inside me freezes as I close my eyes. Her nails graze the bottom of my scalp; it feels so damn *good.*

"Is that okay?" she whispers.

It's difficult to rasp out, "Yeah. It's just been a long time since someone touched me like this."

Her voice is barely a whisper. "Do you want me to do it again?"

Do I? I'm frozen by indecision. It's Rhuth's fifth death anniversary — am I really sitting on our couch, letting a woman touch me, even if it's an offer of comfort?

But I think Rhuth would want me to be happy. Trinte isn't wrong — it's been five years. Not everything has to be a betrayal.

With a mix of relief and dread, I say, "Yes."

I squeeze my eyes shut as her nails trail across my skin in a delectable rhythm. It's hypnotic, and for a moment, I forget what I'm doing. For the last five years, Trinte's the only person who's touched me. And it's not like he's renowned for his affection. Rough hugs and backslaps only go so far.

It's the first real physical affection I've received since Rhuth's death.

With shaking hands, I press the spoon into the ice cream. The first scoop curls into itself easily. I hold the bite up, examining it. Orliana watches me intently.

With a morose twist of my lips, I raise the spoon toward the picture of my wife. "For you, my love."

Then I take the first bite of five-year-old ice cream.

It tastes like goodbye.

29

Orliana

Watching Fynn take the first bite of ice cream softens something inside me. The way his eyes close and his mouth seals around the spoon, savoring it ... it makes me wish for a camera. To capture this important moment for him.

He grimaces, and I laugh. It is a truly terrible flavor. His eyes open, and he scoops up another bite. To my surprise, the spoon steers in my direction.

"I can't eat this, Fynn," I say, trailing my fingers over his nape where it meets his hair. It's enough contact for me to siphon, and it appears to relax him.

Fynn looks so serious. "I would be honored if you shared this repugnant dessert."

I laugh. "Okay, if you insist." I open my mouth, and he slides the spoon in. *Ugh.* The marriage of chocolate mint and chunks of pistachio is a freak of nature. Plus, the freezer burn really adds to the complexity of the grossness. I swallow it though, focusing on the gratitude I feel for him sharing at all.

"Two down, a couple dozen to go," he announces, taking another bite.

By the time we're halfway through the pint, we're resting against the couch pillows and he's leaning toward me. I don't think he even realizes he's doing it. His hair is soft between my fingers, and the scales on the back of his neck are smooth. Are the rest of his scales as smooth? When I pressed my hands to his face the other day, they felt slightly more rough than my skin.

I can feel the peace it gives him, so I happily continue running my nails over his nape, reveling in what he's sharing.

It's at this moment I solidify my decision to become a Siphon therapist. Not just from the subtle high I receive from using my ability, but because right now, in his time of need, I'm able to support Fynn in a way few others can. After today, he'll feel a little lighter than before.

It makes me so excited for him.

After he offers me the next spoonful, I ask, "Can you tell me about her?"

Unlike the times prior, he doesn't appear sad as he shares. "Well, we met when I was twenty-five and she was twenty-four. At a bakery, of all places. I had bought the last chocolate chip cookie and heard this sweet voice ask if there were any left."

I smile, knowing exactly how Fynn would've reacted.

He returns my smile, looking sheepish. "Yeah, I definitely offered half of my cookie to the beautiful woman. We sat outside, eating our portions, and she just began to talk. Oh, Rhuth could talk. I've never been one for lots of words, but Rhuth acted like she invented the spoken word."

I laugh, gazing at the photo above the mantle. He follows my gaze, growing misty-eyed as he says, "I knew from that first bite she was for me. It took me four years to work up the courage to ask her to marry me. By then, we were living together in this home. Yet, I never thought someone as wonderful as her would wish to be shackled to someone like me."

I scan at his profile. The way his nose has a slight bump in it; the scale on the edge of his jaw that's slightly darker than another; the way his Adam's apple bobs as he swallows thickly.

"I asked her in here, actually." He glances at the window overlooking empty skies, then points to a large Monstera fern. "Right there. I filled the whole room with candles, so when she got home, she was greeted with a proposal."

I try to visualize candles everywhere. "That sounds beautiful."

Tears shimmer in his eyes. "It really was. Of course, she said yes. We married a year later." He looks back at the photo. "The day was perfect. We eloped, bringing only the officiant and our photographer."

His voice cracks. He rests the pint of ice cream on his lap. "She died because of me, you know."

My hand freezes. "What?"

He nods, lower lip trembling. "I forgot to call an experienced Dragxi to pick her up because of this." He lifts the pint halfheartedly, as if it weighs too much. "They never found her body. Sometimes, I have nightmares where I'm in the sky, watching her screaming, plummeting to the ground thousands of feet below us."

"Oh, Fynn." I scoot closer, resting my fingers to hold his neck more tight. "That's horrific."

His chest shakes with emotion. "She was pregnant, Orliana."

The words are a physical blow. I bring a hand to my stomach as it cramps from his anguish. I can barely breathe. "What?"

Fynn's hands fly to his face as he lets out a sob. I quickly let go of his neck to catch the pint of ice cream and spoon before they tumbled out of his lap. Placing them on the coffee table, I watch him unravel.

Pregnant? She was *pregnant?* He's never once mentioned this fact. Without thinking, I wrap my arms around him. His shoulders are so broad, my fingertips barely brush, but I try my best to hug him. He cries in a way I've never heard a man cry. All I can do is sit with him inside the grief.

It's not the time to siphon them; it's the time for him to process. Because even though he's made grief a home in his heart, that doesn't mean he's processed a single thing. In fact, I'm willing to bet this is the most he's spoken about her since the day she died.

When it feels right, I run my hand over the tight muscles of his shoulders, trying to soothe him. I can sense it gives comfort, so I don't stop. It takes him a long while to work through the anguish. I'm patient, confident that Trinte either still has Joulian or has called Mom. Glancing outside, I can tell I've been here for at least seven hours. My body, mind, and spirit feel every minute of it.

But the man in my arms needs it, so I ignore my growling belly and the headache beginning to form. The ice cream resembles a soupy, chunky mess. I grimace, not sure how he'll react when he discovers that.

The sun's sinking past the horizon by the time his sobs shift into quiet sniffling. He finally opens his eyes, looking haunted. "Can you take it?"

I nod. "How much?"

"All of it."

I hold his stare, not sure I've heard him right. "*All* of it?"

Fynn looks unsure now. "Is that bad?"

"No ..." I hedge, loosening my hold around his body so I can sit back. He appears earnest in the request. "But Fynn, and I mean this as kindly as possible, but your grief means a lot to you."

"So it would disappear forever?" This seems to alarm him.

"Well, no," I say quickly. "It's not like I can permanently remove the ability to feel something. As long as you grieve, you'll experience grief. But I don't know how long it'll take for it to return to that level. If you're truly ready to move on, you'll most likely feel it on days like today, or in random moments, but it won't be ..."

I trail off. He finished the sentence for me. "It won't be this bad anymore?"

"Right."

Fynn contemplates the option, staring at the melted ice cream. Darkness lengthens the surrounding shadows, casting him in an eerie light. A very faint glow emanates from his chest, where his Fyre resides. Not nearly as bright as it was the other night. I ache to touch it again, to bring it back to life.

"Is it cheating?" A muscle feathers in his jaw; he can't seem to look at me.

I splay my palms and shrug. "I can't answer that for you, but I siphon my emotions away all the time."

He glances sharply at me. "So you never feel anger or sadness?"

I chuckle. "Of course; all the time, actually. Personally, I believe that the mind can become addicted to an emotion, uncomfortable with anything unfamiliar. Even if grief is painful, it's the brain's new comfort zone. Our brain's job is to stay safe; to stay with what's familiar. Sometimes, giving your brain space from an emotion helps you gain perspective."

I grab my pendant, rubbing my thumb over the pointed bottom. "You've sat with this for years. Sometimes, we need a little help to move forward." I cock my head, contemplating. "Think of grief as a pile of boulders you're dragging behind you. I'm just helping you take some boulders out, and you'll be there too."

Fynn audibly swallows. "It would be nice to feel less ... suffocated."

"I know what you mean," I say wryly. "Trust me on that."

He focuses on spinning the silver wedding band still gleaming on his finger. My instincts desperately want to help him. Not for any reason other than a yearning to help heal others. Fynn deserves to be happy. If I can facilitate that, it would be unethical to turn down the opportunity.

Decision made, Fynn looks at me through his lashes, expression unguarded. "Take half?"

"Half of grief removal; coming right up," I joke, pressing his shoulder until he turns to face me. He adjusts until we're both sitting on our heels with our knees touching. Even on this level, he's so damn big. What do they feed these male Dragons in the cradle?

Bringing my hands to his face, I spread my fingers. His lips part as he peers down at me, so full of vulnerability.

"You ready?" I whisper.

He nods.

I close my eyes and plunge into his grief, taking stock of the breadth. At first, it feels endless, like the universe stretching forever into the

Ether. Using my somapathic connection, I find the edges eventually and surround it entirely. Then, I take a mental knife and begin gently severing it in half.

I've never done anything like this before, but my Siphon instincts are at the helm now. While it's easier to siphon into the pendant with my hands, I keep them firmly on his face, mentally connecting to the pendant resting against my chest.

I encourage the grief to leave. It fights at first, too comfortable inside his hardened heart. Grief is often a living thing, full of threats and lamentations. It roots deeply, sinking as far as possible so it's difficult to dig up.

But I'm more stubborn; when it resists, I grow bigger. I hear Fynn gasp and slump forward, but I maintain contact as I mentally yank.

It's reluctant as it slinks out of him into me. As it passes through my body to the pendant, I get a taste of it. Tears fall down my cheeks as I marvel once again at how much he loves her. Now, he'll be able to continue loving her, but without so much grief piling on.

When it's done, I release his face with a groan, hit with a wave of exhaustion. Both of us lean against the couch, breathing hard and crying. Fynn's expression is solemn.

"You're incredible," he murmurs, reaching up to tuck a tendril of hair behind my ear.

I smile faintly. "Just doing my job."

Fynn raises an eyebrow, but he's so drained, it's a half effort. "This is a job for you?"

"No," I chuckle. "I'm just uncomfortable with the compliment."

This lifts the edge of his mouth. "I like how honest you are."

"I spent years lying," I admit. "I try really hard not to lie about important things now."

The clock continues to tick as he appraises me. Adjusting so his head is resting against a pillow, he asks, "Because of Mikan?"

"Because of Mikan," I confirm with too much sadness in my tone.

Fynn's eyes search mine rapidly before he murmurs, "What happened?"

He's been so vulnerable with me; it's only fair that I do the same. Nauseous, I start the terrible story.

"I hid what he did for years. Kyri had no idea. Mom was clueless. Let's just say I was very good at using makeup and wearing layers." I pause, contemplating what my family thought of Mikan. "Neither of them liked him, but Mikan was the type to charm the skirts off a celibate priestess. He spent years convincing people that I was the problem."

Fynn's face twists with disgust. "I hate men like that."

I huff out a bitter laugh. "Yes, well, by the time I realized he was like that, he had me trapped. At first, when he started to hit me, I thought it was an accident. He'd apologize and buy me things. He'd go weeks, months, without another incident."

My eyes close, struggling to make eye contact. "When he got me pregnant, I thought my life was ending. In a way, it did." A thumb rubs away a tear on my cheek. "He used Joulian as a pawn. He was a lawyer, you see. The first time I tried to leave, he convinced the sheriff that I was having a Siphon-related breakdown."

Fynn's expression is thunderous, but he says nothing. "I tried a couple more times, but each time, it failed. All it resulted in was more beatings. Then it got worse."

At this, I choke on a sob. Shame shackles my ability to share more. "I'm sorry; I'm not trying to make this day about me. We don't have to talk about this."

"I want to hear it, Orliana," His hand rests on my cheek, a warm balm to my tears. "You've been nothing but patient with my grief; please don't rob me of doing the same."

Struggling to speak. I bring a hand to his wrist, clinging onto him like a life raft. Not even my family knows knows what Mikan did, but this feels like a moment where unburdening myself from the truth is okay.

"When Joulian was about five, he began to ..." I choke out a sob. "He ... he would force me every night. No matter what. Even if I was sick or tired. He wanted me pregnant again, I think. Another way to control me."

The palm on my face burns hot, almost too hot. I can feel pure, unadulterated fury coursing through his body. Fynn looks ready to strike at the ghost of my husband. This is the first time I can see the deadly reptilian side of him. The way his pupils contract raises the hairs on the back of my neck.

"And you're sure he's dead?"

I nod. "Positive."

Fynn's velvet voice is full of violence. "Exactly *how* positive?"

And this is it. The moment I should tell him what I did. At this point, I don't think he'd judge me. Considering the way he's reacting, he might even celebrate my choice to slice my husband's throat.

But what if he isn't? So many people told me there were other options other than murder. No one understood that there were no options left. Sometimes, it's easier to look in from the outside of a situation and assume you'd know exactly what to do. But when you're in it and the fists never stop coming, it's hard to find a better way out.

Fynn has given me everything today. It would be cruel and disrespectful to not do the same.

"I killed him."

Instead of being disgusted, Fynn looks genuinely intrigued. "How?"

"I took a butcher knife to his throat."

Fynn's face is in half-shadow, but even so, I see his eyes flash with something like pride. "Good."

Good. Every inch of tension inside me disappears like vapor in the wind. "You ... don't care?"

Fynn runs a hand down my cheek to my jaw, then to my neck. It's the most physical affection I've received since the years Mikan was grooming me. Yet, this touch feels ... freeing. It isn't exploratory or invasive — it's intended to be a comfort.

Continuing to rest the hand where my neck meets my shoulder, he says, "I care that you had to do that. I care a whole fucking lot about what he did to you. I care that people have clearly made you think what you did was a terrible thing."

His fingers squeeze gently as his thumb presses against my pulse. "If he were still alive, I would have introduced him to the wrath of Dragons." Fynn leans in close. Our faces are so close, I can smell chocolate mint on his breath. "And our wrath is dictated by strict laws for very specific reasons."

"Oh."

Fynn leans back, smirking. I try not to frown when his hand leaves my neck. "Yes, *oh.*"

We hold our stare for at least a minute, as if allowing everything that's passed between us to absorb into our bones; our souls.

This isn't at all what I expected. Not when I met him at the career fair all those weeks ago, and certainly not when I woke up today.

Using the last of my bravery, I say, "I'm really glad we met, Fynn."

The room is almost completely dark now, so I can't really see his expression, but in the silent home, I hear him whisper, "Me, too, Orliana. Me, too."

30

Fynn

Even in the dark, my sight is good enough to see Orliana's every expression. The way her mouth pinches with shame. How her brow creases in worry when she admits what she's done. When doubt flickers in her eyes, assuming I'd judge her, I can't help but touch her. It's not a want; it's a need.

We're so deep in it together right now, I don't think she realizes she's sharing her emotions with me. As she tells me about that piece of shit hurting her, I experience every ounce of pain. It's different from mine; it's full of fear, loathing, and dread. Emotions she shouldn't have experienced, let alone carry through her days.

When she told me she cut his throat, what I truly wanted to say was, *you should've done more.* Not quite appropriate, but I can already think of a dozen ways I could've drawn it out for days. Weeks. I'd do it without an ounce of guilt or even breaking a sweat.

Dragons are many things, but if a Dragon is discovered to be harming their mate, exile is immediate. In certain circumstances, the entire Weyr exacts revenge. Said revenge always results in dismemberment and death.

Mikan is more lucky than he'll ever know.

If she feels half of the exhaustion weighing on my body right now, she's probably struggling. Assessing her state, I hear her stomach growl. A small, fleeting grimace confirms she's hungry.

Sitting up, wincing at the crick in my back, I say, "I think, if it's okay with you, that we should give this a break. Maybe eat something?"

Orliana nods, a shy smile spreading across her full lips. "I'm famished. No offense, but that ice cream wasn't filling."

I study the melted ice cream. To my surprise, I don't feel bad about it being ruined. Orliana taught me that my grief isn't directly tied to my love of Rhuth — one can exist without the other. And if I *really* want, I can always go visit Virinia to find another pint. I could make it a daily reminder if I wanted.

I *definitely* don't, but it's nice to have options.

It takes effort, but I'm able to stand, then help Orliana stand. As I lead her to the kitchen, it strikes me that we're touching one another without hesitation now.

I'm unsure of what it means, but I do know it doesn't bother me. Quite the opposite, actually.

While I pull out the few snacks I have in my cupboard — I really need to start buying actual food — Orliana sits at the table and goes through her phone. I look over when she laughs.

I squint, taking in the photo she's showing on her phone. "Is that ... Trinte? With your mother?"

She laughs again. "Apparently, the three of them went to dinner?" Shaking her head in disbelief, she says, "Your brother is so incredibly odd."

I huff out a chuckle as I pull out some bowls. "He truly is. I don't know what I'd do without him, though."

She watches as I approach with full arms. "He loves you very much."

"It's mutual, unfortunately," I joke, sitting across from her. Opening a bag of chips, I pour some into one bowl. "Sometimes, it's more like he's the older brother."

"I wish I had a sibling," Orliana says glumly, biting into a chip.

"Your parents never tried for more?"

She waves dismissively. "Absolutely not. It's a miracle I was conceived, considering how much they dislike one another. He wasn't a present father."

"Was he a Siphon, too?"

She nods. "He wasn't a good husband or father. He left us to go live in Telume when I was five. Never heard from again."

I frown. "I'm so sorry. That's awful."

She shrugs, genuinely looking like she doesn't care. "It doesn't bother me much anymore. Perks of getting older, I guess."

Still. It makes me wonder if any man has been kind to her. "How old were you when you met Mikan?"

Her expression flattens, and she rolls her eyes. "Twenty-two. He was thirty-four."

Somehow, that fact pisses me off more. "You were so young."

"The better to manipulate, I guess."

We eat in silence, both of us lost in our own thoughts. I'm dying to know what she's thinking, but we've already shared so much. I think for right now, we deserve a tiny break from sharing.

After a few minutes, Orliana sits back with a sigh. "I need to go get Joulian. He's probably wondering where in the Hells his mother is. I've never disappeared this much before."

"Does he know you're with me?"

She nods. "He actually said that if you needed help, I should go to you."

The words warm my heart. "He's a good kid."

"The best," she agrees. We stand at the same time. A blooming ache appears inside my chest, prompting the words, *don't go,* to sit at the tip of my tongue.

As she grabs her purse, she says, "Thank you again for ..." She motions all around us. "Everything, honestly. It was ..." She nibbles on her lower lip, and my eyes can't look away. "... intense," she finishes lamely.

We both laugh, then I say, "Intense is a good word. Come on, I'll walk you out."

It's a quiet walk to the landing pad, and I shoot off a quick text to order her a Dragxi. While we wait, she turns to face me.

"Do you maybe want to finally try that hug?" she asks, sounding unsure. I watch the way her mouth twists as it always does when she's uncertain.

Without hesitating, I wrap my arms around her. We've spent so much time touching today, I'm not sure where my emotions end and hers begin. All I know is that she's soft in my arms, and squeezes me so tight, a grunt escapes up my throat.

She hums with appreciation as my Fyre responds by expanding, demanding attention. Her face glows as she presses a cheek to the heat.

The Dragxi appears too soon. Right before she releases me, Orliana peers up with wide, innocent eyes. I brush a strand of hair stuck on her mouth. How anyone could hurt her is beyond me.

"Are you going to be okay?"

Of course she's thinking about me. I offer a soft smile, murmuring, "I suspect this will be the first time in a long time that I'll be okay."

The answer appears to satisfy her. A grin spreads across her beautiful face. "Okay, good. But text me if you need anything?"

"Deal."

I resist the urge to reach for her again as she pulls away. My whole body feels drunk from her touch. After years of not touching anyone, it's all I can think about now, like the dam has shattered.

Curtis, in his white Dragon form, snorts out smoke in greeting. I wave, smiling. I know he'll keep her safe. As he takes to the skies, I watch a newfound piece of my heart fly away.

***

Fynn: I can't believe you sent her to my house.

Trinte: Well, you weren't going to let me in, and I knew you wouldn't be mean to her.

Fynn: Still. That was dumb.

Trinte: Are you okay? Is she okay? When she came to pick up Joulian, I couldn't tell, and she refused to speak with me.

Fynn: Serves you right.

Trinte: ???

Fynn: Yes, I'm okay. I'm fairly certain she's okay. Do you want to come over tomorrow evening? I'm going to grill.

Trinte: ...

Trinte: Grill? You're grilling again?

Fynn: If you say another word, I'll char your steak.

Trinte: I'll be there.

***

Trinte walks in without knocking. He struts into the kitchen like he owns the place. He's wearing a simple maroon button-up shirt and jeans. I watch him glance at Rhuth's hairbrush. Holding my gaze, he nudges it with a finger. Like a fucking sphinx testing boundaries.

I narrow my eyes. "So you enjoy really well done steaks?"

"Just checking," he says smoothly, walking over to the salad I'm preparing. When he's close enough, I slap his calf with my tail, hard enough to sting. He doesn't even flinch, already anticipating my reaction.

He peers around my shoulder to inspect the lettuce I'm cutting up. "So you're cooking again?"

Closing my eyes, I place the knife down on the cutting board. "Are you going to point out *everything* I'm doing differently?"

"It's literally in the job description of little brother: to annoy the fuck out of my big brother until he changes his behavior."

My fingers tighten around the handle of the knife. Taking in his blazing blue eye, I narrow mine. "I'll stab you."

He scoffs, but steps back. "No one else will put up with your broodiness, brother. Admit it; you need me." I think of Orliana and how much she doesn't care about my broodiness.

Trinte misses nothing — his face homes in on my expression with suspicion. "What is that?"

"Nothing." I said it too quickly, though.

Trinte straightens. "It's her, isn't it?"

"No," I say sharply, refocusing on the salad. "It's nothing. Stop prying."

"I knew it," he mutters, walking over to where dusty bottles of booze sit. Grabbing the old Minga from my wedding day, he pops the cork and takes a swig.

With a burdened sigh, I turn to face him. Placing the knife on the counter to remove temptation, I say, "And *what,* pray tell, did you *know?*"

Trinte won't answer, though. "You should bring her to the Weyr reunion."

"What?" I stare at him in disbelief. "Why would I bring Orliana to the reunion? We aren't together."

His golden orb crackles with bursts of light. "Exactly! It's perfect if you think about it. You're just friends, right?"

"Right ..." I say slowly, crossing my arms.

He motions with his hand for me to keep up. "Right, so if you *pretend* to be together, and you're *not* because you're *just* friends, then it's perfect. Aunt Teale will be satisfied; no one will ask about Rhuth in front of her, *and* you can get out of any Weyr reunions for at least another three years. Perfect amount of time to continue brooding."

With a shake of my head, turn back to the lettuce, placing handfuls into the salad bowl. "That's ridiculous. She'd never leave Joulian that long."

"But what if she would?"

His question pauses my hands. What if she would? Bringing Joulian to the Weyr reunion would be out of the question; it'd make the relationship look too serious, and I'm not comfortable involving Joulian in that deception.

But a few days with Orliana?

My pulse thrums. Yet ...

I shake my head. "No, she won't go for it."

"You mean *you* won't go for it?" he presses.

Grabbing the bowl and dressing, I bring them over to the table. "We're only friends, Trinte. Can you imagine having to spend all that time together? We'd have to share a room, which could be weird since—"

"You're just friends?" he supplies, expression neutral.

I flash him a look of irritation. "Yes. Exactly."

"Friends share hotel rooms all the time," he adds, focusing on shredding a paper towel. "I won't pretend I know Orliana really well, but she doesn't come off as the type of woman who's had a vacation in a while."

Knowing what I do about Mikan, that's probably an understatement. Trinte must see my expression shift to something insidious because he latches onto the change.

"What?"

I shake my head, unwilling to share her story fully. "She shared some things last night, and I honestly don't think she's *ever* had a vacation."

This was the wrong thing to say. Trinte grins with victory. "*Exactly.* Perfect set-up: you're left alone by the meddling aunts hoping to find you a new wife. She gets her first vacation in *Slous,* of all places."

New wife. Thinking about their meddling makes me feel ill. He's not wrong: some of the aunts will interfere harder than Aunt Teale. It would offer a respite, and Orliana would be able to enjoy herself. I'd pay for everything, so it would literally be a stress-free experience.

Going in for the kill, Trinte announces, "If you don't invite her, I will. It might get a little lonely during those walks on the beach."

A growl escapes before I can stop it. Trinte's eyes widen for a second before he hides his surprise. The thought of him being near her pisses me the fuck off. "You will fucking *not* be doing that."

My smug, dunghole of a brother is clearly unbothered. "Then do it first."

We hold each other's stare; in a flurry of movement, we're both snatching up our phones.

Fynn: Hey, I have to go to a Weyr reunion in a couple of weeks. Do you want to go? It's in Slous.

Trinte's fingers pound at his phone. He's grinning like a maniac, clearly enjoying this moment of pressing my buttons.

Orliana: I don't know. For how long? I don't know if I can leave Joulian that long.

Fynn: It's just for three days. Over a weekend. I'll pay for everything.

Orliana: Why is Trinte asking me to go, too?

I look up at my brother, then look down at the salad bowl. I throw it at him. He laughs, bolting out of the kitchen, still texting. Pieces of salad plop from the wall to the floor as I respond.

Fynn: Ignore him. He's trying to piss me off.

Orliana: Why did he text my mom?

I storm into the living room, where Trinte laughs maniacally.

"Stop fucking texting her and stop fucking texting her mom!" I roar, rushing at him to grab his phone.

We circle the couch. He goes one way while I go the other. I leap over the couch's edge then the coffee table, tackling him to the ground. His phone skids across the tile, but he's laughing too hard to care. I slap him in the face, but he won't stop laughing.

"Come on, Fynn," he says through belly laughs. "You're *just* friends, so *prove* it."

Straddling his chest, I glare at his blue face, taking in the mischievous look.

"You're baiting me," I say flatly.

Grinning, he lolls his head from side to side. "No, not at all. I simply don't want to hear you crying through the hotel walls because Aunt Teale decided to bring along her best friend's daughter as a way to entice you back into the real world."

I stare at him, aghast. "She is not."

He grows serious. "Her name is Maureen. She's a really pretty Dragon, to be honest. If you don't want her, I'll—"

I slap his face again. Not hard, but enough that he shuts up. "You're worse than tail rot, you know that, right?"

My phone buzzes from a few feet away. Both of us glance at it, then back at each other.

"Her mom already said yes," he says, grinning with a split lip. "Talia and I are pretty close now."

I shove off his chest and reach over for my phone. "Please don't tell me you're on a first name's basis with the mother of my—"

I stop speaking, unsure of what to call Orliana. *Friend* feels insufficient, but nothing else feels appropriate.

"Friend?" he supplies.

"Friend," I agree, checking my texts.

Orliana: Mom is a go. Where is it, though?

A tiny flutter of excitement makes me smile.

Fynn: A swanky beach resort. Ever been to one?

Orliana: No, but I've always wanted to.

Trinte groans as he stands, brushing off his jeans. "When are the steaks done?"

Without looking, I throw a pillow at him. He grunts when it smacks him in the face.

Fynn: You'll love it. There's one tiny caveat/request though.

Orliana: Oh, *now* you tell me there are strings attached?

Fynn: I know we're just friends, and I respect that. But could you maybe pretend to be my partner, at least when we're around the family? Trinte said my aunt is bringing a woman for me, and nothing sounds worse.

Orliana: So we're going to pretend to be dating?

Fynn: Is that asking too much?

Orliana: Not at all. I'll proudly be the friendly cockblock.

"What did she say?" Trinte says, walking into the kitchen. I hear him picking up the bits of salad.

"She said yes."

"Great," he chirps. "Maybe Maureen will let me take her on a date."

I snort. "It'll be the worst date of her life."

"At least I'm funny. Orliana is stuck with your broody ass."

"For three days," I retort.

"Sure," he says dismissively. "For three days."

Fynn: Alright, Captain Cockblock. I'll send you the details.

Orliana: Looking forward to it.

31

Orliana

Today, Fynn and I are going to try out another hobby. This one is called Canvas and Cocktails, where we drink while painting. I can't claim to have an artistic bone in my body, but it'll be fun to do something new with Fynn.

It's the first time we'll have seen one another since the shared ice cream; I have no idea what to expect. He's invited me to Slous with Trinte, but all of it leaves me overwhelmed. What does he expect? *Does* he expect anything? No, of that I'm confident. He's been nothing but respectful. There's no reason to think Fynn would want anything in return.

After dropping Joulian at my mother's, I meet Fynn outside the bar where the event's happening. He's already there, wearing charcoal slacks and a dark blue shirt. Two buttons unbuttoned. Thank Emet for that. I'd end up painting the floor if it were less buttons.

His grin is brilliant when he spots me. Suddenly, I'm self-conscious about my simple white T-shirt, long green cardigan duster, and jeans. Moxie immediately sprints for him, zooming around in front of his face like an excited bumblebee.

After we exchange hugs, I inspect his outfit. "I feel under-dressed."

"Don't be; you look great."

The words hang between us; our stare lasts a beat too long. He clears his throat and steps back. "Shall we? I'm in the mood for some femire."

"I hope they have champagne," I say, smiling. He opens the door for me, and a jolt of awareness lights up my body when his hand brushes my lower back as I walk in.

A group of people are already situated at easels, drinks in hand. Fynn leads us to a table, checking us in. He'd insisted on paying for this event because it was another one of his ideas. I'm trying not to read into it, though. Just because he's paying doesn't make it a date, right?

"Our spots are over here." Fynn points to two easels in a far corner. "If you go sit, I'll grab the drinks."

"Sounds good." I walk over to the stools in front of blank canvases. Next to them is a small table with paintbrushes and cups of paint. Next to the items is a mini-easel featuring a small painting of a pair of Pegasus grazing in a meadow with a sunset. Painting Pegasus looks intimidating, but I guess that's why we're trying a new hobby.

Moxie lands near the paint, and I cringe. She's going to cause chaos if allowed. Pointing at her, I command, "No diving into paints or water filled with paints."

She snorts and gives me her rear end as she tries to eat the reference painting.

"Good news — they had champagne." Fynn hands me a flute filled to the brim.

I grin, taking a quick sip before saying, "Thank you."

"Of course." He sits, holding a glass of femire as he takes stock of the supplies. When he spots the reference painting, he frowns. "We're expected to paint that?"

I laugh. "My same exact thought."

We exchange amused looks as the instructor guides us through the process. Even though it's intimidating, when it's time to pick up the paintbrush, I promise myself to try. It's important to try.

"Is it just me, or is painting a Pegasus a bit daunting for a first painting?" Fynn asks, eyeing his blank canvas with dread.

I laugh. "Stole the thoughts right out of my head. Figure it's worth trying, right?"

He flashes me a grin. "I vote to see who can make the ugliest one."

My heart beats a little faster at the boyish grin lighting up his handsome features. "I'm not sure I have to try anything; mine is going to be hideous."

He shrugs, picking up a paintbrush. "Only one way to find out."

A newfound sense of competition rears up inside me. "You're on."

Moxie flies to my shoulder to supervise while I try my hand at painting.

Turns out I'm terrible at it. It doesn't help that Moxie found a workaround to my command by dipping her horn into the paint, then smearing it across my canvas. Her version of helping, I suppose.

Can't fault the ugopeg for being smart.

But now there are random smears of paint dragged across the canvas. Well, at least the goal is to make the painting ugly?

When our drinks run out, Fynn is quick to grab more. We've been discussing some funny Dragxi stories, but when he mentions relaxing after fares by playing video games, it makes me curious.

"So you and Trinte originally bonded over video games?"

He nods, adding a yellow swipe of color to the sunset on his painting. "When we were young, my father got us a console to keep us busy. So after school, when all the homework was done, we'd play for hours." He eyes me curiously. "How did you get started?"

"Definitely haven't been playing that long," I admit, cringing at my version of a horse's mane I'm trying to paint. Why do they look like noodles? "After Mikan's death, I couldn't leave the house for months, unless it directly affected Joulian. I couldn't be around people. Kyri bought me the console."

I cringe. "It sounds pathetic, but it was a way to connect with people; to remind myself they aren't all bad. In fact, most are good. Mikan had me afraid for so long ..."

I trail off, not wanting to turn this paint into watercolors from tears. Fynn gives me a sympathetic look. "I understand. It became an escape for me after Rhuth. Easier than sleeping, that's for sure."

Huffing out a laugh, I nod. "Agreed." Giving a shy smile, I say, "What are the odds we even found one another there?"

"Slim, but I'm glad we did."

Our stare holds a beat too long until Moxie lands on his lap. With hot pink hooves. On his pants.

"Moxie!" I hiss, mortified. An old prick of fear rises, terrified of his reaction. "I'm so sorry, I told her not to dive into the paints and she took it very literally."

He laughs. "I'm fairly certain it'll come out in the wash."

The easiness of his response lowers my shoulders. "Thanks for not being mad."

Fynn gives me a sharp look. "I will never be mad over something so easily fixed, Orliana."

I'm starting to believe him.

The next few minutes, we focus on the finishing touches of our paintings. The instructor announces it's time to put our paintbrushes down. I wince, seeing my Pegasi resembling an experiment gone wrong. Their legs are like overcooked noodles. The hot pink tails, with cloven hoof prints in the center, explode from their butts. Blue, terrified eyes fill their too-small heads. Moxie chose red paint for her horn, making the whole scene look like it's bleeding. All in all, it's disturbing.

"Impressive," Fynn lies smoothly, eyeing my hack job.

With a scoff, I look at his painting. Surely he did better.

Fynn did not, in fact, do better.

Where there should be two, he's made them conjoined, with two heads and four legs. Their rudimentary white faces are full of terror. Mouths peel back in silent screams of terror. Moxie has also dragged slivers of red across his canvas. Both of our paintings appear bloodied.

My laugh is so abrupt, so loud, that the woman next to me drops her paintbrush. After giving her an apologetic expression, I say to Fynn, "I think you might win this round."

"You think?" he beams. Lifting it off the easel, he admires the art. "I think Trinte can have this. It'll look perfect in his bachelor pad."

Knowing Trinte, he'd proudly hang it. "Joulian is going to be upset if I hang this on the wall." I'm already perpetually on thin ice by simply existing as his mother — this might make him truly have a meltdown. I'm not interested in *that* argument.

"I'll take it," Fynn offers. "It would look good in my kitchen. Kevin and Louie can keep me company in the morning over coffee."

"Kevin and Louie," I say flatly.

He motions at my two deranged Pegasus. "Yeah; Kevin and Louie."

"Well, now I have no choice but to agree. You *named* them." The smile comes too easily as I shake my head. "Ridiculous."

"Hey," he says, faking outrage as he grabs both paintings. "Madge and Freckles are insulted."

The sensation of lightness fills my skin like helium; it feels good to talk to him. "Madge, Freckles, Kevin, and Louie?"

Pursing his lips, Fynn raises a sassy eyebrow. "Did you truly expect them to have coffee every morning without names? Orliana, that's *rude.*"

I laugh, leading the way out of the studio. "My deepest apologies to the equine abominations."

"I had no idea you were so callous," he snarks, but there's a grin in his tone.

Opening the door for both of us, I shoot back, "What's a little honesty among friends?"

Fynn steps out, spinning to walk backward. Raising the paintings to his ear, he pretends to speak with them. "What's that? You aren't friends? Sure, I'll relay the message." With a flat expression, he says, "They want me to tell you that they are not your friends because you used the 'a' word."

"Abomination?"

"Shh!" Fynn steps closer, bringing a finger to his lips. In a theatrically loud whisper, he says, "Orliana, for a Siphon, you're *very* insensitive."

Lifting my chin, I grin. "Some might say the opposite. Their opinion is suspect."

He dips his head, grinning from ear to ear. In a low voice, he says, "Everyone knows unicorns are never wrong."

My voice lowers. "No one knows that. You made it up."

"Maybe ..."

His words stall because I think we've realized at the same time how close we are. His mouth is mere inches from mine. Heat warms my cheeks as my heart gallops. My lungs take shallow sips of air, afraid to exhale.

"Maybe what?" I murmur, resisting the urge to shift a little. Enough to cross a line or two.

Gold eyes scan my features, expression devoid of any clues.

His voice is like coffee grounds and syrup as he rasps out, "Maybe I did just make it up. So what are you going to do about it?"

What am I going to do about it? Fantastic question; one without an answer.

No, that's incorrect.

My answer is: I'm not initiating anything with him. So instead of moving, I focus on not sounding breathless as I say, "Nothing. Everyone knows it's bad luck to argue with unicorns."

Fynn's mouth twitches. "No one knows that. You just made it up. Also, they're Pegasi"

"True." I cock my head; only about an inch, but it's enough to flare his nostrils. I see it; the moment this trance breaks. His mouth purses, and a deep valley gouges his brow as he steps back.

Clearing his throat, he says, "I'll send a photo when Kevin and Louie have their new slice of heaven on the wall."

Feeling more than a little foolish, I force a smile. "Yes, please. Do I get shared custody?"

Fynn pauses, significantly less light-hearted than a minute ago. Just as I think he's going to leave, he smiles. "Shared custody it is." Holding up the paintings, he says, "I should get these home. Since we leave in a few days, I also need to start packing."

Right. That's this weekend. "Me, too. Kyri insists on certain outfits." Ones undoubtedly to be both stunning and uncomfortable.

"Trinte is dressing me like a doll," he says dryly. "Claims I owe him." Fynn pauses, a muscle feathering under his red scaled jaw. "Should we hug?"

My arms are around his waist before he finishes the sentence. He's warm against my body. The paintings knock into one another as he folds arms around me.

"Thanks for joining me," he whispers.

"Thanks for inviting me," I say into his shirt.

Tonight feels different. Even he hesitates as he opens his arms, stepping back. "Have a good night. Text me when you're home?"

"Sure." Smiling, I turn and walk away, feeling him watching. It's a hot spotlight, prickling my skin. Right now, I have no idea what to expect from Slous, but something tells me it's going to be interesting.

32

Orliana

"Why would you want to go to a place full of *water?*" Kyri gripes, sprawling out on my bed while I pick through my closet.

I'm struggling to figure out what to pack. Kyri showed up with bags of clothes, including swimsuits that would be better suited to flossing than covering anything up.

But Fynn said there would be a nice event, almost like a gala, and games on the beach. I want to make sure I'm prepared for everything.

"It's probably not going to be that great," I admit. "I'm there to make sure he isn't bothered by his family. Apparently, they're really pushing for him to move on from Rhuth."

Kyri sits up on her elbows, watching me hold up two swimsuit cover-ups. "I like the black one. And what do you mean, pushing him?"

I place the black one on the pile and re-hang the other one. "I mean, it's been five years, and they think that's plenty of time for him to move on."

"And you don't think so?"

I glance at her over my shoulder with irritation. "I think it's inappropriate to tell anyone their feelings have a timer."

“Do you feel the same way about Mikan?”

I whirl on her, shocked. “Excuse me?”

She flippantly waves in my direction. “I mean, it’s been three years. And don’t even try to convince me Mikan was good in bed. I once had the displeasure of watching him lick an ice cream. That man had zero skill.”

“Skill for what?” I deadpan, knowing exactly what she’s alluding to.

“Exactly,” she says, sighing. “Did he ever even try?”

I let out a bitter laugh, turning back to the outfit options. Pulling out a rather modest dress, I hold it up. She shakes her head. I place it back. “Once. It felt ... weird. So I never let him do it again.”

“It’s definitely not supposed to be weird,” she says, sounding disgusted. “Have you ever had an orgasm with a partner, Orliana?”

“Sure,” I say, although I’m not actually sure.

“Orliana,” she says in a chiding tone.

Grabbing a couple of tank tops, I toss them into the suitcase. “What? Why does it matter?”

She sits up fully. *“Orliana,”* she hisses. “Please tell me you at least get *yourself* off.”

“I’ve been busy,” I say lamely, trying on a pair of shorts. They’re a little tight, but I don’t have time to buy another pair. I toss them onto the pile.

“Y-you don’t have *time?* To *orgasm?*” My fiery friend’s clearly outraged. “That’s the most absurd thing I’ve ever heard. How have we been best friends for almost twenty years and you’ve *never* orgasmed?”

“Because I never let you go down on me?” I supply, amused at her reaction. “I really don’t understand what the big deal is. I’ve survived thirty-five years without good sex. I can survive another thirty-five. I have no desire to find another partner, only to discover he also lacks ‘skill.’”

She’s quiet as I pull out a handful of underwear. All of them are unflattering, but practical. It’s not like anyone will see them. I swear she hisses as I tuck them into a pocket of the suitcase. Kyri has always embraced her sexuality, when I’ve spent my entire adulthood avoiding mine.

"You know, maybe Fynn will be into helping you out."

I offer my best glare. "We're just friends, Kyri."

"Sure," she hedges. "Which is why it could be a good idea. Friends helping friends." She blinks innocently as I narrow my eyes.

"Friends don't have sex."

She shrugs. "Some do."

Placing a hand on my hip, I raise an eyebrow. "Is that so? Are you saying you'd like to take our relationship to a new level?"

To my shock, she says, "If you asked, I would. I don't see what the big deal is. You're my friend, and it would make you feel good."

"Kyri!" I shriek. Picking up a pillow from the ground, I toss it at her. She catches it, grinning.

"What? I'm serious. I'd do it for you."

"Well," I say primly, fed up with the direction of this conversation. "We are not having sex, and that's final."

"But maybe you and that big red Dragon?" she says hopefully.

"He's married," I remind her.

"She's dead," Kyri says dryly. "The man has needs."

Standing, I walk over to my shoes. "I know nothing about Fynn's, *a-hem*, needs."

"I assure you, he has needs. Their Fyre and cock are tied together, emotionally." She lays back on the bed and adds dreamily, "It's why Dragons are so good in bed."

"Stop talking." I do not need to be thinking about Fynn's dick.

Kyri ignores me. "I think it's because they're territorial and serial monogamists. It's like once they set their sights on a female, it's all they can focus on. They take it *very* seriously."

"And I'm *very seriously* considering kicking you out," I snarl. "Stop talking about him like that."

She watches me pace around the room, grabbing items. I'm not even focused on what's in my hands anymore — this conversation is too distracting.

"But don't you want to know how he can control the thickness, so you get the perfect—"

I jab a finger at her. "You shut up right now. If you complete that sentence, I'll—"

"Fit?"

I march to the door. "Out. Now."

It's a surprise when she obeys, but I should know better. She slinks by me, positively mischievous. "Fine, but I'll be back in a couple of hours."

I gaze into her ember eyes, fuming. I love her, but sometimes she drives me crazy. "Why? I'm kicking you out."

"Because there's no way in all twelve Hells I'm allowing you to go on vacation with panties the size of a Pegasus' ass."

"No one will see them," I insist.

She gives me a long look. "Sure. You're sharing a room with a *very* handsome man, and there's *no possible way* he might accidentally see your panties."

"Good," I cross my arms, giving the direction of my front door a pointed look. "I'm glad we're finally on the same page."

She gives my cheek a kiss. "Be right back."

***

As promised, she returns a couple of hours later with new clothes, including panties. She's wrong — Fynn isn't interested in me that way — but I pack the new underwear, regardless.

Just in case they fall out of my suitcase or something.

Joulian comes home from school shortly after, bursting with energy. Greg squawks and Moxie gallops around the kitchen while Joulian dumps his backpack on the table.

"Mom! I have a project due next week. I'll need help this weekend!" He starts digging into his bag, pulling out the assignment sheet.

I scan the instructions. "You're going to have to have Gammy help you, bubs. I'm going out of town, remember?"

"Oh. Yeah." He deflates, spiking my anxiety.

"What's wrong?"

"Nothing," he says glumly. As he sits in a chair, he says, "I'm going to miss you, Mom."

My poor mother's heart warms at the words. With this newfound teenage attitude, I never know what to expect from him.

"I'm going to miss you too." I sit across from him. "Are you sure you're okay with me going?"

He nods his head furiously, grabbing a muffin from the pile I prepared for a post-school snack. "Duh. I said that it's fine."

"Yes, but how do you *feel* about it?" I push.

As he chews, Joulian considers my question. "I think you've been lonely for a really long time and deserve to be happy."

I cock my head. "You think I'm lonely?"

"Aren't you?" he says, looking confused. "Isn't it normal for adults to have partners? Since Dad, you haven't been out on a single date, not since Mr. Fynn."

"He's a friend," I repeat robotically, getting tired of everyone alluding to there being more.

Joulian's face twists in confusion. "But you go on dates. You helped him when he was sad."

"How did you know he was sad?" I ask, surprised.

"Mr. Trinte said to Gammy that Mr. Fynn was sad because of his wife."

"He was," I agree. "And friends help each other during difficult moments."

"It would be okay if you dated him, though, Mom." My son looks so concerned for me. It makes my heart squeeze painfully. I reach for his hands. They're cold and clammy. Doing a quick scan of his emotions, I'm alarmed to discover something deeper.

"Jouls, why are you anxious?" His gaze drops as he takes a bite of his muffin. My own anxiety spikes. "Joulian?"

When he looks at me, it's like he's aged ten years. "I know what you did."

There's a roaring in my ears, met with blood pounding in my veins. "What I did?"

"To Dad."

I yank my hands away from his, unwilling to inadvertently my share emotions. "What did I do to Dad?"

"You killed him."

Both Greg and Moxie stop in their frolicking to watch us curiously from the floor. Moxie flies to the table, sitting in front of me. I pet her absentmindedly, trying to soothe the panic raising my blood pressure.

"Who told you that?"

"Gimer showed me the newspaper clipping."

Whoever this Gimer kid is needs a good smack upside the head.

"That's an awful way for you to find out," I whisper, unsure of what else to say. His aura is shades of purple, red, with the gray-blue of grief.

"It should've been from you," he accuses, tears shimmering in his blue eyes. "Why didn't you *tell* me, Mom?"

"Because!" I'm panicking, so my voice is louder than intended. He flinches, and I feel worse. Lowering my volume, I continue. "Because you were just a kid, Joulian. You still are. I took so much from you by not leaving; I didn't want you to hate me, too."

He bolts upright; I think it's to curse me out.

Instead of yelling, he openly weeps as he shouts, "He tried to *kill* you, Mom. Why would you think I'd hate you for saving yourself?"

"Oh, baby," I stand, opening my arms. He rushes toward me, launching himself into an embrace. I squeeze him hard, weeping. "I'm so sorry you had to find out that way."

"Why didn't you tell me?" he wails, the words muffled by my hair. I rub his back, trying not to have a breakdown. It feels like I'm being shredded from the inside. I shouldn't have waited this long to tell him.

"Because your father was never unkind to you. I've never wanted to taint that memory for as long as possible."

Joulian yanks himself out of my hold. With a ferocity more than a man twice his age, he hisses, *"I would've killed him for you."*

"Oh, Joulian," I say, wiping away his tears. "I would have *never* asked that of you. Ever. I did what had to be done when it needed to be done."

His small fingers find my neck, gently pressing where the bruises used to exist. "The clipping said he almost choked you to death."

I nod. "That's true."

"And that you sliced his throat?"

"Also true."

"Good," he snarls. Hate widens his pupils. This kid is half my heart — the more ferocious side of it.

It's difficult not to smile thinking of Fynn's same response. "Don't say that. Mikan was your dad."

"No," he declares. "I have no dad. No dad would ever hurt my mom. So, no. I've never had a dad."

Now's not the time to point out how silly that sounds, so instead, I say, "You're allowed to feel however you'd like. That's your right."

He wipes at his tears furiously. "Mom, you need to find someone who makes you happy. Someone who would never hurt you." A thought lights up his face. "Like Fynn."

If I didn't know any better, I'd say there's a conspiracy occurring. "Fynn is only a friend, but I appreciate the sentiment, kid."

"Maybe he could be more?" he asks hopefully.

"Probably not." I'm not getting his hopes up. "But regardless, I'm okay. I don't need a man to make me happy."

"I don't make you happy?"

I laugh, pushing hair out of his eyes. "You're a man now? Are you going to do extra chores?"

"Okay, maybe I'm not a man yet," he says quickly.

I laugh. "Still my baby?"

"Always," he says quietly, wrapping a hug around my neck. For the next few minutes, I hold my son tightly, the sands of time slipping through my fingers. Soon, he'll be old enough to leave the house and start his own life.

But he'll always be my little boy.

33

Fynn

It should be exciting going to Slous. Orliana is here, wearing a stunning light yellow sundress and brown sandals. Her dark hair falls past her bare shoulders in loose waves. When she strolls up with two large suitcases — I refrain from pointing out it's only three days of travel — she's grinning from ear to ear. Having her nearby enhances my excitement.

That's not the problem.

The problem is that my meddling brother is on the same Pegasus chariot ride, looking like he's ready to stir the pot. Deep down, I know exactly what he's trying to do, but for Orliana's comfort, I'm going to intercept as much as possible. We've agreed to be friends, no matter how badly Trinte wants to make it otherwise.

He sits across from us, grinning like an idiot, while she sits next to me. Orliana's texting her Mom, and I pretend to be busy on mine.

The whole goddess damned time, Trinte watches us with the most annoying grin I've ever seen.

Even when I return it with a glare, it never wavers. He's happier than a Gorgon inside a stone cave.

We're an hour into the two-hour flight when he finally breaks. "So how are the two of you going to do this?"

Orliana glances up, confused. "Do what?"

Trinte motions at me. "You know, play defense while my aunts try to fix him up."

My teeth almost crack as I grind them. "It will be fine. Her being around will be enough."

Trinte shakes his head forlornly. "I'm afraid not, brother. You know how Aunt Teale is." He focuses on Orliana. "In case Fynn has neglected to inform you of Dragon family politics, our aunts think every eligible male should have a mate. As the higher ranking Dragon, she's permitted to show at least two options."

Orliana's eyes ping-pong between us. "Options?"

Trinte nods excitedly. "Yes. I know Maureen will be there, and Aunt Esther said maybe one called—"

"Enough," I hissed, mindful of the other passengers. "Her being next to me will be sufficient."

Orliana twists her mouth. "Are you sure? I mean, we can hold hands. We've done that before?"

"You have?" Trinte says, flashing fangs with a broad smile. "Perfect. But what if there's a need for more?"

"There will be no need for more," I growl, clenching my fists.

A gloved hand slides over one of my fists. My fists relax, and she threads our fingers together. "I mean, what more could be needed?"

Trinte misses nothing, homing in on the physical affection. When his eyes snap to mine, my stomach drops. I might be a total orphan by the time this flight is over, depending on exactly what comes out of his mouth next.

"A kiss?" he suggests sweetly.

"A kiss?" she echoes, sounding shocked. "You really think a kiss would be necessary?"

"No."

"Yes!"

Trinte and I speak at the same time. My tail snaps in frustration. He's an opportunistic dunghole.

To Orliana, I say evenly, "You are never required to do anything you don't want to."

"But would it make them leave you alone?" she says, brows twisted with concern. "I want you to be comfortable on this trip, too. It's the whole reason I'm here, right?"

"Is it?" Trinte asked. "I heard Fynn was also hoping someone would join him on a flight to a private island. Its pink beaches are renowned."

My body jerks with the urge to launch myself at him.

Orliana's eyes light up. "Oh! I'd love that!" Searching my face with those brown eyes, she says, "When are we doing that? I've always wanted to see the pink beaches of Slous. It's a bucket list item."

"I know," Trinte says. "Your mom told me the other day, actually."

Do not crush her hand. I repeat the mantra as my hands twitch, desperately wanting to punch him in the face.

"I think you've said enough," I say, careful to keep my fury locked down. I don't want Orliana to know exactly how I feel about this situation. Because her kissing me is *not* an option. I'd never let her feel like there's a physical transaction requirement for this experience.

Do you want *to kiss her?*

The quiet inner voice has me pausing. Do I? I take in the shining expression lighting up her face as she gushes to Trinte about spending years wishing to see the beach.

Her mouth moves quickly as she speaks, but as she pauses to lick her lips, I know my answer.

When I glance at my brother, he's wearing the most self-righteous, smug, stupid smirk I've ever had the displeasure of seeing.

I'm going to kill you. I mouth the words, and all my brother does is shrug a shoulder. To him, it's worth it.

***

As soon as the flight is over, we're greeted by an attendant, a Merman shifter. Yellow iridescent scales smatter his dark skin as he flashes us a broad grin.

"Welcome. Are you here for the Weyr reunion?"

"Yes," I say, rolling the suitcases over to him. "We should have two rooms reserved. One for my brother and one for me and my—" I peek at Orliana, who grins. We are supposed to be together. "Partner."

The word is natural on my tongue, but my stomach clenches as it appears.

The attendant doesn't notice the hesitation. Instead, he beckons us to follow. "Come right this way."

I lead Orliana by the hand, allowing her to pay attention to the hotel as we trail behind the Merman. It's built to allow the breeze to move around freely, with tall ceilings supported by smooth stone pillars. Everything is painted different shades of blue. A lot of the employees appear to be Merman, sirens, and one of the managers is a Kraken.

There are no windows, only large curved openings showing a brilliant blue ocean outside. Small islands with pink sand and pink palm trees dot the horizon. The air is thick with humidity.

The attendant leads us to the front desk, where a hotel clerk takes our identification to check us in. In the corner of my eye, Orliana fidgets with her pretty dress.

With a smile, the hotel clerk hands over a key. "The room has one bed." She eyes our hands still intertwined. "I assume this is alright?"

Fuck. I had requested two beds in the room, but clearly, that isn't happening. My hand tightens. Will she be okay with this? Calmness comes from Orliana, so it must be okay.

With a stiff nod, I say, "Yes, that's fine."

Stuffing the room keys into my pocket, the three of us head toward the elevator.

"Fynn and Trinte Gleanscale!" A shrill voice calls out from behind us. I flinch and turn to find my Aunt Biliza hustling over with her daughter in tow.

"Shit," Trinte mutters under his breath.

Aunt Bilize stops in front of us, yellow face beaming. Her daughter, with burnt orange scales, gives me a shy smile. What's her name? Cora? Coraline?

"You're too skinny," my aunt says, cataloguing my features. To my brother, she loves him over with approval. "How you're still single is beyond me."

Trinte offers a dung-eating grin, raising an eyebrow. "That sounds very close to saying I'm very handsome, Aunt."

The daughter, our cousin, titters, catching my aunt's attention. Wrapping an arm around the orange Dragon's shoulders, my aunt purrs, "Courissa thinks you're very handsome." They exchange a smile, like a hatched plan is being born.

We've been here barely thirty seconds, and already the aunts are foisting women on us. It takes immense self-control to not curl my lip. "Courissa, our *cousin*?"

Aunt Bilize waves away my pointed fact. "Technically, since she's your Unce Erihc's step-daughter, she isn't blood related."

"Isn't she twenty-three?" Trinte adds, taking a step back.

Aunt Bilize frowns, eyes bouncing between us, not even noticing Orliana. "I don't understand the issue here. Are you both here for matchmaking or not?"

"Or not." I say flatly.

"Actually ..." Trinte waggles his eyebrows. "Find me someone over the age of thirty and—"

"Mother?" Courissa's dusk-colored eyes water with tears. Like this response was unfathomable, and therefore she's left unprepared.

"Shh," my aunt says, rubbing Courissa's shoulders. "It's okay. Your cousin, Vilor, will be here soon. I hear he doesn't care about a stupid little age gap." She gives Trinte a nasty look.

Trinte rears his head back, looking bewildered. "I'm thirty-five, Aunt."

This time, she sniffs, looking at him down her nose. "And you look every second of it." To me, she says, "And you? Are you not ready for a new mate?"

"He has one," Orliana says icily, draping an arm over my elbow. I grin, giving my aunt a smug smile. "What she said."

Huffing out in agitation, Aunt Bilize whirls around, dragging a crying Courissa behind her.

"Emet, save us, because that was absurd." Orliana lets out a chuckle.

Trinte lets out a low whistle. "Surprising, but not unexpected." He looks down at his belly, giving it a pat. "Should I inform her this is all muscle, hidden under a love of sweets?"

"I never want to speak with her again," I declare, motioning for us to continue toward the elevators. Flashing Orliana a grin, I say, "Thank you for being the cockblock. I might be married to my cousin this evening if you hadn't."

Orliana presses the elevator button, tossing her curls over a shoulder with a smug smirk. "Free vacation and staving off incidents of incest? All in a day's vacation."

"More like in a Weyr reunion," Trinte mutters, inspecting his reflecting in a sliver of metal. He turns to the side, sucking in his stomach. "It's not *that* bad, right?"

"To be fair, she said you were handsome first," Orliana muses. "Besides, you have that body type that women love."

I look at my brother, in all of his thick-thighs-and-arms glory. Then down at my flat stomach. Anxiety spikes inside my heart.

"So you think I'm handsome?" Trinte jokes, winking at her. I grit my teeth and smack my tail. My brother is wholly unphased, and the elevator doors opening gives us something to focus on.

The elevator ride is short, and soon we're splitting across the hallway to our respective rooms.

"Have fun with that one bed," Trinte singsongs a few doors down before locking his door behind him.

"Dunghole," I mutter while Orliana huffs out a laugh. When we step into the hotel room, I know things might get a little weird. Trinte wasn't too far off — the bed is large enough for most fliers, but it's still only one bed.

Orliana's mouth twists with insecurity. "Are you sure this is okay? We can go downstairs and try again for a room with two beds."

"It's fine," I assure her. But it's not. The only person I've shared a bed with in the last five years was my brother, right after Rhuth died. But I haven't shared a bed with another woman in fifteen years.

I shove down the dread and panic — I don't want to make things more weird for Orliana. She was kind enough to come on this trip; she doesn't deserve to feel like a burden to my emotions. Again.

Something flickers inside me: a yearning. A small voice whispers, *Wouldn't it be nice to not wake up alone?*

Out of the question.

I motion to the ground. "I can sleep on the floor. Just toss me a pillow and blanket — I'll be fine."

Orliana opens her mouth to speak, but a knock at the door interrupts her. We exchange frowns, and I check the peephole. It's Trinte.

Muttering a curse, I open the door. He's already in a tropical-print shirt and white shorts, with sunglasses holding his long black hair back.

"It's been less than thirty seconds. How are you already changed?" I growl.

He jerks his head down the hall. "Let's go get a drink before this inevitable meat market is activated."

"A drink?" Orliana chirps from behind me.

He stands on his tiptoes, trying to see her. "Yeah. Come on, you have to try their Noura Colada. Rum and strawberry puree. Delectable."

"Sounds delicious." Orliana says excitedly. I feel her heat at my back as she pushes me aside. With a sigh, I shift, allowing her to look at my brother. My knuckles whiten around the door frame.

"They give free fruit with it," he adds helpfully, grinning wide enough to flash both fangs. If he wasn't annoying the fuck out of me, I'd appreciate how relaxed he seems.

"I love fruit," Orliana says solemnly. When she peers up at me, a twinkle of joy in her dark brown eyes softens my irritation. "Can we please?"

I snort. "I don't control you." When disappointment collapses her expression, I quickly add, "I'd love to go get a drink."

The disappointment evaporates. She claps with excitement, refocusing on Trinte. "Lead the way!"

My brother casts his one blue on me with a smirk. In spite of myself, a kernel of excitement sparks. We're here in Slous, with a salt-licked tropical breeze in the air. Orliana's on her first vacation. My brother appears to be happy.

With that trifecta, what could go wrong?

34

Fynn

The bar is an aquarium.

My scales crawl with all the water tanks pretending to be walls, with the colorful fish too plentiful and bright to not catch the eye. Orliana squeals, clapping her hands with a tiny hop; Trinte and I exchange queasy looks. It's a mystery why the Weyr reunion is at a place dedicated to water, when Dragons would much prefer a place like Oasha. Not everyone seems to feel this way though — driftwood tables and chairs are scattered around the room, full of colorful Dragons laughing and enjoying their fruity alcoholic beverages.

A Kraken attendant steps up, his tentacle beard grasping at the air.

"Shall I take your shoes?" he offers, webbed hands motioning to our feet. Orliana complies immediately, handing over her delicate sandals. As Trinte does the same, I hesitate; the attendant notices.

"You don't have to, sir." The Kraken frowns. "But the sand *will* get into your shoes."

"Come on, Fynny," Trinte cajoles. "Loosen up, will ya?"

"Fine," I mutter, kicking off my loafers. Our shoes are placed in a labeled bin, and Trinte's given a ticket to pick them up later.

The floor's made of sand devoid of Slous crystals, soft between my toes. I wriggle them, hiding my smile.

"Hello, welcome to A'hoy Lady." A Water Sprite wearing a white sarong greets us, her pointed ears covered in sea glass piercings. Trinte eyes her with appreciation, but she ignores him, picking up three menus from the hostess stand. "Is it just the three of you?"

"We'd like to sit at the bar," Trinte declares, motioning to the rustic bar top across the room. Only a few Dragons sit on the stools, each holding vibrant drinks with small umbrellas poking out over the edge of oddly shaped glasses.

"Of course," the Sprite says, motioning for us to follow.

Orliana falls in step next to me, touching my hand with soft fingers. "Do you want to pretend we're together here?"

Eyes track us. My excellent hearing picks up whispered phrases like, *"The Gleanscales came!"* and *"I hear Fynn can create entire thunderstorms!"*

More than a few women watch us with hunger and interest. This is probably worse than we've anticipated, especially as some stand, preparing to approach the moment we sit down.

Without hesitation, I tuck Orliana's hand into mine, pressing it into my arm. "Goddess, yes."

"Like sheep let to slaughter," Trinte mutters with good humor, slinging his broad frame onto a barstool. Orliana sits between us, quietly accepting the offered menu.

"You can order from your bartender," the Water Sprite informs us before leaving us to be a spectacle for the entire room to observe.

Maybe this was a mistake. No, this was *definitely* a mistake. My anxiety spikes again, and it's a struggle to control the twitching end of my tail. Clutching the back of Orliana's stool in a display of ownership, I scan the menu.

"Since it's our first time in Slous," Orliana whispers conspiratorially, leaning close enough to fill my nostrils with her soft scent, "We should try new drinks, right?"

"Yes," I theater whisper, smiling at the way her face lights up with even more excitement. She's practically a lightbulb from the way she beams with joy.

"What'll it be?" A green Merman stands in front of us, hands braced against the bar top. His hair is long and tangled, coarse from sea salt. Small gills line the bottom of his jaw, flexing and closing.

"I'll have a Noura Colada," Trinte announces, smacking his menu as if it solidifies his decision.

Orliana nibbles on her plump bottom lip. "How's the slootberry mojito?"

"Pretty good." The Merman eyes her with too much interest, but backs off when I subtly curl my lip.

"I'll have one of those," she declares. "And a plate of fish nachos, please. Extra cheese."

He nods, turning his yellow eyes on me. "For you, sir?"

"I'd like the slootberry daiquiri and a plate of the urchin tacos."

"Coming right up." He collects the menus and leaves us in peace. My neck prickles with awareness, and without looking, I know someone is approaching.

"Incoming," Trinte mutters, leaning against his stool to watch whomever is invading our privacy.

"Fynn Gleanscale."

My name is like a sounding trumpet, causing me to wince. Orliana spins, forcing me to break the grasp I have on her stool. Inhaling a bracing breath, I do the same, watching my Uncle Waltor approach. His forest green scales complement the soft blue glow from the fish tanks. Like Trinte, he's wearing a garish tropical print shirt; its mustard yellow flowers bring out the bright green of his eyes.

I exhale sharply in a mix of relief and apprehension. This is one of my favorite uncles. I stand, sinking into the sand as he wraps strong arms around my chest, slapping my back enthusiastically.

"Uncle," I say with no shortage of deference. He's married to Aunt Teale. How, I'm not sure. Their personalities are night and day.

Clutching my arms, he pushes me back, looking me over. "You don't look a day over thirty-five."

I let out a laugh. "Are you also trying to flatter me in order to marry me off?"

"I'm *actually* thirty-five," Trinte quips, accepting his Noura Colada from the bartender.

"And you're not married because?" Uncle Waltor raises an unimpressed eyebrow at my brother.

Trinte focuses on his drink, the straw missing his mouth a couple of times before he successfully sucks it into his mouth. Uncle Waltor appears bemused as his eyes flick to Orliana.

Extending a hand, he asks, "Who do we have here?"

Orliana looks at the hand. She's not wearing any barriers against touching, but I know she hates shaking hands. Indecision wars across her expression, undoubtedly trying to decide what would be considered rude in Dragon culture.

I sit back down, daring to place a hand on her knee. "This is Orliana. She's with me."

My uncle's dark green eyebrows shoot up. "Oh? Teale told me you'd be arriving alone."

"How odd," I say mildly. "Because she told me I had no option but to bring someone."

He chuckles. "You know how the matriarchs are."

Orliana shifts closer to me. "It's nice to meet you ...?"

"Waltor," my uncle says proudly.

"Nice to meet you, Waltor." She slides her mojito across the smooth wood and takes a sip. Her hum of appreciation is almost too salacious. Waltor raises a single eyebrow, eyes flicking to me. There's a question there, one I have no interest in answering. Instead, I curl my tail around the leg of her stool. He takes a step back.

"Well, I'll let you kids get to it. Mind yourself around the aunts. They're on the prowl." With a wink at Orliana, he turns and returns to his table where other uncles smoke cigars.

The moment he sits, three female Dragons stand.

"Good goddesses," I mutter, grabbing my daiquiri. Orliana grins as I take a deep pull of the drink through my hot pink straw. It's sweet and refreshing, unlike the three women approaching. They eye me and my brother like snacks.

"Am I here to be eye candy or can I be possessive?" she teases.

"*Please* be possessive," I plead, plastering a welcoming smile on my face.

"Fynn. Trinte." The middle female Dragon, a pale shade of red, almost pink, smiles broadly, deepening two dimples on her plump cheeks. "I heard you were both attending and well—" She glances at her two accomplices. "—I just knew we had to say hello. There are so few bachelors here."

"Well, hello there, pretty ladies," Trinte croons with a lopsided grin. "And your names are?"

The instigator points at herself, then at each female Dragon beside her. "I'm Minerva. This is Loural and Turna."

I eye Turna, who looks too fresh faced to be near us. "How old are you?"

The opalescent Dragon titters. "I'm twenty-five."

"Damn," Trinte mutters. "Is *anyone* here of appropriate age?"

"Aren't you both too old to be single?" Loural snarks, her silver eyes flashing with a challenge.

Trinte points at me. "He's a brooding widower." He presses a hand over his heart, pretending to pine for something that doesn't exist. "And I fear I'm too gorgeous and clever to be locked down by just any woman."

Minerva eyes me critically. This entire time, she hasn't looked at Orliana, but the Siphon is done being ignored. Orliana's golden hand grabs mine, threading our fingers together. My whole body heats at the contact, and the true ferocity emanating from her.

"He's mine."

The three females jerk back, looking at her as if she finally matters to the conversation. Turna sniffs with disdain, glancing at Orliana's empty middle finger. "Aren't you also too old to be just dating?"

"What is this? The geriatric dating club?" Loural whispers, knowing damn well we can hear her.

"Why, you little bra—" Orliana snarls, looking genuinely affronted. I squeeze her hand, encouraging temperance. Her mouth shuts, but a vengeful glint sparks in her eye. Instead of calling the three women brats, Orliana looks at them with a smug expression.

"Maybe we're geriatric, but I'm the one here with the Gleanscale brothers. Who are *you* here with?"

This shuts them up quickly. Casting us nasty glares, the three whirl around, stalking back to their table. That's when I notice the dozens of eyes glued onto the interaction. The women who looked at us with interest when we arrived avert their gazes. Orliana has made her point.

"Marry me," Trinte gasps with admiration, batting his eyelashes to cauterize the serious declaration.

Orliana laughs, plucking the slice of pineapple off the rim of her glass. "That was fun. What's next?"

***

We don't stick around for a second round of drinks. The reception is in less than two hours, and we need to freshen up. Sliding the keycard into our room's door, I hold it open, trying not to inhale Orliana's scent as she passes by.

I'm failing. Between the generous amount of skin she's showing and the unique scent her curls hold — distinctly Orliana — my mouth waters at the mere thought of touching her again. This is already more complicated than expected. We've been approached more than I thought possible, and the weekend is just beginning. I'm grateful she's here, but something tells me this Weyr reunion will test us past our limits of platonic friendship.

Would that be such a bad thing?

I don't know anymore.

It's safe to say that I know nothing. So much has changed in this short period of time; I'm turning into a version of myself both foreign and familiar. I like who I am around her; the side of myself thought long dead.

This weekend probably isn't the best time to figure out what's between us, but change is inevitable. The aunts are going to continue foisting their daughters on me unless Orliana stakes her claim immediately. Which means she needs to be prepared for more public displays of affection.

I hate it when Trinte is right.

While she sifts through her suitcase, I clear my throat. “You know, Trinte was being a dunghole, but he might onto something.”

She peers up, clutching a piece of purple lace in her hand. It looks eerily like—

Orliana notices what I'm staring at and tucks it behind her back. “What is he right about?"

I rub the back of my heating neck. "That we might have to kiss. You saw how pushy they were. It's only going to get worse."

She nods, gazing past my shoulder as she contemplates my words. "Um, I know. It's okay, though, if you need it. We're both adults, and we're friends, right?" She laughs. "Kyri says friends can do all sorts of sexual things together and—"

Her lips zip up tight, clamping teeth down on them as her cheeks flush a dark red. Almost as red as my scales.

Intrigued, I raise my eyebrows. “Oh, really? Kyri said friends can have *sex?*”

She blows out a breath. “Yeah, but I'm not saying we need or should or could have sex. It's just what she said, and besides, it's only a kiss, right? It doesn't have to mean anything.”

She's so unbelievably cute when she's nervous. Suddenly, kissing her doesn't feel so scary.

“Well, I'm not proposing we have sex right now,” I say, smiling. She can't even make eye contact. “Kisses don't have to lead to sex, ever.”

Her eyes darted up to mine, then away again. “Yeah, you’re right. If it’s one kiss, that’s fine.”

“It’s what friends can do sometimes,” I add, biting back a chuckle. I cannot believe Kyri said that to her. Now it makes me wonder if they ... Nope, not going there, ever.

“Right.” She rocks on the balls of her feet, chewing on that plump bottom lip. “Well, we can do that whenever you want.”

I take a step forward, and she freezes, watching my feet. Still unable to look at me. “Of course. But maybe ...” I trail off, thinking things through. Kissing now will make sure it doesn't happen for the first time in front of an audience. It's the smart and respectful thing to do.

Right?

I pause long enough for her to finally gain the courage to look up. There’s such a mix of emotions on her face. I have no doubt mine mirrors the conflict. Am I really about to say this?

Do this?

“Maybe what?” she whispers. Her pulse pounds in her neck as her breathing turns shallow.

Breathing is hard for me too; it feels like my heart is going to break through my rib cage and run far, far away. Everything grows hot; my Fyre heats.

“Maybe,” I rasp out. “We shouldn’t do it in front of others for the first time. To make it believable.”

“Believable?” she echoes.

I take another step closer, my body shaking. “Yeah. Could you imagine if I’m a bad kisser and you discovered this right in front of Aunt Teale? She’ll scent it from miles away.”

“*Are* you ... a bad kisser?” she says quietly, her head tilting up as I take another step. Her cheeks flush again, and I’m certain it isn’t from embarrassment.

“I don’t think so,” I say mildly, taking another step forward. “I’ve never had any complaints. You?”

“I-I don’t know,” she admits, voice raspy. We’re a foot apart now, near enough to share body heat. Close enough for me to inhale her unique, delicate scent. I swallow hard. This might be one of the most difficult things I've ever done.

"We can find out," I murmur, scanning her face, settling on her parted lips.

She licks them again, and I hold back a groan. My hands visibly tremble as I bring them up to frame her face, but I don't touch her quite yet.

"Can I touch you, Orliana?"

She nods, and I place a hand on each cheek, tilting her mouth up a little higher. We both breathe as if we've been sprinting. The awareness of her breasts against my body strikes my senses like lightning.

"Can I kiss you, Orliana?" The words are barely audible.

She nods again, and I slowly lower my head, briefly brushing my lips against hers. This is a no-turning-back moment for both of us. I'm not a fucking fool — this isn't about being friends. I may not quite understand how I feel about her, but I do know that I don't kiss or have sex with my friends. No matter what Kyri thinks.

Her breath mingles with mine as I hesitate. One of her hands tentatively slides up my cheek to the back of my head. When her nails gently scrape my scalp, I finally let loose the groan I've been holding back and press my mouth to hers.

35

Orliana

I've kissed people other than Mikan, but it was always lackluster. I've truly never understood what the big deal was about kissing, dating, sex — none of it.

When Fynn's lips barely touch mine, that opinion shatters immediately. Even the brush of his mouth is enough to light up every nerve ending. Instantly, my ability activates, seeking his emotions like a beacon.

He's filled with longing, fear, and desire. So much desire. All the same emotions as mine. It feels incredible to not be alone in this experience, knowing both of us are on the same page.

My fingers curl into his hair. He groans, pressing harder. Our lips part at the same time. When his tongue licks my lower lip, pleasure zings down between my thighs, thrusting my hips forward. I gasp, shocked at the unfamiliar feeling? Is this ... lust?

Fynn groans again, sliding one of his hands to the back of my head. Another round of electrifying pleasure shoots down to my core when his fingers thread into my hair.

Our tongues find one another, and at the first swipe, nothing else matters. My reality narrows down to the way they dance, like this is the most natural thing in the world.

I bring my other hand, the one still holding my underwear, to his bicep, digging my nails into the muscle. Fynn deepens the kiss, and we've catapulted off the concept of practicing, promptly landing me in a state of confusion. He isn't kissing me like he misses his wife; he's kissing like he *wants* me.

Fynn's hips thrust forward, letting me feel *exactly* how much he wants me. Heat pools in my belly; I have the inexplicable urge to jump up and wrap my legs around him.

But that would be crazy, because we're only ... friends?

I don't know anymore.

What I do know is that as his hand leaves my face and trails down my neck, I want it to go lower; so much lower. It settles at the juncture of my neck and shoulder, his thumb rubbing slowly. My fingers tighten in his hair. I moan into his mouth, craving so much more. My hips jerk forward of their own accord, striking a match of need that blazes down my spine all the way to my toes.

Then the moment shatters. In my hands, Fynn freezes. It's a painfully slow process of his fingers releasing my hair and those delicious lips leaving mine without a lingering touch. When he steps back, it forces my hands to let go.

Both of us are panting, his stricken expression matching mine. I have no idea what to say. Are we really going to say we are just friends now? I can almost hear Kyri laughing and saying, *I told you so.*

Rubbing his hands over his face, he makes a sound of frustration. "That was ..."

"Very friendly?" I supply, hoping it will add some levity to this messy moment. There was nothing *friendly* about that kiss, though. Was the chemistry and intensity only one-sided?

He gives a very unimpressed look. Running his hands through his hair, he growls and begins walking to the front door, then freezes. "I took that too far. I'm so sorry."

I stand there, arms slack at my side, trailing his pacing form. "I mean, I was a willing participant, Fynn."

He won't look at me. "Yes, but I pushed it because ..."

"Because why?"

His golden eyes find mine. "It doesn't matter." He stops pacing to face me. Some of his hair sticks up where he's run fingers through it. "Obviously, we aren't kissing like that in public."

"Obviously," I say dryly, growing irritated. Frankly, with this reaction, I'm surprised he wants to do it ever again. The rejection stings, forming a lump in my throat. I glance at the balled up lacy underwear in my hand. He follows my focus, then averts his eyes.

Spinning, Fynn strides to the door. Hand on the handle, he glances over his shoulder. I inspect his aura, and while I'm pleased to see how much he burns with passion and desire, the grief around his heart is growing bigger by the second.

Now I understand.

He opens his mouth to say something, but I hold up a hand. "You don't have to explain yourself, Fynn. I get it. Come back when you're ready."

His mouth snaps shut, and then he walks out.

36

Fynn

I've made some dumb decisions in my life. When I leave Orliana in the hotel room, I immediately know that's one of them. I instantly regret leaving, but I need space to breathe. My body still sings with need for her, and I can't think straight right now.

Like a fool, I let myself get swept up in the taste of it, drunk on the way she kisses. So open and eager. Trusting.

And Rhuth. Now Rhuth will never be the last person I've kissed. It feels like another erasure. Another piece lost. Nausea rolls in my stomach, cramping like a gut punch.

I didn't think of her.

I didn't even think of my dead wife.

Shame, which feasts on my doubt greedily, stirs my stomach into cramps. Should I have thought about Rhuth? Wouldn't it cheapen my connection with Orliana if I had? She deserves my full attention; not sharing it with my dead wife.

Then there's the roiling guilt burning my insides up, because I don't regret it. I'm *glad* it was Orliana. What does that say about me? I've clung to this grief for so long, I don't remember who I am without it.

That's not true. I know the newest version of me kisses a woman passionately, then leaves her standing in a hotel room because he can't stand to look at himself after.

Stalking down the hallway, to goddess knows where, I contemplate the line we've crossed. Because a line *was* crossed. Orliana consented, and the enthusiasm was incredibly clear, but we set a boundary of being friends. I took advantage of the conversation for selfish reasons. I *wanted* to kiss her. I wanted it so badly that I did it at the earliest opportunity.

And I fucking *left* her.

The hallway dumps me out into the lobby. It's still crowded, which is the last thing I need. Shoving my hands into my pockets, I spin, aiming to brood in a quiet corner.

My Dragon hearing catches the worst sound in the world.

"Fynn Gleanscale? Is that you? Come say hello!"

I freeze, shoulders hunching as my teeth grind. Closing my eyes, I take a steadying breath and turn, pasting a ghost of a smile on my face. Pleasant enough to hopefully not be called rude.

Aunt Teale's bustling over with Trinte and a purple female Dragon in tow. My aunt is wearing a bright pink jumpsuit with strings of pearls slapping her body haphazardly. It's probably one of the worst outfits I've ever seen.

Trinte's scanning my face, catching every micro-expression. When his eyebrows draw together, I know what he sees: his formerly semi-happy brother brooding again. Knowing him, he's already jumped to conclusions, because his eyes flick behind me, where Orliana isn't.

When his eyes jump to the female Dragon beside him, I know instantly what's about to happen.

Drawing up straight, I greet my aunt with a little more energy than I feel. "Aunt Teale. Good to see you."

She raises ring-encrusted hands and yanks my face down so she can kiss both cheeks. As her lips loudly smack my left cheek, I catch Trinte's grimace.

"Oh, nephew, you certainly look leagues better than when I saw you last. Have you finally put on weight? And that haircut! How dashing."

She motions to the female Dragon. "Fynn, this is Maureen, my best friend's daughter. I was just telling Trinte that she's thirty-one and single. Isn't that marvelous?"

Maureen's lavender eyes twinkle as she smiles demurely. "It's lovely to meet you. I've heard wonderful things about you and your brother."

"Doubtful," I mutter.

My brother puffs out his chest. "I'm positive most of those compliments were about me."

Maureen gives him an uncertain look. "I'm sure your aunt mentioned Fynn—"

"Impossible." He grins. "Fynn is with someone, so that would be inappropriate for our aunt. *I'm* the most dashing, single male of our Weyr."

Aunt Teale titters, waving her hands dramatically. "Is this true, nephew? You have someone?" She makes a show of scanning the lobby. "And where is this sweet, lucky Dragon?"

Through my gritted fangs, I say, "She's freshening up. And she's not a Dragon."

"Oh." She seems disappointed as she and Maureen exchange looks. "Well, no matter. It's new, so things can change, I'm sure."

"I'm sure," Maureen agrees.

Trinte looks between the two of them, possibly sensing the loss of control. "But Maureen, don't you—?"

"No," she says dismissively. "I do not."

With that, she walks away. I resist the temptation to taunt him and ask him exactly who is more handsome. The crestfallen expression on his face actually keeps my mouth shut. Did he actually think she might be open to dating him? With Aunt Teale pulling the strings?

Aunt Teale sighs dramatically, flapping out a fan and fanning her face. She inspects me with a critical eye. "I'm eager to meet your new squeeze. What's her name?"

"Orliana."

Something flickers in her eyes, but she says nothing. She hums and walks away, leaving me alone with my brother.

He steps closer, looking worried. "Where's Orliana, and why are you so pissed off? What did you do?"

My facade drops. The temporary mental moratorium shatters, reminding me of my choice to leave her. Trinte is just being a good friend, a good brother, but I can't stand his goodness right.

"Of course you're more worried about her," I snark. It's another thing I regret doing today, but my frustration has no outlet, and he's the nearest punching bag.

My brother's face darkens with anger. "You're supposed to show her a good time, Fynn. Not hurt her."

Instead of admitting that I've done just that, I step up to him, snarling. "Who said I hurt her?"

Lifting his chin, he motions at the length of me. "This whole angry, broody attitude you have going on. Where is she?"

"Why don't you go find out?" I say bitterly. "If you care so much."

Trinte grabs my elbow and yanks me down the hall. When we're out of everyone's line of sight, he smacks me upside the head.

"What the fuck?" I snapped, instantly ready to fight him. "Are you eager for a beating?"

Instead of backing down, he does it again, shoving his chest into me. We're almost nose to nose, close enough for me to see the fury sparking in his blue eye. My Fyre roars, begging to shift and shred him with my claws.

"Do that again and I swear to Fortuna, you won't have a brother anymore."

To his credit, he still doesn't cower. "If you make me fight for her, on your behalf, maybe you don't fucking deserve her, anyway."

This makes me pause. "What are you talking about? Orliana? Why are you fighting for her?" The thought of him wanting her in any capacity has my claws lengthening. *"Are you in love with her?"*

"Fortuna, save me from this fucking imbecile," he mutters, rubbing his face in frustration. Throwing his hands in the air, he yells, "No! I'm not in love with her." He jabs a finger into my chest. *"You are."*

"I'm not ..." But I can't finish the sentence because I'm not sure if it's true.

He shakes his head in disbelief. "You are the smartest dumb person I've ever met."

"Watch it," I snarl, still itching for a fight. I point a claw at him. "It's really none of your business, Trinte. I'm married. I can't be in love with another woman because I love *my wife.*"

"It's been five years," Trinte roars, shoving me again. His words echo down the hallway, past the small alcove we've been in. "When will you stop punishing yourself? When will you start living? I thought you were; I thought she was bringing you back to life. But clearly, you're so determined to be miserable, you can't fucking see what in the Hells is right in front of you!"

"*Nothing* is in front of me," I snap, shoving him back. I can't handle this truth. It's too much. All of it's too much. That blasted kiss blew apart everything inside me, and all I want to do is run from it. Because admitting the truth, that I'm ready to move on from my dead wife, is too difficult to admit.

My feelings for Orliana are intense, beyond what I've wanted to acknowledge. But I knew the moment our lips touched that I was a goner. Everything I've been afraid of disappeared and intensified, all at once. It makes me want to rip my hair out.

The lies scald my tongue as I fling them out into the world. "I don't think of her in that way, Trinte. Stop trying to force something that doesn't fucking exist."

There's a small gasp; we look over to see Orliana watching, her brown eyes full of tears. A hand flies to her mouth as my stomach drops to the lowest Hell. How much did she hear? How much of it did I even mean?

None of it.

I meant none of it.

Yet she heard me say it. It can't be taken back. And the way she steps away from me with devastation twisting her features, I'd rather Fortuna herself strike me down than ever see this expression on her face ever again.

"Orliana, wait, I didn't—"

She takes another step back, staring at Trinte. My brother steps forward, and she doesn't move. She's not afraid of him because she knows at least he cares about not hurting her, unlike me.

"Come on," he says softly, steering her down the hallway. "Let's leave him to brood in peace."

My shoulders slump in defeat. I rub my chest, aching for the ability to remove my worthless heart. I always said I wouldn't hurt her, but look at me now.

A fucking liar.

37

Orliana

Trinte keeps an arm wrapped around me, letting me cry without judgment. We stop at a hotel room, and he unlocks it with a key. It must be his. The door closes behind us, and he guides me to a chair in the corner.

I rest my elbows on my knees, crying into my hands. I can't get Fynn's words out of my head.

Nothing is in front of me.

I don't think of her in that way.

Something that doesn't fucking exist.

The last one is what hurts the most. In a split second, he reduced everything we've experienced together to nothing. Like I was a vessel for his healing. Now that it's becoming too serious, too unpredictable, he's over it. I don't matter.

Trinte squats in front of me, offering a cold bottle of water. "Here."

I shake my head. "I don't want it."

"Orliana, take a sip. Take a breath." His tone brooks no argument, so I sigh and sit back, snatching the bottle out of his hand and taking a sip.

He smirks. "Good."

I wipe my mouth with the back of my hand. "Your brother is a real piece of work."

He chuckles, standing and crossing the room to sit on the bed. "Yes, well, not everyone can be as perfect as me."

"You're *insufferable*," I snap, then immediately, "I'm sorry. That was unkind."

Trinte tosses his head back with a deep laugh. "No, that's a valid thought. I fear I feel like I know what's best for everyone before they do, because normally, I do."

"Oh, really?" I challenge. "And you thought I was best for your brother? So he can heal and be with someone else when he's done with me? So you employed some half-baked machinations to make this happen? Are you happy?"

His head jerks back like I've smacked him. "*That's* what you think I've done?" I immediately feel bad when he gives me a look of disgust. "Orliana, you and he are two sides of the same coin. Sure, I assumed your ability could be helpful, but if you *recall*," he says, sounding actually pissed. "I didn't know about your ability when I had the genius idea of joining you at the club. Only when we were there. My *machinations* were already in place beforehand. I saw what the two of you have been too stubborn to see from the start."

Guilt has me staring at the ground. "I'm sorry."

Trinte lets out the loudest, most burdened sigh in history. "Don't be sorry. I understand what this must look like, but I promise you, I had only the purest of intentions. I honestly didn't think he'd fight it this much."

I scoff. "He's not ready." My lips quiver, struggling to say the words. "*I'm* not ready." Tears fill my eyes. "I can't be with another person who treats me like I'm a plaything."

Trinte snaps to attention. Leaning forward, his different colored eyes hold a promise of violence as he asks quietly, "What *exactly* did my brother do?"

"Nothing like that," I say quickly. "He just ... we just ...kissed." It sounds so lame, with all of this drama as the fallout. All over a stupid kiss. The best kiss of my life, sure. But it was still only a kiss.

"And you consented?"

"Yes," I rush out. "It was entirely consensual, I promise."

Trinte exhales with relief. "Good. I would've really hated having to kill him." Something tells me he isn't kidding. "So let me get this straight: the two of you kissed, and it was good?" When I nod, he continues. "It was so good, my brother panicked and left?"

When I nod again, he lets out a bitter laugh. "He walked straight into Aunt Teale, me, and Maureen. Where my aunt immediately tried to practically gift this female Dragon to him, even after learning about you."

"She did?" I ask, shocked. "That's ..."

"Annoying. And as a heads up, she'll probably do it again. You really were here to help him as a buffer." He runs a hand through his hair, reminding me so much of his brother. Standing, he motions to the water. "Take another sip, please."

This man is the most thoughtful, overbearing person I've ever met. I do what he says, though, because it's easier than arguing. After I take the sip, he stands. "Come on, let's get you back."

"I'm not going back to him, Trinte. I'll rent another room; I don't care."

Trinite studies me, as if evaluating how serious I am. Whatever he finds has him lifting a lip in frustration. "He really made a mess of things, didn't he?"

"I think that's quite obvious, don't you?" He walks over to his suitcase. He begins loading the few belongings he'd already pulled out.

"What are you doing?"

He raises an eyebrow. "I think that's quite obvious, don't you?" When I still look confused, he says slowly, "I'm giving you my room, Orliana, so I can spend our time here making it as unpleasant as possible for him. I'll bring your things over, so you can stay here."

"Oh."

He zips up the suitcase. "Yes, *oh.*" He shakes his head, rolling the suitcase toward his door. "I swear, between the two of you, I should get paid as a therapist."

When he reaches the door, he says, "Look; if you have any lingering affection for him, could you *please* maybe hopefully *please* consider still being his date to the events during this trip? I'm not kidding when I say Dragon aunts are a fucking nightmare for bachelor Dragons."

Finally, he gives me that trademark grin. "I can only take so many of the ladies for myself, you know?"

I grab the pen next to me and throw it. He laughs, ducking. "So, is that a yes?"

How hard will it be next to Fynn after hearing his words? Even if he looked immediately devastated, he still said the words. There has to be some form of truth in them.

But maybe he's right. We made this mess by kissing in private. Everything was fine before that. I came on this trip with the agreement to help him navigate the events. Not doing so would be incredibly disrespectful. It's not like he insulted me directly; he's just in love with his dead wife.

I can't — *won't* — hold that against him.

"Fine." When he grins like he *knew* I'd give in, I warn him with, "You tell him I'll play the pretty girlfriend, but we are *just* friends. And I mean it, Trinte."

There's not an inch on his face that tells me he believes the words, but still he says, "Got it. *Just* friends." He opens the door and pushes the suitcase out. The sight tugs at my heart; I was supposed to share a room with Fynn. Now I'll be all alone.

Poking his head around the edge, Trinte adds, "Totally *just* friends who had a kiss *so hot* it ruined their friendship?"

He's gone by the time the worship book next to me slams into the door.

38

Fynn

I'm pacing, practically wearing a hole in the carpet, when the lock of the door beeps. My heart leaps into my throat, fully expecting Orliana's beautiful face. I'm ready to apologize, to grovel, to explain.

Instead, it's my fucking brother with his stupid fucking smug smile.

"Hey baby," he purrs. "Did you miss me?"

"Get out," I growl. "I still owe you a beating for what you did. It's your fault she heard all of that."

For a second, he only stares at me. Then his face twists into fury. He slams the door behind him and stalks over, suitcases flung aside.

We're chest to chest as he snarls, "*My* fault? *My fault?!* You *kissed* her and then *left* her. Your own tongue said it meant *nothing* to you. I didn't force that out of your too-big mouth."

He shakes his head in disgust. "If you weren't my brother, if I didn't love you so much, I'd genuinely break the tip of your tail. You broke her goddess-damned heart, Fynn."

His words feel like glass rubbing against my insides. "Where is she?"

"My room. Where she'll be sleeping tonight."

I see red, and in a flash, my claws are out. With a vicious shove against his chest, I snarl, "The Hells she will. If you lay a single hand on her, I'll—"

"You'll what?" he taunts.

I know my outburst doesn't intimidate him — he spends five days a week at the local battle gym. Without magyck involved, he could probably kick my ass if he wanted to. Somehow, his reaction makes me feel a foot tall and thirty years younger.

Sensing my flagging anger, he sneers. "Brood? Kill me? Act possessive over a female you won't take possession of?"

"She's not a *thing*, Trinte."

"Oh, really?" he snarks, crossing his arms. "Could've fooled me, considering the way you made her feel."

This deflates my fury. I blink, trying to process his words. "What do you mean?"

With every ounce of derision possible, he curls a lip. "And I quote, 'I can't be with another person who treats me like I'm a plaything.'" He raises an eyebrow. "Do you care to explain what she means by that, *brother?*"

My Fyre winks out. Every fiber of my body eager for a fight sags. "She said that?"

He cocks his head. "Yes."

"Did she ... say why?"

"No, but I can take a guess."

The mattress groans as I sit on the edge of the bed, defeated. "She told you about her dead husband?"

Meeting my energy, his voice softens. "No, but her mother did. She showed me the news report."

I look at him with a bleak expression. "There's a news report?"

He sits next to me. "Do you remember that prominent lawyer who was killed in his home three years ago? Killed by his wife while he tried to murder her?"

Everything goes silent. My heart doesn't dare beat while I struggle to understand what he's saying. "He tried to kill her?"

"Mhmm. Came pretty damn close, too. She spent two weeks in the hospital with broken ribs, a broken eye socket, a partially crushed trachea, and other old, badly healed injuries." I watch silently as he pulls out his phone and pulls up a news report.

My hands shake violently as he hands it over. It features a photo of a handsome Elf in a professional suit. Next to the image is what is possibly a picture of Orliana, but she's unrecognizable. Haunted, bloodshot eyes. Face full of black, blue, purple, and green. Multiple splits in her lip. Emaciated.

I never once asked her why she killed him. I was simply glad he was dead, but how could I *not ask?*

Trinte's low voice interrupts my thoughts. "Can you understand why I'm going to fucking kill you if you hurt her?"

Without a shadow of a doubt, I'd hand him the weapon if it came down to it. "I didn't mean to."

"I know," he murmurs. "But you need to decide, Fynn. You and I both know you can't be just friends with that woman. She's smart, compassionate, and patient. If you let her slip through your fingers because you're stuck living in the past, I promise you'll regret it."

It hits me like a lightning bolt; how right he is. How wrong I've been. The day she came over and stood next to me in front of the freezer, my perspective shifted. When she siphoned my grief away, it let me see her with new eyes.

I think I've slowly fallen in love with her.

Things might be different if we weren't on parallel journeys — but we've been doing this together. Having first time experiences together felt more like jump-starting a new future.

Hells, she's done more for me than I've done for her.

What I've done has caused more harm than she's ever caused me.

I need to fix this. I *want* to fix this. Trinte's right, the smug bastard — I'll regret ruining things with her. I'm too old to be too proud for an apology. To tell her how I feel.

But ▯part of me still doesn't feel ready. To be honest, I'm terrified. To love someone else ...

What if I lose her, too?

What if she decides I'm too much and leaves?

What if she dies?

The thoughts make me nauseous.

"What is it?" Trinte asks, watching me work through my thoughts.

Leaning against my knees, I stare at the floor. "What if I'm not enough? What if I lose her, too?"

"You've already lost her if you don't get your head out of your ass."

Leave it to my brother to cut right to the point. I laugh bitterly. "Exactly. I was selfish, Trinte, and it hurt her."

"She still wants you," he says softly. "I know she does. She's hurt, and she's furious, but she ... feels deeply for you."

The words make my heart skip a beat. "Do you think she'll forgive me?"

He nods again, putting the phone away. "Well, you have a long road ahead of you because I'm sleeping with you tonight, and she's taking my room."

I gape at him. "You baited me."

Standing, he says smoothly, "And see how quickly you bit the hook?"

I kick his tail, but he ignores me as he walks over to Orliana's things. They're still spread out. I see the pair of lacy purple underwear outside the suitcase.

I bolt upright. "Let me do that."

With *another* knowing look, he steps back, hands up. "Fine, but you aren't taking it to her."

Carefully placing her clothes into the suitcase, I frown. "What? Why not?"

"She doesn't want to see you until it's time for the meet and greet reception."

My shoulders slump as I zip up the suitcase. "She said that?"

"Yes. She also requested that I convey that you are actually *just* friends now. She was quite vehement about it."

I glance over my shoulder, dismayed to see a serious expression. "How do I make it better?"

He shrugs, walking over to his suitcase to move it out of the way. "I've done enough meddling. It's up to you now."

As much as I want to snap at him, I keep my tone quiet. "I'm grateful for your meddling."

Trinte grabs the suitcase. "I want you happy, brother. Truly. I know Rhuth was an incredible woman, but we don't get a specific allotment for happiness. You need to stop acting like you ran out of rations."

Not for the first time, I wonder how my little brother became wiser and smarter than me. Not like I'll ask him — his big blue head is big enough.

To my surprise, he wraps his arms around me. We hug longer than we ever have, healing what words cannot.

39

Orliana

Trinte shows up with my suitcase a few minutes later with a smile. "He'll be here in about thirty minutes to escort you to dinner."

My stomach flips. I'm still not sure how I feel about everything, or how to approach the coming days. "You can't take me?"

He doesn't miss a beat. "Absolutely not. See you there."

With that, he's gone, strutting down the hall, whistling like he has no care in the world. I saw the way he went after his brother, pushing Fynn literally and figuratively. I knew male Dragons were aggressive, especially brothers, but seeing the two of them physically brawl was shocking.

Now is not the time. Tossing the suitcase onto the bed, I begin pulling out clothes. I inspect the dress Kyri added. Naturally, it's more revealing than I'd prefer. It's made of shimmering satin and is the color of the deepest ocean. The neckline plunges to the middle of my sternum, with the hem down to the floor ... with a thigh slit almost up to my hip.

I thought it would be too much. As I press it against my body in the mirror, I realize it'll be perfect for my intentions.

Pulling out my phone, I send Kyri a picture.

Orliana: Fynn kissed me, panicked and walked out. I went to go find him, and overheard him say what we have means nothing to him. So now I seek revenge. Do you think this works?

Kyri: He did WHAT?!

Orliana: He kissed me?

Kyri's face appears on the phone screen as it rings.

Putting her on speaker, I answer. "Hello?"

"Tell me *everything.*" Her tone is both demanding and excited.

Placing the dress on the bed, I flop down beside it. "That's it, really. He kissed me, panicked, left, got into a fight with Trinte and I overheard things I shouldn't have. Now, I barely want to speak to him."

She sighs, sounding a mix of resentful and dreamy. "Right out of a romance novel, I swear. Was it a good kiss?"

I stare at a hanging sconce as I begrudgingly admit, "Reality-altering."

She hums, considering my words. "How angry are you?"

I contemplate the question. There's so much muddling my brain, but most of it is based in the fear of history repeating itself. "I'm afraid he's like Mikan."

She growls. "Why?"

Regret and self-doubt chokes me up for a moment. So many mistakes stemming from ignorance and naïveté. "Because. Mikan tricked me so easily. He tricked all of us. What if Fynn is using me to feel better?"

"Oh, Orliana." She sounds so sad on my behalf. "I mean, of course it's possible, but I don't know. Mikan was dedicated to his appearance in everything. He was a smooth talker." She laughs. "Fynn is nice and all, but he doesn't strike me as a smooth talker."

I chuckle. No, Fynn isn't a smooth talker. He's more real than anyone I've ever met. "You're right. I still don't know what to do."

Kyri makes a dismissive sound. "*Pffi,* make that man sweat. Put him through his paces. See how he reacts if you reject him outright. You told me Mikan would freak out if you didn't let him walk you to the bathroom. If Fynn is even close to that level, your rejection will trigger him."

I eye the dress. Do I really have it in me to make him uncomfortable? She's right though; I need to know how Fynn will react if I don't 'behave.'

Letting out a sound of frustration, I sit up. "Alright. I need to get ready. Just needed a pep talk."

I can't see her, but I know Kyri is grinning. "You're a sexy woman with stunning hair *and* a great butt; I *know* that man regrets fumbling it."

I eye the dress. "Only one way to find out."

"Good luck, and send me a photo. Love you."

"Love you, too." I toss the phone onto the bed and begin getting gussied up.

Thirty minutes later, on the dot, there's a knock at the door. I check my reflection one last time, admiring the slender gold chains hanging from my ears and the deep red lipstick decorating my lips. My pendant settles between my breasts.

"Alright, come on," I summon my familiar.

Moxie pops up beside me, incensed. She lands on my palm, bickering at me with disturbing bleats. Through our bond, I sense her frustration at not being able to defend me.

I smile. "I had enough to take care of. You would've stabbed his eye if you'd been here."

She huffs in agreement. There's another knock, and she glares at the door. Her intent is clear: *Can I go?*

"Oh, not only can you go, but I want you to cause havoc," I murmur, grinning.

Moxie stomps one hoof, bobbing her head. A ugopeg's version of a salute.

With her floating behind me, I answer the door.

For a moment, I can't breathe. Fynn is wearing a dark blue shirt that annoyingly complements my dress. The first *four* buttons are undone, revealing his muscular chest. His hair's perfectly styled, and he smells so damn *good*. Like smoke and sandalwood.

His eyes trail from my black heels up to my eyes. Those golden eyes heat with desire, and despite my resolve to make him beg for it, I swallow hard.

I'm steeling myself for being *only* friends, with a minor caveat: I plan on torturing the absolute fuck out of him. Because now I *know*. The second he kissed me like that, like I was a drink of water in the middle of the desert, I knew he wanted me.

I'm sure he feels guilt about Rhuth, but after what he said about me in the hallway, I've decided that's not my problem anymore. I'm tired of catering to men's emotions. If he wants me, he's going to have to prove it. If Fynn is the guy I think he is, he won't mind me making him sweat a little.

For the first time, the power is mine — I will wield it without mercy.

If only he hadn't unbuttoned the fourth button.

Ignoring the brilliant red scales covering his chest, I give my best scowl, firing the first shot. "I'm only doing this because your brother asked."

"He meddles too much," he says smoothly.

"Agreed." Giving him a return once-over, I sniff dismissively, trying too hard to appear nonchalant, when that unused fourth button has me very much chalant.

Confusion flickers in his expression before smoothing out into a genial smile. Moxie flies at his face, and he ducks. "What the Hells?"

My familiar squeals. I think she might genuinely be trying to take out his eye. Instead of reeling her in, I laugh.

In a singsong voice, I say, "Oh, she's *mad* at you."

Moxie bops him on the head while he stares at me. Again and again, she hits him with her butt. Deadpan, he asks, "If I apologize, will that make it better?"

"No." But I silently command her to reel it back. We don't *actually* want to blind him.

To my amusement, she lands on his shoulder with a huff. He watches her warily. "Is she going to burst my eardrums?"

Don't actually harm him. Moxie's tail wags. "Just be nice and she'll be nice."

"Somehow, I don't think that's how it works," he mutters. There's an awkward beat of silence where we're just staring at one another. I'm not starting this conversation.

I won't.

He can do the labor. I'm done building bridges with men who carry axes.

Fynn rubs the back of his neck, peering up at me through dark lashes. "Orliana, can we please talk?"

I frown, but secretly, I'm thrilled he's initiating the conversation.

Wait, no.

My standards need lifting, because how pathetic would it be to let him come in? And just accept whatever apology he drums up? I'm not actually trying to be mean, but I need to be mean a little, right?

Right.

"We'll be late."

Fynn lifts his chiseled chin. "I don't care. This is more important."

Okay, well, there goes the rest of my self-righteous anger.

Indecision tears at me. He needs to understand he can't treat me this way, but we're adults — we should be able to talk things out.

But what if he's here to actually send me home? I don't think I can handle it if he tells me we aren't friends anymore.

Betraying my dedication to being angry, I ask, "You aren't here to end our friendship, are you? Because if so, I don't think I have the energy to fake it in front of your family later."

"No." He steps closer, brow pinched tight. His sandalwood and smoke scent intensifies; it makes my mouth water. "Please?"

My shoulders sag. As much as I'd like to torture him, it isn't in my nature. Siphons aren't naturally angry. Other people's pain *is* my pain. Causing harm to someone will only cause myself harm.

With a sigh, I step out of the way. Moxie follows him like a sentry, ready to cause pain. For a minute, we stand there, staring at one another. His lips part a couple of times, drawing my attention to them. Reminding me of what happened less than an hour ago. I wish it had lasted longer, especially if we won't do it again.

Stop it, you sex fiend. One epic kiss and I'm suddenly obsessed with them.

Fynn runs fingers through his hair, mussing up the style. "I'm sorry for what you overheard."

The hurt of those words flares again. "Sorry I overheard it, or sorry you said it?"

"Both." Fynn walks to the chair situated in the corner of the room. He leans forward, resting his elbows on his knees.

Clasping his hands together, his gold eyes search my face. "Orliana, I cannot express deeply enough how sorry I am. I should have never said those things."

"Did you mean them?"

"No," he says fiercely.

Moxie flies to my shoulder in camaraderie. "So how *do* you feel about me?"

"I ..." His eyes fly around like the answer might appear. "It's complicated, Orliana."

If this had been three years ago, I would've let it go. Stopped speaking to him — although, let's be honest, I wouldn't have spoken to him in the first place. I would have feared that a punch would meet any attitude.

But I know Fynn now. I know his heart. And I know that no matter what I say, he's not going to physically harm me. My heart, however, is another matter.

My pulse pounds wildly while alarm bells scream in my head. There's only one way to move forward from trauma, and that's by making different choices, one at a time.

Starting by expressing my true feelings.

Cocking my head, I curl my lip. "You said what we've had together meant nothing, Fynn. Everything we've already been through together, everything I've *done* for you, was *nothing.* In a single sentence, you diminished everything we're becoming for one another. You think a simple *sorry* will fix that?"

Shame draws a frown on his face as a muscle feathers his jaw. "No, absolutely not. I know what I said, and I will not pretend it was okay. It's just complicated for me."

I throw my hands up. Placing my hands on my hips, I make a sound of frustration. "*Ugh.* Yes, we *know;* it's *complicated* for you." I point a finger at him. "Did you ever think for one *second* that it's complicated for me, too?"

His eyebrows raise. I've never spoken to him like this, but maybe it's what he deserves.

Allowing myself to feel how much this hurts, I say, "Since I've met you, I've not only given you the space to work through things, I *never* once pushed things. Ever. I've had nothing but compassion, and literally stood next to you for hours while you went through one of the hardest things you've ever done."

Fynn stands, taking a step toward me.. "Orli—"

"I'm not done," I seethe, stepping up to his chest, raising my chin, jabbing a nail into the hard muscle. He stares at it, then back at my face. For a split second, I'm afraid this is the moment he'll snap.

When he doesn't lash out, I exhale sharply and continue with a shaky voice. "And you told your brother that meant *nothing?*" I draw myself upward, even as my insides curl inward from pain and fear. "*Fuck you,* Fynn Gleanscale. You've made me feel *worthless,* and *used,* and ... and ..."

I have to stop speaking because I've started crying. It feels like I'm always shedding tears. I'm so goddess damned tired of crying over *men,* of all things.

Fynn goes to put hands on my elbows, but thinks twice and drops them. His face contorts with a mix of shame and guilt. Always those two. When he speaks, his voice is layered with an agony no one deserves to feel.

"Orliana, I swear I *never* intended to treat you like that. I see now how selfish I've been. I've let this ... this ..." He throws up his hands in frustration. "... this fucking *grief* devours *everything* inside me, and it's so fucking insatiable, it's gobbling *everything else* up in my life."

A tear streaks down his face. "I don't *want* to be like this for the rest of my life. I don't want to think, 'Rhuth is no longer the last to do this' or feel guilt because I didn't think about her at all."

This time, he doesn't hesitate to touch me. His hands come to my face, and I stare into the despair twisting his expression. The way tears stream down his face. "Please, Orliana. Feel what you mean to me. I may not be able to truly explain it yet, but please, *feel* it."

Immediately, I lower my shield and allow his emotions to consume me. My whole body jolts at the intensity. It's so much desperation, shame, longing, guilt, happiness, and ... love. It's small, so frail. Not because what he feels is small, but because he's crushing it down desperately.

But it's there.

My hands come to his uncovered elbows. "Fynn—"

"Orliana." He breathes my name like a prayer. Irises the color of warm sunsets search my face desperately, hoping for a clue to my feelings. "I left because I realized that when I kissed you, I didn't think about her at all. That's why it's complicated. Because at that moment all I wanted was *you.* Only you. Can you understand why this tears me up? Please tell me you can understand."

His voice chokes, and he swallows hard before saying, "Because I truly don't think I can survive you being mad at me. We can just be friends. That's fine. That's perfect, if it's what you want. But letting you walk around this world, thinking you mean nothing to me, I simply cannot bear it."

We're two broken people standing in this hotel room, clutching one another like a lifeline. It's taking enormous effort to not burst into sobs with him.

As much as I want to cling desperately to that glimmer of love for me nestled inside of him, I need time to think this through. It's probably the greatest apology of all time, but I can't let myself get swept up by sweet words again. I did that once, and look what happened.

I'm about to tell him we need to talk about this later, but the memory of him in the club, holding me with fear in his eyes, stops me. The way he fed me ice cream on the deathaversary of his wife. Every patient word he's given Joulian.

Fynn isn't Mikan. Never once, in all those years, was Mikan vulnerable and raw. Everything in Fynn is more earnest and pure. And even if I weren't a Siphon, I can't meet his exposed soul with derision. It's not who I am.

"I'm scared." My voice trembles, much to my embarrassment.

His fingers twitch against my arms, as if resisting the need to make fists. "Why are you scared?"

A tear slips down my cheek. "I spent over a third of my life with a man who made me question reality. I ..."

Sudden, deep exhaustion makes me sag. I'm so *tired.* Fynn sees my body weave, and he coaxes me to sit on the bed.

With him next to me, I gather my strength. "I haven't spoken about Mikan because I hate thinking about it."

I blink, and a tear falls to my lap. I press at the wet stain with my thumb, distracting a part of myself. "Every day, he would feed me his rage. He held me by the throat and forced himself on me."

My hands reach for my pendant, remembering what those moments were like. "And I did it, you know? It's what Siphons are good for — helping others." Devastation mars his beautiful face. "It made him nicer for the rest of the day. Nicer to me; nicer to Joulian." I pet Moxie. "Nicer to her."

I inhale a jagged breath. "The day I killed him, it was the first and only time I set out to hurt someone." Desperate for him to understand, I grab his hand without thinking.

I'm so lost in my grief, I don't even realize I'm sharing my emotions with him as I whisper, "I didn't *want* to kill him, Fynn. *I didn't.* He was Joulian's father. I thought that maybe one day the opportunity to leave might happen. That maybe he'd get bored with me and find someone new. Which felt awful to think about every day."

Renewed tears simmer in his eyes, and he places a hand over mine. "I believe you."

Those three words crack my soul in half. So many people didn't believe me, even after seeing the bruises and fractures. For months, Mikan's old friends and associates spread rumors and lies to help his parents gain custody of Joulian. It was a terrifying time.

"What happened?" He brings a hand to my back, making comforting circles.

Rubbing Moxie between her ears, I say, "It was a normal day." I give him a sardonic smile. "Normal for us, at least. Joulian was at school, and I was late for Mikan's release." The last word's bitter in my mouth. "That's what he called it. His releaseRelease. Sometimes, if he was drunk, he would call it 'releasing the beast' as if what festered inside him made him powerful, and he was gifting me this 'power.'"

Fynn's palm becomes scorching against my skin, and he raises his hand so his Fyre doesn't hurt me. But before he does so, I can feel the deep hatred pumping in his blood. Hatred for Mikan.

"Rage at the undeserving is cheap," he mutters.

I scoff. "He didn't agree, but it wasn't really up to me. That day, after he did it, he wanted a *different* kind of release."

Fynn goes deathly still, and I pause, wondering if I should say these things. I give him a worried look. "Is this too much?"

"No," He brings a hand to my face, so tender in his touch. Another tear cuts down his cheek. "You can never be too much for me, Orliana. Ever."

My expression wobbles with emotion. I have to avert my gaze before I lose my courage. "I told him no. I ... I still hurt from the night before. But when I refused, he decided he was tired of my so-called attitude."

My hand trails up to my throat, where sometimes, the ghost of his grip lingers. "I was terrified. He spoke about raising Joulian without me, and I snapped. I kicked him between the legs and ran for the knife. I almost didn't win; but the whole time, I kept thinking, *don't stop.* For my son, I couldn't stop."

Sobs rattle against my rib cage. Fynn's hand comes to my back with a gentle press, a silent bolster against my nightmare. "He was going to literally stomp my face in. It's sheer luck and willpower that I got my hands on the knife again. I sliced his Achilles tendon, and when he collapsed, I returned everything he's ever given my pendant."

A shudder spasms through my body at the memory of those emotions. Some of which still exist in this pendant. "And as he wept like a baby, faced with everything he'd ever given me, I slit his throat."

He watches me, rapt and furious. "I slept like a baby that night, which somehow makes things worse. Shouldn't I have felt guilt? Remorse? Something? It was Joulian's father; yet, some days when I'm sad, I think of the way his skin split and the blood coated my arms. And I feel *better*, Fynn."

The words never said before feel like both chains and wings. Being honest to this degree is like plunging into an ocean storm and praying you don't drown. I watch him, desperate to read his aura or emotions, but I can't use it as a crutch for connection.

Fynn's red scales glimmer against his gold eyes, as if glowing from the inside. An orange fireball peeks through his shirt, showing his deeper, unshared emotions. "If he were still alive, the things I'd do to him are utterly unspeakable, Orliana. And I would never lose sleep over it. I'm not going to tell you how to feel, but just know that even if you never felt guilty, I'd still be proud of you."

When my crying shakes my body, he uses those big arms to tuck me into his chest. In his hold, I let it all go. With Fynn here, his heat keeping the cold dread away, I've never felt safer.

40

Fynn

Dragons are renowned for their fury. As well as their possessiveness and bluntness, but our fury is terrible enough that there are laws in place that prohibit some actions, even under the sanctioned laws of revenge.

For example, it would've been punishable to use my claws to flay her husband alive, then slowly roast each inch of his flesh over weeks until his entire body was jerky. Too barbaric, they would've said.

It would've been a punishment gladly accepted.

Because Mikan deserves worse. So much worse.

With Orliana in my arms, it's all I can do to not shift into my Dragon form, take to the skies, and find a mountain to turn to glass with my Fyre. I desperately want to hurt something on her behalf.

I can't destroy the guilt eating at her. The only thing I can do is to swear never to hurt her again, and pour nothing but love into her. Mikan might've wanted to give her his rage, but I want to give her so much more.

When she's done crying, she sits up, dabbing at the tears marring her makeup. Even this distraught, with mascara smudged under her dark eyes, she's still one of the most beautiful women I've ever seen.

Inhaling a shaky breath, she says, "I didn't expect to say all that. I never talk about him. It gives life to the guilt, and I can barely tolerate it most of the time."

Smoothing hair from her face, I give a sad smile. "I understand."

"I know you do, which is why you're the only person I've said all of that to. Kyri and Mom can't understand, and I don't have the energy to explain."

Giving a sympathetic nod, I brush hair off her shoulder and lay a hand on the soft exposed skin. "We never have to speak about it ever again if you don't want to. But please know I'm here to listen if you do."

"Thank you," she whispers, looking like a broken fawn with her big brown eyes and dark lashes.

The urge to kiss her again is overwhelming, but I have no choice but to resist. "Do you want to skip tonight?"

She shakes her head. "No, but I think I need a drink before we go and play Dragon politics."

Releasing a deep chuckle, I reach over to the nightstand and pull out some tissues. "That's an excellent idea. Champagne?"

"Oh, yes!" she says excitedly. And that's one of the things I love about her — she never wallows. Some of it's a defense mechanism, but I truly believe she's always eager to see the good in this world.

As she dabs her face with a tissue, I peer around the room. "So, you're sleeping in here tonight?"

It's impossible to not sound disappointed. I didn't realize I'd looked forward to waking up next to her, even as just a friend, until this moment. What does she look like with hair mussed from sleep and ... other things?

Orliana gives me a half smile. "Is that okay? I'm not mad at you anymore, but maybe we should take a night apart? To process? It's been one of the most intense hours of my life."

I let out a laugh. “First off, of course it’s okay. Second, I agree, and that’s really saying something, considering our past experiences.”

Finally, she truly smiles. “Right?” Her expression falls. “We need to talk about the kiss, Fynn.”

The light buzzing pressing up under my skin fizzles out. “Okay.”

“How ... did you ... did you like it?”

Like it? I liked it so much that I almost ruined everything over it.

I go to touch her face. “Can I touch you?”

When she nods, I cup her cheek. My thumb brushes away a lingering tear, resting against the small freckle under her eye. “Like isn’t a strong enough word, Orliana.”

The words appear to unravel some sort of fear. Relief softens her expression. “Okay, good. Yeah, me too.”

Balling up the used tissue, she says, “I was talking to Kyri—” she gives me a sidelong grin, and I roll my eyes. “—and since we’re being entirely open and honest, I have to admit ... I may have a son, but I’m not very experienced with kissing or anything like that.” She scrunches up her face. “What I mean is that out of all the sex that’s happened to me, I’ve never, uh, enjoyed it.”

“Where exactly is Mikan buried?” I ask smoothly, trying to appear innocent and probably failing. It brings me great pleasure knowing we will never share oxygen.

This gets a laugh and a smack on the arm. “I’m being serious.”

“Me too,” I deadpan. Because what does she *mean* she’s never enjoyed it?

Her eyes dance as she grins. “Anyway, if the kiss was bad—”

“It wasn’t,” I refuse to let her think it was anything less than spectacular. “It was one of the best kisses of my life.”

She blinks, speechless. I brush a thumb to her lip, gently tugging it down. Without thinking, I lick my own lips, eager for another taste. “I’d also be very interested in doing it again.”

Orliana looks away, and my stomach sinks. I let go of her lip. She nibbles on the spot where my thumb was before saying, “I don’t want to mess up our friendship, Fynn. It means everything to me, and I know Joulian would be crushed if I took you away from him, too."

"Orliana." I take a finger and tilt her head toward me. Dread tugs at the corners of her eyes. "Even if *I* somehow mess this up, because we both know it would never be you, I would *never* take it out on your son. Ever."

"Promise?"

"On Rhuth's grave."

Her eyes flare, understanding the severity of my promise. "Okay, thank you." The corner of her mouth pulls down as if it pains her to say, "But still. I'm realizing how inexperienced I truly feel. And I was thinking ..."

Her cheeks redden; she fidgets with her pendant. In her lap, Moxie opens a sleepy eye.

I'm starting to connect the dots. Pulse hammering, I murmur, "Is this a conversation better said over champagne?"

Orliana laughs with relief. "Yes, I think so. Probably."

If she's about to ask what I think she is, I'll need at least half a glass of whiskey in my stomach. Standing, I offer her a hand. I don't think I'll ever tire of her bare palm on my body. When her hand slides into mine, delicate and tentative, my cock twitches.

No.

Ignoring my growing desire, I help her stand. Moxie follows her as Orliana grabs her purse, the ugopeg giving me dirty looks every chance she gets. To me, it's a sign that Orliana is still apprehensive.

Breathing becomes impossible when Orliana bends over, grabbing the purse on the ground where she dropped it. Her plump ass is like an offering, and my hands twitch with the deep need to dig my fingers into it.

She straightens and gives me a bright smile. "Ready?"

Forcing myself to breathe, I croak out, "You have no idea."

41

Orliana

When Flynn leads me down the hallway with his fingers intertwined with mine, I don't let go. After asking an employee for a bar not surrounded by fish tanks, we find ourselves in a small, boat-themed bar. Sand still covers the floor, but instead of fish tanks as walls, it's painted driftwood, with string lights and hanging lanterns illuminating the cozy space.

We find a seat toward the edge of the bar, lending some privacy. Moxie lands on the bar top, grabs a napkin, and chews on it.

Fynn turns his body toward mine, bracketing my legs with his thick thighs. The split of fabric above my right thigh reveals long inches of skin. I'm overcome with the urge to grab the fabric to hide my leg, but I see Fynn stare at it for a beat too long. That lingering look flutters shy excitement inside my chest. It can stay as is.

This unfamiliar feeling of *want* and *need* makes me bold. Anew. I'm fully inside a new chapter of my life, and there's an irresistible urge to jump in, feet first. Despite what's happened so far, it's such a relief to share my deepest fears with someone who understands.

Which is why I'm comfortable — well, comfortable *and* terrified — to ask him if maybe he might want to help me explore my sexuality. Maybe he'll scream at me, and I'll truly ruin things entirely ... but he said that kiss was incredible. That kiss showed me there are things I've discounted due to negative experiences. Maybe he'll laugh at me right out the door, but maybe ... he won't?

Throat bobbing, Fynn clears his throat. "So. What is it you wanted to ask?"

Desire and embarrassment heat my skin. What if he makes fun of me? I'm thirty-five and considering asking him to help me ... what? Help me discover what all the fuss is about with sex and orgasms?

We aren't adolescents — this feels so infantile. How would he *not* laugh at me?

"I need to wait for the drink," I squirm in my seat. It's not sexy to squirm in a dress this beautiful, but I never claimed to not be awkward.

The bartender appears, saving me for a moment while Fynn gives the drink order. I watch the bartender walk away — I need him to bring that liquid courage faster. Because I opened my big mouth. By the way Fynn's watching me with hunger, it's like he already knows what I'm going to say.

Fynn leans against the bar top, raising a thick brow. "Now I'm extremely intrigued."

A bead of sweat rolls down my spine. I'm feeling cornered. It must show, because Flynn softens. "We can talk about the weather or how we'll kick Trinte's tail later."

I chuckle, a little relieved. "I feel silly."

His focus drops to my thigh again, and his hand twitches, as if he wants to grab it. It bolsters my courage.

"I've never orgasmed," I blurt out. The second the words exist, it's clear I should've waited for the drink. My mouth goes dry as the Oasha Desert.

Flynn's head flies back in shock. Nearby patrons glance over, causing me to cringe. That was absurdly loud, judging by the expressions on everyone's faces.

My cheeks burn. Fynn leans forward, lowering his voice. "I'm sorry, did you just say you've never had an *orgasm?*"

Now my knee jiggles as my anxiety reaches a fevered pitch. "It's not a big deal, I promise, but—"

A warm, firm hand lands on my exposed thigh, right above my knee. My breath hitches, watching his fingers press into my flesh. Fynn's eyes are burning. "It's a *very* big deal, Orliana. You're how old?"

Grimacing, I say, "Thirty-five."

"How long were you married?"

"Too long."

His fingers tighten. "And you haven't ...?" When his gaze briefly flicks to between my thighs, my stomach flips.

I shake my head. "It's never seemed important. With Mikan, it's like my whole body didn't even belong to me. After ... My focus was on surviving and moving on. It's hard to miss what you've never had."

He nods thoughtfully, taking a swig of his drink and points at mine. "Take a sip; you're going to need it."

Baby Pegasi flutter in my belly as I sip my champagne. Moxie trots over to me, makes sure I'm not having a visible meltdown, and returns to her half-eaten napkin.

After three sips, I can't wait any longer. "You don't think I'm broken or something?"

"Absolutely not, Orliana," he says fiercely. His hand slides up a little higher as he leans a little closer. It's becoming difficult to think as that hand shifts. "It means you still have so much to experience." With a wicked grin, he says, "And isn't that exciting?"

How does he always know what to say? I huff out a laugh; the tension coiling in my muscles releases. "I guess you could look at it like that."

"It's the only way to look at it," he declares, releasing his hold on my leg to sit back. Cold air prickles where his hand was. I want to glue it back.

We sip our drinks, watching one another. Now I'm positive he knows what I'm hedging at, but he's going to make me say it. My anxiety spikes again. Here goes nothing.

"So ... I was wondering ... if ... maybe you might be interested in ..." My mouth goes dry *again,* forcing another sip of champagne. Impulsively, I downed the entire thing. Fynn watches me with an amused half-smile and raises a finger to the bartender, ordering another.

"Interested in ...?" he prompts, sipping his whiskey again. The way his eyes dance with amusement, he knows exactly what I'm trying to say. Why is this so hard? I'm a grown woman asking a grown man to help me with something entirely natural.

Except it never felt natural. It's been boring, painful, a waste of time, and even annoying.

The kiss with him showed how little I know of pleasure, and that was a *simple* kiss. Having kissed only three men ever means my pool of experience is small. However, something tells me there's more to it. If everyone felt that kind of chemistry, society as a whole would've developed around people needing to kiss all the time. Instead, we decided to have jobs that take all day, taxes to pay, and so many alternatives for activities.

No, what we have is special.

If it were any less spectacular, I wouldn't ask. But I can't resist the opportunity to not only know myself better, but to know Fynn better. He said it was one of the best kisses of his life. Considering how much he loved Rhuth, I've decided that means something profound.

Fynn watches me work through these thoughts, showing only patient and growing amusement

Refraining from letting loose a growl of panic-fueled frustration, I rush out, "Helpmehaveanorgasm?"

With impeccable timing, the bartender arrives with my drink. He gives us wide eyes before walking away.

My entire body burns from the effort of being this vulnerable. I'm petrified that Fynn's going to laugh at me. Or worse, reject me.

Nausea rolls in my belly. What if he—

"I'd be delighted," he says without hesitation, pulling out his wallet. I watch him pull out corals and place them on the bar top.

After taking a deep gulp of the champagne, its fizz lighting up under my skin, I squeak, "You would?"

Fynn hesitates. "Yes, but we also need to have a serious conversation about what you said to Trinte."

I think of all the things his brother and I discussed. When it's obvious that I don't understand, he clarifies. "He was clear that you were quite adamant about being friends. That clashes with the idea of seduction."

"I can see how those two can clash," I murmur, watching Moxie finish the vestiges of the napkin, her tiny tail flicking with happiness. I rub her little rump with a finger. A part of me regrets declaring we're only friends again. The other part is screaming, pointing out that we've had deep, connective conversations with undeniable chemistry.

The final part of me is terrified that we're going to complicate things. Again.

Fynn shifts forward, and that blessed hand finds my thigh again. "You can revoke consent at any time. *Any* time. I could be deep inside you, and if you say stop, I'll freeze like ice."

Liquid heat pools in my core, and I have to stifle a whimper at the visual of him naked, on top of me, and thrusting ...

My instant desire must show, because his expression is feral. "I'm glad you like the idea, but I'm dead serious, Oriana. Your friendship is important to me, and I will never put it at risk ever again. May Rhuth return and throttle me in broad daylight if I ever even come close again."

I laugh. "She'd really do that?"

"Oh, yes." His smile becomes soft and wistful. "I've thought many times in these last few weeks how she'd thump me upside the head for being so stupid."

Hesitating, I weigh my question before asking, "Are you ... ready? I don't want to do anything until you're ready." I give him a sardonic smirk. "I went thirty-five years without an orgasm — I'm fine with waiting longer."

Fynn's mouth opens, then closes. He stares at his whiskey, swirling the ice. I can appreciate he's thinking his answer through. There's no reason to rush anything, even though I can't stop visualizing him inside—

"Yes." My attention turns back to him as he says, "When we kissed, I didn't think of her at all." His voice cracks, and he pauses, taking a sip of the whiskey. After another few heartbeats of silence, he says, "I think that means I'm ready."

We lock eyes. "I'll never not love my wife, Oriana. She was and always will be a vital part of who I am."

Emotions thicken in my throat. My bottom lip shakes. "I would *never* want you to forget or stop loving her. Your love for her is one of the best things about you, Fynn."

"And that's why you're so perfect," he murmurs, turning his focus back to the drink. Even though it stings that he looks away, I understand how hard it must be to say all of this, so I sit patiently, taking a sip of my drink. Just as he did for me.

"It might not be easy for me," he confesses. "I'd be humiliated if I started crying during sex, but I genuinely cannot guarantee it wouldn't happen."

It's my turn to lean forward, placing a hand on his thigh. Heat slowly licks up from my toes to my lips as those golden irises home in on my touch. "I'll be there to support however you need."

When those irises reach mine again, there's a promise of something I don't quite understand yet. But something tells me I will soon.

He tosses back the rest of his whiskey and stands. While I've never seen someone smolder, I'm fairly certain he's smoldering. "Then it would be an honor to facilitate your first orgasm."

When he holds out a hand, I stare at it. "Right now?"

His chuckle is deep, like the softest velvet. "I mean, certainly if you insist, but I'm a big fan of seduction."

My eyebrows jump. "Seduction?"

Fog coats my thoughts as he leans forward. One of his hands braces against the bar top while the other cups my jaw. Gently, he turns my head to the side. Breath shudders in my throat as he inhales my scent deeply. My lungs forget how to work when his warm breath tickles my ear as he whispers, "Would you like me to show you?"

Would it be inappropriate to scream yes? Goosebumps explode all over, sending a shiver down my limbs. Without meaning to, my thighs clench. "*Yes.*"

Fynn grabs my drink. I watch, confused, when he holds out a hand again. "Superb. Time for dinner."

Dazed, I stand, enjoying his rough palm against mine. What will they feel like all over my body? The visual turns my thoughts to quicksand, swirling straight down to my core. Moxie flies off the bar top and lands on his broad shoulder. She rubs her face into his stubble, and he tilts his head into her affection. She gives the tiniest honk. Through our bond, I feel what I've been fighting.

There's no use in fighting it or lying to myself anymore.

I'm too sick and tired of doing both.

42

Fynn

Long forgotten levels of happiness bubble up in my stomach, inflating my heart. My thigh still tingles from where her hand pressed. I swear my own hand burns from where I touched her thigh — twice. It's silky soft. Does the rest of her body feel like that? How is she so goddess damned perfect? I can barely keep my hands to myself since that first intimate touch.

Our conversations went better than I could've dreamed of. I'd never given my fears a voice, but it's always been a deep concern that someone new would become hurt or angry that I can't completely put Rhuth behind. So many people would.

Of course, Orliana isn't like other people.

Watching her visibly squirm as she asks for help with her first orgasm gives me great pleasure. Not because I want her uncomfortable, but because I enjoy watching her chest flush and the way she keeps licking her lower lip. When she's nervous, she plays with the ends of her long hair, continuously twirling the strands. I don't think she knows she's doing it.

Bringing my hand to the delectable curve of her back, I steer her through the bar toward the bought-out restaurant where Aunt Teale has the meet and greet planned. I've spent weeks dreading this event, but with Orliana on my arm, everything will be okay.

There's a large group of Dragons already waiting. Some are easily recognizable, but not all. The restaurant connects to the main lobby, which is also full of familiar Dragons. Our Weyr contains about four hundred family members. Not all of us know one another or are attending, but it's still a large mass of shifting colors.

At the front, Trinte stands with some cousins, but his focus finds us immediately. He studies us, sees the way I touch her, and a small smirk quirks his lips. I can't find it in me to be irritated. He meddled deeply, but I'm grateful. He saw something I was too blind to notice at first, but if there's one thing I know about Trinte, is that he'll do anything for someone he loves.

He excuses himself from the conversation and weaves through family members, meeting us on the edge of the crowd.

"So," he says, looking between us. "How are my two favorite *just friends* doing?"

Okay, maybe he still deserves a solid punch in that broad jaw. "Fine. Remind me to sit away from you today."

Trinte gives Orliana a soft smile. "Are you okay?"

She returns the smile. "Yeah, I'm good."

Seemingly satisfied with our relative non-answers, he glances over his shoulder and lowers his voice. "I fear Aunt Teale has meddled once again."

"Are the two of you in cahoots or something?" I growl. When he says nothing, I ground my jaw. That's an answer I *will* get later. But for now, "What has she done?"

"She's doing the *Têasté*."

Blood drains from my face, my Fyre burns with possession. "No."

"Yes."

Orliana's forehead wrinkles. "What is a *Têasté?*"

Fuck. This is the *last* thing Orliana and I need right now.

"It's a Dragon tradition for new couples." I let out a growl of frustration. "It's when the lead matriarch chooses a potential match for each Dragon and then makes the couple sit together next to each match."

"I won't be near you?" She sounds panicked. "I'm not even a Dragon."

I rub my thumb on her spine reassuringly. "I'll be right next to you. It's not only Dragons subjected to this dumb tradition. However, I suspect Maureen will be on my other side and ..."

"Warnock will be on hers," Trinte finishes.

At the name, I freeze. This cannot be happening. Giving my brother a scathing glare, I snarl, *"Warnock?"*

Orliana touches my arm, concerned. "Who is Warnock?"

"I'm Warnock," a deep voice says. Behind Trinte, a disturbingly handsome Dragon approaches. He's my height, with scales the color of the brightest tropical waters. His dark blue hair curls around a strong neck.

For the first time in years, there's a twinge of inferiority. Where I've let my body wither from grief, he's clearly hit the gym daily. The burnt orange linen shirt reveals his musculature, including his stupidly impressive pectorals.

He appraises Orliana with an appreciation that makes me whip my tail in warning. My childhood nemesis, who just so happened to seduce my girlfriend when we were adolescents, grins.

"Long time no see, Fynn. Good to have you here."

"I can't quite say the same," I clip. Since we're roughly the same age, and his magyck isn't as powerful as mine, I don't have to abide by a hierarchy of respect. "Why did Aunt Teale choose you?"

"Oh, I'm seeking a possible mate," he says nonchalantly. "When she asked which bachelor could take part in your *Têasté*, I was the first to volunteer."

"You're playing with fire," Trinte warns.

Looking at Orliana, Warnock breathes a tiny bit of fire onto his tongue, licking lasciviously at the air. "I like fire."

At her tiny gasp, it's a nearly impossible task to not scoop her up and ravish her in the hotel room. Make her forget all about that stupid trick I could never master.

Moxie flies up to Warnock's face and, to my pleasure, the little goat screams at him so loud her tongue sticks out. His head snaps back in alarm. My smile defines the word *smug.* If he can't handle her familiar, he can't handle her.

"Moxie, knock it off," Orliana says nervously. The tiny ugopeg lands on my shoulder, still incensed.

Careful to not display too much of a challenge, so Aunt Teale doesn't tail whip me for impropriety, I take a small step and flick my tail again. "You will *not* touch her."

Orliana's hand tightens around my arm. "I can speak for myself, thank you."

Warnock holds my glare, regardless. He breaks it to give her another once over. "I'm eager to learn more about you, Orliana."

Her name on his tongue makes me want to rip it out. But if Aunt Teale insists on the *Têasté,* we can't decline. It's usually for show, a formality to prove the connection between a couple, which is exactly why she's chosen this.

She and I need to speak. Immediately.

Ignoring Warnock, I gently guide Orliana to Trinte's side. "Where is our esteemed aunt?"

He jerks his head toward the inside of the restaurant. "The receiving line."

Great. An audience will be privy to my frustration. Giving Orliana a tight smile, I say, "Stay with Trinte. Please."

She nods wordlessly with an expression that is a mix of confusion, intrigue, and amusement. With one last warning glare at Warnock, I stalk off through the crowd.

Aunt Teale stands with the other aunts, greeting each family member as they find their assigned seat on the massive chart by the door. Since I'm taller than most Dragons, she spots me immediately. I swallow hard at the delight broadening her smile.

As I approach, she says, "Oh, Fynn. Again so soon?"

"It's so good to see you," Aunt Venil says, happiness raising her voice.

"Good to see you, too." While she throws her arms around me, I try to return the hug while asking Aunt Teale, "Why are you making us do the *Têasté?*"

Aunt Teale inspects me with appreciation. "You look good. Maureen will appreciate it, I'm sure."

"I'm here with Orliana," I hiss, mindful of those listening.

"Yes, but as head matriarch, it's my responsibility to test all connections." She sniffs dismissively.

"Orliana isn't a Dragon," I remind her. "She's not required to participate."

"No, but you are," she reminds me with a smirk. "Besides, if you think she's good enough for a Dragon, she should be treated as such."

I loathe how right she is. It's rare for Dragons to be with a non-Dragon, simply because the politics and temperaments prove to be more than most can handle. Something I've failed to fully prepare Orliana for.

"Why Warnock?" I ask, coming perilously close to sounding petulant.

Aunt Reena gasps, then claps her hands. "Oh, Teale. Excellent choice. Did you hear he was the first in his family to become a millionaire? Invented the radiography tech that allows physicians to obtain scans through the dense structure of Dragon hide."

Something inside me wilts. A millionaire inventor? How can I compete? I'm a Dragxi; a widower barely able to see past his grief who hasn't seen the inside of a gym in years. And there are certainly not a million corals in my bank account. Not even close. I'm not destitute, but not *that* wealthy either.

Aunt Teale must see my bleak realization because she places a hand on my forearm. "If she loves you, there's nothing to worry about, right?"

Orliana doesn't love me, though. I'm not clear on exactly how I feel, either. I've barely had a moment in the last hour and a half to process everything that has happened. My thoughts race, trying to assimilate, but there's no time.

Whatever she sees in my expression makes her falter. "She does love you, right? And you, her?"

I can't answer because I don't *know* the answers. She draws up straighter, wiping the concern off her face. "The *Têasté* is exactly that: a test. It's tradition for the most eligible options to be presented, and that's what I've done. I wish you luck, nephew."

She greets an uncle I don't recognize, dismissing me.

The other aunts watch me with pity, but say nothing. I stalk back to my brother and Orliana. They're waiting, deep in conversation. Warnock is nowhere to be seen. Good. I see the tension between them, and I furrow my brow. Orliana hisses something and Trinte shrugs, saying words I can't hear over the different conversations.

Trinte spots me first, says one more thing to her, then stops when I'm close enough. I'm about to ask what he's said that has clearly upset her, but he says, "What did she say?"

"It's still happening," I growl. "I tried to point out that Orliana isn't a Dragon, but she basically said if she's good enough for me, she's good enough for any other eligible Dragon."

Trinte swears under his breath. "She has me sitting across the room. Now I understand why."

"What is she up to?" I snarl, my Fyre clanging against its mortal cage of ribs. What I really want to ask is, *Will Orliana be wooed by someone better?*

"It'll be fine," Orliana says, sounding confident. "It's just for dinner, right?"

I close my eyes. After exhaling harshly, I open my eyes. "Yes. It will be fine."

The lie scalds my tongue.

43

Orliana

Watching Fynn come undone by this surprise *Têasté* is fascinating. Granted, he knows more about what's going to happen than I do. It appears to be an unexpected thing, so I can't be mad for not knowing about it earlier.

While Fynn stalked off, Trinte says, "This could very well be a disaster."

Anxiety spikes. "Why? I thought it was only for dinner."

"Fynn hasn't mentioned it, so I will: You won't be permitted to speak to him during the entire meal."

I pale. "The whole time?"

"Correct. You will sit side by side, but you're only allowed to speak with Warnock or anyone else who engages in the conversation."

I gawp, then sputter out, "B-but ... t-that's absurd. He's right next to me."

Trinte grimaces, shoving hands into his pockets. "Yes, but *Têasté* means 'test' in Dragonian. It's a test on multiple fronts; can you obey the laws of the Weyr? Do you trust your connection enough to go a single meal without speaking? When presented with the most eligible option, can that connection be upheld?"

I can't see Fynn right now, but I know how panicked he felt in my hand. "Why is Fynn so worried?"

Trinte gives me a sidelong look. "Oh, I don't know, Orliana. Perhaps it is because you both just had a meltdown? He's barely had time to figure out how he feels? He knows you're probably in the same place?"

Pointing a finger, he pretends to have a great idea. "Oh, I know! It's probably because he and Warnock have had an absurd competition since they were children. Warnock successfully seduced a partner away from Fynn when they were about eighteen."

"But Fynn had Rhuth," I insist. "What does that have to do with anything?"

Trinte chuckles bitterly. "I fear you have much to discover about male Dragon pride, Orliana. It could've been thirty years ago, but a Dragon's pride has a long memory."

My mind races for a solution. There's no time for another conversation with Fynn to reassure him. I stare at my bare hands. "Can I use my ability without violating the *Têasté?*"

Trinte looks confused, then realization dawns. "I mean, on a technicality, it wouldn't be a problem. You aren't to speak, but there's no rule about touching. Come to think of it, I've seen Dragons wrap tails in silent comfort." He grows excited. "Without a tail, I could see this being a suitable compromise."

"Do you need to ask?" I'm afraid my growing hope is folly.

Trinte considers my question. "Yes. To honor the *Têasté* to the fullest, it's vital to be transparent. When Fynn returns, I'll go ask Aunt Teale."

"Don't tell Fynn," I say quickly.

A glint of amusement twinkles his blue eyes. "Want him to squirm a little?"

"Maybe a little," I admit shyly. "He might've given a sincere apology. I won't make him grovel, but a little squirming isn't being cruel, right?"

"No, it's not cruel." Trinte studies my face with a small smirk playing at his lips. "You know, I once had a conversation with Rhuth I never shared with Fynn." He adds, lowering his voice. "And I will never share, understood?"

Understanding the unsaid words, I nod.

Looking around to make sure no one is listening, he murmurs, "It was about a year before her death. We were at their home, and he was at work. The topic of soulmates came up, and I said they weren't real."

Checking again to make sure no one is listening, he continues, "She said they were. I joked that she was lucky to have found hers. Orliana, she looked me dead in the eye and said she wasn't his soulmate."

I gasp, a hand flying to my mouth. Trinte stepped closer, his words coming out faster. "I asked her how she could even say that, but she said it was a feeling she had. An abstract understanding that while she loved him, something always told her she was never going to be his final chapter."

My stomach cramps at the words. "Why ... why won't you tell him that?"

"At first, it wasn't my story to tell." Trinte rubs the back of his neck with a grimace. "After she died, it seemed moot. When you first met him, do you think that version would've responded well?"

"No," I admit. "He would've probably disowned you."

"Exactly. And he was like that for *five years.*" He straightens. "Maybe I'll tell him one day." Trinte looks at me knowingly. "When the time is right."

What he's implying has me staring at my shoes, resisting the urge to hold the queasiness in my belly. "I wish you hadn't told me. How am I supposed to keep this from him?"

The more I think about it, the more my anger builds. How could he tell me and ask me to say nothing?

Trinte opens his mouth, then shuts it, eyes homed in on something behind me. I follow his gaze; Fynn's walking back, looking anxious.

To me, this infuriating brother says, "I told you because Fynn is the type of male who needs his tail dragged to the truth, kicking and screaming sometimes. A little squirming won't hurt him, but it can certainly shine a light on what needs to be known."

"What are you implying?" I hiss with no short amount of panic.

I almost slap him when he shrugs. "I know Rhuth would've adored you. When you think of my brother, can you think of forever?"

"You ask me this *now?*" My palms are clammy, and blood pounds in my ears. This is turning into one of the most challenging days of my life.

"There's plenty of time to contemplate, Orliana. In fact, you have an entire dinner planned for just that."

Fynn comes to stand next to us, breathing hard. His aura reads all of the colors showing panic, fear, dread, and grief. The grief is significantly smaller than ever before. What does that mean? When he looks at me, shades of red and pink flare.

"What did she say?" Trinte asks.

As Fynn tells him, I examine his features. I've never seen fear crease the edges of his eyes, but it's there. Why is he afraid? Feeling my concern, Moxie hops onto his shoulder, nuzzling his cheek. Comforting him in a way I can't yet.

But I will.

44

Fynn

Dread makes my feet feel they're caught in quicksand as I guide Orliana to where we're assigned to sit. Placards sit on gleaming plates, showing Maureen on my left, and Warnock on her right. Pulling out her chair, I help Orliana sit and tuck the chair back in.

"Hello, again."

My body tenses as Warnock strolls up, eyeing Orliana again. He won't even acknowledge me. It's a purposeful insult.

Orliana offers him a tight, polite smile. "Hello."

Once I sit, the *Têasté* begins. Maybe if I stand here all night, we can prolong this insanity. When I don't sit, Warnock remains standing; a silent challenge. He's still watching her, and I want to claw out his eyes.

Since the *Têasté* hasn't begun, I'm permitted to lean down and run my lips along her check. Into her ear, I whisper, "I'll be thinking of our kiss the whole time."

Orliana stiffens, cheeks flushing. Inhaling her scent once more, I take a seat, sealing the beginning of the *Têasté.*

Warnock sits with grace, turning to face her. I hate the genuine interest in his expression. I'm desperate to scream, *she's mine,* but that would not only be inappropriate, it would be untrue. She's not mine.

Not yet.

"We meet again," a feminine voice murmurs, the chair beside me pulling out. It would've been polite to help Maureen sit, but I'm not engaging in the farce more than necessary.

"Hello," I respond stiffly.

Objectively, Maureen is a beautiful Dragon. Her lavender scales are stunning against her luscious form. She's wearing a revealing dress to show her finer assets, but I keep my eyes on her face. I refuse to give Orliana any opportunity for concern.

"I hope you don't mind that I insisted on being your option for the *Têasté,*" she says, voice shy. "I've heard many great things about you. You have your own company?"

Do not be mean to the perfectly nice woman. "Yes, for the last ten years."

"That's so impressive," she says, reaching for a glass of ice water. Around us, everyone is finding their seats. Only thirty seconds have passed.

This is going to be the longest dinner in history.

She glances around my chest at Orliana. "And that's the infamous Orliana?"

"Infamous?" I raise a brow.

Maureen chuckles, grabbing the napkin off the table and primly placing it in her lap. "There have been discussions about the friend you've brought. Teale said you've spent the last five years mourning your wife." Her face twists with sympathy. "I was so sad to hear of the tragedy."

The first mention of Rhuth is like a physical blow. Air leaves my lungs, and for a split second, I can't think. This is exactly why Orliana is here, but during the *Têasté,* Maureen is permitted to ask or say anything she wants.

Hand shaking, I take a sip of my water, buying a moment to think. This might be the first time, but since this is the first Weyr reunion since her death, Rhuth will be brought up. It's only natural. The downside of Aunt Teale delaying the reunions on my behalf.

When I'm able to speak, I say, "Yes. It was a tragedy."

"You must miss her very much."

The grief I'd put on a mental shelf, in an attempt to give Orliana the attention she deserves, reappears in full force. This is exactly what I've been dreading.

I'm about to answer — what I'm going to say, I still don't know — when I hear Trinte come up behind Orliana. "It's been approved."

I turn to look at him, brow furrowed. My brother winks, then walks away. What in all Hells has been approved?

"Fynn? Did I say something inappropriate?" Maureen's sweet voice is full of concern.

She deserves honesty. Inhaling a fortifying breath, I explain, "I've spent every day for the last five years missing Rhuth. In fact, it's become a deep personality trait. Trinte likes to call it broodiness."

Maureen smiles. "I think that's beautiful."

Her response makes me falter. "You think it's beautiful that I can't stop missing my dead wife?"

"Of course. She was also with child, right?"

Panic slams my heart into overdrive, and my legs twitch, desperate to run. It's too far. Too much. I can't talk about Titus. I *can't.*

A familiar hand finds mine. I glance at Orliana, but she's still talking to Warnock. I'm flooded with a sense of calm, and just like that ... Everything is fine.

This must be what Trinte confirmed as permitted. We can't entangle tails, so hand-holding is an accepted modification. She's supporting me in the best way she knows how.

A flash of magenta catches my attention. Aunt Teale is marching to a podium. When she spins, she catches me watching. Her eyes flick to where Orliana holds my hand. She dips her chin in approval.

Relief allows me to inhale deeply. To Maureen, I say, "Yes. With my son."

"How awful," the lilac Dragon murmurs. "I'm glad you're doing better now."

Am I doing better? Orliana's hand squeezes mine, as if she can feel my faltering sense of self. In the time we've been getting to know one another, I've come alive. I already know that when I get home, things will be drastically different. Even if I never get to kiss Orliana again — which would be a travesty — she's awakened my dormant Fyre.

Smiling, I say, "Yes, I'm doing better now."

Aunt Teale taps the microphone and clears her throat. The crowd quiets; a rapt audience. "Welcome Weyr Wingside to the fifty-second reunion. It's been far too long since we all gathered." When her eyes flick to me, it really sinks in — the mercy she granted by delaying the reunions until now. "It's been a pleasure meeting new Dragons, and old. Some of you are *too* old."

The crowd chuckles. She grins. "This weekend is about reconnecting and strengthening our Weyr's magyck. If you haven't already received the timeline, just know that photos are tomorrow morning. You'll have free time after, but tomorrow's evening gala will introduce new couples that have passed the *Têasté* and wish for a formal announcement. We have a dozen *Têastés* occurring right now. I'd like to introduce you to all twelve couples."

Orliana's hand tightens, and I'm worried that she might not want to be announced as a couple. Aunt Teale is throwing all sorts of curveballs right now. I really should've asked what else she had planned.

Through our touch, I sent her my concern. She sends back comfort that warms my chest. That's the best answer I'll get; it'll have to be enough.

Aunt Teale announces the couples one by one, each standing with big grins. Should *I* smile? Orliana gives me the sweetest smile of encouragement, sending comfort again.

"And it's my pleasure to introduce Fynn Gleanscale with his new partner, Orliana Veritas. We all know the tragedy that occurred, and we all deeply miss Rhuth Gleanscale, may she fly in the skies."

"May she fly in the skies," the crowd murmurs. Emotions thicken in my throat, and my legs shake as I stand with Orliana. Through our touch, she sends me what could be love, but that would be ridiculous.

She doesn't love me. I'm just confused.

I plaster a smile on my face, relieved Aunt Teale didn't mention Titus. I might have an actual breakdown if she does. One mention tonight is more than enough.

"Welcome to you both. May you revel in the *Têasté*, and find the answers you are seeking."

With that, we sit. My aunt speaks of the accomplishments within the Weyr, including Warnock's scientific breakthrough that helps all Dragonkind.

Meanwhile, I collect stories while carrying people on my back.

My doubt is again met with reassurance from Orliana. It's as if my emotions are the sole focus for her, even as conversation resumes.

"I'm so excited for dinner," Maureen gushes, watching the waitstaff bring out plates. "I heard it's roasted piglet and potatoes, with a side of blood jam."

My mouth waters, and I can't help but admit, "Piglet is my favorite."

Maureen beams. "Excellent."

Yet, as the dish arrives, smelling divine, all I can think about is what I'd rather be devouring.

Staring at my utensils, I realize the issue: I have to let go of Orliana's hand to cut into the meat. I'd rather starve, even as my stomach roars. Dragons can continue to hold tails, but we can't ...

I'm speechless as Orliana guides my hand to the smooth, golden leg that's taunted me all evening. She places it higher than I would've dared and shifts it inward. As her thighs tighten around my hand, my entire body throbs.

Without asking, she grabs my plate and, as she continues talking to Warnock, Orliana cuts into my piglet, creating bite-sized pieces. It'll be clumsy eating with my left hand, but I'd rather drop food in my lap than remove my hand from hers.

That's when she lets me feel it: the desire pulsing through her. It matches mine, and blood shoots to my cock. *Fuck.* My body jerks, and I almost drop the water in my hand.

Flabbergasted, I peek at Maureen. She's staring at where my hand is, then up to my face. In that moment, I can see she understands. There's literally not a single chance on this continent or universe where I'd choose anyone other than Orliana.

Smiling to herself, Maureen cuts into her piglet.

45

Orliana

I'm barely able to focus with his palm so high between my thighs. It doesn't help that Warnock is absolutely boring. So far, he's asked questions about me, but they're all intended for him to answer.

I'm pretty sure he only volunteered to be the eligible option to fuck with Fynn. His eyes narrowed with irritation as I placed Fynn's hand between my legs and grabbed the piglet to cut into. I don't care. The various emotions ripping into my friend are too much. He needs my support more than anyone else in this room.

Which is why I think of that kiss and send my feelings to him. It's clear the second he feels it because those fingers dig into my thigh with barely there restraint.

When the piglet's cut up, I place it in front of him, receiving another squeeze on my thigh. Goddess, I want more of that.

Instead, I'm forced to speak with this self-important Dragon. Warnock continues speaking, not even realizing how little I've said in return.

"I've always known I was meant for greatness, you know. Ever since I was young. My mother said I was meant for great things, too."

"Mmm," I murmur, shoving a potato in my mouth so I don't have to speak.

He takes a sip of the wine a waiter brought. I take my champagne, trying not to drink it too fast, but each sip numbs the growing boredom.

Flicking his eyes to Fynn, Warnock asks, "So, how long have you been together?"

Instead of admitting we aren't together, I say, "We've known one another for a little over a month."

"Oh, just a month?" he says, leaning forward. I lean back, keeping the same distance between us. Fynn's arm presses against my back. I feel him shift, attention turning to us.

"Yes, it's been a very interesting month." I loathe his scent of sharp cedar.

It was the wrong thing to say. Warnock takes another sip of his wine. "Wasn't the five-year anniversary of Rhuth's death a couple of weeks ago?"

My stomach plunges to the floor. The hand on my thigh grips, almost painfully, then instantly softens, as if Fynn realized he had hurt me. He's clearly listening to the conversation. Is Maureen not speaking to him?

"Yes," I clip, glaring.

The Dragon doesn't notice. Or maybe he does, knowing Fynn is listening. "Yes, it was such a tragedy. And to be a Dragxi from his own company? I'm sure it haunts him."

The hand on my thigh loosens. His devastation weighs on my heart. I slap a hand on his, refusing to let it leave my thigh.

Now it's clear why Warnock has me on edge. It's not only because he's so incredibly self-absorbed. It's because he reminds me of Mikan. Well put-together. Ready to brag. Antagonizing people for no reason. Treating me like a toy to fight over. *Fuck that.*

Anger shoots adrenaline through my veins. I straighten, lifting my chin. To Warnock, I snipe, "Are you truly concerned? When was the last time you called to check on him?"

"Well," Warnock says, taken aback. "We aren't exactly on those kinds of terms."

"So, is the speculation of his emotional state right now in empathy, or are you attempting to antagonize him?"

Fynn's hand relaxes. Warnock is at a loss for words. Clearly, everyone has fawned over him for some stupid invention, but I don't care. There is nothing eligible about him.

Letting the anger ice my tone, I lean forward and hiss, "If you continue to talk about Rhuth, I will not hesitate to stab you with this knife."

I grab the serrated blade next to my plate. Vicious promise bares my teeth. Warnock's scales pale. With as much fury as I can muster, I whisper, "I've used a knife on a man before. It didn't end well for him, and it won't end well for *you.* Am I clear, or do you need a demonstration?"

"No need," he says quickly, leaning as far away from me as possible. "Understood."

"Good," I purr, sliding the knife back into place. My growing anger is satiated. Adjusting my napkin, I say primly, "It would be a nightmare to get blood out of this beautiful dress. Although I wouldn't mind a good night's rest. Let me know if you change your mind."

"Psychotic female," he mutters, grabbing his wine. All I can do is grin. Around us, voices have grown quiet.

I may not have the stellar hearing abilities of a Dragon, but I swear someone says, "Well, she certainly has the heart of a Dragon."

46

Fynn

Pride isn't a strong enough word for how I feel about Orliana right now. When she grabbed that knife, I almost tackled Warnock to stop her from making a mistake. When she threatened him loud enough for at least twenty people to hear, I couldn't help but grin like a madman.

Warnock is undoubtedly trying to bait me, especially with the underhanded comment about my company being responsible for Rhuth's death. Orliana didn't hesitate or falter in her threat. If she hadn't said anything, I'm unsure of what my reaction would've been. The initial reaction was pure rage, followed by devastation.

But Orliana was there immediately, coming to Rhuth's defense. Protective of a woman she'll never know; protective of my heart to the point of violence. Her emotions confirmed that she meant every word. She would've hurt him.

I've never been so proud.

At my side, Maureen lets out a quiet chuckle. Under her breath, she says, "Well, she certainly has the heart of a Dragon."

Yes, she does. With a steady hand, I grab my whiskey. Voice full of joy, I say, "You have no idea."

The rest of dinner is quiet. Since neither of us is speaking to our neighbors, we eat in silence. My hand stays in place until dessert. It's a slice of cake, but I don't want that for dessert.

So as Orliana takes the first bite of hers, I slide my hand up a little higher. The heat between her thighs is intoxicating. It feeds the ember of lust beginning to simmer under my skin.

Her slice of cake falls off the fork.

She stabs into the piece again, clearly determined to act like nothing is wrong. I let my fingers crawl a little higher; not as high as I desperately want, but enough that she traps my hand with her thighs. That's fine. I'm exactly where I want to be.

Raising my whiskey glass, I'm about to take a sip when a sharp pulse of desire strikes like lightning down my spine straight to my groin. *Sweet fucking Fortuna.* I jerk so hard, whiskey sloshes onto my lap.

Orliana chuckles softly, finally taking a bite of her cake.

Oh. We're playing *that* game.

Gladly.

Taking a long sip of my whiskey, I imagine lifting the satin dress and spreading her legs like a buffet. Lowering my mouth between her thighs; tasting her with my tongue. I return exactly how that makes me feel.

Her thighs tighten; it's almost painful. Still, she cuts into her cake like nothing happened. I would never have known it phased her if it weren't for her thighs clenching.

Time to play really dirty. Pretending to be distracted by a painting on the wall, I imagine crawling between her shaking thighs. Pressing myself against her entrance. Sliding into her wet heat. Feeling her from the inside. My cock pounds with my boiling blood. It's almost excruciating.

This time, when I send her that level of need, her fork clatters onto the plate. The people sitting across from us watch us with concern.

"Sorry," she mutters. A flush works its way from her chest to her neck and up to her cheeks. With a shaking hand, she grabs the fork.

No, that simply will not do. I promised her seduction; since we can't speak, she needs to feel exactly how much I want her.

Smiling blandly, hoping my face doesn't betray my thoughts, I imagine slowly thrusting inside her; consuming her whimpers; her hips rising to mine. Grinding her pelvis as she pursues pleasure. Wrapping these amazing thighs around my waist as I sink deeper.

The fork clatters again, and she sits ramrod straight. Her breath quickens, and from the looks she's receiving, and how eyes flick between the two of us, I know people have an inkling of what's occurring. They might not know she's a Siphon, but at the wild look in her eye, it's impossible to misinterpret.

"When is dinner done?" She asks the woman across from us, breathless. It's an aunt I don't recognize.

"In fifteen minutes, I do believe Teale will announce the official end of the ..." My unknown aunt's eyes trail to where my hand hides under the table. "... dinner."

Dragons have no shame about their sexuality, as a general rule, so I know Orliana isn't being judged. It's unconventional at dinner, but I'm not worried about getting in trouble.

The heat between Orliana's thighs increases, and the second the pressure of her thighs weakens, my hand slides up higher. My fingers are so close, yet so far. Maybe if I wriggle my pinky, I could see exactly how much she's enjoying this.

The sensation of overwhelming desire gut punches me. My cock thickens to a painful degree, more than I've ever allowed it. Standing is going to be difficult if we don't stop this. Despite my efforts, I grunt.

Next to me, Maureen whispers, "Do you want me to go ask Teale to end dinner early?"

Unable to look at Maureen, I can only nod. Words have failed me. Maureen stands and disappears. I should've been nicer to her. Her intentions, unlike Warnock's, were pure.

The next few minutes are a painfully delicious volley between us. My thoughts have devolved to the most basic instincts of touching and fucking the ever loving Hells out of her.

This redefined seduction to a whole new level.

It took over a decade for Aunt Teale to approach the podium again. Looking like the hydra who caught the hero, she announces dinner's end. I sense her stare as she says, "The *Têastés* are completed. I hope the answers sought have been discovered."

Discovery isn't the right word for my situation.

I'm fucking ravenous.

Not giving two fucks about my erection, I bolt upright. Orliana does the same. Around us is a chorus of understanding chuckles. It's impossible to resist smirking at Warnock, who is fuming.

I use the rest of my self-restraint by not bending Orliana over the table to show him exactly who she belongs with.

We hustle out of the restaurant, Orliana's legs pumping at an impressive speed in those heels. She veers to the right, heading to her hotel room, but if I bring her there, she's never coming out. Trinte will find me, insisting on our overnight separation.

Instead, I grab her hand and practically drag her down an empty, dim hallway. When I'm sure it's far enough from the lobby, I stop. My lungs can't receive enough oxygen as I stare at her.

"That was a very dirty game you played," I say, voice so low it's made of gravel. Her breath hitches when I step close enough to inhale her scent. "Who knew you could be so naughty, Orliana?"

47

Orliana

When he takes a step closer, I step back. Every nerve ending in my body lights up in anticipation.

"It could've been dirtier."

His eyes narrow. "It could've. But I'm not about to let Warnock get a free show while I make you moan with pleasure."

Oh, goddess.

He takes another step closer; when I retreat, the wall hits my back. My heart beats wildly as he closes the distance, leaving only a couple of inches between our bodies. Breasts heaving, I lick my lips, trying to hold on to my sanity as he lowers his voice.

"If you want to be *just* friends, I'm okay with that. Truly. But if this is how you want to play — a cat-and-mouse game of emotions — then know you won't win. Because the thought of losing you made me realize *exactly* what I want."

Everything else disappears as he lowers his head, bringing a finger to my chin. As he tilts my mouth up, oxygen stutters in my lungs. Desire threads from his finger into my skin, mingling with mine.

Voice hoarse, I whisper, "W-what do you want?"

This maddening man … instead of kissing me, soft lips brush at the corner of my mouth, then along my jaw. I whimper, bringing my hands to his biceps, digging my nails into the thick muscle.

"I want …" he murmurs.

Tilting my head to the side, he inhales at the spot where my jaw meets my ear. A groan rumbles in his chest, and the Fyre glows between us.

"I want …"

Those lips trail down my neck. When my knees buckle, his free arm wraps around my waist.

I'm panting now, desperate. All of my anger's forgotten, ashes under this sizzling heat surrounding everything.

"Fynn," I whisper. "We can't …"

His movements stop, but he doesn't let go. Warm breath caresses the spot where my neck and shoulder meet. My head tilts to the side, exposing the sensitive skin.

"Do you want me to stop?"

I can barely hear him over the pounding of blood in my ears. I've never felt this level of lust before. Although the all-consuming desire he feels right now elevates mine to new heights.

Searing heat throbs between my thighs, and I want to beg for something, anything, to relieve it. "D-do friends do this?"

With blatant amusement, Fynn says, "Apparently, some friends do. Would you like to be that kind of friend?"

This is either the stupidest or the best decision of my life. With one word, I can ruin this delicate connection we have. Or bring it to new heights. Even the part of my brain that would offer caution is ready to spread its legs for this man. *Fuck it.*

"Yes," I breathe.

A moan fills the empty hallway as his tongue tentatively licks my skin, followed by his lips. His tongue trails up my neck with a vexing slowness, as if he's savoring the flavor of my flesh.

When he reaches my jaw, he uses his hand to tilt my face toward him. Our noses brush, and my eyes flutter. When his lips come close enough, I can feel the heat emanating from them.

His hand leaves my jaw, and my body jerks as he runs knuckles down my sternum. Never kissing me directly; placing his lips everywhere but my mouth. I let out another whimper when his hand slides under my dress, his fingers grazing the edge of my breast.

"Can I touch you, Orliana?"

I can't squeeze my thighs any tighter, desperate for friction. I nod my head.

"Say it."

"Yes."

With tender slowness, his fingers spread, cupping my breast. Just as I'm about to sob from the pleasure, his lips crash onto mine. He consumes the sound with a moan of his own. When a rough thumb brushes over my sensitive nipple, his whole body presses into mine.

If I didn't know any better, I'd say we've been set ablaze by his Fyre, because my body *burns.* When his hips roll into mine with a possessive growl in his throat, my body softens. Fynn brings one of his large thighs between mine. Without hesitation, I grind against it. My moan is salacious, but he only snarls with approval. Releasing my breast, he brings his large hands to my hips.

Still ravenously kissing me, he moves my hips, guiding me as I chase ecstasy. My hands fly up, clutching his neck for stability. When our kiss breaks, we're panting like wild beasts.

"Fynn," I moan into the dark space between us.

"That's it," he murmurs with a jagged breath. "Use my thigh."

He moves my hips at a punishing pace. It's all I can do to hold on, lost in the intense pleasure that wipes away my identity. It builds, threatening to rearrange my sense of self. My whimpers meet his quiet mutterings as he encourages me.

"Keep going. Take it, baby. It's for you. All for fucking you."

I've never felt anything like this. My heart hurts from its wild beating. I've never felt more alive.

"You're so fucking beautiful," he groans, pressing his forehead against mine. "Let me make you feel good, Orliana."

It's those words that unravel everything. Forgetting where we are, I press my mouth into his shoulder to muffle my scream. It tears at my throat as my entire body pulses. My legs fully give out, shaking. Fynn holds me up, not easing the pace until my moans turn to sobs, then back to whimpers.

When my hips are still, we stay there, our sweat-slicked chests heaving. Fynn nuzzles his nose against mine, then ducks his mouth to deliver a tender kiss; the perfect ending to my first orgasm.

It's now abundantly clear why everyone seems so obsessed with sex.

Fynn pulls away, and my heart beats at a different pace. Anxiety replaces my satiating pleasure. Is this when he pulls back? I might actually die if he does this time.

Fynn's eyes search mine, full of concern. "Are you okay?"

I exhale with relief. He must understand the sound because he brings a hand to my face. "I'm not leaving again, Orliana." His thumb strokes my cheek. "I'm so sorry I left before, but it will never happen again. I swear it."

I believe him.

Swallowing hard, wishing I had a glass of water, I smile. "You might officially be my new best friend."

A brilliant grin, deepening his dimples, splits his handsome face. "I'm a big fan of our friendship."

The sound of footsteps has me scrambling to dismount his thigh, but he's reluctant to let me go. "Fynn, someone's coming."

"Let them watch," he says mildly.

I laugh and push against his chest. He sighs, removing his thigh. I quickly readjust my dress. He scans the hallway, hair still mussed from my fingers.

"There you are," Trinte says, striding toward us. At Fynn's unfettered grin of happiness, he almost trips. He scents the air and shakes his head with a grin. "I pray the two of you have a relationship that does not reflect the last few hours. I'm exhausted."

Fynn guides a hand to my back as I steady my legs. "There are a few moments in those hours I'd like to do again."

I smack his arm. “You’re so crude.”

He gives me a boyish grin. I melt at those dimples and fangs. “Only for you.”

“And apparently me,” Trinte says dryly. “I’ve come to escort your *friend* to her hotel room. I was serious; you both need a breather.”

Fynn groans, but doesn’t argue. We know his brother is right. Sadly. Heedless of our audience, Fynn kisses me gently on the lips. Against my mouth, he whispers, “I’m going to think of you all night.”

“Goddess, not next to me,” Trinte grumbles.

Nuzzling his nose, I ask, “Will I see you in the morning?”

After another chaste kiss, he says, “Sunrise brings a new day. This fool can’t keep me from you after that.”

“I can’t wait to have my room back,” his brother grumbles.

We share another smile. Fynn pulls back. Readjusting his pants, which still show an impressive erection, he turns to his brother. “Don’t touch her.”

“Hadn’t planned on it,” Trinte says, motioning me forward. He keeps a careful distance between us.

As he escorts me away from Fynn, I look back one last time. The red Dragon watches me with an expression that promises a very interesting day tomorrow.

48

Fynn

I might actually suffocate Trinte with a pillow tonight. Smother him into oblivion for taking her away from me. Even though I know he's right.

As much as I loathe watching her walk away — and also really enjoy the view — I need space to process everything that's happened.

Rubbing my hands over my face, I wait in the hallway until the blood returns to my brain. It's not like I can satisfy myself with my brother in the same room.

Besides, I want my next orgasm to be with her.

When I'm finally presentable, I leave the hallway. Dragons flood out of the restaurant. As a result, I'm stopped by a few cousins and elders. To my surprise, when they bring up Rhuth, it hurts less. I'm able to smile when they share an anecdote. I don't need Orliana here to regulate my emotions. I'm finally strong enough to do it on my own.

I don't think it's an exaggeration to say that she's saved my life.

When I'm able to get away, I find my way to the large terrace that overlooks the lush landscape of Slous. Twilight sprawls against the horizon, with both moons halfway up the sky. Stars twinkle in greeting.

Sitting on the edge, I let my legs dangle as I take a deep breath in, exhaling the rest of my worries.

We were supposed to come here, Rhuth and I. The ticket stayed in my email, unused, all these years. It never expires, but I've never wanted to come. Aunt Teale hadn't given much of a choice, but I don't regret coming.

Tears shimmer in my eyes; I allow myself to explore the emotions showing up like a summer wave. In another life, maybe Rhuth and I would've taken our son here. Played in the ocean. Laughed on the pink sand. Flown in the sky.

Instead, I'm going to do those things with Orliana.

I wait for the guilt, the sense of betrayal, but there's nothing there.

Just peace.

And that's what makes me cry. There wasn't a single moment in the last five years that would've led me to believe the guilt would disappear. Maybe it won't forever, but the reprieve is a gift.

I'm not a fool — Orliana siphoning away a large part of the calcified grief is the only reason I've been able to make this much progress so quickly. Who knows what state I'd still be in without it. Regardless, I'm appreciative of the gift. I can hold Rhuth in my heart without punishing myself.

To the skies, where I'm sure Rhuth is flying, I whisper, "I miss you so much. And I'll always miss you."

The breeze responds, caressing my face as she used to. A tear falls down my cheek. I don't wipe it away; I want to feel all of this. The grief will always exist, but I'm able to live beside it now. It can't swallow me whole anymore.

I've relearned how to fly.

"There you are."

Instead of being irritated, I'm pleased to hear my brother's voice. I look up as he comes to stand beside me. He notes the tears and sits. Our shoulders press together, a show of silent solidarity.

"I was just saying hi to Rhuth," I whisper.

The breeze picks up again, and he gives a low chuckle. “Looks like she’s saying hello back.”

We sit in silence for a few minutes, watching the moons separate as they find their designated places in the sky. When we were kids, we’d lie on blankets to watch the moons, staring at the constellation of Borath, Fortuna’s lover.

We’ve led long, complicated lives. Trinte’s life has been difficult, especially since he’s spent the last five years essentially parenting me. I’m eager to prove he doesn’t need to do that anymore.

“You love her.”

Trinte’s words interrupt my thoughts, but instead of fear appearing, I feel ... a calm sort of acceptance.

My answer comes without hesitation. “Yes. I do.”

“She makes you happy?”

I gaze at my brother, touched by the concern. “Yes. Very much.”

He looks away. “You need to tell her.”

I smile. “Stop meddling.”

“Can’t. It’s my lot in life.”

I gently push my shoulder against his and chuckle. “What a chosen burden.” Swallowing hard, I say quietly, “Thank you for fighting for me, brother. I know these last five years have been miserable, but you never stopped. I can’t thank you enough.”

My words choke, and I inhale a shuddering breath before continuing. “You saw what I couldn’t. You never stopped fighting for me. I owe you my life.”

Trinte’s eyes shine as he stares straight ahead. “You’re all I have. I could never let you go, Fynn.” He goes quiet, fidgeting with his fingers. “I miss Rhuth. She was wonderful. I loved the way she lit you up.” Looking at me, a tear drops down his blue cheek. “It’s wonderful to see you light up again.”

The words simmer, sinking into my bones. Wiping away my tears, I exhale roughly. “Okay, enough mushy stuff. Do you want to go flying?”

Trinte’s eyes light up. We haven’t flown together in five years. “Really?”

I grin, allowing myself to tilt forward. As the air embraces me, I shift into my true state. Trinte does the same, his massive blue Dragon form coasting alongside mine ruby red form.

For hours, we fly among the stars, racing against the wind and through the clouds.

The whole time, I patiently wait for dawn.

49

Orliana

The moment I'm sequestered in the hotel room, I call Mom. She answers on the first ring.

"Muffin! How's Slous!"

Hearing her voice unravels some of the remaining tension coiling my muscles. "You're never going to believe what happened, Mom."

"Tell me everything," she commands, a smile in her tone.

As I tell her the entire saga — minus the hallway orgasm — I get ready for bed, removing my makeup and carefully hanging up the beautiful dress.

I'm crawling into bed as the story finishes. She's breathless as she says, "Orliana. That's so much."

Propping myself up with a pillow, I say, "Definitely. I can't tell if we've made things more complicated or not."

"Of course it's more complicated." She laughs. "But I can't say I'm surprised."

My eyebrows shoot up. "What do you mean?"

"I mean, every time you spoke about him after the first couple of weeks, you had a look on your face."

"A *look* on my face?"

"Oh, yes. Enamored."

I bark out a laugh. "I did not look enamored."

"Yes, you did," she says firmly. "Kyri will agree with me. So will Trinte."

"I'm not sure how I feel about you talking to Trinte about my supposed expressions."

"Orliana, that boy has been scheming to get you and his brother together since the first day he met you at headquarters."

I sit upright. "What?"

Mom laughs. She's taking too much joy in this revelation. "Sweet Muffin, yes. Weeks ago, he told me about how Fynn scooped you up on the dance floor, ripping off his shirt. How could you not tell me about that?"

My cheeks flush at the memory. I still don't really quite remember what him shirtless. "I was a little out of it, Mom. Plus, I siphoned some of his grief that night. It was intense for both of us."

"Well, I'm glad. Fynn seems very lovely, and he's very good with Joulian."

At the mention of my son, an ache pangs my heart. "How is he, by the way?"

"Oh, you know, being spoiled rotten. Told me to tell you to have fun and to not worry about him."

"Of course he did," I murmur, smiling. Tone shifting to more serious, I say, "Mom, I have a question."

"Oh?"

I pause, pilfering through my thoughts to come up with the right question. "Do you think it's too soon to have deep feelings for Fynn?"

She's quiet for a moment. "No. I don't think so. From what I understand, you both have explored yourselves emotionally, together and separately. Does he require you to regulate his emotions?"

I nibble on my lip, considering everything we've gone through. "He never asks. I'm the one who offers."

"So your siphoning is given freely and happily?"

"Always."

"Does he do anything that reminds you of you know who?"

I laugh. "You can say Mikan's name, Mom. It doesn't bother me anymore."

"That's enough for me," she says. "You wouldn't have said that a month ago. That boy has been as good for you as you are to him." There's a beat of silence before she says, "Do you love him?"

"Yes," I whisper. "I really do. And it scares me, Mom. What if he's lying to us like Mikan?"

"Do you truly believe that?" she asks softly. "When you really look at the situation, does he behave in a way that reminds you of that scum?"

I smile at the nickname. "No. I've thought about it. Honestly, he's so open with sharing his emotions and exactly where he's at. He never gets mad, even when I was yelling at him. He's so good with Joulian."

"And Joulian adores him," she agrees.

A new fear appears. "Wait. What do you think Joulian will say if I'm with Fynn? I've never dated anyone before."

"There's only one way to find out, but I suspect he'll be happy."

My instincts say the same. I check the clock. It's barely ten at night. Somehow, I have to wait eight hours to see him. "I need to sleep. I have a feeling Fynn will be here the second the sun breaks the horizon."

Mom's laugh is full of delight. "Go have fun. Don't worry about Joulian; he's fine. Go be just Orliana tomorrow. And for the love of Emet, get laid."

"Mom," I groan. "You aren't supposed to say things like that."

"Why?" she asks innocently. "You're going to tell me you aren't thinking the same thing."

"No," I say begrudgingly. "But it's none of your business."

"Agree to disagree. I'd like some more grandbabies."

"Goodnight," I growled.

"Goodnight." Her laughter warms my heart.

I hang up and toss my phone to the other side of the too-large bed. Staring at the ceiling, I'm not sure how I'll survive the night. My body feels like it's burning alive. The conversation with Mom made me more confident in my feelings. I wish Fynn were here.

Moxie comes to my side, curling into my chest, immediately letting out tiny snores.

Somehow, against all odds, I fall into a dreamless sleep and wake up as the sun peeks over the horizon, filling my room with dawn light.

There's a knock at my door.

My eyes spring open.

50

Fynn

Sleep barely existed all night. Even after flying for hours and crawling into bed next to my brother, I toss and turn.

I can't stop imagining Orliana in my arms, writhing with pleasure. Screaming my name. The sheets become tangled from my restlessness and incessant sighing. My body burns with the need for it to be a reality.

Just as the sun's rising, Trinte slams a pillow in my face. "For fuck's sake, go. Leave me in peace."

Grabbing my phone, I bolt out of bed. I'm only wearing a white T-shirt and gray sweatpants, but I don't have time to get dressed.

I *need* to see her.

It's a blessing she's only a few rooms down. It takes the last dregs of my restraint to not pound on the door and roar her name. Within five seconds of my first knock, the door opens.

She's gorgeous, with tousled hair, sleep still in her expression — at least one of us slept — and wearing a short, lacy nightgown the color of spring meadows. She blinks those big brown eyes. Instantly, blood refocuses its trajectory to my groin.

"Hi," she says, voice raspy.

My heart pounds, stealing my breath. "I literally cannot wait anymore. Please, I beg of you — let me touch you."

Orliana's smile is more beautiful than any sunrise. "No begging required."

I lift her up, groaning when those glorious legs wrap around my waist. Our lips collide. I kick the door closed and blindly walk toward the bed. When the edge hits my shins, I tumble us forward, cradling her head with a hand.

Here, between her thighs, is the only place I want to be. Her hands roam my body, frantic in their exploration. I rest on a forearm and bring a hand to her breast, groaning in her mouth. They're just as delicious as I remember.

Tugging the top of the nightgown, I catch a nipple in my mouth, giving it a hard suck. Her moan is the most stunning sound. While I swirl a tongue around the tight bud, my hand lowers, sweeping her thigh.

"Fynn." My name's husky on her tongue.

Her thighs widen, allowing my hand to stroke upward to her center. Lace blocks my exploration, but the wet heat of her arousal already soaks the material.

"Is that all for me?" I growl, licking her nipple.

She whimpers, nodding her head frantically. I slide my knuckle up and down the lace. Her hips jerk with desperation.

Sitting on my heels, I rip off my shirt. She watches it fly in the air, then homes in on my bare chest. I suck air through my teeth as her hands trail my muscles. A moment of insecurity sparks. She must feel it because she smiles, sitting up. Running a hand over my torso, she explores with her fingers. When a hand brushes over a nipple, I inhale sharply.

A devilish glint shines within her eyes. "You like that?"

"I like *everything* you do," I growl. My chest brightens as my Fyre flares, eagerly devouring this insatiable desire in my body.

Her breast peeks out from the top of her nightgown. I *need* to see both of them.

Grabbing the hem, I ask, "Can I please remove this?"

There's a moment of indecision flickering through her expression, stopping me cold. "What is it?"

Orliana's hands curl over her belly. "I'm self-conscious."

"Of what?" My eyes skim her body, unable to find a flaw. "You're fucking perfect."

Unacceptable shame flickers in her eyes. "I mean, I had a baby, and my body—"

"Orliana, I would normally allow you to express any insecurity, but I'm going to stop you right there. I want you, and I don't care if your body is different from giving Joulian life."

Tears shimmer in her soft eyes, and her hands part. Reining in my voracious need, I lift the nightgown with tender care. Slow enough that she can stop at any given inch.

When it's pushed up to her ribs, I admire her soft curves. Her belly is plush, with stretch marks like adorable lightning strikes from her cute belly button. I trail one of the silver scars along its jagged path where it ends at the flare of her hips. I want to lick it.

She whimpers, and my eyes immediately find hers. "Is that okay?"

Orliana nods, but her brows furrow as her lips flatten. Alarm bells ring in my mind. Instantly, I remove my hands from her body and place them on my lap.

"We don't have to do anything you want to do. But please know I still find you *incredibly* attractive."

"I know. I ... I don't know what's happening." Her face crumples. "Please stop."

That's all it takes for me to fully pull back and assess her reaction, trying to hide my panic. Did I do something wrong? Her demeanor is devolving fast. She begins to cry in earnest, and for a second, I'm ashamed that I might've caused this.

Like plugging a shattered dam with a finger, I adjust the nightgown. It only makes her curl into herself.

"Orliana ...What's wrong?" Panic gallops inside my veins, roaring in my ears. What did I do?

She doesn't appear to hear me, her body shaking with sobs. Can I help? What would she do for me? What has she done for me already?

One of my hands finds hers and gives it a gentle squeeze. Silently, I ask her what she can share. Her ability responds immediately, like the emotions are wild beasts clawing for purchase.

I almost blackout from the intensity.

It would hurt less if she'd kicked me in the gut. The fact that she has this level of agony inside her makes me want to scream. It's a deafening wave of doubt, terror, pain, and dread. It's like every bone in my body being broken and stitched back together all wrong.

A month ago, I wouldn't have been strong enough to handle this without succumbing to my own. But now, I can be there for her like she was for me. I shift from between her thighs, still holding her hand as I come to lie beside her.

Resting my head on a pillow, I watch silently as she pours into me, sobbing. Her entire body shakes violently; I grab the comforter, bringing it over us.

Moxie zooms around, frantic. The poor ugopeg lands on the bed, bleating repeatedly, panicked. I point to the pocket of space between me and Orliana.

"Come on, little one."

She dives in headfirst, her rump wriggling to get as squished as possible. My heart hurts for her; it can't be easy to be small, voiceless, and feel a part of yourself shattering.

The need to curl around Orliana, tucking her in with my tail, is overwhelming. But I suspect touching will be too much.

So I wait. I let her feel how loved and safe she is.

With Moxie's tiny snores keeping me company, I let Orliana unravel.

51

Orliana

The memories pommel me into submission. My body feels like it's pressed against an electric fence.

"Get in here, Orlee."

"Lay there, Orlee."

A warm body lays next to mine; fear trembles my limbs. Is it Mikan? *No,* it's over. He's dead. He's gone. I slit his throat myself.

I squeeze the hand holding mine for dear life, not even caring that I'm shoving every emotion into it. Thoughts are impossible. Air refuses to enter my lungs.

"Breathe, Orliana."

Fynn's soothing voice from far away calls to me. I curl inward, making myself small. Covering my vital organs. He's still here. Still everywhere. In every cell, picking apart my essence, one rageful attack at a time.

I can't breathe.

"Be a good girl and open wide."

My lungs compress.

My throat tightens.

"Give me some, Orliana. Please."

No, I can't give Fynn this. He's only just now healing. I can't add to it.

"That was a terrible performance. When I get home, you better be ready to show me a better time, Orlee."

I can't breathe.

Fynn's hand strokes my hair. "You're safe, Orliana."

"You're so disgusting, Orlee. What happened to that tight body?"

I open my mouth and try to breathe. This sob is so excruciating, it's swallowing me whole. No matter how hard I try, *I can't breathe.*

"Please. Breathe. Fortuna, please bring her breath."

I crack on the inside, then shatter into a million tiny shards of glass. A hand presses on my chest, almost willing my body to do its job.

Air heaves into my throat, my lungs turning into a vortex as I inhale. A wave of relief rolls over my body as my blood gains the oxygen it needs.

Then I scream. I scream and scream and *scream.*

"There you go. Let it out."

There's a pounding from far away.

I'm set adrift from reality. The hand continues to run through my hair, and I keep pouring into the other one. From far away, I recognize it's Fynn.

I'm so broken. So, so broken.

"Why do you make me do this?"

"Go shower. You're disgusting."

The door lock beeps and someone else is near. Is it Mikan? Reality feels unobtainable, blurred with memories. What if it was a dream, and he's still alive? Releasing the hand, I scramble into the pillows, curling in tighter. Smaller. Invisible.

"What's wrong?"

That's not Mikan. That's Trinte. Sweet Trinte. Why is he here?

"She's triggered. I'm trying to figure out what to do." Flynn sounds pained. So much worry. I don't want to worry him. Will he think I'm dirty? Broken? Unloveable?

The footsteps draw closer. I shrink. No matter how much I remind myself it's Trinte, my body doesn't believe it.

"Hey." Trinte's voice is soft. "Orliana. You need to focus on breathing."

I shake my head, pressing my mouth into the pillow.

An incredibly warm hand touches my elbow. I jerk away, but it stays.

"She doesn't like that," Fynn snarls.

"Just trust me," Trinte murmurs. A rough thumb swipes along my elbow. "Orliana, give me some. I can take it."

A tiny invitation pokes at my somapathic connection. It seizes the opportunity and slams into a new home. Except ... It's not new.

My darkness is greeted with its cousin, a shifting inky depth inside his heart. No matter what my ability brings into Trinte, it's met with familiarity. There's nothing I'm feeling that he hasn't experienced or contains.

What has happened to him?

With Fynn, I still instinctually held back. With Trinte, I *give.* His grip stays firm and steady. Not a tremor or a flinch.

"I love you. That's why I do this."

"Stop crying. You know you like it."

Disgust. Shame. Horror. It's an overwhelming waterfall of despair.

"There you go," Trinte whispers.

His words are muffled, overwhelmed by my panting breaths, the throbbing pulse in my ears, and the sweat covering my body.

Little by little, Trinte allows me to crawl back to reality. Focusing on those sensations, I claw myself back into the present. It takes too long. Like wading through a dense fog determined to keep me lost.

My senses slowly return. I can feel the sheets beneath my body. The comforter over it. The heat of a body behind me. Instinctually, I curl into the warmth, desperate for a kind touch to replace the bad one. There's a tiny squeal as Moxie lands in my hands. My sweetest friend. She nestles inside my curled fingers.

"Just stay with her." The hand disappears. "She should feel better in a little bit."

Trinte's feet head toward the door.

"Thank you, brother."

"Anytime." Trinte's voice is hollow. The door closes.

I shift into him. Fynn stills, then softens. "Can I hold you?" I nod, but he frowns. "I need you to verbally consent, baby."

"Yes." My throat is so sore, I can barely speak.

I'm enveloped by strong arms, followed by the scent of smoke. His body curls around mine, his chest at my back and his tail coming to my front. With one hand holding Moxie, I use the other to hug the thick tail closer. He tightens his hold.

"You're safe. I won't let anyone hurt you," he murmurs, pressing his forehead into the back of my head. Slowly, my breathing steadies. The tears dry up. Exhaustion weighs down, and sleep takes me under.

52

Fynn

We lay there for hours while she sleeps. Her reaction was unlike anything I've witnessed, but I'm fairly certain I can relate to her feelings. The moment she stopped breathing, it brought me back to the day I found out Rhuth died. How Trinte had to beg me to breathe.

It was a scary moment as her face turned purple, with her body simply refusing oxygen. I nearly wept with relief when she inhaled.

Trinte barged in here, saying he heard her screaming down the hall. When he saw her prone form, even though I covered her, he quickly put two and two together. Maybe I should feel inadequate for not being able to help her like he clearly has, but I'm not too prideful to be grateful that she received the support.

I'm hungry, and I'm sure she is too, but her shaking body's still covered in sweat. Even as she sleeps, her body is working through unseen traumas.

The irony is that I thought I'd be the one to trigger. Orliana gave no indication that it might happen for her, so maybe she really didn't expect it. If she hasn't dated anyone for the last three years, but spent over a decade being abused, it's not really a surprise.

When I'm alone, when we're not touching, I'm going to let myself feel the agonizing fury that only helplessness can bring. Helpless to help her fight the ghosts; helpless to *kill* that ghost. But right now, I remain as neutral as possible. Her body sheds the emotions, bringing them through my body, then sucking them back in. It's an odd sensation, like an unwelcome visitor constantly walking into my home.

She did it for me, though. I'll do it for her.

The intensity eases over time. In the early afternoon, she stirs. Her arms, still holding onto my tail, flexing, then softening. between us, Moxie pops her head up and crawls over Orliana's shoulder to snuggle into her chest.

I gently kiss the back of her head. "How are you?"

She groans, unfolding her body, forcing me to do the same. I want to keep her wrapped up, safe between my tail and arms.

"Like I just had to fight a hydra and one of the heads chewed me up and spat me out."

I can't help it; I laugh. "That's an insane visual."

She snorts, rubbing her face into a pillow. "Well, I feel insane."

My heart squeezes with empathy. "You're not insane, Orliana."

I reach up to brush her hair back until her neck is exposed. I press my nose into her shoulder, quietly inhaling her scent.

"Thank you," she whispers. "But that was kind of crazy."

"It was definitely more intense than anticipated."

"And not in a good way," she mutters.

"Hey," I murmur. "There are never any expectations. Ever."

Her ribs shake as she cries again. It's quiet, but I can feel the shame in her body. Reluctantly, I release her and sit up.

"Orliana, please look at me."

She presses her hands to her face, shaking her head. "No. I'm so ashamed. I can't believe I did that. I know that you wanted it, and *I* wanted it too."

Prying a hand from her face with gentle care, I get graced with one bloodshot eye. She's pale, and her hand is clammy. "Come on. Look at me."

Finally, she lowers the other hand, but they both cover her chest. Like she's trying to hug herself. Reaching over, I grab a small pillow and hand it to her. "Here."

She takes it quickly, hugging it closer. Orliana's eyes search my face. "I would understand if you left. I'm complicated, Flynn." Her expression turns bleak as she adds bitterly, "And let's be honest; that's going to happen again. I'm broken."

"Okay," I say. "So it happens again. Now we know what to expect, and we can discuss beforehand if you need me to do anything different."

"Why?" she says, expression twisted in confusion. "Why would you want to deal with my shit too? When you have so much of your own?"

"Can I touch you?"

She nods. Since she's aware, I accept the silent consent. I wipe away the lingering wetness on her cheeks. "I'm going to say something, and it's probably not the most ideal time, but I need you to understand why I don't care, okay?"

She nods. I plunge into the point of no return. I thought it would be terrifying, but with her, *for* her, I'm brave.

"I love you, Orliana. I think I've loved you from the start, but it took me so long to see it. I'd say I regret how stubborn I've been, but I'm not. Because I wouldn't want to go through all of this with anyone else."

Taking in her open, vulnerable expression, I repeat, "I love you, Orliana. I'll be your safe space as you heal. Because you deserve to be happy."

"But why?"

Her question takes me by surprise. My brows furrow to the point it hurts. "Why what?"

Her voice is so small when she says, "Why do you love me?"

Oh. That's easy. I hold up one hand, ticking off each finger. "You're smart. You're compassionate. You're kind. You're patient. You're a fantastic mother."

I hold up the other hand. "You're brave. You strive to see the good in people. You give without taking, to a fault. You put up with my brother."

At this, she giggles. Returning her shy smile with one of my own, I point to the last finger. "Because when you laugh, everything feels like it's going to be okay, even when it's not."

This sobers her. She hugs the pillow tighter. "But I have flaws, too."

I shrug. "Me, too."

"But I might freak out again," she insists, the edge of panic returning to her voice.

I hold my tail out to her. "Here's your new security blanket. Compliments of the house."

This time, her expression is as brilliant as it had been hours ago. She tosses the pillow and snuggles up to my tail. It sends a shiver up my spine.

"I really do like it."

This beautiful woman makes my heart ache in the most wonderful way. "I love you, Orliana."

With eyes as big as the moons, she whispers, "I love you too, Fynn."

Those four words thrust me high into the heavens, leaving me cradled in the clouds. As I place a kiss on her forehead, she asks, "Was Trinte in here earlier?"

"Yes." I don't think it's possible to express the amount of gratitude I have for his hard-earned instincts. What he did for her is something I clearly cannot — we have led very different lives.

"He helped me," she says quietly.

"You'll learn he's like that."

She hums. I lay down, pulling her into my chest. Her warm breath feels wonderful against my bare skin. "Do you want to stay here?"

As if conspiring against us, both of our stomachs rumble simultaneously. She sighs. "I'm really hungry, honestly. And I need to move around."

I stroked a hand down her back, relishing finally having her in my arms. "Okay. Do you want to eat here? There are still photos to be done. Plus, the surprise I have planned."

She cranes her head to peer up at me. "Surprise?"

"Oh, yes. A very wet one."

She's quiet for a moment. "I think I can get dressed and leave the room. But there aren't any ridiculous Dragon rituals to do later, right?"

I'm glad she can't see me grimace. I forgot about tonight. "Well, there is the gala tonight where we are presented as an official couple."

Into my chest, she asks, "*Are* we a couple?"

With a grin, I say, "No, baby, we are *just* friends."

When her teeth connect with my chest and bite down hard, all I can do is laugh.

53

Orliana

Despite Fynn telling me he loves me, doubt still exists. How could he want to be shackled with someone who might freak out before, during, *and* possibly after sex?

I've never triggered like that. I didn't even know that was possible. Obviously, there's trauma around sex for me, but there was never an opportunity to truly understand the ramifications. Now, I'm feeling like my insides have been scraped raw by a rusty spoon.

I desperately need space from thinking about it. Staying in bed, wallowing in this unexpected side to my future is too depressing.

With a kiss on my forehead, Fynn leaves so we can both get dressed. We're going to arrive at the tail end of pictures, but I truly cannot muster the energy to put a lot of work into my appearance. I settle on putting some water on my hair to sleek back fly-aways in a ponytail, one of the nice shirts I brought, and a pair of linen shorts. Underneath, I'm swearing a bikini, since Fynn said we're getting wet.

Staring at my bleak expression in the mirror, I realize there's no way I have the energy to put on makeup. So I guess these dark circles are playing third-wheel today.

Within fifteen minutes, Fynn is walking through the hotel room door, looking anxious until his eyes land on me. His expression softens. "Are you ready for some food?"

I smile and grab my purse. Moxie lands on his shoulder, and the three of us walk to the restaurant with Fynn's hand wrapped protectively around mine.

Fynn's family is all over the hotel, so we're stopped multiple times. Even at breakfast, relatives appear to ask questions. Thankfully, no one tries to foist a daughter onto him. Some bring up Rhuth and their son. Others ask me questions about myself. All of them congratulate us and ask if we'll be announcing ourselves at the gala post *Têasté.* Fynn informs me that the *Têasté* is the reason he's being left alone.

In a way, I'm a little disappointed. It was fun being possessive of him.

Fynn takes it all in stride, answering whatever questions he can. When he notices my energy sinking further — because how are there so many *questions?* — he begins asking for privacy while we eat.

Once our bellies are full, we find the sprawling lawn set aside for hundreds of Dragons to have their photos taken. There's a line, so we hold hands and wait patiently. I lean against him, resting my head on his arm. The entire time, he's a refuge. Fynn never stops watching or anticipating.

When it's finally our turn for photos, the photographer directs us to stand with our backs to the sun. Rolling turquoise waters are a beautiful backdrop. Paired with the scent of brine, it heals a little something in me.

"Wrap your arms around her," the photographer directs. Fynn brings his hands to my waist, hugging me tight.

"Is this okay?" he whispers.

I plaster a mask on my face, hiding how tired I am. "It's fine. I'm glad this is almost over."

Fynn chuckles, twirling a strand of my hair around his finger. "Yes, but we're supposed to think this is fun. Don't let Aunt Teale hear you complain."

The photographer's camera clicks. "Give her a kiss."

Fynn's eyes search mine. "Are you okay if I kiss you?"

"Go on, give her a kiss!" the photographer encourages.

"I think so," I whisper, but I can't hide my nervousness.

"Just one kiss!" the photographer yells, sounding impatient.

Fynn glares at the photographer. His arms tighten around me as he snarls, "Can you back the fuck off for a second? Good goddesses, can't a man get some consent first?"

The photographer appears stunned. I duck my head into Fynn's shirt, smiling. I love this man so much.

"Orliana," he murmurs. "I'd very much like to kiss you."

Tilting my head back up, I grin. "Please do."

He waits a beat, giving me a moment to show any nerves. When he sees nothing, his lips press against mine, feather light. No, that won't do. I can't be treated like some porcelain doll ready to crack at any second.

My hands come to the back of his head to press him closer so I can lick his lips. He groans, and suddenly, the kiss is deeper and hotter than is probably appropriate. Bursts of fire lick my body as the familiar burn of his kisses appears.

Large, steady hands trail up my back, pressing me closer to his chest. He inhales the air between us, stealing my oxygen.

"Um, okay, you can stop kissing now," the photographer says nervously.

Fynn feels reluctant as the kiss mutually ends. Golden sunset eyes search my face. "Was that okay?"

I sigh happily. "I love you."

His smile is better than ... It's better than *everything.*

"I love you, too." A chaste kiss lands on my forehead. "Are you ready for your surprise now?"

I hop up and down. "Yes!"

He grins, long fangs flashing. "You say that now, but tell me how you feel in a little bit."

54

Fynn

"We're riding seahorses?" Orliana says, incredulous, staring at the colorful seahorses resting patiently at the docks, their equine halves bobbing above the turquoise water. A small group of travelers waits a few feet away while we all check-in.

Slinging an arm around her shoulders, I grin. "Yep. Thought maybe you might enjoy the local water sport."

Even though I can't see her eyes behind the owlish black sunglasses, I know they're sparkling with delight. "I've always wanted to do this. Do you need experience with riding them?"

"They told me when I booked that no experience was required."

It's our turn to check-in. Once we sign waivers, we're given ridiculous orange life jackets. I'm sad to see Orliana's maroon bikini top covered, even for safety reasons. They struggled to find one for my broad chest, so it's a size too small — I look absurd.

The Elf guide, with tanned skin, sun bleached hair, and layers of muscles, leads everyone to the seahorses. Orliana grabs my hand, squeezing. A flutter of her nerves skitters onto my skin.

"We don't have to do this if you don't want to."

The breeze sways her dark strands as she scrunches her nose. "Of course I want to. But look at them; they're huge!"

She's not wrong; seahorses are enormous. They're as big as Pegasi, at least the top half. The bottom portion is a sleek, scaled tail with wispy fins undulating under the clear water. Their manes are braided with trinkets like shells and sea glass. All of them are passive as everyone's assigned to their mount.

"Just stay next to me," I assure her. "Worse comes to worst, I'll pluck you out of the ocean with a talon."

This causes a laugh. "I don't know if that *actually* makes me feel better."

I kiss the top of her head and give her a tiny push toward her assigned purple seahorse. "Go on. It'll be okay."

I watch her swing a leg over the kelp saddle. Her seahorse cranes its head to inspect her empty hands. She smiles as she rubs its forehead.

Taking that as a positive sign, I approach mine. It's a huge blue seahorse, with feathering covering its two hooves. Dark, fathomless eyes watch me as I approach, assessing the creature carefully. As a fire species, I'm less inclined to be in the water. It's better than the species with actual wings, but there's something about water that makes me feel so helpless. Trinte and I both learned how to swim when we were younger, but it's been a long time since I've been in a body of water like this.

"Nervous?" Orliana teases, noticing my hesitation.

Trying to set a brave example, I shake my head. "Just thinking how I might want some shells in my hair later." With no short amount of courage, I swing a leg over the saddle. It's slimy and slippery. How in the Hells I'm staying on is beyond me.

"That one's name is Gaeston," the guide says, coming to check everyone's tack. The blue seahorse snorts, a hoof splashing at the surface of the water. I pat his smooth shoulder; he turns to survey me with one big eye. I swear he's saying, D*on't pet me like a chimeragon*, but I can't be positive.

"What's mine's name?" Orliana asks, petting hers without receiving an equine glare in return.

"Sandela," the guide says, adjusting the bridle. "She's gentle."

"Sandela." Orliana echoes the name with a faint smile, playing with a shell in the mane. "We're going to have fun, right, girl?"

"Alright, everyone! I'll mount up and we can get to the wide open waters!" the guide says excitedly. He hops onto a lime green seahorse who nickers when he's close enough.

When Gaeston shifts, heeding some unspoken signal, I wobble in the saddle. This is going to be a lesson in humility; I just know it. This kelp is ridiculously slimy. Would it be a breach if I used my magyck to keep me and Orliana in the saddle?

Behind me, Orliana squeals with delight, distracting my thoughts. I turn to watch her face light up with a laugh as Sandela glides through the water, her purple fish tail cutting through the waves. Water sprays over Orliana's face, dampening her dark hair. She catches me staring and grins wider. The sight makes my stomach flip-flop; I want to see her this happy forever.

All the seahorses appear to know what to do because they crowd around the guide as we face endless open water. The guide swivels in the saddle to say, "We're going to start off with a race. When your mounts go underwater, don't panic. They use magyck to keep you in the saddle and make sure you can breathe."

"We're going underwater?" a young girl says at the front of the group, her eyes wide. Frankly, I want to have the same reaction, but with more panic. As is, it feels like my heart is going to break free from its cage of bones at the thought of going underwater.

The guide grinned with a nod. "Wait until you see the kelp forest."

I don't want to see the kelp forest; I want off this ride.

"This is so exciting!" Orliana gushes as Sandela sidles up to me and Gaeston. Her cheeks are red with anticipation. Swallowing the growing fear — because I'm a grown male Dragon and immune to fear, supposedly — I give her a wavering smile.

"Very, uh, exciting."

She frowns, her brown eyes flicking over me. *Please don't check my aura.*

"Why are you scared?"

Damnit, she checked it. Time to bluff. "I'm not—"

"And let's go!" the guide cries out, as if calling us to ride into war. Before there's a chance to finish my sentence, Gaeston locks me into the saddle with an invisible sliver of magyck and we're cutting through the waves at breakneck speed. Behind me, Orliana lets out a shrill shriek of surprise, then cackles. At least one of us is having fun.

The seahorse's front legs pound at the sea-foam, their back halves swaying at a rapid pace. It's not as bumpy as expected, but salty ocean spray pelts my face. It gets in my eyes and mouth. Leaning forward, I use Gaeston's thick neck to block some of it.

Chancing a glance down, I can see through the clear water where chunks of brightly colored coral zips by in streams of rainbow. Fish bolt out of the way, of all shapes and sizes.

"To the arch!" the guide cries out in front of everyone. Ahead is a massive stone arch. All the seahorses aim for it, probably having done this trail hundreds of times. My pulse roars in my ears as my fingers white knuckle the reins. I swear I'm trying to have fun, but my Fyre curdles at all the ... *wetness.*

But when Orliana laughs again, her hair falling in soaked strings, it bolsters my bravery. She deserves to have a moment free of worry.

When the arch is close enough, I nearly screech like an upset toddler when Gaeston plunges into the water. Instantly, a bubble of air covers my face, allowing me to breathe. Which is great because now I'm actually screaming like an infant.

Why are we underwater? This was *not* in the ride description when I booked the tour. I imagined bobbing like life rafts at the surface, not plunging into the deep where krakens could eat us or something equally awful.

Right now, I've never felt so far away from my power.

Relax. Enjoy. Inhaling, I try to slow my rapid breathing. A fire creature has no business being underwater like this, but I'm trying *really* hard here. Looking around, I try to appreciate the towering scaffolds of coral that crane toward the sunny surface with crooked fingers. Schools of yellow and blue fish flee in explosive movement when we're close enough. The sight is so wondrous, my fear takes a backseat.

Chancing a moment of terror, I glance at Orliana. Her skin is washed out by the blues and greens, casting an eerie glow. When our eyes meet, it's impossible to be afraid anymore. She's been brave from start to finish — the least I can do is suck it up.

We're charging through a thick kelp forest. Soaring stalks of dark green kelp slaps against our bodies, but Gaeston is undeterred. He lowers his head, seemingly determined to gain distance.

Deciding to embrace this chaos, I lean toward Gaeston's ear. "Let's go, boy."

His ears flicker forward and back; he picks up speed. Without his magyck, I would have sunk to the ocean floor by now. With over fifty feet of water above us, all I can do is trust this creature.

So that's what I do: trust. When we explode out of the kelp forward, I'm pleased to see we're taking the lead, with Sandela hot on our fins. Grinning, I peer over my shoulder and jerk my head to Orliana, unable to yell out encouragement.

There doesn't appear to be a clear finish line, but Gaeston gains speed, so there must be a specific destination in mind.

Boulders, caves, and coral fly by. More kelp. It all rushes by, with the group far behind me and my mount. Only the guide and Orliana keep up, but Gaeston is a stubborn beast. A spark of pride in him makes me grin.

Then I see it: a huge underwater arch. We're headed straight for it, and my instincts say that's where we'll win. A blur of purple levels with us; the race is neck and neck, Orliana's adorable face twisted with determination. Sandela's ears are flat against her purple mane, and she goes to bite Gaeston's face. It veers my seahorse slightly off the path, causing Orliana to take the lead. Gaeston fixes it, but it's too late.

Just like that, Orliana wins.

In my oxygen bubble, I let out a crow of laughter, my racing blood throbbing in my throat. The rest of the group catches up. When we're all gathered, grinning from ear to ear, the guide brings us to the surface. As soon as the oxygen bubbles are removed, everyone chatters excitedly.

Reining Gaeston over to Orliana and the cheating mare, I laugh. "Sandela has some dirty tricks up her mane."

Orliana shrugs, looking pleased. "A good female always knows how to put a male in his place."

I snort, patting Gaeston on the neck. "He put in a good effort."

"Alright, everyone!" the guide calls out. "Time for some sightseeing!"

The rest of the tour is exactly how I imagined it, with us sailing by islands with pink sand and purple palm trees. He shows us the skeleton of a long-dead leviathan on the ocean floor, covered in vibrant coral and thousands of fish.

By the time we're back at the dock, I'm not afraid anymore, but I'm desperate to dry off. That's enough water for the trip. Tomorrow's surprise excursion for Orliana will *not* involve plunging into the depths.

Giving Gaeston one last affection pat, I dismount and step onto the dock with wobbling legs. Orliana does the same, wrapping her arms around my stomach. Peering up at me with wide, trusting eyes, she says, "Thank you for that. I can't remember the last time I had so much fun."

And that's why we did it. Instead of saying the thought aloud, I kiss her on the forehead. "How about we go rent some beach loungers on dry land for the rest of the day?"

I'm graced with another bright grin. Orliana lifts onto her toes and kisses my cheek. "I can't wait."

55

Orliana

The rest of our day's spent lounging in beach chairs, enjoying the sunshine. We order endless fruity fancy drinks decorated with little umbrellas. Moxie enjoys gnawing on orange slices and diving into the sand.

After the trigger this morning *and* seahorse racing, my body is exhausted. But my heart has never felt lighter. He'll never admit it, but I knew Fynn was terrified to be in the water. It wasn't only the flares of orange in his aura; he looked absolutely panicked at times.

But he did it for me, and that creates a warm, fuzzy feeling to fill me up to the brim. I'm not alone in this, judging by the way Fynn smiles easily. More easily than I've ever seen. When we meet up with Trinte for dinner, the blue Dragon can't stop staring at each smile, so it's not only me noticing the change.

By the time we're getting ready for bed, I'm more than ready to snuggle in with him. Moxie waits on the bathroom counter as I slide on my pajamas, which is nothing more than a blue lacy nightgown. It's skimpy, creating fluttering Pegasi in my belly. Moxie bleats her approval, but unfortunately she isn't the one who will be sleeping next to a man she struggles to be intimate with.

I frown, examining my reflection. Insecurities whisper I'm both too much and not enough, but I remember the way he looked at me this morning, with reverence and need. While I'm not quite ready to try sex again, it's important to maintain perspective. If he hasn't run by now, he probably won't. At least, that's what the objective part of my mind is saying.

My heart, however, is screaming to run. To protect itself.

Be brave.

Inhaling a shaky breath, I step out of the bathroom. Fynn's already in his pajama pants, shirtless, leaning against the headboard with a book in his hands. He blinks rapidly.

Clearing his throat, he pats the space next to him. "Come 'ere."

Trying not to seem *too* sexy, I hurry to climb into bed and slide under the blanket. Resting my head on his pectoral, I snuggle into his side. Moxie lands on the pillow beside him, folding her legs to lie down.

Fynn wraps an arm around my shoulders and kisses my head. "How are you feeling?"

Placing a hand on his chest, I say, "I'm exhausted. It was a lot today."

"Was it too much?"

The worry in his tone makes me smile. "No, it's not too much." After a moment of contemplation, I add, "Well, this morning was a lot. But necessary."

Fynn makes circles on my shoulder with a finger. Under my palm, his heart beats steady. "What can I do to make things easier for you?"

I shrug. "I don't know if there is anything to be done, other than working through it together."

"Easy enough." His voice rumbles in my ear, tickling it. "Do you want to talk about anything?"

There's so much that needs to be said, but there's one thing that has been niggling me since we've escalated everything up to this point. I sit up to look at his expression. "Actually, yes." His eyebrows jump, but when he says nothing, I rush out, "I want to talk about how we're moving forward after we get home."

His expression doesn't shift. "What do you want to discuss?"

"Well," I say slowly. "I have Joulian to think about. He's never seen me date anyone before, and while he's a big fan of yours, I want to make sure we have boundaries in place so he knows what to expect." With a shy smile, I add, "And me, too."

Fynn closes the book and sets it on the nightstand. Shifting to face me better, he says, "Orliana, I have no desire to date you."

The words strike my heart like a sword. He must glimpse the blooming devastation because he cups my face. "I don't want to date you, Orliana, because I want to do *more* than date you. I want to greet each sunrise and sunset with you by my side. Whatever this is between us deserves more than a weekly scheduled date, wouldn't you agree?"

Instantly, I'm better. More than better; I'm ecstatic. "Yes, I agree. But I don't want to confuse Joulian. What if we ever ...."

I don't want to say the words *break up* because we aren't officially together. Maybe I'm applying too much pressure, too soon, but as a mother, this conversation can't be shoved aside. Joulian's already hurting over everything with Mikan; the last thing he needs is to get attached to someone, then be disappointed. Crushed, even.

Fynn wraps a strand of my hair around a finger, twirling it thoughtfully. "Why don't we talk to him about it? Really, he should be involved in this discussion, don't you think?"

"True. I think he'd like being involved," I admit.

Fynn hums in agreement, readjusting so I'm leaning against his chest again. Resting a hand on my arm, he rubs it with his thumb. "Last night, I decided it was time to embrace this connection between us. Which means I'm willing to move at the pace that makes you most comfortable."

The hand leaves my arm to tilt my face up. "We could never have sex, and I'd still want to be with you, Orliana."

"I don't want that," I say quickly, earning a grin.

“I don’t want that either, but you need to understand that I don’t love you because of it. My love isn’t transactional, Orliana.”

I let out a happy sigh. “Mine, either.”

When I let out a yawn, he chuckles. “Let’s go to sleep. You sound as tired as I feel. Tomorrow, we’ll go get some breakfast; then I have some place to bring you.”

“Is it more seahorses?” I tease, shifting under the sheets to cuddle closer.

“Hells no,” he drawls, turning off the lights. “I love you, but I never want to do that ever again. Unless it makes you happy.”

I laugh. “We have to bring Joulian here at least once. He’d love it.”

Fynn’s arms wrap me up in a heated cocoon. “Okay, for him, I’ll waterboard my Fyre one more time. No more.”

“No more,” I agree with a grin.

His fingers rake through my hair in a comforting rhythm. “Get some sleep. I’ll be right here if you need me.”

Burrowing into the heat of his Fyre, I close my eyes and breathe him in. Moxie snuggles in between us, letting out a little happy, bleating sigh. Tucking her in close, the three of us fall asleep.

***

The next morning, Fynn tells me to prepare for a beach experience, but that’s all he’ll say. Since the surprise yesterday was so fun, I’m blindly trusting him. When we’re ready, Fynn guides us through the hotel lobby, Moxie leading the way.

To my surprise, Trinte’s waiting for us by the front desk. He has an impish grin on his face.

After giving me a hug, he says to Fynn, “Everything is ready on the landing pad.” A smirk curls his lips. “Even some extra blankets, if you know what I mean.”

“I do *not,*” Fynn growls. More softly, he adds, “Thank you.”

"Have fun, kids," Trinte sing-songs, shoving his hands into pockets before striding away.

I look up at Fynn. "What does he mean by extra blankets?"

But the love of my life ignores the question, tugging me along to the entrance of the hotel. We stop at an assigned landing pad, where a blue backpack waits. It's stuffed to the point of bursting.

Fynn hands me the bag. "Will this be too heavy for you?"

I stare at the backpack. "What's in there?"

"Picnic supplies. And apparently more blankets than necessary."

A picnic? Anticipation has me beaming. "Where are we going?"

With a smile as devious as his brother's, Fynn says, "We're going to that private island, remember?"

My jaw drops. "I thought Trinte was joking."

"He was," he admits. "But the second I discovered it's a bucket list item, I knew there was no way we'd leave Slous without doing that for you."

I stare at the empty landing pad. My stomach jumps with excitement. "How are we getting there, Fynn?"

He grins at the apprehension in my voice. "Dragonback, baby."

Even though this isn't much different from being on a Dragxi, my heartbeat thumps roughly against my ribs. "But there's no saddle."

Fynn cocks his head. "You think I can't keep you safe without a seating saddle?"

I love how this Dragon cannot fathom why I wouldn't want to get on the bare, unsecured back of a flying creature. "Isn't it unsafe without seating?"

He grows serious as he closes the distance between us. Brushing his fingers through my hair, he murmurs, "Do you truly believe I would do anything to endanger you in the slightest?"

"No," My answer is swift and adamant. "Not at all. But ..."

"Aren't you the tiniest bit curious about how handsome I am in my true form?" he teases. Well, he's not wrong. I'm actually very curious. I've seen Trinte, but not Fynn. Which, now that he mentions it, is odd.

"How will I stay on?"

"Magyck, my love," he purrs, sensing my acceptance. Handing me the backpack, he begins walking backward, beaming. "Prepare to be awed by the majesty of the most handsome Dragon you've ever seen."

I laugh, slinging the heavy backpack over my shoulders. "So Trinte's coming?"

At the joke, his eyes narrow. "So, you want to do loopdeeloops?"

"Don't you dare," I shriek. "I'll never get on ever again!"

Fynn laughs as he stops in the center of the landing pad. Then he's ... a Dragon. The air shimmers, expands, and a dragon the color of rose petals appears. Fynn is enormous. In his bi-pedal form, his tail shows boney spots where spikes can be. I haven't seen it yet, but from what I know, they're on his back, too.

Now, those black spikes jut from the crest of his wide, rectangular head to the tip of his long tail, ending in a deadly spiked clubbed. Wings the color of blood unfold, the membrane a darker shade of pink. Golden reptilian eyes turn to me, and smoke curls out of his nostrils. Fangs overlap outside his mouth, and a forked tongue tastes the air.

He's magnificent.

Now, come over here, beautiful.

Smiling, I approach. Fynn lowers his head, and when I'm close enough, he presses his snout into my arms. I laugh. While I've been around plenty of Dragxi in my life, I've never truly touched one. His skin is hot to the touch, but not so hot that it burns. He smells of sulfur and smoke. It makes me curious about his fire.

Rubbing a hand between his nostrils, I giggle when he makes a purring sound deep in his chest. "Are you just an oversized cat?"

Will you let me curl up in your lap if I say yes?

"Not like this." I study his bare shoulder. "How in the Hells am I getting up there?"

Go where you'd normally load.

I obey, walking over to his front leg. The long black claws scrape against the metal platform, leaving deep scratches. I crane my head, trying to figure out how to get up.

Don't freak out.

Before I can ask what he means, I'm flying. Okay, not *exactly* flying, but more like floating. Still, I yelp, my legs pumping against the air. "Fynn! A little warning would've been nice!"

The chuckle grumbles in his throat. Slowly, carefully, his magyck places me right behind one of his spikes. Fear pumps through my blood; I know deep in my bones he'd never put me in danger, but still!

"Do you honestly expect me to hold onto these the whole time?" I complain, trying to stamp down my panic. Immediately, the sensation of a belt around my lap appears.

No, baby. I'll keep you there. Don't insult me by thinking I can't keep a small person on my back. You're riding one of the most powerful Dragons alive, Orliana.

"Not yet," I tease, rubbing his rough scales.

There's silence in my head, but I can feel the desire vibrating deep in his Fyre. I yelp again as he moves. The massive wings unfurl. Fynn launches himself into the air with one powerful sweep of ruby wings. Dragxis never do that, so it's unexpected.

My hair whips into my face as the air streams past. We climb into the blue sky. Gravity yanks at my belly, but the uncomfortable sensation disappears when he evens out.

I peer over his neck, enjoying the stunning view of sparkling water, tiny islands dotting the surface, and their pink sand. The clouds are perpetually in oranges, pinks, purples, and iridescent whites.

On each island, I see various sized crystals jutting from the pink sand. The trees are a mix of green and pink palm trees, with flowers blossoming on bushes in-between.

Out in the distance are lime green mountains, with rainbow clouds shifting through their peaks.

"It's so beautiful," I whisper.

It is, he agrees. ***I've wanted to come here for years.***

"With Rhuth?"

With Rhuth.

"Is it okay that it's me?"

I would not want it with anyone else.

His admission flutters my wakening heart. We fly in silence, and I enjoy the sensation of the misty wind on my body. Dragxis normally use pockets of air to shield passengers from the elements, but I love the rawness of this experience.

When we plunge into a cloud, the mist beads on my skin. The sun immediately dries it away. Between my legs, his Fyre hums with heat. Up here, there's nothing but the sound of his beating wings.

"I love this," I murmur.

Me, too.

Fynn begins lazy circles down toward a deserted island. Excitement perks me up even further. It's my first time having a picnic.

Fynn lands with care, his magyck helping me onto the sand. I immediately kick off my sandals, curling my toes into the sand. It's a rich shade of pink, like a shade cut straight from the sunset sky.

Dropping the backpack unceremoniously, I watch Fynn shift back. A wild, happy look lights up his face as he stalks over to me. My heart hammers, realizing this gorgeous man is all mine.

"Tell me you think I'm the most handsome Dragon you've ever seen," he insists with a smirk, scooping me up. His arms hold me tight, fingers digging into my thighs.

I wrap my legs around him with a giggle. "You're *definitely* the most handsome."

After planting a smacking kiss on my mouth, he says, "Fantastic. Please make sure to inform Trinte."

I flick his nose. "I'm not saying that to him. It'll hurt his feelings."

Fynn narrows his eyes. "My brother's feelings matter more?"

Throwing back my head, I let out a deep belly laugh. "Mr. Gleanscale, I fear you're setting a trap."

He pretends to pout. "I'm going to brood now."

Over his shoulder, I point to the backpack. "As long as you set up the picnic while doing so. I'm hungry again already."

"Yes, ma'am," he murmurs, bringing his lips to mine again. This time, it lingers. A silent question. Wrapping my arms around his neck, I happily deepen the kiss. The breeze caresses us, and the sound of gentle waves is soothing. There's nothing out here but us.

The realization is thrilling.

With a burdened sigh, he carefully places me on the ground, then turns to unpack the picnic. While he does that, I examine the rest of the island. It's small, no bigger than the Dragxi headquarters. I can see each end, and while pink palm trees rustle in the center, I'm betting the other side isn't too far either.

The ocean stretches out to the horizon, with civilization existing in another world. Turning back to Fynn, I smile at the carefully laid out blankets. He's organizing the food, humming to himself. His back muscles flex as he removes a bottle of chilled champagne from a small bag of ice. Glasses tinkle as he pulls them out from the front pocket.

Sensing my stare, he peeks over his shoulder and flashes a grin. "I told Trinte to get the best one they had available."

Giving a giddy clap, I skip over to the blankets and plop down. Summoning Moxie, I watch the purple ugopeg inspect the condensation on the bottle. She licks it up, tail wagging. Fynn pops the cork and fills both champagne flutes. Handing me one, he settles to sit on a hip while I sit on my heels.

"This is amazing, Fynn," I say, taking in the small sandwiches, fruit, and crackers.

"I'd do anything for you." His expression is serious. *"Anything."*

"Even murder?" I joke without thinking.

At the flare of my eyes, about to take back the joke, he confirms, "Especially murder."

I hold up my glass. "To finally seeing Slous for the first time."

His glass clinks against mine. "To Slous."

We take a sip, never breaking eye contact. The champagne is like stars in my mouth, filling my belly with joy. I sigh happily, eyeing the backpack.

"So, what do we have in there?"

Fynn unzips the main compartment and begins pulling items. "Let's see what my brother thought would befit a picnic on the beach."

Trinte, apparently, is incredibly thoughtful. There's fruit, cheese, some chocolate-covered slootberries, and a variety of crackers. He also packed a small jar of honey, two plates, and even included utensils.

"Your brother actually did pretty well," I admit, plucking a grape from one of the containers.

"A blind sphinx can catch a mouse on occasion," he mutters, but amusement tugs at the corners of his mouth.

We nibble on the food in silence, reveling in the warm sunrays that make him as bright as a ruby. When I can't eat anymore, I take to sipping my champagne and watching the waves lap at the crystals jutting up from the sand. My muscles are languid, as if all they needed to relax was a private island, honey-covered crackers, and a bottle of champagne.

"How much space do you have for a serious conversation?"

Fynn's watching me with an unfamiliar intensity. Twisting my mouth, I consider the question. "How serious?"

After taking another sip of his champagne, he says, "It's about what happened yesterday morning."

"Oh." Anxiety sparks, and I take a long sip of my drink. "Well, I guess we should talk about it. A beautiful beach is as good a place as any."

"We don't have to," he says quickly.

I shake my head. "We do."

Turning to fully face me, he asks, "Has that ever happened before?"

"No," I admit. "I really didn't expect it. I'm really sorry—"

He holds up a hand. "I'm not looking for or needing an apology. I'm trying to understand." Fynn considers my words. "In the hallway, you felt fine?"

I laugh. "Definitely more than fine."

"But ... the bed was a struggle?"

I think I'm understanding what he's trying to get at. Silently, I examine what might've triggered me yesterday. Mikan and I only had sex in the bedroom.

"Maybe the bed was a trigger?" I offer.

"Was it me being on top a part of the issue?" he asks.

"Maybe." It's difficult to admit, but we can't discount the possibility. "It was also ... feeling so exposed." Closing my eyes, I tentatively consider what was going through my mind. My heart rate picks up. "It was also how you watched me."

Fynn blanches, and I quickly say, "It's not how *you* watched me, but I think my brain immediately thought it was like an examination. You weren't actually examining me, but my brain couldn't tell the difference."

"Okay, so I need to take down my admiration a notch?" he jokes.

My smile is shy. "I don't ever want you to stop admiring me. Maybe ..." I gnaw on my lip, playing with the blanket. From a few feet away. Moxie's head pops up from under the sand where she burrowed. Sand coats her face and eyelashes. Her eyes shake, and granules of sand fly in the air.

To Fynn, I say, "Maybe you can look at me, but not sitting up like that? It didn't bother me when you were closer. It didn't really bother me, having you on top. It was the distance, I think."

He nods thoughtfully, taking a sip of his drink. "Okay, this is good. If you trigger again, I'd like to have these conversations. I never want you to feel like you can't tell me what might be or actually is an issue."

"Thank you," I murmur, warmth filling my body. This is what it's like to be loved by him. It suddenly hits me that the love he has inside his soul, deep enough for that level of grief, might actually find a home with me. While he'll always love Rhuth, and it's one of the reasons I love him, maybe I can have a slice all for myself.

Seeing my expression, he asks, "What are you thinking?"

Finishing my champagne, I say, "I'm thinking that I've spent weeks feeling the depth of your love for Rhuth, and maybe ..." The words choke for a second as fear blooms. What if he takes this the wrong way?

I shove away the concern. He'll always lead with empathy, just like me.

"Maybe I might be blessed enough to know what that feels like." When his eyebrows fly upward, I panic and add quickly, "Just a little bit. I'm not trying to take anything from her."

In response, Fynn drinks the rest of his champagne and tosses the glass onto the blanket. He crawls up to me, our knees touching.

The breeze whips around us, flying hair into my face. With a soft expression, his eyes search my face as he gently tucks strands behind my ears. "Orliana, because of you, I'm learning about the different kinds of love."

"Different?"

"Different," he confirms. "The love I have for Rhuth is permanent. Not just in the way it'll never go away, but also that it can never grow further. It's solidified; even calcified, maybe. But since love is a living thing that grows and evolves each day, it needs to be fed."

My heart hammers as his eyes lower to my mouth. I lick my lips as he says, "Every day, even without acknowledging it, my love for you grew. It changed as I learned more about you. Each challenge, each conversation, changed the way I love you. For the better."

His strong hands come to my hips and lift me easily. My legs instinctually part so I'm straddling his thighs. Our chests are flush, our pounding hearts thumping in tandem. My forehead leans against his, soaking up the sweet words as his fingers run along my spine.

"You'll never have to compete against my love for Rhuth because it's not in the same realm. It's uniquely ours. My capacity for love is not altered, even if I spent years thinking it was."

Our noses nuzzle, then his lips are soft on mine. Emotions tighten my throat. I bring my hands to his neck, playing with his hair. He lets out a soft moan, and I smile against his mouth. I now know his weakness.

"I love you, Fynn." It's probably impossible to tire of saying that.

He hums, deepening the kiss. Showing me his love in the way his fingers make comforting circles between my shoulder blades. Fynn's other hand trails down to my hip, fingers digging into the softness.

With a rough voice, he says, "I want to see if being in a different environment helps your mind and heart. It's okay if it doesn't work out, but I figure it's worth a try."

In an instant, all I want is him. I'm willing to chance it for the opportunity to be with him. "I'm ready to try."

56

Orliana

The second the words are out of my mouth, Fynn's kiss deepens. My hips roll forward. Through his shorts, I feel the hard length pressing against the fabric. Grinding into it, I moan at the pleasure.

"Fuck," he growls, breaking the kiss to trail his lips down my neck. Both of his hands come to my hips like the other night, coaxing my them into movement. There's not an inch of sunlight where our bodies press together. The urge to pry his chest open and crawl into his heart makes me whimper. I need him closer.

My fingers find the hem of his shirt, and I yank. He lets go of me to raise his arms. Tossing the shirt, our mouths collide again, the frenetic energy building. I pepper kisses down his neck, to the curves of his collarbone. He groans, leaning his head back so I can lick the column of his throat, ending with my lips on his again.

Taking charge of my experience, I grab the bottom of my shirt and pull it over my head. My breasts brush against his chest, and pleasure shoots from my nipples straight to between my thighs. When our bodies press together for the first time, a sense of peace settles over me. Everything will be okay.

"Orliana," he murmurs, kissing the point where my neck and shoulders meet. His fangs scrape and press. "Can I mark you?"

I wrap my hands around his neck. "Please."

Fynn doesn't hesitate; the fangs gently sink into my body, and I arch my back, relishing him marking me. His satisfied growl vibrates through our bodies, and I moan, thrusting my hips with force. When his fangs retract out of my body, he pulls his head back to look at my face. A smear of my blood smudges the bottom of his lip.

"Goddess, that's so fucking hot," I rasp out, crashing my mouth to his. I taste my blood, but I don't care because it mingles with the taste of Fynn.

His arms wrap around me, and he gently turns us to lay me on my back. He's careful to not sit up, leaning on an arm as he trails his other hand from my sternum to the button of my shorts.

"Is this okay?"

"Yes," I breathe, arching my back as a finger teases my skin. The button snaps, offering more space for Fynn's warm hand. I squeeze my eyes shut, feeling the barest sensation of panic flare.

He stops.

My eyes fly open, confused. Fynn's watching me with unwavering intensity. "What's wrong?"

"Just checking in," he says smoothly. One of his fingers makes maddening circles right above the top of my panties. "I'll be doing that a lot if that's alright with you."

I search his face; he must have felt that niggle of panic. I smile. "It's absolutely fine with me."

His fingers move a little lower, and my breath hitches in anticipation. They're *so close,* right *there,* but not where I *need* them. Yet, he doesn't get to the desperate destination. Those fingers slide back and forth, making circles, and never quite hit the spot.

With a sound of frustration, I snatch his wrist and shove his hand deeper. Fynn chuckles, allowing a finger to trail along the wet seam of my underwear. "Making sure you *really* wanted it."

My hand stays wrapped around his wrist, enjoying the way it anchors me to his movements. "I *really* want it."

"Tell me."

His words tear my focus where that damn finger slides up and down. "What?"

After giving me another sensual kiss, he says against my lips, "Tell me what you want. Direct me."

"Your hand," I whimper. "Please put your hand between my legs."

My back arches off the blanket when he obeys, the heat of his palm covering my soaking panties.

"Good," he rumbles. A finger teases the fabric's edge, brushing against the inside of my thigh. "What next?"

"Inside," I croak, my hips desperate for something. The finger tentatively slides under, and when it finally touches my slickness, I let out a moan so loud I'm glad we're on a deserted island. My hand pushes his wrist down, but he resists.

He growls, his forehead coming to my temple. "What else, Orliana?"

"P-please," I beg. "I-I don't know. Something. *Do something.*"

"Say it," he snarls, keeping that damn finger still. It needs to sink a *little* deeper. A *little* more.

Growing desperate, I demand, "Put your finger inside me."

I cry out as it plunges inside. He moves it with a slowness that threatens to shatter my mind. In and out. In and out. *"More,"* I plead, on the precipice of weeping. When he adds a second, I think I babble incoherently.

The heel of his hand presses down, multiplying the intensity of my pleasure as he obeys. The pace increases, rocking in tandem with my hips. Our frantic breaths mingle. Sweat coats his chest. He groans as my tongue flicks out to lick some off.

The pleasure builds, coiling like a snake ready to strike. Everything in me lights up. Sensations overwhelm. The breeze soothing our sweaty bodies; the waves lapping gently at the sand; the press of his muscular body against mine.

"Cum for me," he says, voice husky. "I want you to come undone around my fingers, baby."

When he curls his fingers, my entire body falls apart. My bones vibrate as my nerves electrify. I cry out, and his kiss swallows the sound.

"You did so well." He brushes small kisses along my jaw. When my hand loosens around his wrist, he slowly pulls it out. Looking me dead in the eye, he licks his finger.

"Mmm," he hums. "Delicious." I stare at him. Fynn smirks. "What?"

"You ... like it?"

His face twists in bewilderment. "Of course. Why wouldn't I?"

"Um." My face burns and my legs draw together. He notices and scoots my body closer to his.

"Baby, I want to taste you every single day you'll let me," He kisses my forehead. "If you need me to prove it, I'll gladly let you know how I feel with you on my tongue."

"No," I say quickly. I'm not ready for that.

Fynn's smile is small, quirking to the side. "Okay, but I'm excited for the opportunity." He assesses my half-clothed body. "How are you feeling right now?"

I pause and gauge my internal state. Blood still pounds in my veins, and I've yet to fully catch my breath. Otherwise, "Fine, I think."

"Do you ... want to do more?" He sounds so hopeful and shy. The tiny bit of anxiety burns up in an instant.

"Can we get naked?" I ask, silently cringing. One part of my brain knows he will never judge me, but the other part is consistently nervous that his kindness is a farce, and at any second, he's going to lose control.

"Yes. How would you like that to happen?"

My eyes widened. "How?"

Fynn's smile gentles. "Yes. I don't know what triggers you might have around removing clothes."

"Me either," I admit. "There wasn't exactly a pattern to it."

His eyes sweep down my chest. "Do you want to undress me?"

Instantly, I get nauseous from memories I'm forced to shove away. "No."

"Okay. So I need to undress myself?"

"Yes."

"Do you want me to undress you?"

I shake my head. "No."

His smile broadens, amused. Okay, so we undress ourselves?"

I grimace. "This is so stupid."

"No, baby, not at all." He rubs a thumb across my cheek. "I don't think it's stupid. I think it's wonderful that we have the ability to talk about this, don't you?"

A lump forms in my throat; my fear spikes, afraid of another trigger. But he's right. I'm safe. Inhaling a shuddering breath, I nod. "Yes. It's wonderful."

The words are more bitter than intended, causing him to chuckle. "I'm going to sit up, okay?"

When I nod, he pulls away to sit up. To my surprise, he doesn't look at my body. He faces the water, saying over his shoulder, "Do you want to get undressed, too? And on the count of three, we turn around?"

A laugh bursts out of me. "Are we doing a nudity reveal?"

He chances a quick glance at my face to grin. "I'd like to see what surprise is behind door number one, please."

A giggle shakes my chest as I sit up. He turns away when I do. Facing the palm trees, I close my eyes. This feels ridiculous. It feels like this should kill the mood and stall the momentum. Yet, even as I shimmy out of my shorts, I grin.

Mikan would never have done anything like this. It was never about my comfort. For Fynn, it's his only concern.

Knowing that makes it easy to slide off my underwear.

Behind me, he says, "I'm ready; are you?"

Goosebumps raise the hairs on my body as the breeze slides past my legs. I bring my hands up to my chest, feeling exposed. "I don't know."

"That's okay. The ocean is beautiful," he says conversationally. "I mean, you're more beautiful, but I can tolerate this view."

I laugh. "The palm trees are lovely."

"I have a question."

"What?"

"If and when we turn around, can I look? Or should I close my eyes and pray I don't trip on a coconut?"

"There aren't any coconuts," I say, laughing.

"A crystal?"

Breaking into a fit of giggles, I say, "Okay, what about a five second rule?"

"Do you plan on flying toward the blanket, and I need to pick you up within five seconds?"

Grinning wildly, I put my hands on my hips. Staring at a swaying palm tree, I retort, "No! You can look at me for five seconds."

"And you look at me for five seconds?"

The thought of finally seeing him naked makes my mouth go dry. "Sure."

"Okay, but there are parts of me that may take longer than five seconds to look at."

Thinking of the length I've felt pressed against me, my cheeks heat. "Are you seriously implying your dick is long enough to take five whole seconds to look at?"

"Orliana," he admonishes. "Get your head out of the gutter. *Yeesh.* I was talking about my very impressive tail. I've been told it really brings out my *ass*ets."

I'm laughing so hard, I'm clutching my stomach. "You aren't taking this seriously!"

"Orliana," he says quietly. "I've never been so serious in my entire goddess-damned life." After a second, he adds, "My tail is *very* impressive."

"Okay!" I say, still giggling. "On the count of three, you can show me the tail I've already seen a hundred times before."

"You've been *looking?*" He pretends to sound outraged.

Exhaling, I say, "One."

Immediately serious, his voice rumbles, "Two."

I gnaw on my lip nervously. *"Three!"*

I whirl around at the same time he does. We stand there, arms at our sides. I thought it would be weird, that the six feet between us would feel too far. Instead, he doesn't ogle my body. He watches my face with an intensity that makes me gulp.

With an eerily calm voice, he says, "Why aren't you looking at my tail, Orliana?"

Grinning, I stare at way more than his tail. My gaze stops between his legs, and a thrill shoots down my spine, straight to my core. No, this doesn't feel weird. Anticipation lights up my skin.

His hand motions my eyes upward. "My face is up here, you little pervert."

"You're ridiculous."

"Do you mean ri-*dick*-culous?"

I point at the blanket. "Get over there *now.*"

Instantly, he's dropping onto the blanket, sitting back on his heels, hands resting on his thighs. He resembles an acolyte, ready for worship. Staring at his knees, he says, "You know, I'd really like to gaze upon what Fortuna has provided."

I step closer and, for the first time in my life, I feel powerful. Here's one of the strongest men in literally all of Gondora, on his knees. And he thinks his goddess *sent* me?

I stand straighter, shoulders pressing back, feeling beautiful. "Okay. Then gaze upon what Fortuna sent."

57

Fynn

My eyes raise slowly, starting at her ankles and trailing upward. To her thick, golden legs. At the vee of her thighs. Generous hips that cradle a soft belly. Beautiful scars on said belly. Full, round breasts. A graceful décolletage. Lips like divinity.

All of the blood in my body shoots straight to my cock.

"Perfect," I whisper, my eyes meeting hers.

Her mouth twists as her fingers find strands of hair to twirl. "Really?"

"Really." I beckon her forward. She takes a hesitant step forward, then another. My eyes never leave hers. "How would you like things to go?"

Orliana's beautiful face flickers with uncertainty. "I think I'd really like to go at a pace that doesn't involve check-ins every ten seconds. I really appreciate it, but I think it'll make me feel like a burden if we constantly do it during ..." She motions at my naked body. "This."

Flashing a wicked grin, I say, "So can I please have enthusiastic ongoing consent until otherwise revoked?"

"Yes."

"Would you like a safe word?"

She cocks her head. "Safe word?"

"Yeah. Something silly that would not exist on this island, so if you say it, I know to stop immediately."

Orliana scans the beach, chewing on that damn lip. "Coconut? Since they aren't here?"

"Coconut it is. Now, get your delicious body over here."

As soon as she's close enough, my hands are at the backs of her knees, jerking her forward. She gasps, forced to use my shoulders for balance. Bringing her breasts to the perfect height. I catch a nipple in my mouth and suck hard.

"Oh, goddess," she moans, knees buckling. I use the momentum to straddle her across my lap. My painful erection throbs at the hint of her heat.

I open my mouth to ask if she's okay, then remember I need to trust her to communicate if something isn't. So I let my hands explore while she settles around me, hooking her feet under my tail.

Palming her bare, delectable ass, I groan. "Fuck, Orliana. So fucking perfect."

She moans, thrusting her hips forward. The second her wetness slides against my cock, I almost lose my damn mind. My groan is guttural. My tail twitches with the need to wrap around her waist and hold her in place while I fuck her senseless.

Later. Right now, this moment is for her and only her.

I suck air through my teeth when a hand comes to my length and pumps once. Twice.

"I need you inside me," she groans. "Please."

I've wanted nothing more in my life. Ever. Panting, I nod. "Take me whenever you'd like."

"Lift me up," she orders. I raise her higher, and she reaches between us, directing my tip right to her entrance. "Bring me down slowly."

I like it when she's bossy. I obey, teasing her with the tip as I slowly work her down. Dragons are capable of increasing the thickness of their cocks, but I'm refraining right now. She can tell me exactly what she likes later. For now, I want to keep it as easy as possible.

"Fynn," she whimpers, dropping her forehead to my shoulder.

"That's it," I encourage. "Take a deep breath in and relax." Her body softens a little more when she does what I've asked. It's still not enough; her body is resisting. She's certainly ready, more than ready, but her body is clenching.

"Breath," I murmur, kissing from her jaw to her throat. "You're safe."

Her arms wrap around my neck as she whimpers. I want to pause and check in so badly, but I need to trust her. I don't feel any fear or anxiety, so I keep talking her through it.

Bringing her back up to the tip, I work her down slowly again. Sweat coats my body from the effort because all I want to do is *plunge.*

It's pure, delicious torture.

Little by little, her body relaxes. "That's it, baby. A little more. Breathe." She exhales, and her muscles release, gaining a few more inches. It feels like a quiet victory. "Good. One more time."

This time, I'm able to fully sink into her body. It's exquisite. In my arms, she trembles. Sweat coats her body, and she clings to me for dear life. I could stay here, inside her and staring at the ocean, for the rest of my life. She doesn't need to move; being right in this moment is enough.

"You're doing so well," I whisper, cupping her head. My other hand rests on her lower back. Through our connection, I finally sense the fear and doubt, so I wait.

"I don't understand," she whimpers.

Running my hands through her hair, I ask, "What don't you understand?"

"How this feels so *good,*" she says quietly, tears in her voice.

I smile, even though she can't see it. "It's supposed to be this way."

"Really?"

"Yes, really."

She sniffles, and a tear drops onto my shoulder. "So much has been taken away from me."

I nod against her ear, resting my chin on her shoulder. The shaking slows, and her body softens further. "I agree, but if you'll let me, I can give you some wonderful things."

Orliana inhales a shuddering breath. "Show me."

Keeping the hand on her head, I shift the one on her back a little lower so I can move her forward. She gasps, then relaxes even more. Taking that as a good sign, I do it again. I'm trying so hard to focus on her and ignore how it feels, but it's ... transcendent. There's no doubt in my mind she's goddess-sent, because how is she so perfect in every way imaginable?

Soon, her body shakes for a different reason. She comes alive in my arms. Her hips begin with hesitant movements, gradually becoming more confident. Against my chest, her pulse beats wildly; as wildly as mine. In my ear, her little panting breaths are like music.

"That's it," I murmur, closing my eyes briefly to tune into how she's feeling. "Take whatever you would like."

The breeze caresses us as she shifts back. I open my eyes, pleased to see her watching my expression. Now her hips pick up their pace, and she tilts her hips to grind her pelvis against mine. Sweeping her long hair away from her face, I hold it behind her neck. She rests her forehead against mine, fully in control of her own movements now.

"You feel so good," she whimpers.

"Likewise," I say, bringing a hand to her breast. When I give it a firm squeeze, her breath hitches. The pace quickens; I grit my teeth, trying to hide my struggle.

Orliana tilts back, baring her chest to the sun, closing her eyes. I glance at where we join, deeply pleased at the visual. Gently tugging on the hair to expose her neck further, I lean forward and lick up her chest. Her mouth meets mine, our tongues slamming into each other with hunger.

Her body tightens, and her breaths quicken. She's close. Orliana's grinding against me like she has a vendetta, and I fucking love it. "There you go," I purr, latching my mouth onto a nipple. She jerks, her pace becoming more erratic. I bring my free hand to her ass, encouraging a steadier movement for her.

"Fynn," she moans again. My name is now my favorite word on her lips.

"I'm here with you," I say, allowing myself to truly immerse into what she's doing. The wet heat wrapped around my cock, undulating waves of pleasure that lapped at my sanity.

"Fynn," she cries out, mouth parting with a scream.

"Yes," I snarl, keeping her steady as she comes undone. Her pelvis jerks again, and she's wailing to the skies. An offering to my goddess.

I do the same, holding her tight as I release inside her. It feels like coming home for the first time. It's taken me a lifetime to reach this moment. A road of devastation, with a trail of despair left in the wake. But as we find our pleasure together, I know this is exactly where I'm meant to be.

And all of it is suddenly worth it.

58

Orliana

Can fantastic sex feel like being reborn? Because I feel reborn.

Straddling Fynn, with him still inside me, is incredibly intimate. Our breaths mingle as our heart rates slow. He's leaving a trail of kisses from my chest up my neck while his hands stroke my back in soothing motions.

Sex has definitely never been like this. Mikan would be gone by now, only returning for next time. Fynn isn't Mikan, though, and it's never been more clear.

"How are you feeling?" His voice is hoarse from breathing so hard.

I grin. "I'm amazing. You know, I was telling Kyri that I didn't understand what the big deal was about sex."

Intrigue has his eyebrows raising. "And now?"

"Now, I don't know why people aren't doing it all the time."

Fynn lets out a low laugh. "Because unfortunately, we need things like sleep, food, and jobs." His fangs nip my chin. "I'm willing to fill your free time, though, in more ways than one."

I slap his shoulder playfully. "Ridiculous."

"Do you mean ri-*dick*—"

"That is not turning into an inside joke," I say vehemently.

Fynn looks mischievous. "No guarantees."

I peer down to where we're still joined. "What now?"

He frowns at the sun. "And now we have to head back for that damn gala."

I groan. "You promise there are no surprises?"

Fynn grunts. "I cannot make that promise, unfortunately. My aunt is always up to something, and it's a Weyr reunion. We're actually lucky yesterday was so low key."

"*That* was low key?"

"Yes," he says with a smile. Fynn shifts, wincing. "While I am deeply obsessed with being inside you, I fear my legs are going numb."

"Oh!" With a pout, I separate from him. My body already aches for more, but it aches, period. I'm going to sleep well tonight.

I gape at Fynn's naked body as he shifts, coming to stand. Okay, maybe not *that* well. Maybe we can have round two tonight.

I glance at my sandy, sweat-covered body, with our cum still between my legs. Getting into the ocean will make things worse. I sigh, leaning down for my shorts.

"What's wrong?" Fynn's immediately alert, in sync already with my moods.

I motion to my body. "I feel filthy."

A glimmer of something enters those golden eyes. "Would you like a shower?"

I make a show of looking around the deserted island. "I mean, yes, but there isn't exactly indoor plumbing here."

Fynn's Fyre glows in his chest. "Look up."

I crane my head to peer at the clouds suddenly rolling in. What in twelve Hells? There's a crack of lightning, then the surging boom of thunder. Moxie, who has been napping on a palm frond, squeals.

"Oh, goddess," I shriek. "Where did that come from?"

Fynn lets out a deep laugh. "We aren't in Gondora, so I can show off a little."

Incredulous, I ask, "This is from you?" A fat raindrop plops on my head. Then another. And another. It begins pouring, soaking my hair and clothes. The mess covering my body sloughs off.

Flinging my arms out, I laugh and open my mouth, catching the drops with my tongue. Moxie plays in the puddles, sand coating her body. I can't believe he brought a storm to us, like it's nothing. My gaze snaps to him.

"What else are you hiding, Mr. Gleanscale?"

"Look." He points out to the ocean. As the water pours, a strike of pink lightning slams into the roiling waves.

"Again!" I squeal, clapping my hands.

Fynn comes to stand beside me, grabbing my hand. It's a shock to feel the power radiating off him in waves. Three more lightning strikes light up the sky and disappear into the water. I grin up at him. "You're way too modest about your power, you know."

Fynn hums. "Hmm, probably. But if more people knew, I'd be conscripted into the government to do weather management of some sort, and I'm not interested. So I don't advertise my abilities much."

Peering up at him, I see the way raindrops fall from his lashes and lips. The need for him overwhelms again.

"Kiss me?"

Without hesitation, Fynn wraps me up in another kiss. Warm rain runs down our bodies while his lips coax mine into opening.

Against my belly, he hardens again. I push my belly into it. "Already?"

Fynn growls softly. "I'm going to be insatiable for you, Orliana."

"Take me to the blankets," I murmur. Fynn lifts me up and marches us to the soaking blankets. I don't even care when he carefully lays me down, settling between my thighs. He pauses, waiting to see my reaction. My hips lift in offering.

Forearms bracketing my face, he searches my face. I can tell he desperately wants to do a check-in; thankfully, he doesn't. Instead, I watch him guide the head of his very impressive dick to my entrance.

Watching my expression closely, he slides into me again. A harsh groan rumbles his throat. When he's fully seated, I wrap my legs around him. Our mouths meet again as Fynn moves. It's slow at first.

I'm not interested in slow.

Reaching down, I smack one of his ass cheeks. "Stop taking it easy on me, Fynn. Show me what you've been wanting to do."

The pace he sets is vicious and deep. It's all I can do to hold on while he pounds into my body with voracious greed. I scream when his fangs clamp into my shoulder again. He holds the bite as he thrusts. All I can do is soften my body and allow him to guide our pleasure.

He releases the bite and sits back. Gathering my legs, Fynn lifts my hips. It sends a thrill through me, knowing he's trusting me to tell him if watching is a problem. The single-minded way he gazes where we're joined makes me moan louder. He runs a hand up from my belly to my sternum, then roughly grabs a breast.

"*Yes,*" I gasp, arching to take him deeper. "More, Fynn. I need more."

My Dragon snarls, "As you wish, baby."

Rain slicks our bodies as he unleashes his control, grabbing my body with aggression. I whimper as he pulls out, and I let him organize us until one of my legs is slung over his while I lie on my side. This time, when he sinks into me, I cry out, clutching the wet blanket. It feels so *good.*

His breath is ragged as those strong hands dig into my skin. "Touch yourself, Orliana."

The command bunches my brow. I'm barely coherent as I gasp, "What?"

"Your fingers. *Touch yourself.* Now."

I freeze. Fynn slows his pace — barely. With a slightly softer voice, he says, "I want to see you come undone."

"I've never done that," I whimper, still consumed with the way he feels inside my body. He slams into me, rocking my head back as I let out a scream.

"Now," he barks. Treating me exactly as I asked. Giving no time to overthink my insecurities. The hesitation burns up as my fingers find my clit, exploring.

Immediately, my body turns boneless as the pleasure reaches all new heights. How in the Hells have I never done this before? No wonder Kyri was appalled. My fingers circle my clit faster and faster, finding the pattern that makes me see stars.

"Good," he snarls. He's so animalistic right now, at odds with the Fynn normally by my side. But it fits. *He* fits.

Another orgasm tunnels into my core, filling my limbs with warmth. Fynn's hips slam into mine, but he holds me in place, rasping out breaths.

"Fynn," I gasp. "I'm going to cum."

His fingers find one of my nipples, and when he pinches, it's all over. My muscles flex as my legs shake. His depth becomes almost too much as he seeks his own undoing. I let out a guttural scream; his fingers dig painfully into my hips as he roars, slamming into me one final time. Around us, thunder rolls, and more lightning cracks into the water.

When we're done, we stare at each other. Through our connection, I can feel his bewilderment.

"Is it always like that?" I ask, voice low.

He shakes his head, causing raindrops to fly. "No."

Satisfaction makes me smile. "Can we do it again?"

Fynn tosses his head back with a laugh. "I'm god-like, but not an actual deity, my love. Give me a few minutes before round three." I pretend to pout and gyrate my hips. He raises an eyebrow. "How are you not tired yet?"

"Hey," I say defensively. "I literally just discovered sex can feel good. Cut me a break."

His jaw grinds at the reminder. "Maybe I can rally for a third time?"

It's my turn to laugh. Already, I'm sore. With an exasperated sigh, I signal with my hips for him to pull out.

As he does, I say, "Unfortunately, I've also discovered good sex can equal being sore."

Fynn falls forward, landing on his hands, hovering over me. Drops of water sluice down his nose, dropping onto my face. I laugh as he nuzzles me. "Baby, when you're ready, I'm going to show you it can be painful to sit sometimes."

The idea is intriguing. "Tomorrow?"

"Tonight?"

I place a kiss on his wet nose. "Tomorrow?"

"Tomorrow."

We both sit up; I look at the wet sand and roiling waves as I hold up my clothes. "We're sort of clean now, but what about this?"

The rain stops abruptly, and the clouds dissipate. Like they never existed. Sunshine blankets us, warming my skin. Fynn grabs my clothes; within seconds, they're dry. Holding out his hands toward a soggy Moxie, she flies onto his palms. Within two seconds, her fur is dry and a miniature wind gale blows off all the sand. She honks, wagging her tail excitedly.

I eye him suspiciously. "You know you're now required to give me exact details on what you can do, right?"

"Naturally," he says brightly, grabbing his clothes. I'm sad to see his body covered up, but I'm also ready for a hot bath, followed by a nap.

After spending a few quiet minutes eating the food Trinte packed, it's time to pack up. I'm sad to leave the island, but Fynn promises we can come back any time I want.

We pack up quickly, and within a few minutes, he shifts, placing me on his back. Moxie nestles into my tank top, her tiny head popping out between my breasts.

The flight feels faster this time, which is great because by the time we land, I'm weaving on my feet. To my chagrin, Fynn scoops me up and brings me to his hotel room. Trinte has already packed up and moved back to his room. My things, including tonight's dress, are hung on hangers.

After depositing me on the bed, Fynn starts the bath. I don't even have to ask — he just knows. While I'd like to linger in the bath, I make it quick, eager for a few hours of sleep.

Fynn goes through the motions of toweling me off, dressing me in pajamas, and tucking us both under the blankets. Moxie bleats and shoves herself into our little cocoon. Fynn tucks me into his chest tight, curling us into a ball. When his tail reaches my chest, I wrap my arms around it.

And the three of us sleep the rest of the afternoon away.

***

We're still exhausted after the nap, but Fynn assures me that we only need to be at the gala to announce our relationship status and we can leave. Something tells me that won't be all that happens, but I nod along like it's the truth. Not that he's lying; he's probably trying to reassure me.

For the gala, Kyri packed me a floor-length blood red dress. It has another absurdly high slit, with a tight bodice. The neckline is modest, barely showing cleavage. It doesn't have traditional sleeves — instead, it has floor-length sleeves, creating the illusion of a chiffon cape.

It's breathtaking.

Fynn's decked out in an actual tux with a maroon silk shirt, looking absolutely delicious. How we ended up matching again is a mystery, but it's probably just a coincidence.

I'm standing in front of the mirror, attaching gold earrings, when he comes to stand next to me. A red scaled hand sweeps my hair away from my shoulder. He presses a kiss on the place where he marked me. Satisfaction settles deep in my gut. It's the first mark on my body I've wanted *and* enjoyed receiving.

"You're ravishing," he whispers, kissing up to my jaw.

I giggle when he nips the shell of my ear. "You don't look so bad yourself."

"We look good together," he murmurs, studying our reflection. His arms wrap over mine, holding me tight. "I still can't believe you're here."

Moxie flutters up from the bed and lands on his shoulder. She's going to have to take a break today — it's an effort to prevent as little drama as possible tonight. With any luck, we'll be back in bed within three hours.

"So ..." I say coyly, nestling deeper into his hold. "When we're asked exactly what we are, what do we say?"

Those gold eyes appraise me in the mirror. "Whatever you're comfortable with."

My brows raise. "I do believe I came here under the guise of being a friend because you didn't want anyone asking about Rhuth."

It gives me deep pleasure to see his aura continue to stay red and pink as he watches me. The grief still exists, but it's phenomenally smaller.

Fynn considers his words. "I want you to be my friend, Orliana." At my darkening expression, he smiles. "I'll always want you to be a friend first. Everything else is a bonus."

Gently shifting me to face him, he smooths my hair away from my face, searching my face. "Be my partner, Orliana. Let me worship you every day and hold you each night. Tell me your fears and your joys. Let me be there for Joulian. I need you to feel less alone in this world."

With each word, my heart pounds harder. This feels like a dream. How is this the same man from six weeks ago who could barely look me in the eye? Surrounded by grief?

Wrapping my arms around his waist, I say, "Fynn, it would be an honor."

When he kisses me, I think of nothing but what our future holds. It's the most exciting thing I've ever imagined.

59

Fynn

The closer we get to the gala, the more dread builds in my belly. There simply isn't enough time to explain to Orliana all of the possible options that could occur tonight. Dragons have many traditions — too often they're plucked out from dusted tombs for arbitrary reasons.

The *Têasté* is a great example of that.

While I'm pleased that it brought Orliana and me closer together, it's difficult to lead her into an event that could cause unexpected issues.

Beside me, she looks like Fortuna come alive. Her hair is in gentle waves, with lipstick that I'd love smeared somewhere in particular. The sweeping sleeves that brush the ground are regal and spectacular.

As we walk through the lobby, each step increases my apprehension. Through our connection, I feel her nervousness. What a pair we make.

Aunt Teale is greeting family members at the entrance, wearing a poofy electric purple dress beaded with pearls and crystals. Her magenta hair is in a beehive, featuring fake butterflies swirling to the top.

When she spots us, she motions for us to speed up. I don't. The smirk on her face is unnerving. Like the sphinx that caught the canary.

When we're close enough, she gushes, "You're so handsome, Fynn. And Orliana! That dress is mythical." A genuine smile of pleasure spreads across her wrinkled face. "I'm so glad Trinte's plan worked."

This shocks me out of my anxiety. "What?"

"What?" Orliana echoes. We exchange confused looks.

"Oh, yes," Aunt Teale says, waving to an aunt walking by. "It's really quite impressive. That boy schemed for weeks."

My brain moves slowly as I try to catch up. "What *exactly* did my brother do?"

Aunt Teale waves away my question like it's a bothersome fly. "This and that. Mostly aimed at getting Ms. Orliana here to the reunion. I told him you didn't seem to be ready, but he insisted. The words he used, I believe, were 'she's waking him up.'"

My blood freezes in my veins. I have no idea how to process this. The amount of effort he put into everything. Things begin to come together. All the ways he convinced me to spend time with her, making it seem like it was my idea.

I tilt my head at my aunt. "Maureen?"

Again, she waves away my words, then pats her hair. "Oh, she definitely wants a mate, but when I told her of the plan, she happily agreed to help with the *Têasté*."

That explains how helpful she was. "Warnock?"

Aunt Teale laughs gayly. Like it's all a game we won. "That is something you can thank your brother for. He knew Warnock could be, well, Warnock." She gives me a knowing smirk, then says to Orliana, "Please forgive me. I may not know you well, but by the looks of things, it appears that there will be ample opportunity in the future."

Orliana is speechless. Frankly, so am I. Trinte did everything. All because of how much he worries about me.

I want him back.

I owe my brother anything he wants.

"I can see there are things to absorb," Aunt Teale says, already shifting her attention. "Please enjoy the festivities."

And just like that, we're dismissed. I guide Orliana away from the crowd. When we're out of earshot, I say, "Who picked out those dresses?"

She looks down. "This? Kyri."

"And the blue one? Where we also matched?"

"Kyri."

I narrow my eyes. She quickly puts it together. *"No."*

"Fairly certain."

"Those two," she mutters. "Has the whole world been conspiring at this point?"

"Probably," I muse. "Can we even be mad?"

"Yes!" she says indignantly, then deflates. "Okay, no. It's kind of genius, to be honest."

"I'm still going to tail whip him," I promise. "Just once."

"I'll soften it with a hug?" she suggests.

"Maybe," I growl, eyeing my mark on her. He'll know to keep his distance for a while. Everyone will. Glancing over my shoulder, I see the crowd growing. "Come on, let's go find our seats."

Together, fingers intertwined, we head into the large ballroom. Circular tables fill the large room, with Dragons of all shades conversing and laughing. After we find our assigned table, I leave Orliana to get us both drinks.

When I return, Trinte is sitting next to her. I swallow my irritation and plaster a tight smile on my face. "Brother. What good timing."

He's leaning against the table, cheek resting against his fist, watching Orliana speak. Now his attention flicks to me. He raises a black eyebrow. "Orliana was informing me how you both have discovered my diabolically genius plan that made you two fall in love. It's okay to name your firstborn after me. No one would blame you."

Orliana slaps the back of her hand against his chest, chuckling. "Knock it off. You've antagonized your brother enough, don't you think?"

My brother gives a solemn shake of his head. "It will never be enough. I'm fulfilling my duty as a little brother."

I sit on her other side and hand her the champagne. Her eyes light up. My heart flutters with love as she takes the first sip. Trinte watches me watch her, smiling softly. I can't be mad at him in any capacity. My brother has been through enough.

Sipping my whiskey, I scan the crowd for familiar faces. Some cousins come up to say hello. When they share their condolences, the grief doesn't make an appearance. I'm pleased to introduce them to Orliana as my partner.

Things get underway quickly. It's actually relatively painless, considering. The aunts lead most of the presentations. When it's time for the *Têastés* to announce their standings, it's easy to stand next to Orliana and announce that we're together. The whole time, Trinte beams and claps louder than anyone else in the room.

After dinner is done, exhaustion weighs down my body in earnest. Considering I didn't sleep last night, and everything that has happened since I woke up yesterday ... I deserve some sleep. Orliana does as well.

But first, she deserves to show off that dress. Turning to my partner, I hold out a hand.

"Would you like to dance?"

As she did all those weeks ago, she looks at my hand. "I've only danced once before, and it didn't work out well for me."

My heart swells as her hand slides into mine. She stands with profound grace, smiling.

Tucking her arm into mine, I say, "I would disagree. It would appear to have worked out *very* well."

She giggles as we stride onto the dance floor. A slow, crooning song fills the air from the nearby band. Having slow danced plenty of times with Rhuth, I ease Orliana into position, eager to take the lead.

She allows me to guide her through the group of couples, head pressed against my chest. My hand trails along her back, feeling at peace. From the platform where the head matriarchs sit, Aunt Teale watches us.

Thank you. I mouth the words. She tilts her head in acknowledgement, then turns to talk to the matron beside her.

As the song comes to a crescendo, my soul settles back into place. It's a profound sensation, feeling like everything has finally aligned exactly as intended.

Orliana's hands tighten, and she sends me her own contentment. I let it mingle with mine, exhaling like I've taken my first breath.

My eyes trail to the crowd, where Trinte sits. He's sitting at the table, staring into his whiskey glass.

A male Dragon walks up from behind him. He's a burgundy, with scales darker than mine. White hair flows down to his shoulders. A sharp nose juts from his square face. I know if I were close enough, I'd see amber-colored eyes.

I know this because that's my father.

When he stops next to Trinte, my feet freeze in place, startling Orliana. She looks up, confused. "Fynn?"

"We have to go," I rushed out. "Come on."

My brother has no warning as the big red hand claps on his shoulder. My brother, who is always careful about who and what he touches, visibly flinches. The man I've called father whispers into Trinte's ear. Something slimy writhes around in my gut at the expression of annihilation on Trinte's face.

I pull Orliana along faster than she can keep up with.

Trinte whirls around and almost falls out of his chair trying to scramble from my father. Blood roars in my ears; my heart aches painfully at the speed it's forced to take. He shouldn't be here.

He shouldn't be here.

"Fynn," Orliana hisses. "What's wrong? Who is that?"

Trinte stands, his blue scales paling. His body ripples. I let go of Orliana's hand and sprint toward my brother, panic screaming inside me, blanking out my thoughts. The only thing I can focus on is getting to him before he shifts.

My father barely appears alarmed, but I know it's a farce. The surrounding people notice what's happening. I leap over a chair, desperate to get to Trinte before he makes a horrible mistake.

"Trinte!" I roar. All eyes are on us as I leap over another chair, pouncing on my brother. Before he can fully shift, I wrap my body around him, using my magyck to keep him small. I know it's going to cause him excruciating pain as he fights against me, but I can't let him accidentally kill someone.

Not because of *him.*

"Fynn." Orliana lands at my side. Smoke emanates from my body, and my skin's too hot. *He's* too hot. We're turning into infernos as he fights me. His whole body writhes; he's strong as all Hells — I'm still regaining my strength.

"Trinte," I say, frantic. "Stop!"

"Fynn, how can I help?" Orliana says.

Trinte bucks and roars. It's too much. I won't be able to stop him for much longer. Soon, he's going to shift and destroy everything in this room. "You have to take some of it from him, Orliana," I pant. *"Take it."*

She hisses as her hand comes to his face. His skin will blister hers, but she doesn't stop. Grabbing the pendent, she buries a scream behind clenched teeth as she siphons from him. Whatever she's consuming is going to be dark. Probably darker than mine, even in my darkest moments.

Around us, people are panicking. I hear someone call for Aunt Teale. But I can only focus on Orliana and Trinte. They're all that matter. She's weeping, face flushed.

My Fyre roars, then falters. I can't hold him much longer.

"Please," I whimper. "Stop, Trinte. You're going to kill someone."

Trinte openly sobs and screams, trying to claw across the floor toward him. My father. *Why the fuck is he here?* He stands there, staring at one son trying to kill him, while the other is desperate to stop it.

He does nothing.

"Trinte," Orliana murmurs, never releasing the press of her hand. "It's okay."

Something must shift inside him. Maybe she takes enough that he can pause and consider his actions. Orliana rubs his arm and smooths back his disheveled hair. If I had a moment to think, I'd appreciate how much she loves him.

Instead, my Fyre begins to peter out. He might actually be stronger than me, especially in my exhausted state. To my relief, I sense his doing the same.

Seizing the opportunity, I hiss, "You're going to hurt Orliana if you don't stop."

That appears to do it. Trinte goes limp in my arms, sobbing. I keep my body wrapped around him, not sure if it's a ruse. Orliana continues to stroke his arm, whispering comforting words to him. Telling him how brave he is and how kind. Tears blur my eyes.

Weyr reunions are the fucking worst.

"Let me through!" Aunt Teale roars, her magyck pulling rank. The crowd scatters, but *he* stays. Watching impassively.

I'm going to kill him myself.

Aunt Teale's big dress comes into my vision. "What in twelve Hells are you doing here, Racidious? You aren't welcome here."

A voice that causes nothing but dread says, "I wanted to see my sons."

"Clearly, they do not wish to see you. Leave. Immediately."

My father looks at his sister with a smirk. In my arms, Trinte curls into himself. I think he's finally running out of steam. For now.

I share a look with Orliana. Her face is pure devastation.

There's nothing but sorrow in her voice when she says, "What did he *do?*"

"All of it," I croak. My muscles are vibrating from exhaustion and anticipation. My father needs to leave, but he's my aunt's twin brother. She literally cannot order him to do anything. As head matriarch, she has a lot of pull. But twinship is a whole other magyckal ballgame.

"Racidious, you're going to drive this boy mad if you stay," Aunt Teale says, almost sounding desperate.

"I merely wish to speak with him. What is the issue?"

Orliana and I don't break eye contact, but her expression turns thunderous. With one final gentle stroke on my brother's face, she leans down and whispers, "Just watch."

Trinte's body shifts, and he peels his eyes open with great effort. Calmly, Orliana stands. I want to let go of my brother to protect her, but I don't know what to do.

She's shaking, but it's with fury. Not fear. My father watches her approach, and the crowd pushes in, eager for a show. I fucking hate that they're witnessing this moment for Trinte.

Orliana points at my brother. "Are you the reason why he's like this?"

My father scoffs, shoving hands into his pockets. "I can't speak for this absurd reaction. What grown man acts like this?"

"Are you?!" Orliana shrieks. Everyone around us flinches. Aunt Teale inhales sharply. I'm stunned; she's never raised her voice.

My father narrows his eyes into an expression I don't like. "Who are you, anyway?"

"You can call me Orliana," she says, holding out her hand. Her bare hand.

"Orliana, don't," I rasp out. She ignores me. My father's attention flicks to me, then her. But to him, it's a lowly woman only holding out her hand.

The second his palm hits hers, that assumption is corrected.

Trinte and I watch as our father falls to his knees. Orliana stares down at him with such unforgiving hatred, she's barely recognizable. Gone is my sweet friend. In her place is Emet's wrath.

My father inhales deeply and lets out a guttural scream. Everyone around us is silent, watching with wide eyes. She pours everything into my father, just as she did for Mikan before she killed him.

"What is she doing?" Trinte says with awe. He's fully enraptured with her ability to bring our father to his knees.

"Giving him what you gave her."

"Incredible," he murmurs. He pushes against the floor. "Get off me."

"Are you under control?" I demand, refusing to let go otherwise.

"Yes. *Stop touching me.*"

I release him. He ignores my offered hand to stand. Our bodies are coated with sweat. Trinte watches Orliana, stunned. My father is on the floor in the fetal position now.

"It's almost over," she snarls. Trinte flinches and draws back. Then he's shoving past me and everyone else. The crowd parts as quickly as possible. Again, I'm torn. I can't leave Orliana here alone, but Trinte shouldn't be alone.

I walk up to her and place a hand on her arm. I fully expect to feel something, but there's nothing. She's fully shielded and pouring only into him.

"Baby, we need to go find Trinte."

Her hollow eyes find mine, then searches for my brother. Immediately, she drops my father's hand like a discarded toy. "Where is he?"

"Go," Aunt Teale says. "I'll take care of this mess." She walks up to her twin brother with nothing but disgust on her face.

Yet, I can't quite leave yet.

"One moment," I murmured to Orliana. "You might want to ... look away."

There's steel in her gaze as her jaw sets. "No."

I glance at Aunt Teale. Motioning to my father's face, I ask, "May I?"

She sighs. "Fine."

I stalk up to my father and lift him by the collar. He weighs nothing against my rage. For Dragons, there are intricate codes of honor, but some of them are quite clear. 'Don't hurt your family' goes without saying. My father couldn't honor that one simple rule.

I elongate my claws and shove them into his eye socket. He screams in convulsions. It's a disgusting visual as I rip it from his skull.

Maybe it's Trinte who should be the one to do this, but that's the great thing about eyes: there are usually two of them.

Ignoring my wailing father, I walk to the nearest table and grab a napkin. Wrapping it around the eyeball, I walk back to my father.

He probably can't hear me through the pain, but I don't care. "An eye for an eye, you piece of shit. Don't come near us again, or I'll kill you."

Walking up to Orliana, I offer my arm. She takes it silently, expression still full of fury. The crowd parts for us as we leave this goddess forsaken Weyr reunion behind.

60

Orliana

Blisters coat the palm that held Trinte's face, but I barely feel the throbbing there. Instead, it's my soul that pulses with a deep, unabiding ache.

For the first time, I doubt wanting to be a Siphon therapist. Mom always said that she's felt some dark things. I thought Mikan's hatred or Fynn's grief was what she spoke of.

Trinte's darkness? Its inky blackness coating his insides? It felt like being catapulted into the vacuum of space and left to float into nothingness.

Next to me, as we exit the ballroom, Fynn vibrates with unleashed fury. Watching him tear the eyeball from his father's weeping form hadn't even phased me. If he caused what's inside Trinte, the anguish, he deserved significantly worse.

When we touched hands, I had a brief moment to scan him. His soul is the embodiment of Uaeju, the goddess of chaos. Except I'm not sure she'd claim his filth.

As I took what I could from Trinte without going mad, all I kept hearing was, "It's almost over." Again and again, it echoed in my mind.

I couldn't tell if it was a promise or a threat. But as I fed Racidious everything Trinte gave, plus whatever was left of Mikan in the pendant, it felt fitting to say it.

"Where did he go?" I ask, panicked. Trinte shouldn't be alone right now.

Fynn sounds equally distraught. "I don't know. He's never lost control like that before." He sags. "I almost couldn't control him. That nearly became an actual disaster."

Our steps echo in the mostly empty lobby. No one is here. Where is Trinte? I summon Moxie. She appears, already frantic from my energy.

"Go find Trinte," I command. She zooms off like a hornet, heading down one hallway.

Fynn stops, pulling out his phone, presumably to call his brother. The phone rings, but no one picks up. When he looks at me, it's with a bleak expression. "He's not answering."

"We'll find him," I assure. "Do you think he's in his room? The skies?"

"I don't know. He's never lost control like that." A wild look enters his eyes, and I realize Fynn isn't really in control either. In his other hand is a soggy napkin containing an eyeball. This situation isn't one for the Gleanscale brothers to command.

"Okay," I say, pressing a hand to his arm. "Let's go check his room first."

Silently, I summon Moxie. As we march down the hallway to the hotel room, she catches up. When she's close enough, she lands on Fynn's shoulder, nuzzling his cheek.

Stopping in front of the hotel room, Fynn pounds on the wood. There's no answer. My concern is a lump in my throat as I swallow hard. "Let's go to the landing platform. Maybe he's there."

When we arrive, an attendant confirms he never saw a blue Dragon. Fynn tells me that there's a chance Trinte jumped off the terrace of the hotel like they did last night. He brings me to our hotel room, then rushes off to check the skies himself.

My hands tremble as I get out of the dress. Starting a hot bath to reset my system, I siphon my anxiety into my pendent. I need to be level-headed right now.

I stay in the bath as long as necessary, but not longer than that. When my shakes subside, I'm out and toweling off. Just as I'm slipping on a sweater, there's a knock at the door.

Tying my hair up into a bun, I look through the peephole.

It's Trinte.

I swing the door open. "Oh goddess, Trinte! Where have you been?"

He's a man reduced, hollow-eyed and sallow. Like Fynn, his clothes are in tatters. When that beautiful sky-blue eye meets mine, there's nothing inside them. His voice is full of unspoken aches as he whispers, "Orliana."

"Come in," I say, ushering him inside. "Fynn's out searching for you in the skies."

His tone is dull as he says, "He is? I should go find him."

As much as I hate the idea of Fynn out there, stressed, I know he'll be relieved to find his brother here.

"It's okay. He'll be back soon." I guide him to a chair. He slumps into the piece of furniture, his focus both here and elsewhere.

Moxie lands in his lap, and he jolts with surprise. My familiar has never touched him before. I keep an eye on him as I grab him a bottle of water. He tentatively touches her little back with a finger. She honks and curls up on his lap.

"Here, take a sip." I offer the water bottle.

He shakes his head. "I'm fine."

I shove it closer. "Drink. Some."

Giving me a dirty look, he takes the bottle and mutters, "So bossy."

"Learned from the best," I retort with a smile that he doesn't return.

Sitting on my knees in front of him, I say, "I'm sorry I took from you without asking. Fynn told me to, but I generally don't just take it like that."

"It's fine." He stares at the floor. My friend, usually full of sarcasm and smiles, isn't here right now. "I'm sorry I freaked out. It's inexcusable."

"How do you feel?" I murmur, aching to grab his hand.

Trinte stares at the opposite wall like he can drill a hole to climb into. "Like every wall I carefully built was shattered."

I nod with empathy. "I hope you know I made him suffer."

Trinte's eye slowly drags to mine. "Thank you."

"Also, Fynn took one of his eyes."

This actually perks him up. "Really?"

I chuckle and stand. Grabbing the eye-ball filled napkin, I offer it like a gift. "He saved it for you."

Trinte stares at the napkin in my hand. "He ... did that?"

"Mhmm. Also said if your father comes near you ever again, that Fynn will kill him."

Trinte scoffs, placing the napkin on the nightstand. "I don't know if that's true."

I think of how calm and purposeful Fynn was when he picked up his father and plucked out the eyeball. "I wouldn't be so sure."

Sitting on the floor again, I hold out my palm. "Would you like me to take some more?"

Trinte stares at my hand. "No. In fact, I want you to give back what you took."

My brow furrows. "You ... want it back? All of that ..." I don't know how to describe what was inside of him.

A muscle feathers in his jaw. "Yes."

"W-why?" This is something I'm really struggling to understand.

"Because it's my burden to bear."

Frustration begins to build. "For someone who makes fun of Fynn's broodiness, you sure are taking after your brother." I try to make it sound like a joke, but it doesn't land.

Trinte ignores my comment. "Are you going to give it back?"

I grimace. "I ... I can't. I gave it back to him. It's inside him now."

He finally looks intrigued. "Forever?"

"Most likely, unless he also goes to a Siphon, a traditional therapist, or deals with what he's done head on."

"Good."

I want to laugh. Both Fynn, Joulian, and now Trinte love confirmation of revenge. Is this a boy thing? "Do you want to talk to me about it?"

Trinte sighs. "Honestly, I don't want to talk about this at all, Orliana." He stands. "Tell Fynn I'm fine. Don't come find me. I'll be gone."

Panic has me standing. "At least wait for your brother, Trinte. He's so worried about you."

Trinte collects the eyeball and stalks over to the door. A lump of emotion almost chokes me as I trail behind, desperate to grab him; to help; to do *something.* Fynn's going to be devastated if Trinte leaves.

"Tell him I'm fine, Orliana. He has you now — he'll be okay."

I inhale sharply. "*Trinte.* That's preposterous. He needs you just as you need him."

Trinte stops at the door, white knuckling the handle. "He didn't need me for five years. He can handle a day or two now."

"Are you actually going to throw that in his face?" I hiss. "After putting all of that effort into helping him? Us?"

Trinte gazes at me with a deadened expression. "You can't help someone who doesn't *want* to be helped, Orliana. I'm sorry that you had to see this at all. There's a reason I hide this from everyone, even him. It's an ugly side of me."

I close the distance between us until I can smell his cologne of smoke and citrus. "Trinte, you can ask your brother; I don't think this side is ugly. I just want to—"

"Help," he finishes flatly, turning the knob. "I know. And it's appreciated, Orliana. But focus on my brother. I'll be fine. I'm always fine ... eventually."

The door opens, and anxiety sizzles within my body. Without thinking, I snatch his hand. It's warm and trembling. I don't read his emotions because I know he'd perceive it as a violation, but I plead, "Please, Trinte. Don't go."

He squeezes my hand softly, then gently pulls it out of my grasp. "You're a wonderful person, Orliana. My brother deserves you." Tears shimmer in his eyes. "I'll reach out when I'm ready."

Before he walks out, I read his aura. Just a tiny peek, but it's enough.

It's pitch black.

A sob slips past my lips before I can stop it. Holding my hand up to my mouth, I watch the door close.

61

Fynn

By the time Orliana tells me what happened, Trinte's gone. He's not answering my calls. All I can do is honor his wishes. I'm sure he'll be back at work in a couple of days.

At least ... I hope so.

Crawling into bed, we hold one another with Moxie snuggled between us. The hotel room is quiet, painfully so.

"Will he be okay?" she whispers, fighting sleep. My eyelids are heavy, seconds from closing.

"I don't know," I admit. "I've never seen him react like that. If I'd known my father was here, I would've clipped his wings and tossed him off the terrace."

Her face snuggles further into my chest. One of her legs rests between mine. I tighten my hold around her. Without my brother, I'm unsure this moment in time would exist for me. I need to figure out what to do for him. To fight for him as he fought for me.

"What did your father do? You never talk about your parents."

Running my fingers through her hair, I say, "Mom died during childbirth. I barely remember her. Trinte, obviously, never knew her." I clear my throat, already struggling to share this horrific story. "My father raised us, but I learned too late that he hid his hate for Trinte."

Her nails caress my back in soothing motions.

"When I turned eighteen, I left for my internship with a Dragxi company in Oasha. I thought Trinte would be fine ..." My voice cracks; the words are like chilled honey in my throat.

"But he wasn't?" she guessed.

I nod. "The years made my father change more than I'd realized. For five years, I focused on work, never visiting home. Trinte and I stayed in touch, of course, but he never told me." Breathing becomes difficult as my heart races with this admission. "He ... he was doing more than using his fists."

I can't say it. I can barely think of it. What my brother endured is unspeakable. He could barely explain it to me, and we've only spoken about it once. Over fifteen years ago.

Orliana's arm freezes. "He was sexually abusing him?"

Hearing the words feels like claws digging into my chest, trying to rip out my heart. Trinte never speaks of it, but it shows in small ways. He's never been in a serious relationship. While he approaches almost everything like a game or puzzle to be figured out, I know it's a way for him to control the world around him. And physical affection is near impossible unless it's exactly on his terms.

"Yes."

Orliana sucks in a sharp breath. "Why was Racidious here?"

She can't get much closer without smooshing Moxie, but I want to tuck her into my soul and never let her go. If all of this had happened without her here, I don't know how things would've turned out. "Because he's a narcissistic piece of shit. He assumed correctly we'd be here, and he's been trying for years to get us to talk to him."

"But why?"

"Last I heard, it was to apologize. As if an apology is suitable enough."

Orliana's voice is quiet as she asks, "Your father took Trinte's eye, didn't he?"

"Yes," I admit. "It happened the night he told me what was going on. They'd gotten into a fight, and Trinte snapped. Attacked him. My father ripped it right out. Called it self-defense, but no one really believed that. Trinte was barely eighteen."

She lets out a small cry of dismay. "It really is a miracle that he's okay."

Her sweet heart is breaking for my brother, and it makes me love her even more.

"I don't think he is," I murmur. "Today proves he's not."

"But he's still kind and thoughtful."

"Yes," I agree. "But the brightest masks often hide the deepest sorrows." She hums in agreement as she snuggles in closer. She yawns, which makes me yawn. "Baby, let's put this to rest for now. I'm exhausted and desperately need to sleep next to you."

"Agreed," she mumbles, already half-asleep. Between us, Moxie snores quietly.

Still running my hands through her hair, hoping it helps soothe her transition to slumber, I stare into the dark. Wondering how the Hells I'm going to help my brother as much as he helped me.

***

The trip back to Gondora is somber. I don't bother saying goodbye to my family. The risk of running into my father is too great. Plus, Orliana is anxious to see Joulian again. I promise to bring him next time.

It's difficult saying goodbye after everything we've gone through. When Orliana loads up onto a Dragxi, a new anxiety bubbles up. I requested the specific Dragon, Curtis, but I don't think the fear of a repeat disaster will ever fully disappear. Even as they fly away, it feels like I've sent off another piece of my heart into the unknown.

My first stop, before home, is visiting Virinia. I haven't seen her in a couple of weeks, and I miss her.

She's at the same register as always. When I walk in, she stops mid-scan, the loaf of bread hovering above the counter. Her voice is incredulous as she says,"Fynn?"

The customer turns to look at me, confused. With a grin, I point toward the ice cream aisle. This morning, I asked Orliana her favorite ice cream flavor. It's less hideous than Rhuth's; white chocolate raspberry. The flavor sits right next to the chocolate mint and pistachio. I grab a pint of both.

The register is empty when I walk up, placing the ice cream on the counter. Virinia narrows her eyes, inspecting me. "What the Hells happened?"

She picks up the first pint of chocolate mint and pistachio. Her eyes fill with sympathy. Without saying anything, she picks up the second. This time, she does a double take. She knows my favorite ice cream is cookies and cream. So that could only mean one thing.

A vibrant smile splits her face, revealing sharp teeth. "Fynn, have you met someone?"

"Maybe," I say slyly, unable to hide my proud grin. "You're the first person I wanted to tell, actually."

Her lip wobbles, and she abandons the pints, rounding the counter to wrap me up in a hug. It's the same hug she gave me five years ago, but this time, it feels wonderful. Using all of her considerable strength, she squeezes tightly, briefly lifting me off the floor.

I laugh. "Put me down, Virinia. What will people think of a male Dragon getting picked up?"

She drops me, and I land with a loud thump. Scowling, she says, "That female Orcs are strong as Hells."

"Touché," I say, grinning.

Returning to the scanner, she rings me up. "So, tell me about this very lucky woman."

After giving her a quick synopsis of the last six weeks, she practically has hearts in her eyes. "Oh, Fynn, what a romantic story!"

Handing me the bag of ice cream, she pulls out a container from under the counter. Inside is a pasta dish. "I brought this in today, hoping to see you."

Smiling, I take it. Still warm. "Thank you. Although I think cooking will come easier again."

"I hope so," she says softly. "I'd really like to meet her."

I hold up the ice cream. "Once she knows my supplier, I'm sure you will."

With one final hug, I leave the market and take to the skies.

Up until today, I've spent five years dreading going home. Walking through the front door, I'm finally able to see it with a mix of familiar and new eyes. Rhuth is everywhere, and it no longer hurts.

After unpacking, starting a load of laundry, and taking a shower, I go through the motions of botanical care. I turn on some music, inspecting wilting leaves while having no idea what to do about them.

For the first time, that doesn't make me panic.

Going into the kitchen, I look at the hairbrush. Picking it up for the first time in five years, I finger a strand of blue hair. I'm not ready to get rid of it, but I think creating a box of some items wouldn't be so bad.

The sweater on the chair is next. Lifting it, I bring it to my face and inhale. There's the tiniest, infinitesimal scent of Rhuth on it. Instantly, my heart aches. I know the grief will never fully disappear, proven by this tidal wave of emotion.

Sitting down at the table, I put the brush on top of the sweater. Wiping a tear away before it can fall, I feel the soft material. It's fuzzy and warm. It's something another woman might benefit from.

That's when it hits me: Rhuth's things can't stay here, at least the vast majority of them. I can't hold onto her pants and socks until the day I die.

But a domestic violence shelter would put it all to excellent use.

Smiling, I collect the sweater and hairbrush. On my way to the bedroom, I grab her shoes collecting dust by the front door.

Starting a pile on my bed, I walk to the closet, the side I've avoided for five years. Running my fingers across the collection of clothes, I inhale slowly. When I exhale, I begin pulling down clothes.

Making space for my future.

62

Orliana

Joulian bolts for me the second I walk into Mom's home. The second he's in my arms, the pressure in my chest eases. With him here, everything is okay.

"Mom! How was it?" he says, squished against my chest.

Running a hand over his hair, a compulsion to check him from head to toe, I say, "It was very, very eventful."

He steps back, face flushed with excitement. "Are you and Mr. Fynn finally together?"

My mother walks into the room. After looking me up and down, she smirks. "I'm willing to bet I know the answer."

What the Hells does she see to make her assume correctly?

He looks at her, then at me. "Yes?"

Unable to hide my happiness, I nod enthusiastically. "That's a yes."

Joulian fist pumps. "Yes! Now I'll definitely get a job as a Dragxi attendant."

Pretending to glare, I say, "Do we need to discuss the concept of nepotism now?"

"What's nepotalisman?" he says, face scrunched in confusion.

Ruffling his hair, I laugh. "We'll discuss it later." To Mom, I say, "I think I'm going to avoid Weyr reunions from now on."

An eyebrow goes up. "Oh?"

Giving Joulian a pointed flick of my eyes, I repeat, "We can discuss it later. But for now, I'm eager to get home." To my son, I ask, "What do you think?"

Greg flies to his shoulder as he declares, "I'm very excited to sleep in my own bed!"

Joulian talks the entire ride home, telling me about the cake my mom let him have for dinner and the zoo they visited. It's clear he didn't miss me much, which gives me a little relief. Maybe this transition to dating someone won't be as difficult as anticipated.

When we get home, our familiars make a beeline for their resting places. After we unpack, I start dinner while Joulian sits at the table, catching up on homework.

Heating up the stove, I ask, "How would you feel if Flynn and I dated?"

He looks up, pencil poised against the paper. "I would feel really good about it."

Placing a couple of slices of chicken on the hot pan, I say, "I have to be honest with you."

I study him to gauge his expression. It's inquisitive, which I'm going to take as a good sign. "Fynn and I are pretty serious already. We didn't do it on purpose, but sometimes that's how things unfold."

"Okay. Is he moving in?"

I choke on a laugh. "Moving in?"

"Yeah. Isn't that what people do when they love each other?"

Shaking my head in disbelief, I place cut up vegetables in a pan. "We haven't discussed that. I wanted to have a conversation with you to hear your thoughts first."

"Is he nicer than Mikan?"

Everything freezes from the way he refers to his father. "Do you mean your dad?"

"No. I mean Mikan. I don't have a dad."

Alright, then. “Um, yes. Incredibly nicer, calmer, and better than Mikan.”

“Good enough for me,” he announces, turning back to his homework. I watch him, at a loss for words. I expected ... more. I don’t know what, but this simplified conversation wasn’t it.

Sometimes, being a parent is like riding an untrained unicorn.

***

The next day, I meet with Kyri for coffee. It’s at the Glyradite coffee shop where Fynn and I had our first conversation. To my delight, the same table is available. Grabbing Moxie’s cookie and my muffin, we sit down and wait.

My phone buzzes. Thinking it’s Kyri, I pull it out and check.

Fynn: I need help with something later. Can you come help?

Orliana: You don’t even have to ask. What is it?

Fynn: I need to empty out Titus’s bedroom.

My fingers freeze. He’s emptying the baby’s room? The magnitude of this decision doesn’t miss me. Is he doing the same with Rhuth’s things? Is it because of me?

Orliana: You’re sure?

Fynn: Yeah, but I’d really like you there.

Orliana: To Siphon?

Fynn: No, I'm okay. I want to share this with you. I feel like you're the only person who will understand.

Orliana: I'm having coffee with Kyri and I'll head over?

Fynn: I'll be waiting with a surprise for you.

Orliana: Does it involve taking a five second look at something?

Fynn: Maybe.

Smiling, I put my phone away. Kyri's breezing through the door, like a living flame with her creamsicle curls and wings. An ethereal angel straight from the Hells. People watch her, enthralled, as she steps into line, giving me a little wave of acknowledgement with orange fingers.

It reminds me of Trinte and how they might have conspired together. We haven't heard from him for the last three days. When Fynn and I played online last night, Trinte never showed up. We had to find a random person to join the team; we lost.

I'm sick to my stomach about Trinte's silence, but his phone goes straight to voicemail.

I'm hand-feeding Moxie when she finally sits down, full of energy. She gives me a quick once over. "Hi! You look fantastic!"

Smiling, I say, "You should've seen the way time went into slow-mo as you walked. I swear that the Cyclops in the corner was going to fall out of his chair."

Kyri preened, her wings ruffling. "Is he still looking?"

I laughed. "Yes."

She gives a discreet glance over her shoulder. The Cyclops looks away immediately. Kyri shares a grin with me. "Maybe I should go talk to him?"

"He might panic," I joke. Thinking of Trinte, I say, "I know you both conspired."

It was a guess, but the way her eyes flare, I know Fynn was right. "He told you?"

"No," I laugh. "You just did, though."

She scrunches her nose. "Damn, I walked right into that one." Turning pensive, she asks, "Have you ... heard from him? He went radio silent a few days ago."

How did they even get one another's numbers? Are they actually talking that often for a few days to matter? I shift uneasily in my chair. "There was some drama at the Weyr reunion involving him. Trinte kind of ... disappeared."

Alarm raises her eyebrows. "Is he okay?"

Moxie marches up to my muffin, taking a bite. Her cookie's already gone. "Um, we don't know. He didn't even come into work."

Kyri looks properly worried now. "That's not normal."

I'm dying to know what's going on. "No, it's not."

She pulls out her phone and shoots off a text. Placing it on the table, she says, "So tell me about the Weyr reunion. Did you and Fynn finally hook-up? Did he properly grovel?"

Grinning, I tell her everything that happened up to Trinte's meltdown. It feels too private to share, even if it was in front of an audience. Clearly, they talk enough that she's worried. If he wants to tell her, he will.

Kyri's fanning herself, cheeks flushed, after I tell her about the deserted island. "Orliana, that's probably the hottest thing I've ever heard."

Smug satisfaction makes me smirk. "Right? Honestly, I don't think I could've asked for anything more or better."

After taking a sip of her coffee, she asks, "What now? Does Joulian know? Is Fynn ready for something serious?"

"Joulian's actually good with it. And after this, Fynn asked me to help him go through the baby's room. I'd say this is a very good indication of being ready."

She nods slowly. "I agree. Honestly, it wouldn't surprise me if you two are married within a year."

I gasp with genuine shock. "Kyri! That's outrageous!"

She raises a white eyebrow. "Is it? You're in love with him; your son adores him; he's cleaning out his home. If that's not commitment material, I don't know what is."

"Well, when you put it that way," I mutter. Swallowing the dregs of my coffee, I consider her words. Am I ready for that kind of commitment? The idea of marrying Fynn sounds ... incredible. He would be kind, attentive, generous, and dedicated. A life of peace and security.

"Oh my goddess, you're thinking about it!" Kyri whisper-shrieks.

Wiping the dumb smile off my face, I say, "I have no idea what you're talking about." Checking the time, I gather the wrappers. "Time to get going."

We both stand. As we walk out of the shop, Kyri says, "Um, do you think you can ask Fynn for Trinte's address? I want to check on him."

I give her a sidelong look. "Are you ever going to tell me what happened between the two of you?"

"Maybe," she hedges. I frown. She's never been reluctant to share details about a man. Ever. This is becoming odd.

Either way, I don't mind helping her. I send a quick text to Fynn and he immediately responds with the address. Feeling a bit vengeful, I send it to her.

"If he asks how you got the address," I grin. "Tell him it was a gift from Fynn and me."

"Will do." She brushes a kiss against my cheek, then struts off to the nearest launch platform. As I summon a Dragxi, I think about how she might be able to help my friend.

I hope Kyri can drag him out of whatever depths he's found himself in before he drowns.

63

Fynn

Orliana barely knocks once before I fling the door open. She's a vision in the sunlight, the light beaming behind her like a heavenly glow.

Reaching for her, I bundle her up in a hug. Moxie flies to my shoulder and rubs my cheek. The anxiety that's been eating me alive eases a little.

"Hey," She mumbles the word into my shirt.

Kissing the top of her forehead, I release my tight hold. "Thanks for coming."

"Of course." She steps inside and takes off her shoes. Her being in here feels right. "So, what exactly are we doing today?"

My stomach flutters. "I want to start emptying the ... room."

Orliana grabs my hand, instantly reading me. "Why the rush?"

This barks a laugh out of me. "Five years is a rush?"

"Well, no," she admits. "I think it's more that when I met you not even two months ago ..."

I squeeze her hand. With a half smile, I say, "I was already getting sick of my broodiness when we met. You've been an integral part of my journey, but please don't think I'm doing this just for you or rushing through it."

"Okay." She still looks doubtful, but that's okay.

Her eyes wander toward the living room, where boxes are piled. "What's that?"

"A lot of Rhuth's things."

Orliana approaches the boxes, and I follow, suddenly nervous. She pauses where the large image of the wedding day rests against a taller pillar of boxes. With a furrowed brow, she asks, "Why did you take this down?"

Suddenly unsure about my choice, I mumble, "I didn't think you'd want to look at it."

"Fynn!" She whirls on me, outraged. "You said you weren't doing this for me!"

"Well, not all of it," I amend. "I just didn't think you'd want to see the face of another woman in this house."

"Fynn Gleanscale." The full use of my name makes me wince and smile. She points at the framed image. "You put that back right now. You've made it clear from the start how important she is to you; I made it clear that your love for her is my favorite part. Now, I don't think I want pictures of her in the bedroom—" Orliana smiles when I laugh. "—But reminders of her don't bother me. It's a beautiful photo."

Looking unsure again, she says, "Maybe *we* could get some photos, though?"

"Yes," I say quickly, rushing up to hug her again. "I can call Luca, the photographer, as soon as you want. I want photos of us, including Joulian, on these walls."

"Deal." When she pulls back, I reluctantly release her. She peers up at me, blinking slowly. "Do you want to go through the room now?"

With a silent nod, I lead her to the door I haven't opened in five years. Like we did those weeks ago at the freezer, she stands at my side while I stare at the doorknob.

"I haven't been in here since the day I found out," I murmur. "Trinte put all the baby shower gifts in here. I'm fairly certain not a single one was opened."

I think of Curtis, with the new baby on the way. Suddenly, turning the knob isn't so hard. These items will find a good home.

The door opens with a quiet squeal. Dim light fills the space; the scent is like a gut punch. I inhale sharply, smelling Rhuth everywhere. In everything.

When I back up, panicking, Orliana's hand is instantly in mine.

"It's okay," she murmurs. "One step at a time."

It takes a couple more minutes before I can fully step into the room, and it's only after I can wipe away fresh tears enough to see clearly. While I stand in the center of the room, feeling lost, Orliana raises the blinds and opens the window. Fresh air breezes in, and just like that, it feels better. Like the breeze is Rhuth offering encouragement.

We sit on the stunning handwoven blue rug Rhuth chose and begin unwrapping the dozens of gifts. She helps me decide what Curtis would need and what will be donated instead.

As we're going through the newborn onesies, Orliana goes soft and misty-eyed. "I remember when Joulian was this small." She laughs with so many memories I can't see. "He was such an easy baby."

Folding the onesie onto the pile of others, she reaches for tiny socks. I'm enthralled, watching her motherhood appear. The way she inspects the tiny socks, folding them into an itty bitty ball of cotton. A potential future appears, and I can't shake the vision of her with a round belly; a belly full of our baby.

"Do you want more kids?" I blurt out.

She looks up with sharp surprise. "What?"

"Kids. Do you want more?" I've never needed a particular answer so much in my life.

Orliana grins. "Well, if I did, I'd have to do it soon. Those girls told me geriatric, remember?"

I snort. "That's not really an answer."

"Are you asking if I'd want to have kids with you, Fynn?" Orliana gives me a shy smile. My heart picks up speed, knowing the exact answer immediately.

"Yes."

Orliana examines the organized wreckage of my past. She begins grabbing some of the toys from the giveaway pile.

"What are you doing?"

Grabbing a box holding baby bottles, she says, "Well, we might as well save some of this, since we're probably going to need it soon."

Electric with joy, I pounce on her. She squeals into peels of laughter that quickly turns into a gasp when I press my lips to hers. It's been days since she's been in my arms. Even in the middle of this room, surrounded by ghosts, my need for her is unquenchable.

Softening in my hold, Orliana kisses me back. It's hesitant at first, then grows more and more enthusiastic. I worry about triggering her, but I need to trust her to speak up.

Pulling away for a second, I say, "You remember the safe word?"

"Coconut?"

"Yep." My mouth descends on her as if she's my oxygen. My hand reaches up her shirt, and I moan at the sensation of her soft skin.

She freezes, and my hand does the same. Breaking the kiss to inspect her face, I ask, "What's wrong?"

Orliana cringes. "Um, can we do this somewhere else? It feels a little weird."

Looking to the side, I see the unopened bassinet and agree. Standing, I hold out a hand. When she stands, we look around. Almost everything's separated. I'll contact Curtis later to find out what he needs. Everything else will go to the domestic shelter.

"I think we're good for now," I announce. Scooping her up, I walk her down the hallway to my room. She laughs, clinging to my neck.

When we enter, she scans the bed. "Fynn ..."

"I had the mattress replaced yesterday."

She beams. "Really?"

"Really." It had been difficult, but necessary. While I'm not interested in erasing Rhuth, some things need to change for Orliana's comfort. I wouldn't want to screw or sleep in the same bed she shared with Mikan.

Before I toss her into the bed, which would be my preference, I ask, "What would you like to do?"

Doubt flashes across her face. Neither of us wants her to trigger; the last time we were in bed turned out differently than expected. "I don't want to be treated like I'm breakable. If I trigger, we can deal with it. But until then, I want to feel normal. Is that okay?"

Grinning, I kiss her forehead. "More than okay." I toss her onto the bed.

She squeals as I leap with a playful snarl, catching myself before actually landing on her. Orliana is giggling up a storm as I settle between her thighs. The laughter ends the second I press a crushing kiss to her silky lips.

Instantly, we're all passion. Her nails scrape my back as she rips off my shirt. Lifting her shirt, I lick up the soft hills of her belly, nipping the underside of her breasts. She laughs and arches her back, begging for more.

With a growl, I help her pull the stupid piece of fabric off, exposing her luscious form.

"Goddess, you're so beautiful," I mutter, kissing down her sternum. When I reach the waistline of her shorts, I cast a glance in a silent question.

Her face flushes, showing indecision and insecurity. I wait patiently while she considers.

"Okay."

Slowly, one by one, I unfasten the buttons and slide them over her hips.

64

Orliana

The second the shorts are off, my thighs open instinctually, ready for whatever he's offering. Fynn's golden eyes home in on the sight. When he licks his lips, pleasure shoots down to my core, warming up my insides.

When he fully kneels, Fynn grabs my hips and jerks me to the edge of the bed. I gasp, then giggle.

"What's the safe word?"

"Coconut."

"Good." His mouth is on me, hot and greedy. When his tongue swipes up my slickness, I moan. He snarls in satisfaction, holding my hips down possessively. Fynn is an enthusiastic lover, clearly getting pleasure from my moans.

I make sure he knows how much I love what he's doing. Loudly.

When he adds a finger to his ministrations, my hips buck. His talented tongue teases and sucks. This is *nothing* like I expected. Within minutes, I'm a sobbing, pleading mess, begging for release. Instead of following through, Fynn stops. This maddening man just ... stops.

"What are you doing?" I demand, panting and flushed.

With an impish grin, Fynn stands. I watch silently, trying to catch my breath, as he stands. At his full height, he's like a towering god with me prostrated like an offering. My throat bobs as he unbuckles the belt, then his pants. They slide down, revealing the most intriguing part of his body.

His eyebrow raises. "Did Kyri tell you about the specifics of Dragon genitalia?"

I grimace. "Don't use the word genitalia in bed, Fynn."

"Cocks," he croons with a grin. "Did she tell you about our cocks?"

My mouth goes dry as he fists his length, giving it languid strokes. "Um. Yes, I believe she mentioned that it can ... get ..."

"Thicker?" he supplies. I nod, still not entirely sure what it means. I take a shuddering breath as he leans over me, the heat of his simmering Fyre warm against my chest.

Pulse pounding, I watch him gaze at me hungrily, still stroking himself. Like we have all the time in the world, and he's trying to memorize every second.

"You okay to continue?" he asks, voice rough.

"Yes."

"Good." The tip of his cock presses against my entrance. Never taking his eyes off me, he slowly works himself in. He moves his hips until I'm mewling with need, desperate for every inch.

"So good," he murmurs, running a hand up my sternum. "You feel incredible, Orliana."

He sits back on his heels and presses firmly on my belly as he slides the last inch into my body. When our hips are flush, he pauses. His stomach muscles flex as he pants, beads of sweat already trailing down his muscled form.

"Tell me when it's too much."

At first, I don't quite understand what he means. The sensation of fullness inside my core appears, expanding. Stretching. I gasp, clamping my thighs shut. Fynn pauses, watching me carefully.

"Too much?"

"N-no, it just surprised me."

He spreads my legs again. "Let's see how this feels for you."

When he begins to thrust at a leisurely pace, my eyes roll back in my head. It's exquisite. Now I understand why Kyri was excited for me.

"A little more," I rasp. He obeys, and pleasure like I've never known explodes in my body. I feel so full, but in the most perfect way.

"Faster," I demand. Fynn's hands grab my thighs as he increases the pace. The concentrated lust on his face makes me moan louder. My fingers claw into the blanket, desperate for a perch.

My breasts bounce with each thrust, and I grab my nipple. Something I've never done before, but I'm desperate for more sensations. I gasp at the way it feels, the way it shoots more pleasure straight to my core.

Fynn growls in approval, slamming into me now. "Again."

I do it with both nipples, closing my eyes, losing myself in the way he makes me feel. The way I can make myself feel.

The pad of his thumb comes right between my thighs, rubbing in slow, methodical circles. His palm keeps my hips down, no matter how much I try to move them.

"Orliana, look at me," he barks, sounding desperate.

My eyes fly open. The intensity of his gaze thrills me to no end. With a voice made of velvet, he says, "I'm going to love you like this every chance you allow. I'm going to make you feel so fucking good; all you have to do is ask. Do you understand?"

I nod, unable to speak from breathing so hard. Before I can register what he's doing, the pillows are gone. He's pushing me upward so he can fully settle between my thighs and continue with slow, punishing thrusts.

Fynn settles his hands on each side of my face, rubbing a thumb along my cheek. "I love you, Orliana."

My eyes flutter closed when his lips come to mine. The kiss is soft and sweet. Gone is the furious need, replaced by yearning reverence. The intimacy is too much. Tears prick my eyes, and I begin to cry.

Fynn freezes. "What's wrong, baby?"

I shake my head. "It's fine. Keep going. I'm just so ... *happy.*"

The last word comes out a little pathetic. To his credit, Fynn doesn't laugh at me. He gives me the softest smile and continues at a torturous pace. "I'm happy too, baby. So, so happy. I want to spend the rest of my life making you happy."

The orgasm building rushes like a tidal wave now. "F-Fynn ..."

"Orliana," he purrs into my ear, grinding his pelvis against mine. Providing the last bit of friction needed to send me over the edge. I come undone, shattering into pleasure like I've never known before. He gives a guttural groan in my ear, throbbing inside me.

Coming down from the high, we pause, wrapped up in one another. Fynn trails soft kisses on my face, murmuring words of affection. In his arms, I've never felt more safe.

"I love you." I murmur the words against his throat after planting a kiss.

He hums, and the vibration tickles my lips. "That's good, or asking you to have my baby would be incredibly awkward."

I giggle. "True. Actually, I think you might've proposed while inside me, too. Very unconventional."

Nuzzling my nose with his, Fynn rumbles, "When I actually ask you to marry me, you'll know. I'm just testing the waters."

Now I laugh in earnest. "Some might say it's inappropriate."

Fynn scoffs, pulling back to look me in the eye. "I think that word doesn't really exist in our relationship at this point."

"True. But still. The proposal better end with you inside me, but not during."

"Deal." He eases back, breaking our physical connection. Placing an arm on top of my knee, he leans against my leg. "Orliana, will you marry me?" He grins,waggling his brows. "Round two?"

I grab a pillow and smack him in the face with it. "Rude!"

Fynn shrugs. "Maybe better luck next time."

"I swear, if you ask again in five minutes ..."

He makes a derisive sound. "If you think it'll only take five minutes at any given point, then I feel challenged to prove you wrong."

I spread my legs in invitation. "You can try."

Just as he's about to rise to the challenge, Moxie flits into the room, landing on his head. He jerks in surprise with a laugh. Reaching up, he cups her tiny body, holding her out in front of him. "You, little miss, are trouble."

Moxie honks as she hops around on his palm. Because she loves him just as much as I do.

65

Orliana

The moment Fynn lands on the platform, my nerves vibrate with anticipation. His magyck floats me onto the ground. I wait as he shifts, sharing an anxious smile as his fingers intertwine with mine.

"Nervous?" He scans my face with worried golden eyes.

Grimacing, I nod. "What if she doesn't like me?"

"Impossible," Fynn says firmly, guiding me to the automatic doors of the shopping mart. The cool air smarts against my cheeks as fluorescent lights reveal a pretty female Orc who grins the second we walk in.

Virinia claps her hands, ignoring the patron waiting in line with items as she rounds the counter. "Oh, aren't you beautiful!"

Before I can grasp what's happening, I'm bundled up in warm, meaty arms. After two months of practicing, shielding is instinctual at this point, but her joy is impossible to not feel. I've been so nervous to meet Fynn's friend, knowing how integral Virinia has been for his mental health. He once admitted that without her meals, he probably would've let himself starve to death.

Virinia releases me and hugs Fynn. While she does that, I pull out a container of oatmeal cookies from the backpack slung over my shoulders. When she pulls away, I offer the cookies.

"Fynn told me you are basically responsible for keeping him alive and also informed me this is your favorite flavor of cookies."

Virinia looks positively thrilled, immediately popping open the container to inspect a cookie. She grins, then glares at me. "If you hurt her, I'll never make you piglet ever again."

"So, five years of friendship means nothing in the face of cookies?" he says dryly.

Virinia smirks. "Men will never understand."

I grin. "Yet, somehow we tolerate them anyway."

"Fortuna save me," Fynn mutters.

"Uh, excuse me, but can I check out?" The Elf waiting at the counter eyes us impatiently. Virinia shoves the cookie into her mouth and gives us a wave as she returns to her job.

Fynn presses a hand to my lower back, steering me back outside.

"That was quick," I remark, reeling from how fast that introduction was.

Fynn chuckles. "She's at work."

I nod. "Maybe we should invite her family over for dinner? Have you really only ever seen her at the market?"

Fynn frowns. "Well, until now, I haven't really been in the mindset to invite people over." He shoots me a sly grin. "But now that I have a house full of people, there's nothing stopping me from inviting her over one night."

My heart expands three times its normal size from the happiness threatening to burst out of my chest. Two weeks ago, Joulian and I moved into his home. I'm selling my house — good fucking riddance — and our new life together has already been amazing. Joulian loves living in a different home, and Moxie adores all the plants. To my delight, Fynn invited me to begin my dream of gardening by rehabilitating his flower beds. Next week, we're repainting the outside of his home.

Everything is being refreshed, offering a new start to our future.

The flight back home is quick, and by the time we land, my stomach growls for lunch. The moment our front door swings open, the smell of bacon has Moxie reappearing and jetting down the hallway toward the kitchen.

"Hello, hello!" I call out as Fynn closes the door behind us.

From the kitchen, my mom calls, "In here!"

She and Joulian are busy cooking in the kitchen, prepping sandwiches for lunch. Joulian is in charge of the bacon, while my mother slices into a fresh loaf of bread Fynn made yesterday.

Mom smiles when we walk in. "How'd it go?"

"She liked the cookies." I sit on a stool at the island while Fynn grabs us some drinks.

"How could she not?" Fynn pulls two glasses from a cabinet. "Your oatmeal cookies are the best."

"Pfft." I dismiss his compliment. "They're just regular cookies."

"Stop being modest," Joulian orders, pointing tongs in my direction. Behind him, Moxie eyes the slices of cooked bacon cooling on a plate.

As Fynn hands me a glass of water, he kisses my forehead. "You're too modest, love."

"One of my most endearing qualities, I'm sure," I say dryly, but the compliment makes me smile. I raise an eyebrow at Joulian. "Did you finish unpacking?"

He shakes his head, flipping slices of bacon. "There's three left."

"Make sure you get that done tonight," Fynn says in a stern tone.

Instead of throwing an attitude, Joulian says, "Yes, sir."

I spot a small grin as he ducks his head. He's taken to Fynn being parental, seeming to revel in the male guidance I know he's been craving.

Mom lays out the slices of bread and spreads mayonnaise. "So, what's the plan for the rest of the day?"

"Unpacking," I say after taking another sip of water.

Fynn sits next to me, nodding. "Maybe a movie later?"

"Yeah!" Joulian says excitedly, not noticing Moxie snatching a slice of bacon and flying out of the kitchen. Greg follows her on silent wings.

"What movie?" Mom asks, adding slices of white cheese on top of the bread.

My son's eyes shine with glee. "Can we watch the one where the Elven princess is kidnapped by the Orc prince and held for ransom, starting a war?"

Joulian sounds so hopeful, it makes me chuckle. "That might be a little too violent."

"Let the kid live a little," Mom says breezily.

Fynn clears his throat. "I heard there's a sex scene in there."

"Eww." Joulian cringes while adding slices of cooked bacon onto the growing pile. "Nevermind."

"I'm sure there's a cartoon we can find," I say flippantly.

"I'm not a kid," Joulian insists, bringing the plate of bacon over to where Mom adds lettuce to the sandwiches.

"Great news!" I announce. "The water bill just arrived, and I've been meaning to pay it, but ..."

"A cartoon could be fun," Joulian rushes out.

Fynn chuckles. "No need to rush being the man of the house."

Joulian pauses, cheeks flushing. "That's what dads are for, right?"

Everyone pauses; air exits my lungs. We watch different emotions flick across Fynn's face as he processes the unspoken question Joulian has asked.

After swallowing hard a few times and clearing his throat, Fynn nods. "Yeah, son. That's what dads are for."

Joulian visibly relaxes, flashing a toothy grin.

And just like that, I fall in love with Fynn Gleanscale all over again. Mom sniffs, ducking her head as she finishes making the sandwiches. I place a hand on Fynn's thigh in silent gratitude.

This is the kind of life I've always deserved; the kind Joulian has always deserved. As Fynn helps my mother bring the plates to the table, I watch my little family settle into their chairs. Joulian sits next to Fynn, telling him about a recent school project. Just like the first day they met, Fynn patiently listens.

Mom catches me still sitting on the stool, watching the scene unfold. Coming to stand next to me, she wraps an arm around my shoulders and whispers, “I’m so happy for you, Muffin.”

Our heads rest together as I bring a hand to hers, squeezing it tight. “Me too, Mom. Me too.”

66

Fynn

Three Years Later

The day my wife gave birth, I was searching for ice cream. Not just any ice cream; the raspberry white chocolate kind. It's her favorite flavor — now it's mine, too — and it's her nightly pregnancy craving. Stupid me forgot to buy ten pints last time; apparently six wasn't enough.

There's no way in all twelve Hells that I'd let her suffer over ice cream, of all things. Luckily, I know exactly where to find it.

Seeing me walk through the sliding glass doors, Virinia grins. "Third time this week."

I shrug, breezing by, heading straight for the ice cream aisle. "She claims it's all the baby wants to eat."

Her laugh follows me as I enter the aisle. Grabbing eleven pints, balancing them all in my arms, I walk back. Dumping them onto the counter, I laugh. "Do you think it's enough?"

Virinia lifts one with a critical eye. "I think this supply will last Orliana approximately three days?"

Grinning, I pull out my wallet. "That's a good guess."

While she scans each one, she asks, "Due any day now, right?"

Pride puffs out my chest. "The midwife estimates this week, actually. We have the nursery ready, and Joulian has been organizing everything. You'd think *he* was the one nesting."

Virinia chuckles, adding the pints to my freezer bags. "That boy is more excited about a new sibling than any only child I've ever seen."

I think fondly of my son, smiling. "He's a good kid. I think he's going to be a good big brother."

Handing me the bags, Virinia smiles. "Well, tell me when she finally pops. I can't wait to hear the sex and name."

"Will do." With a whistle, I walk out the door. Once I'm positive the ice cream is safe, I shift and grab the bags, making my way home.

The house looks as it always has, but with renewed life in the garden. Two pots, the ones we made when we were just friends, sit on a shelf, housing small shrubs. We've planted extra peony bushes, and last year, we planted a slootberry bush that is finally bearing fruit. It'll make a delicious pancake topping when they're ripe.

Walking inside, I call out, "I'm home!"

"Hey Dad!" Joulian's squeaky teenage voice comes from the nursery. After putting up the ice cream, I head back toward the bedrooms. Joulian's sitting on the floor with Orliana, putting together the bassinet. It's the third one we've bought — Orliana keeps changing her mind on the style she wants.

My wife smiles up at me, exhausted but happy. "Hey, honey. What'd you get at the store?"

"Your lunch."

Her eyes light up. When she struggles to stand, Joulian is up in a flash, helping her stay balanced. One of her hands presses against her round belly as she huffs. "I cannot wait for this baby to evict itself. So over feeling like a beached Kraken."

Smiling, I help her walk down the hallway. Leading her to the couch, I kiss the top of her head. "I'll bring you the first pint."

She hums appreciatively, fondly gazing at her belly, rubbing it in slow circles. I pause, taking a memory snapshot and storing it in my mind permanently. Gazing up at the photos above the ceiling, I smile at the photo of Rhuth and me.

Right next to it is the image of Orliana and me on our wedding day. We'd had a glitter and rainbows themed wedding, in honor of our first conversation at a Glyridite coffee shop. My old wedding photographer, Luca, photographed the event with his wife, Reverie. Our images are filled with glitter and laughter. Just like our lives have been ever since she walked into that career fair.

Grabbing the pint and a spoon, I sit next to my wife. Opening the container, I hand it to her and bring one of her feet to my lap. She sighs happily as she takes the first bite, and I rub the sole of her foot. Moxie appears, curling up on her belly.

"How are you feeling?" I ask.

Orliana lets out a burdened sigh. "As big as a Dragon. I swear, this one is going to be as tall as you."

I laugh. "Hopefully not. She'll find it difficult to date, otherwise."

We've known the sex for a while; we're just keeping it a surprise for everyone else. I'm beyond excited to hold my little girl. Joulian is already fiercely protective, like a big brother should be. Orliana is excited to wear matching outfits.

Within minutes, the ice cream is gone. Orliana licks the spoon like it holds invisible seconds. Taking it away from her, I say, "The overnight bag is packed?"

"And repacked five times," she confirms. "Everything is ready."

"Talia will take Joulian."

She nods. "And Kyri said she can take care of the plants." She glances at the botanical haven we've made our home, doubling the amount of Rhuth's. Orliana grunts as she sits up. I grab one of her arms to help her stand. When she's steady, I rub a hand over her belly. While I'm excited for the baby, I'm going to miss the feel of tiny kicks against my palm.

Just means we'll need another baby soon.

"I want a bath," she announces. "Take some of this weight off for a few minutes."

"On it," I say, kissing her forehead. She totters after me while I head to the bathroom. Sitting on the edge of the clawfoot tub she demanded six months ago as the baby grew in size, I turn it on. Testing the temperature with my hand, I call out, "Do you want it hotter? Just warm?"

"Just warm, please," she responds from the bedroom as she undresses.

Grabbing her favorite bottle of bubbles, I pour it into the stream of water. The smell of lavender fills the room.

"Fynn?" The tone in her voice raises the hairs on my neck.

Instantly, I'm rushing toward her. "What? What is it?"

She's standing by our bed, a puddle of liquid on the floor. "I think my water just broke."

Excitement explodes, and I laugh. Turning off the bath, I say, "Okay. Wait right here." Rushing down the hallway, I yell, "Joulian! It's time!"

"Got it!" he screams back. Moxie and Greg fly off their perches, hopping around with anticipation.

While he gathers the overnight bags, I help Orliana change her pajama pants, then text everyone who needs to be in the know. Everything we've been planning for months sets into motion.

Helping Orliana to the front door, I kneel and place the shoes on her feet. She grabs a jacket and Joulian supports her down the steps outside. I turn to gaze at my home. In a day or two, this space will be more full of love than ever.

Locking the door behind me, I regard my son and wife. At the grins on their beautiful faces. Brushing a thumb against Orliana's flushed cheek, I say, "Let's go meet baby Rhuth."

Acknowledgements

First off, *thank you* for reading First Time Friends. This book was a labor of love, thanks to the deep emotional dive this book required. In fact, it demanded to be written only two weeks after I finished writing Glittering Skies. I had no real plan, just this vague idea of a red Dragon shifter who was a Dragxi by day and loved video games in his off time. Then Fynn was like, "My wife is dead," and I'm staring at the computer screen going, "Poor thing, let's make it worse!"

Like Glittering Skies, this book was a divine download, so as before, I must send my complete gratitude to the Universe for this gift. It taught me so much, healed things, and makes me so excited to see how this story will help others.

To my husband, thank you for not only joining me on the writing journey, but for also beta reading, giving advice, keeping me fed, and allowing me to spend way too much time and money on marketing. You're my biggest support and greatest cheerleader. You're so much like Fynn, minus the scales, inflatable dick, and tail. Oh, and the power over weather.

I love you anyway.

For my Hype Hoes — Bex, Nikki, Sarah, and Emily — thank you for reading the early drafts, weeping and cursing me out while telling me the world needs this story. To the entire community of Happily Ever

Authors, thank you for the late night sprints. When I first read y'all for the first kiss scene and the first chapter, your cheers and tears kept me going. I wouldn't be the author or person I am today without all y'all. I'll always remember the discussion of whether or not Fynn would have two totally normal, red scaled dicks. I ended up giving him one, but head canon will always give him two.

I *have* to mention my amazing author community that I'm building one DM at a time. There are so many of you now, but seeing everyone succeed and thrive and struggle and lament — makes it all feel less lonely.

Again, thank you to everyone who enthusiastically took part in the release of this book, from beta readers to bookstores. Your heart is in these words just as much as mine.

About Jenna Avery

The origin story of Jenna Avery is complex, weird, and requires numerous alcoholic beverages to regale. The current story? She's an elder millennial with a penchant for evolving and growing. This is a polite way of saying her ADHD makes her choose a new hobby every three months. By the time you read this, who knows what she'll be into. Just ask. Otherwise, she lives with her horde of kids and pets, a golden retriever husband, and a rotating residency of soon-to-be-dead plants.

www.ingramcontent.com/pod-product-compliance
Lightning Source LLC
LaVergne TN
LVHW100502110826
845146LV00002B/493

* 9 7 9 8 9 8 7 1 8 9 0 6 1 *